If Looks Could Kill

KATE WHITE

WARNER
VISION
BOOKS

An AOL Time Warner Company

WARNER BOOKS EDITION

Copyright © 2002 by Kate White

Cover design by Shasti O'Leary

Warner Books, Inc.
1271 Avenue of the Americas
New York, NY 10020

Visit our Web site at www.twbookmark.com

 An AOL Time Warner Company

Printed in the United States of America

First Warner Books Printing: May 2003

10 9 8 7 6 5 4 3 2 1

more . . .

"Fast-moving and gutsy, this first novel delivers excitement with a confidence usually missing in first attempts."
—*Dallas Morning News*

"For anyone who likes a good, fun read....It takes you on a wild ride."
—**Kelly Ripa**, *Live with Regis and Kelly*

"A delicious new mystery...well written....Bailey is a lot of fun, smart, tough, and persistent."
—*Sullivan County Democrat* **(NJ)**

"Wonderful...peeks between the lines of America's glossiest magazines from the very top of the masthead...a deliciously deadly glimpse at an insider's world of fashion and style."
—**Linda Fairstein, author of** *Deadhouse*

"An intriguing mystery....White is very good at painting her world—the life of a single woman in high-powered New York—glamorous."
—*Booklist*

"A glitzy and witty thriller...fun."
—*Romantic Times*

"A stunning, self-assured debut...a marvelously written whodunit with so many twists and turns that I was kept guessing to the end. Brava!"
—**Diane Mott Davidson, author of** *Sticks & Scones*

To Hunter and Hayley. Thank you for all your wonderful support and encouragement.

ACKNOWLEDGMENTS

So many people were helpful to me when I was writing this book but several gave especially generously of their time and I want to say a very big thank you to them: Paul Paganelli, M.D., Chief of Emergency Medicine, Milton Hospital, Milton, MA; Sandra Schneider, M.D., head of emergency medicine, University of Rochester Medical School; Chet Lerner, M.D.; Barbara Butcher, deputy director of investigations for the office of the chief medical examiner, New York City; Pete Panuccio, sergeant, NYPD; Roger Rokiki, chief inspector, Westchester County police; and magician Belinda Sinclair.

I'd also like to thank my fabulous editor, Sara Ann Freed, for all her guidance, my terrific agent, Sandy Dijksktra, for not gagging when I said I wanted to write a mystery, and Miriam Friedman for all her amazing efforts.

If Looks
Could Kill

CHAPTER 1

CAT JONES WAS the kind of woman who not only got everything in the world that she wanted—in her case a fabulous job as editor in chief of one of the biggest women's magazines, a gorgeous town house in Manhattan, and a hot-looking husband with a big career of his own—but over the years also managed to get plenty of what other women wanted: like *their* fabulous jobs and *their* hot-looking husbands. It was hard not to hate her. So when her perfect world began to unravel, I might have been tempted to turn my face into my pillow at night and go, "Hee hee hee." But I didn't. I took no pleasure in her misery, as I'm sure plenty of other people did, and instead I jetted to her rescue. Why? Because she helped pay my bills, because she was my friend in a weird sort of way, and most of all because as a writer of true crime articles I've always been sucked in by stories that start with a corpse and lead to crushing heartache.

There's no way I could forget the moment when all the Sturm und Drang began. It was just after eight on a Sunday morning, a Sunday in early May. I was lying under the covers of my queen-size bed in a spoon position with thirty-four-year-old Kyle Conner McConaughy, investment banker and sailing fanatic, feeling him growing hard and hoping I wouldn't do anything to mess up the delicate ecosystem of the moment. It was our sixth date and only the second time we'd been to bed, and though dinner had been nice and last night's sex had been even better than the first time, I had a pit in my stomach—the kind that develops when you find yourself gaga over a guy you've begun to sense is as skittish as an alpine goat. All it would take was the wrong remark from me—a suggestion, for instance, that we plan a weekend at a charming inn in the Berkshires—and he'd burn rubber on his way out the door.

The phone rang just as I felt his hand close around my right breast. I glanced instinctively at the clock. God, it was only 8:09. The machine would pick it up, regardless of what idiot had decided to call at this hour. It was too early for my mother, traipsing around Tuscany, and too late for old boyfriends, who did their drunk dialing at two A.M. from pay phones in bars below 14th Street. Maybe it was the super. It would be just like him to get in touch at this hour with some pathetic complaint, like my bike was leaning up against the wrong wall in the basement.

"Do you need to get that?" K.C. asked, his hand pausing in its pursuit.

"The machine will," I said. Had I remembered, I wondered, to turn the volume all the way down? The fourth ring was cut off abruptly and a woman's voice came booming into the room from the small office directly across from my bedroom. No, I hadn't.

"Bailey? . . . Bailey? . . . Please pick up if you're there. It's Cat . . . I need your help. . . . Bailey, are you there?"

I moaned.

"I better grab this," I said, wriggling out from under the white comforter. I propped myself up on my elbow and reached for the phone on the bedside table.

"Hi," I said, clearing my throat. "I'm here."

"Oh, thank God," Cat Jones said. "Look, something's wrong here and I'm going insane. I need your help."

"Okay, tell me," I said calmly. If I wasn't responding with a huge degree of concern, it was because I'd known Cat Jones for seven years and I'd seen her freak when the dry cleaners pressed the seams wrong in her pants.

"It's my nanny—you know, Heidi."

"This one quit, too?"

"Please don't be funny. There's something the matter. She won't answer the door down in her apartment."

"You're sure she's there?"

"Yes. I mean, I talked to her yesterday and she promised to be here this morning."

"Christ, it's only eight o'clock, Cat," I protested. "She's probably dead asleep. Or she's got a guy with her and she's embarrassed to answer the door." K.C.'s hand, which had been fondling my breast only seconds ago, had now lost much of its enthusiasm.

"But she'd never just ignore me," Cat said. Of course not. Few people would have the nerve to do that.

"Maybe she's not even in there. Maybe she spent the night at somebody else's place."

"She said she was staying in last night. I've got a bad feeling about this."

"Can't you let yourself in? You've got a key, right?"

"I'm scared to go in alone. What if there's something the matter in there?"

"Well, what about Jeff?" I asked, referring to her husband.

"He's up in the country for the weekend with Tyler. I had something to do here," she added almost defensively.

"And there's no one closer? A neighbor?"

"No. No one I trust."

She paused then in that famous way of hers, which had started out as a trick to make people rush to fill the void and divulge their most sacred secrets to her, but which now had become a kind of unintentional mannerism, the way some people bite the side of their thumb as they think. I waited her out, listening to the sound of K.C.'s breathing.

"Bailey, you've got to come up here," she said finally.

"*Now?*" I exclaimed. "Cat, it's eight-eleven on a Sunday morning. Why not wait a bit longer? I bet she spent the night at some guy's place and she's trying to flag down a cab right now."

"But what if that's not the case? What if something happened to her in there?"

"What are you suggesting? That she's passed out from a bender—or she's hung herself from the door frame?"

"No. I don't know. It just seems weird—and I'm scared."

I could see now that this was bigger than a dry-cleaning snafu, that she had her knickers in a twist and was serious about wanting me there, uptown on 91st Street, now.

"Okay, okay," I said. "It's going to take me at least thirty minutes to get dressed and get up there."

"Just hurry, all right?" She hung up the phone without even saying good-bye.

By now there didn't seem to be much lust left in my dashing Lothario. He'd let his hand slip away and had rolled from the spoon position onto his back. I'd once heard someone say that Cat Jones was so intimidating that she had made some of the men she went to bed with temporarily impotent, but even I, who had never under-estimated her, was impressed that she'd managed to do that from about eighty blocks to a man *I* was in bed with.

"Look, K.C., I'm really sorry," I said, rolling over and facing him. He had lots of Irish blood in his veins, and it showed—dark brown, nearly black eyes, coarse dark brown hair, pale skin, front teeth that overlapped ever so slightly. "This woman I work for has a live-in nanny and she thinks she's in some kind of trouble. I've got to go up to her place and help her out."

"Is that Cat, the one you work for at *Gloss*?"

"Yeah. The beautiful but easily bothered Cat Jones. You're welcome to hang around here till I get back."

What I wanted to add was, "And when I get back I'll do things to your body that you've never even imagined before," but at that moment I wasn't feeling very nervy.

"No, I should go," he said. "Can I make a preemptive strike on the bathroom? It'll be quick."

"Sure. I'm gonna make coffee. Do you want some-thing to eat—a bagel?"

"Not necessary," he said, pulling his arm out from

under me so he could swing out of bed. He leaned over the side, reaching for his boxers, and then padded off to the bathroom. Great. There'd been the tiniest hint of snippiness in the "Not necessary," as if he suspected I'd found an excuse to blow him off. Or maybe he was relieved. This way there'd be no awkwardness about how long he was supposed to stay at my place or whether he should take me out for French toast and mimosas.

I forced myself out of bed and stole a look in the mirror above my dresser. I'm fairly attractive, I guess you could say, but lookswise the morning has never been my finest hour. I'd gotten all my makeup off last night, so there was none of that streaky "Bride of Chucky" horror, but my short blondish brown hair was bunched up on top of my head and it looked as though I had a hedgehog sitting there. I swiped at it with a brush a few times until it lay flat and then pulled on a pair of jeans, a white T-shirt, and a black cotton cardigan.

As I headed toward the kitchen I could hear K.C. splashing water in the bathroom. I put on the teakettle (I make my coffee in a French press) and walked from the living room out onto my terrace to see what the weather had in mind today. I live in the Village, Greenwich Village, at the very east end of it before it becomes the shabbier East Village, and my view is to the west, toward an unseen Hudson River blocked by gray- and red- and sand-colored buildings and nineteen shingled water towers scattered over the rooftops. It was cool, and the sky was smudged with gray.

"How'd you get this place again?"

K.C. was standing in the doorway, all dressed, ready to split. There was something downright roguish about him, a quality that was kept almost at bay when he dressed in one of his navy banker suits, but came through loud and clear as he stood there in slacks and a shirt rumpled from having been tossed in a heap on the floor in my bedroom. I was torn between the desire to swoon and the urge to heed a tiny voice in my head that was going, "Run, Bambi, run."

"I got divorced, and this was part of the consolation prize."

"Ahh, right."

He took three steps toward me. "I used your toothbrush, Miss Weggins."

"Then I look forward to using it next," I said. I nearly cringed at the sound of myself saying it. I'd once written an article about a woman with fourteen personalities, including an adolescent boy named Danny who liked to set five-alarm warehouse fires. Maybe that's what was going on with me.

But he smiled for the first time that morning and leaned forward and kissed me hard on the mouth.

"Have a good day."

"Oh, I'm sure I will. I'll be scouring New York for the no-show nanny."

"I hope she's worth it," he said.

"You want to come along?" I asked in a burst of imagination or stupidity.

"Can't," he said. "I'm supposed to go sailing today."

I walked him to the front of the apartment, flipped the locks on the door, and opened it. He spotted *The New York Times* lying on the mat and picked it up for me. Then he flashed me this tight little smile with raised eyebrows and turned to go. No "Call you later." No "That was the most awesome sex I've ever had." I felt a momentary urge to hurl the newspaper at the back of his head, but I just closed the door and begged the gods to keep me from falling hard for him.

Twelve minutes later I was in a cab heading uptown. I'd brushed my teeth, made coffee, and then poured it into a Styrofoam cup. I'd tried sipping it in the taxi, but the driver was going too fast, so now I had the cup on the floor, squeezed between my shoes.

There didn't seem to be anyone on the sidewalks at this hour, just people walking their dogs, and cabbies hurrying out of delis with blue-and-white disposable coffee cups. The last time I'd been outside on a Sunday this early was about a year ago and I'd been coming home, doing the walk of shame in a black cocktail dress. At 23rd Street we turned right, drove all the way to the end, and picked up the FDR Drive. As we sped alongside the East River, the sun burned a small hole through the clouds, making the river water gleam like steel.

I tried to read the front page of the paper, but I couldn't concentrate. I kept wondering if I'd totally blown things with K.C. by tossing him out for the sake of some silly nanny who'd most likely spent the night in a shagathon and would soon be returning home with a major case of beard burn. I'd actually met Heidi on several occasions. She was a stunningly pretty and aloof girl from Minnesota or Indiana who'd been imported to take care of Cat's two-year-old son, Tyler. In fact, I had just seen her on Thursday night when I'd been at Cat's house for a party and she'd appeared briefly in the front hallway to rifle through a closet, searching for Tyler's jacket. She had looked through me as if we'd never met before. I was certain that by the time I got to Cat's house Heidi would have surfaced and I'd be back in a taxi, spending another $15 on a ride home.

The only consolation was that I was getting an early start on the day. Besides, I really didn't have much choice but to indulge Cat on this one. She was not only my friend, but also partly responsible for the fantastic little career I had today, at the age of thirty-three. She'd made me a contributing writer to her magazine, *Gloss,* one of the so-called Seven Sister magazines, which had once specialized in running recipes for chicken dishes made with cream of mushroom soup and profiles of women who'd spent the best parts of their lives trying to get toxic dump sites removed from their towns, but under Cat had metamorphosed into something worthy of its name—a juicy, glossy thing with sexy fashion portfolios, down-and-dirty guides to making your husband moan in the rack, and fascinating crime stories and human dramas. And I got to write those stories. Not the make-him-moan ones—but the crime stories and human-interest dramas, tales about serial killers and vanishing wives and coeds killed and stuffed in fifty-gallon drums by the professors they'd been having affairs with.

I was grateful to Cat, but it was fair to say she got her money's worth. I was good at what I did, and my stories pulled in readers and won awards, and a book publisher just recently decided to package twelve of them together as an anthology.

Cat and I met seven years ago, at a little downtown magazine called *Get,* circulation seventy-five thousand, which focused on New York City happenings—the arts, culture, society, scandal, and crime, not necessarily in that order. Up until then I'd been at newspapers, starting, after college at Brown, on the police beat at the *Albany Times Union* and moving on to the Bergen County *Record* in New Jersey. I loved anything to do with crime, though I'm not sure why. My father died when I was only twelve, and my ex-husband once suggested that my fascination with the macabre was born then. I'm more inclined to think it stems from an experience I had as a high school freshman. Someone began leaving nasty notes for me in my desk and in my locker, and rather than just take it, I methodically figured out who the sender was (a girl), and the thrill that came from solving that mystery was totally empowering. Eventually I realized that magazines would offer me more stylistic freedom than newspapers, and I found my way to New York City and the newly created *Get*.

I met Cat, known as Catherine then, the first day on the job. She was deputy editor, four years older than me, and though she supervised mostly the celeb and arts stuff, not the gritty pieces I wrote, I got to see her strut her stuff in meetings. She took a liking to me, maybe because I didn't fawn over her like so many people, and over time she began coming into my little office, closing the door and confiding in me about office politics and the complications that came from dating several men at the same time, including a married one with two kids. She had recognized me as a secret keeper, a rare breed in New York. Once, I even flew to Barbados with her because she wanted to keep Jeff, whom she'd been dating for four months, hot and bothered. What did I get out of the relationship? I was totally dazzled by her, by her ambition and total self-assurance and the fearless way she asked for what she wanted.

After I'd been at *Get* for just a year, the editor in chief resigned in a major snit because the owner was pressuring him to kill a snarky story about a friend. The ten of us remaining on staff stood around in the hall that afternoon, wondering what the hell we should do, until Cat suggested we should all quit, too, in a show of solidarity. And so we did. That night we gathered in a bar with the editor, who bought us rounds of drinks and told us we'd be talked about in journalism schools for years to come. I wanted to feel giddy and important, but all I could do was wonder if I still had dental insurance, since I was only halfway through a very nasty root canal treatment. Cat, on the other hand, looked preternaturally calm, leaning against the bar with her martini and a cigarette. Three days later it was announced that she was the new editor in chief of *Get*.

I didn't speak to her for five months. Eventually she wooed me back, with some explanation about a magazine being more important than the people who ran it and by giving me the chance to write even bigger stories. Catherine had become Cat by then, the editor who could seduce any writer into working for her and knew if an article was good, as someone once wrote in a profile of her, if her nipples got hard when she read it. She became an It girl in the media world, and just over two years into her tenure, the owner of *Gloss* used an electric cattle prod to force Dolores Wilder, the sixty-seven-year-old editor in chief, to "gracefully" retire, naming Cat as her hot new replacement. Each of the Seven Sister magazines, which included *Women's Home Journal* and *Best House,* was close to one hundred years old—or long in the tooth, in the opinion of some—and if they were going to survive, they needed fresh blood like Cat. She'd extracted a promise from the owner that she could turn the magazine on its head in order to modernize it. Within days she had offered me a contract to write eight to ten human-interest or crime stories a year as a freelance writer and had even given me a tiny office on the premises. I could still write for other places, including travel magazines, a sideline of mine. I'd been yearning for the freedom a freelance gig would offer over a staff job, and the arrangement thrilled me.

We'd kept the friendship up, though like I said it was a kind of weird one. Occasionally I'd be tempted to keep my distance, when the selfish bitch part of her personality reared its ugly head. But then she'd do something fun and amazing, like leave a bag on my desk with an ice pack and a thirty-gram jar of caviar.

By now the taxi had exited the FDR Drive at 96th Street, and from there we headed down Second Avenue and then west on 91st Street to Cat's block between Park and Madison, a neighborhood known as Carnegie Hill. It was an elegant, tree-lined block of mostly town houses, some brownstone, some brick, one painted a soft shade of pink. Catty-corner from Cat's house was an exclusive private lower school, where children were often delivered and picked up in black Lincoln Town Cars. I paid the driver and climbed out of the cab, careful with my coffee cup. The street was empty except for a man wearing a yellow mack and walking a pudgy Westie in the direction of Central Park. A cool light wind began to blow out of nowhere and there was suddenly a snowfall of pink blossoms from a tree on the edge of the sidewalk. Petals landed on my sweater, my shoes, even in my hair.

As I brushed them away, I scanned Cat's town house, looking for signs of life. It was a four-story white brick building with black shutters, erected, she once told me, in the 1880s. The main entrance of the house was on the second floor, through a double set of black painted doors at the top of the stoop. On the first floor under the stoop was a separate entrance to the nanny apartment, which you reached by going down several steps from the sidewalk and walking across a small flagstone courtyard. There was a seven-foot wrought-iron gate that opened to a vestibule under the stoop and the door to the apartment. I stepped closer to the house, leaning against the wrought-iron fence in front of the steps to the courtyard area. From there I could see a faint glow coming from the two front windows of Heidi's apartment, creeping out from around the edges of the closed wooden shutters. Ahhh, so all was well after all. Obviously, the hung-over Heidi had been jarred from her slumber while I was being bounced over the potholes of Manhattan. I wondered if I'd at least be offered a croissant before I was sent on my way.

CHAPTER 2

I CLIMBED THE stoop to the second floor and rang the bell. Cat answered almost instantly, as if she'd been standing there waiting behind the big double doors. She had on black capri pants and an oversize white shirt, and her long, thick blond hair, which she almost always wore down, was pinned up on top of her head with what appeared to be a set of ivory chopsticks. She was wearing absolutely no makeup, something I'd never witnessed before. Her skin was pale and tired, with faint circles under her blue eyes, and for the first time since knowing her, I noticed that her lips were covered with small, pale freckles.

"So I take it everything's okay now," I said.

"What do you mean?" she snapped.

"With Heidi. She's here now?"

"No, no." She pulled me by my wrist into the foyer and closed the door. "Why are you saying that?"

"Her lights are on. I assumed she surfaced."

"But don't you see? That's the point. Her lights are on, she's supposed to be home—but she's not answering the door."

"And you don't think that at the last minute she could have decided to spend the night at somebody else's place? Twenty-one-year-olds do that sort of thing."

"She's twenty-two."

"Whatever. Does she have a boyfriend?"

"She did. But they cooled it a few months ago. Besides, she promised to be here. And like I said, she's always reliable."

"I thought she got weekends off. Why would you need to see her at eight on a Sunday morning anyway?"

"I needed to talk to her. About Tyler. Just some general stuff."

Odd answer. But this didn't seem like the moment to pursue it.

"Okay," I said, "let's open the door to her apartment and see if we can make any sense of this."

"You think I'm being hysterical for nothing, don't you?" she asked.

"I'm sure everything's fine, but on the other hand, you've got a bad feeling and we need to check things out."

Cat lowered her head and pressed the tips of her fingers into her temples. Her nails were the color of pomegranates, and they were as shiny and hard as a lacquered Chinese box.

"Will you do it?" she pleaded softly, taking her hands down. "I mean, will you go in the apartment? I'm scared. If there's anything the matter, you'll know what to do."

"Sure," I said. "Why don't you get the key."

I followed her through the open double doors on the left wall of the foyer, through the khaki-colored dining room, and then into the kitchen, all white and stainless steel and, though not very big, designed to perfectly suit the demands of a caterer. She yanked open a drawer and began rummaging around for the key.

"Has Heidi ever shown any signs of having a problem with alcohol?" I asked as I waited in the middle of the room.

"You mean, could she be lying down there in an alcohol-induced stupor?" Cat said, looking up. "I don't have any reason to suspect that she's a big drinker—or that she uses drugs. But you don't always see the signs. She *has* been acting kind of funny lately—distant."

"When was the last time you actually saw her?"

"On Friday night, when I got home from work."

"Friday?" I exclaimed. "I thought you said you spoke with her yesterday."

"I did, but by phone. I had to go to East Hampton yesterday. We're co-sponsoring that film festival at the end of the summer and I had a planning meeting out there."

"You went out there on a *Saturday?"* I said. East Hampton, the very chic and expensive beach community, was more than a two-hour drive from the city.

"It was the only time I could squeeze it in. You know what my life is like. Where is that damn key?"

"Okay, so you come back, when? At the end of the day?"

"Actually, this morning. I was too tired to drive back last night, so I got a room out there and left before six this morning. Here's the key."

I started to turn toward the foyer, but Cat stopped me.

"This way," she said. "There's an entrance downstairs, off the library."

It made sense that there was an inside door to the nanny's apartment, but I had never seen it. I trailed Cat through the kitchen into the living room, which was at the back of the house. It was a big, square room, almost every inch of it—walls, sofas, chairs, drapes—done in different shades of white and cream. Two sets of French doors opened onto a balcony, overlooking the garden behind the house. Along the right wall a staircase, with a wrought-iron banister, led down to the library. Cat descended it, with me right behind her.

Though the deep red-painted library faced the garden, too, the second-floor balcony prevented it from getting much sun, and it was dim in there this morning, except for the light from two swivel lamps above the couch. The front wall was lined with bookcases, but as I stepped off the last stair into the room, I saw that a section of the bookcase was actually a two-foot-thick door, which had been pulled out, revealing a plain wooden door behind it. I'd been in the room a dozen times and never known the bookcase was anything more than a bookcase.

"This is how she gets in and out of the main part of the house?" I asked.

"Yes, mostly—though if she's coming in from the outside, she might use our front door rather than go through her apartment."

"Who opened the bookcase part?" I asked.

"I did, to knock on her door," she said.

"When you open this door, are you right in her apartment?"

"Sort of. There's a little corridor first. Then there's her room. There's no bedroom. It's just a sitting room with a pull-out couch."

I crossed the room and leaned my left ear against the door. From the other side I could hear, ever so faintly, the sound of music. My heart reared up, like a horse that's just smelled smoke wafting into its stall. It was one thing to leave a light on if you were going out, but why would you leave music on, too?

I lifted my arm and pounded four times on the door.

"Heidi," I called. "Heidi, are you there?"

I waited for half a minute, though I was awfully sure that no one was going to open the door.

"Give me the key," I said, stepping back toward Cat.

She let out a nervous sigh as she passed the ring to me with the key stuck out like a little gun.

"It turns to the right," she said.

I put the key in the lock and tried to turn it, but it resisted. I wiggled the key back and forth a few times and finally tripped the cylinder. I pushed open the door, calling out Heidi's name one more time.

The smell walloped me right away, and it was god-awful. It was the sour smell of vomit and the stink of feces and maybe other bad stuff. Fighting the urge to gag, I took two steps back from the half-open door and turned toward Cat.

"Not good," I said. "She's been sick—or she's dead."

Her hand flew to her mouth and fluttered there like a sparrow. "Oh, God," she moaned.

I took off my cardigan and wrapped it around my face to prevent the smell from making me do a dry heave. Pushing the door all the way, I took a step into the corridor. As a reporter I'd seen dead bodies before, mostly in car wrecks, but I didn't know what was waiting for me in Heidi's room, and frankly, I felt scared out of my wits.

The corridor was longer than I'd imagined, with a small Pullman kitchen to the left and a bathroom to my right. The bathroom was empty, though the light was on, and I spotted a pile of sea foam green towels on the floor, covered with dried vomit. I kept walking, with little baby steps, toward the main room. It was a square space, with a door on the far left leading to a hallway, which obviously led to the front door. The couch was in the middle of the room, positioned so that it faced the street and the windows, its back to me. There was only one light on, a stand-up lamp next to the couch, but I could see all the corners in the room with just a glance, and there was no Heidi pausing midroom in her pj's, looking indignant because I'd barged in. The music, some kind of jazz piece, was coming from a radio on a bookshelf against the left wall. And logic told me that the smell from hell was emanating from the other side of the couch.

I moved closer, and halfway around the couch I saw her. She was lying on the floor between the couch and a little trunk used as a coffee table, face up, arms stiffly at her side, almost as if she'd slipped off the couch while lying on it. And she was dead. The skin on her face was waxy pale and her khaki green eyes, open, were cloudy and tannish, as if they'd begun to discolor from being left open so long. She'd gotten sick from something, that was clear. There was vomit crusted on her lips, through strands of her long blond hair, on the front of the white tank top she wore above her jeans. I glanced toward the coffee table, looking instinctively for booze or drugs.

There was nothing like that—just an empty bottle of Poland Spring water, a gold box of Godiva chocolates, and a wet sea foam green towel snaking over a copy of *People* magazine.

My eyes found their way to Heidi's body again. I noticed that the skin along the entire sides of both arms was purplish red. It looked like bruising, but I knew that it was where the blood had begun to pool after death. She had probably died sometime last night. I glanced toward the little corridor. Cat wasn't in view.

"Cat," I yelled, pulling the sweater down from my face. "Where are you?"

She leaned her head into the doorway.

"I'm right here. Is Heidi in there?"

"Yes, she's dead. We need to get help right away."

I backed away from the couch almost on tiptoes, careful not to touch anything, not even turn off the radio, and then down the hallway. Cat was moaning, "Oh, no," over and over again.

"We have to call 911," I said.

"What happened? How did she die?" she wailed.

"I'm not sure. It looks as if she was sick or something—she's puked all over the place. Let's just get upstairs."

I guided her back through the library and up the wrought-iron staircase into the living room. As I hurried behind her, I felt an irrational panic, as if I were being chased. I looked back once over my shoulder to be absolutely sure no one was following me.

CHAPTER 3

As soon as we got upstairs to the living room, Cat collapsed on one of the creamy white couches. She looked as if she wanted to cry but didn't know how to start. I felt oddly detached, as if I'd been switched on to automatic pilot.

"Cat, I'm sorry," I said, standing in front of her. "This must be terrible for you."

"I can't believe it," she exclaimed, the heels of both hands pressed hard against her forehead. "I mean, I was worried something terrible might have happened, but now that it has, I can't even believe it."

"Do you want me to call 911—or do you want to do it?"

"Please, will you?" she pleaded.

There was a phone right next to her on the end table, a sleek cordless model sitting beside a black lacquered bowl filled with potpourri. It took four rings, and when the operator answered she sounded no-nonsense, almost curt, as if I'd caught her at a bad time.

"Did you try to take her pulse?" she asked after I'd explained what had happened and a few basic details about Heidi.

"No," I told her. "I didn't want to touch the body."

She said she would send an ambulance. I knew she would also send the police from the nearest precinct.

After setting down the receiver, I filled Cat in on the brief exchange.

"What do you think happened to her?" she implored. "You said she was sick. How would that *kill* her?"

"I'm not sure," I said. "Alcohol, drugs, they're both a good possibility, I guess. She might have taken too much of something that first made her sick—and then killed her. Or she could have choked on her own vomit. I didn't see signs of anything like that, though. The police and ME will figure it out. They'll look at everything down there. They'll treat it like a crime scene."

"Oh, great," Cat said sarcastically. She picked up one of the leopard throw pillows from the end of the couch and hugged it to her chest. "But if it's *not* drugs, what could it be?"

"I really don't know. Maybe she got ill from something she ate. I doubt it's any kind of a food allergy. I'm allergic to peanuts, and when you have an allergic reaction your throat swells up and you start to suffocate. Botulism? That supposedly makes you sick as hell. But if she was ill through the night, you think she would have called someone. Did she say anything on the phone about not feeling well?"

"No," Cat said, and then thought for a second. "I think what she said was, 'I don't feel up to going out tonight.' "

"Like she was sick?"

"Shit—I don't know."

"What kinds of things would she eat for dinner?"

She made a face. "It would depend on whether someone was watching."

"Meaning?" I asked.

"If she was eating with us, she'd have tiny portions. But I think she binged sometimes when she was alone."

"You mean she was *bulimic?*"

"No, I don't think so. It's just that she'd play Miss Low-Fat Food Lover around a crowd of people, but later in her room she'd wolf down something big and gooey. I know she stole food sometimes from the fridge."

"You're kidding?"

"I'm making it sound worse than it was. She did live with us, and so technically it was her food, too. She was just sneaky about it, which drove Carlotta nuts. She'd take the last piece of Tyler's dessert from the fridge or the leftover chicken—and she'd do it without asking or admitting it."

"And maybe even a box of Godiva chocolates?"

"What do you mean?"

"There was a box of candy on her table."

"Well, if it's Godiva, it's probably the box someone brought me Thursday night at the party. When I went to look for it later that night, it was gone. That's exactly the kind of thing I'm talking about."

She tossed the pillow over to the far end of the couch and stood up.

"How long will it take the damn ambulance?" she

asked. "I can't stand thinking of her down there like that."

"Look, Cat," I said, "we're going to have to call her family. This would be a good time to do it, before the ambulance—"

"She doesn't have any family," she said. "I mean, she did, but they're dead. Her father ran off when she was born, and her mother died when she was fourteen or something. She went to live with an aunt after that."

"You have a number for her?"

"Somewhere, I guess. It's upstairs in my office, I think."

"Why don't you see if you can find it, okay?"

After she left the room, I just sat there trying to get a handle on what I was feeling. My emotions, I could tell, were on some kind of delayed reaction, and I knew I wasn't going to be knocked over by any grief or sadness or horror until everything had a chance to sink in. What I *was* experiencing was a certain amount of confusion. I had lots more questions for Cat about Heidi, but I would obviously have to wait until later to ask them. My brain was also having a hard time catching up with the reality of the situation. An hour ago I'd been lying in my bed about to be ravished by my wild Irish rogue, and now here I was, sitting with a dead body, crusted in vomit, one floor below.

I got up and headed to the kitchen to look for caffeine. The morning was going to be crazy and depressing, and I needed something to help me compensate for having had only five hours of sleep the night before. There was a Mr. Coffee on the counter, and after rummaging around in the cupboards, I turned up a filter and a bag of Starbucks special blend. I filled the machine with ten cups of water and hit the start button. As the water began to plop into the pitcher, I walked back to the front of the house, to the dining room, and pushed aside the silk curtains on one of the windows. A family of four strolled by, he in a navy jacket, she in a sleek lavender suit, the two little boys all jacketed up, too, and I wondered where they could be headed dressed to the nines at this hour, and then I remembered: Sunday, church. All of a sudden the ambulance came down the street, with its siren making a kind of funny staccato whooping sound. It overshot the house by a few yards, lurched to a stop, and then backed up. I raced to the hallway and flung open the front door.

Three EMS workers sprang out almost simultaneously, from the driver's seat a fiftyish guy, and from the back a young Hispanic woman and a twentysomething white guy with a shaved head. The young guy had an in-charge look, and as he strode toward me, the other two began unloading something from the back of the truck.

"She's in there," I said, pointing toward the apartment. "But she's dead. I mean, I didn't take her pulse, but I know she's dead."

"We can get in this way?" he asked, cocking his head toward Heidi's door.

I noticed the iron gate and realized I was going to have to open it up.

"I'm going to have to find keys. Do you want to come in through the house first and see the body?"

"Show me the way."

As he'd been speaking to me, the two other paramedics had pulled out their equipment. One had a folded stretcher and the other had what appeared to be a portable defibrillator. They looked like people who had over-packed for a weekend out of town. The young guy put up his hand like a stop sign.

"Let me check it out. Stay on the radio, okay?"

He and I hurried up the stoop steps together, and as we stepped inside the house, Cat was descending the front hall stairs.

"The ambulance is here," I told her. "We're going to have to open the outside entrance to the apartment. You need a key for the iron gate, right?"

"Right."

"Do you have it?"

"You do."

"What?"

"*You* do, on the key ring."

I felt in my pocket where I'd stuffed the keys earlier and pulled them out, getting her to show me the one for the gate. She said it also unlocked the front door of the apartment.

"Is there a chain on the front door?" I asked.

She looked at me in bewilderment and then, realizing what I meant, nodded her head.

"I'll show you the body," I said, turning to the paramedic, "and then we can unlock the door and the gate." I led him through the house and down the stairs into the library. He asked me a couple of questions as we scurried along—Heidi's age, when I'd found her, what made me think she was dead and not just unconscious.

"It's through that door," I told him, pointing. I'd pulled it closed as I left the room.

"Okay, just stay here, then," he said. "Where's the body?"

"In front of the couch."

He opened the door and the gagadelic smell burst into the library, accompanied by the sound of jazz. I fought the urge to retch, but he seemed unfazed. I watched as he made his way down the little corridor and stepped around toward the front of the couch. He lowered himself gingerly on one knee and examined the body for less than a minute.

"She's dead," he said as he walked back down the corridor to me. "I'm pronouncing her dead"—he glanced at his watch—"at nine-thirty-two A.M." At this point, that seemed like the oldest news in the world.

"What's next?" I asked. "The police have been notified, right?"

"Yeah. I'll open up the front for them. It shouldn't be very long—not much going on today."

"There's a hallway to the left that will get you to the front door and that opens to the area with the gate," I said, handing him the key ring. "Can you tell how long she's been dead?"

"Well, there's not much decomposition yet—the smell's mostly from the vomit—so I'd say she probably died late last night."

"Any ideas on what killed her?"

"That's for the ME's office to figure out."

Obviously feeling no urge to discuss things with me, he turned to reenter the apartment and I went back up the stairs and through the house. I glanced in both the kitchen and dining room for Cat, calling her name twice, but she had disappeared somewhere. Through one of the front windows I could see that not only had a handful of pedestrians congregated outside to investigate the scene, but there were also two uniformed cops, their car double-parked in front of the house, talking to the other ambulance crew. I opened the front door again and headed down the stoop. Before I'd even reached the sidewalk, a dark navy car pulled up in front of the house, and out stepped two guys who were obviously cops as well, but in regular clothes—probably detectives. With a DOA the patrol cops generally come first to scope out the situation, but if it's a slow day or a hot case, the desk sergeant will have precinct detectives hightail it over simultaneously.

The four cops had a short confab with the EMS guy, who was just emerging from below, and then the two plainclothes guys headed in my direction. The older of the two, a guy in his late forties, stepped forward to greet me. He was about five ten and very compact, like something freeze-dried, with sandy hair and skin that had crinkled around the eyes. In his too tight khaki suit, blue button-down shirt, and red club tie, he looked ready to sell me a mattress at Macy's. When Cat met him she'd have to fight the urge to tell him that khaki suits are a no-no before Memorial Day.

"I'm Detective Pete Farley from the Nineteenth Precinct," he said.

"Bailey Weggins. I'm a friend of Cat Jones, the woman who owns the house. I came by to help her. It's her nanny who's dead."

"Is she in there now?"

"The nanny?"

"I realize the nanny's in there. Is the owner here?"

"Yes, she's inside," I said, feeling like a moron. I half turned toward the steps, expecting him to follow me.

"We're gonna look at the body first," he said. "Please

tell Miss Jones that we'll want to talk to her in a few minutes."

I hurried back into the house, where I encountered Cat gliding down the stairs again.

"Cat, look," I said, not concealing my annoyance. "You've got to stay put now. The police are here and they're going to want to talk to you in a few minutes—after they've looked at the body."

"I called Jeff. He's leaving right now. He should be here in just over two hours since there won't be any traffic."

"Good. What about the aunt? Were you able to reach her?"

"There's no answer. Not even an answering machine."

"Well, you can try again a little later. I made some coffee. Why don't I fix you a cup while we wait."

We went into the kitchen and Cat, looking stunned, sat on a stool at the black granite-covered island counter as I filled two coffee mugs. No matter how stressful things became at *Gloss,* no matter who was threatening to sue her or never allow another celebrity client to appear on the cover, Cat stayed in control of the situation, letting loose with charm when that served her best or turning steely when that was the only strategy that would work. I had never seen her so befuddled.

After she had taken a few sips of coffee, she seemed slightly more focused. She rooted through a Fendi purse for her makeup bag, and as she applied pressed foundation, blush, and lipstick the color of brick from a gold Chanel tube, I filled her in on what the procedure for the day was likely to be. The cops would be there possibly for hours and would call in both a medical detective from the ME's office and their own crime scene investigators. She needed to be prepared for a long day.

"This may seem coldhearted," I added as I set down my coffee mug, "but there are some PR concerns to consider here as well. You need to get ahold of the PR agency. The press is going to eat this up."

"I've called them already," she announced.

"You're kidding," I said. "When?"

"Well, I called Leslie when I was upstairs. She's in town this weekend and going to get in touch with them. She's coming over, too, to help out."

Oh, great. Leslie Stone was the butt-kicking managing editor of *Gloss*. While the executive editor, Polly Davenport, oversaw the creative side of the magazine, Leslie was the person in charge of all the administrative stuff, including managing the budget and expenses, creating schedules, tongue-lashing underperformers, and making sure the magazine got out each month. On work matters she was also Cat's biggest confidante. So Cat had put her battle plan in place. She wasn't as out of it as I had thought.

Suddenly there were footsteps, and each of us gave a nervous start as the two detectives walked in through the back door of the kitchen. It was Detective Farley and the other detective, a younger guy with a blond buzz cut who just might have been the thinnest person I'd ever laid eyes on.

Cat introduced herself, and Farley's eyes widened ever so slightly. He hadn't appeared to recognize her name when I gave it in the street, but it appeared he did now, maybe because he had the face to go with it. After declining her offer for coffee, he told her pretty much what

I had: Someone from the ME's office would be coming to examine Heidi before she was moved. He said it was standard procedure in home deaths, but especially considering the age of this victim.

With Buzz Cut perched on one of the counter stools taking notes, they started with their questions about Heidi: name, age, where was she from, how long had she worked for Cat, what were her responsibilities. Cat's answers were complete, but she never elaborated.

"Where's the child?" Farley asked abruptly.

"Oh, at our weekend home in Connecticut, with my husband," Cat said almost defensively, and went through her spiel about why she was in Manhattan this weekend while her family was elsewhere.

They appeared to take her explanation in stride, and Farley went on to ask how the body had been discovered. When she explained that I had been the one who had actually entered the room and found Heidi, both detectives snapped their heads in unison toward me. I wondered if they could tell by the expression on my face that when Cat had telephoned me, I'd been butt naked and seconds away from being shagged.

"Can I call you Bailey?" Farley inquired.

"Of course," I said.

"Do me a favor, would you, Bailey? Would you show me exactly how everything unfolded this morning? Detective Hyde can stay with Ms. Jones and get some more details about her nanny." He'd emphasized the word *nanny* as if it were a word he didn't use much, like flambé or foie gras.

Guiding me by the elbow in a thoroughly annoying way, he led me toward the back of the house, aiming for the stairs. I knew that he had intentionally separated me and Cat, and I started to feel this wave of totally irrational guilt and anxiety.

Downstairs in the library, the door to Heidi's apartment was now partially closed, and though I could detect movement in the apartment, I couldn't see how many people were in there or what they were doing. But I knew it was either the crime scene investigators or the medical detectives, or both. As we stood by the door, I took Farley verbally through my movements that morning, up to the point of entering Heidi's apartment.

"Do you want me to retrace my steps in the room for you?" I asked, hoping I wasn't going to have to go back in there.

"Not necessary. Why don't we talk out here," he said, cocking his thumb toward the garden. Without waiting for an endorsement from me, he flipped the lock on one of the French doors, swung it open, and gestured toward the wrought-iron garden table, where we both took a seat. From the inside pocket of his suit jacket he pulled his own steno pad and pencil and jotted down a few notes before even asking me a question. His fingers were short and stubby, like a row of cocktail wieners.

"So as you were saying," Farley said, "you unlocked the door, and walked in the room."

"Uh-huh—and I could tell from the smell something wasn't right," I explained. "I walked around the couch and then I saw her." The day had not managed to get much warmer since I'd left my apartment, and I folded my arms around my chest for warmth.

"Did you move or touch the body when you were in the room?"

"No, I did not," I said. Why was I sounding so defensive?

"You sure about that, Bailey?"

"No—I mean, yes I am sure. No, I didn't touch her."

"You didn't look for vital signs, take a pulse, to see if she might still be alive?"

"No. It was very obvious she was dead. Besides, I didn't know how she died and I knew it was important *not* to touch the body."

"It sounds like you kept a pretty cool head through all of this," he said, the skin around his eyes crinkling as he flashed a tight smile. His tone didn't make it sound like the world's greatest compliment.

"Well, I'm a reporter," I said. It was going to come out sooner or later, so it seemed best to get it on the table now.

"Oh, really. What kind of stories?"

"Human interest, crime stuff. In fact, I write a lot for *Gloss,* Cat Jones's magazine."

"Maybe that explains why I don't recognize your name. I generally stick with the men's magazines, if you know what I mean. So tell me what you thought when you saw the body. If you're a reporter, you're obviously observant. Did you suspect foul play of some kind?"

Foul play? Was *that* what he was thinking? "You mean, did I think someone had done something to her? No, I assumed she'd become violently ill for some reason."

"And why was that?"

"Well, there was vomit all over, and she was on the floor."

"Did Ms. Jones come in the room with you at any point?"

"No, she stayed in the library."

"Had you met the young woman before?"

"A few times, yes. Though I work with Cat, we're friends, too, and I've seen Heidi around the house."

He didn't remove his pale blue eyes from me while I answered, but when I was done he took a second to jot down what I said. As he wrote, the right shoulder of his too tight khaki suit strained at the seam.

"She a nice kid?" he asked.

"She was pleasant to me—and I think Cat's son liked her a lot. But I really didn't know her at all."

"Was she doing a good job as a nanny? Was Ms. Jones happy with her?"

"As far as I know."

"Was anyone in the house with the nanny this weekend?"

I paused for a moment. "I believe she was alone."

"You hesitated there for a second, Bailey," he said, cocking his head.

"Well, there's a housekeeper, Carlotta. She works mainly during the week, but I believe she sometimes comes in on weekends." From down the block I could hear church bells begin to peal and then, closer by, the whistle of a teakettle from an open window.

"And as far as you know, Mr. Jones wasn't around at all?"

"From what Cat said, no. His name is Henderson, by the way. Jeff Henderson."

"What about a boyfriend?" he asked.

"I beg your pardon?" I said, startled. It was a split

second before I realized he was talking about Heidi, not Cat.

"Did she have a boyfriend as far as you know?"

"I believe she had one at some point, but Cat said they were cooling it. You need to ask her about that."

"Did the nanny have any health problems? Was her health—"

"You know, I'm sorry, but I barely knew her. Cat would know all of this."

He just stared at me, the pale eyes watering slightly. His look suggested that I'd be smart not to cut him off like that again.

"You live in the city?" he asked after an uncomfortable moment.

"Yes, in the Village."

"Why do you think Ms. Jones called you to come up here today?"

"She was nervous, I think—worried. Heidi's apparently always been very reliable, and so Cat became alarmed when she didn't open her door."

"No, what I mean is, why you in particular?"

"We've known each other a long time. I'm the kind of friend she can call at eight A.M. on a Sunday morning."

"What was her demeanor like when you arrived?"

"Like I said, she was worried—very worried."

"She didn't want to go in the room herself?"

"I think she was just too scared to."

"Can I ask you something, Bailey, between the two of us? Did that seem funny to you? Her not wanting to go in alone?"

"No, not at all. We talked about the possibility of drugs

or alcohol or even suicide, and Cat didn't want to face it all by herself."

"Suicide? Had Heidi been depressed?"

"No. I mean, not that I know of. My point was simply that something seemed off, and as far as Cat knew it could have been one of any number of things. Or nothing. She just didn't know."

He didn't say anything else, just held my gaze momentarily before rising from the table. For now the interrogation appeared to be over. He asked for my phone number and address, jotting them down in the notebook and telling me he might need to get in touch in the next couple of days. He flipped the cover of the steno pad back over with one hand and led me back upstairs, where he collected Buzz Cut and announced they were going back downstairs. As soon as they were out of earshot, Cat grabbed hold of my sleeve.

"Am I being paranoid?" she asked. "Or did they deliberately separate us?"

"You're not being paranoid," I said as I poured myself more coffee. "That's exactly what they did."

"That's beautiful," she said sarcastically, throwing back her head. Most of the hair that had been held up with the chopsticks was down now, cascading around her face. "I suppose that means they think we're hiding something and they want to catch us in a lie?"

"No, it doesn't mean that. Cops interview bystanders and witnesses separately because if they're in the same room, they often unconsciously try to make their versions fit together."

"Look, I haven't had a chance to say this yet, Bailey,

but I don't know how I could have coped today without you."

"I'm glad I came. Your instincts turned out to be totally valid."

There was something I wanted to ask Cat, and this finally seemed like the right moment, but before I could, the doorbell rang. She went off to answer it, and a minute later Leslie Stone was striding through the kitchen.

Thirty-eight years old, with brown eyes and thick brown hair worn in a China chop, Leslie was considered attractive, but personally I didn't get it. Her nostrils were as big as kidney beans, and when I looked at her I always felt as if I were face-to-face with a fruit bat. Today she was all decked out in a beige, rayony pantsuit and strappy sandals, looking as if she'd been dragged away from a brunch in Santa Barbara. I hated being catty at a time like this, but I noticed that she had packed on some pounds since the last time I had paid close attention to her thighs. My problem was that I just didn't *like* Leslie. As a free-lancer I was fairly immune to her bullying, but whenever possible she harassed me about deadlines and my travel expenses. Her husband had made a killing in the stock market a few years back and then cashed out, and the only reason she worked, people claimed, was that she loved being in charge and telling people what to do.

"Start from the beginning," she demanded as she parked herself on one of the kitchen bar stools. The look she shot me registered irritation, as if I must be partly to blame for the mess. Cat took her through everything that had happened. While they talked, I excused myself and headed off to the powder room that was tucked under the hall stairs. I took my time, washing my hands, splashing water on my face, and putting on some blush and lip gloss I found in a basket in the cabinet under the sink. I stared at my reflection in the mirror. I looked about as bad as I felt, tired and drained and wigged out from the whole experience. How had the morning turned out this way? What could possibly have killed Heidi? And where was K.C. now? I wondered.

When I emerged from the bathroom I found that two young and very blond women from the PR agency had arrived, and they launched into a long discussion with Cat and Leslie about how to handle the inevitable press scrutiny, eventually including on speaker phone the head of the agency, who was safely out of town for the weekend. Lunch was ordered. We had drawn the drapes in the dining room, but I took a peek out occasionally. The ambulance had departed, but now there were other vehicles parked outside, including a van from the ME's, and people were traipsing in and out of the apartment below. There were gawkers outside, too, an ever-changing cluster on the sidewalk. So far no TV news trucks.

At about twelve-thirty, Jeff turned up—alone, having dropped off Tyler, he said, with friends in the city. He had his hip fashion photographer thing going—green cargo pants, white T-shirt, V-neck camel sweater—but he looked extremely distressed and white as a ghost. He and Cat hugged, and she clung to him even when he was ready to let go. He wanted to know everything, from start to finish, and she took him off to the kitchen.

Jeff, Jeff, Jeff. He was without qualification an absolute hunk. About six feet one and amazingly buff, he had hazel eyes, a full, sensuous mouth with a small cleft in the middle of his lower lip, and slightly wavy brown hair worn longish, just lower than his chin, and generally tucked behind his ears.

As a photographer he specialized in fashion, and as far as I knew after several years on his own, his career was in high gear. He didn't have Cat's level of success, but then again he was six years younger than her. As for their marriage, it appeared solid, despite predictions to the contrary from people who thought she couldn't last with a guy who had never read a novel all the way through. But Cat had had her fill of moody Wall Street millionaires and prickly Renaissance men. What she desired, she'd told me, was a guy who did one thing extremely well and wanted to spend the rest of his time with her, who was easy to be with and never made her walk on eggshells, who liked massaging the kinks out of the back of her neck—and who knew how to make the sex so good that the neighbors would wonder some nights if they should phone the police. Jeff was that man. Though I liked him enough, things had always been slightly awkward between the two of us. Maybe because I found his looks so disconcerting.

At about two I finally decided I'd better beat it. I felt bad for Cat, because of the jam she was in, and I wanted to help her. I also wanted to be in on the action. But I was beginning to feel like a fifth wheel. Cat preferred what you might call a compartmentalization approach to her friendships. We all served specific needs, with no one person responsible for too much. Right now Cat was preoccupied with damage control, which wasn't one of my specialties.

It would have been helpful to have a chance to talk to Jeff before I left, but Leslie was currently monopolizing him. I figured I'd do better leaving now and calling or coming back later. I told Cat I was splitting and said to call me if she needed me. Picking at a pasta salad as one of the blond spin doctors yammered away next to her, she acknowledged my departure in a state of distraction.

I found my sweater on the hall table, though I didn't recall leaving it there. As I started to open the front door, Jeff stepped out into the hallway.

"You okay?" he asked with just a trace of his Tennessee roots. "Cat told me how you found the body."

"I'm hanging in there. But what about you? This must be very sad for you."

It was hard to tell, though, exactly *what* he was feeling. He looked more agitated than anything else.

"Of course," he said quickly. "And this is going to be awful for Tyler. What do we tell him, for God's sake?"

As I started to ask him another question, one of the PR babes popped her head out into the hall.

"I wouldn't hold that door open if I were you," she chided me.

Jeff gave me a quick kiss on the cheek and I hurried away, down the steps. A TV news van was attempting to park out front, which would give me time to outdistance anyone climbing out of it, but a young guy on the sidewalk with a tape recorder and mike descended on me. I sprinted away, toward Park Avenue, where I flagged down a taxi.

As soon as I'd collapsed into the backseat, I realized that my head ached, my back and legs ached, and my brain ached, too. There were so many unanswered questions about Heidi's death. What had made her sick? Was she a drug user? Had she been alone last night? Why hadn't she called anyone once she began to get violently ill? I also had questions for Cat, things that had been bugging me all morning. Why had she spent the weekend in the Hamptons while her husband was up at their country home? Why had she needed to see Heidi at the crack of dawn on Sunday? And what had made her so terribly certain that something bad had happened?

I was anxious to hear the answers to those questions, but the thought of them scared me. Something told me that over the next few days, Cat's life was going to become a big ugly mess.

CHAPTER 4

THE GLOSS MAGAZINE editorial offices occupy the entire tenth floor of a building on Broadway at 56th Street and center around a large open area, nicknamed "the pit," which holds the cubes for the photo, art, and production departments as well as for some of the junior writers and editors. The space once consisted of traditional offices, but Cat had had it redesigned about six months after she'd taken over, remodeling it in the style of a classic newsroom. I don't think she ever expected anyone to come running through yelling, "Stop the presses! Gwyneth Paltrow screamed for mercy during a Brazilian bikini wax!" She did it, she said, to create the perfect combination of noise, energy, envy, and sexual chemistry. From what I could tell, she'd more than succeeded.

When I slunk into Gloss on Monday at around nine, ~~y~~ blueberry scone and large container of coffee, ~~practically deserted. The photo editor, wear-~~

ing a black shirt with a ruffle down the front, was sitting at his desk leafing through *W,* and about eight cubes away one of the production guys was opening a window. A low level of attendance was standard for any morning at *Gloss* before ten, but I had assumed—wrongly—that on this particular day a few people might have surfaced early to hear more about the death on 91st Street. At the far end of the pit, Cat's office, with its front wall of glass, was pitch dark.

I hung a left and headed down the long main corridor toward my office. I nearly jumped when, passing the alcove with the copy machine, I discovered "Kip" Kippinger, the deputy editor, photocopying pages of a book. He was about my age, a former producer at *Good Morning America* who'd been lured to *Gloss* about a year ago to oversee the articles department. A magazine person by background, he'd made a temporary foray into TV, and though I think he'd produced mainly health segments on topics like irritable bowel syndrome, the way he talked you'd have thought he'd overseen the coverage in Kosovo. His arrival at *Gloss* had created a stir because he was one of the only straight guys on the premises (though with a wife and two kids in the suburbs), and he was considered superattractive: a redhead, with milky, freckled skin and blue, blue eyes. No one seemed to notice that his head, at least as far as I was concerned, was too small for his body. I found him arrogant and smug, and his editing reflected that (he'd once suggested in a sex piece he'd overseen that a way to compliment a guy in bed was to ask him: "Do you have a license to carry that?"). Fortunately, because of my tenure at *Gloss,* my articles were still overseen by Polly, the executive editor.

"Morning," I said.

"Aren't *we* in early," he remarked, not at all pleasantly. It was the kind of passive-aggressive remark I never knew quite what to do with.

"I could say the same to you."

"You hear the news?"

"You mean about Cat's nanny?"

"Yeah, what's up with that, do you know?" He had a scowl on his freckled face, as if he were afraid the death was about to cause a major wrinkle in his day.

"It's in the papers," I said, cocking my head toward the two newspapers sticking out of my tote bag. "I was just about to sit down and read what was going on." I scurried off down the corridor before he could say anything else. The last thing I felt like doing was taking Kip up to speed on what I knew.

I rounded one more corner to my office. I was back in an area of the floor with a more traditional layout, where the fashion and beauty departments were situated and the senior text editors had their offices. My tiny space had once been a small reference library, but with *Gloss*'s reincarnation into a slick, hip women's magazine focusing on what was happening *right this minute,* there wasn't much need for tomes like the *Reader's Guide to Periodical Literature,* and the books had all been put in storage. The room was about eleven-by-seven, with a window that looked out onto an air shaft and a pie-wedge view of Broadway, but I loved the cocoon feeling of it, as well as how off the beaten track it was at the magazine. Besides, as a freelancer, I was lucky to have been given an office at all.

I tossed my bags and leather jacket onto the straight-backed chair in the corner and popped the lid off my coffee. Settling down at my desk, I turned my attention first thing to the two New York tabloids I'd picked up at the newsstand.

MYSTERY DEATH OF MEDIA STAR'S NANNY. That from the *Daily News.* It was in the banner section across the top. The *New York Post,* however, had turned over all of page one to Cat's calamity, and they, of course, had the more outrageous headline: NANNY DEAD IN MEDIA BOSS BASEMENT.

Below the headline was a shot of Cat dashing along a sidewalk, appearing totally frazzled. The picture, at least a year old, had obviously been selected from the photo archives so that it would appear as if the *Post* had caught up with her fleeing police headquarters.

Inside each paper the story continued, but only with sketchy details, both hinting at an overdose. There were several clichéd "Ms. Jones is deeply saddened" kinds of quotes supplied by a "spokesperson," indication that the spin doctors had worked at full throttle after I left Cat's. Both papers had a shot of the town house, and the *Daily News* featured Cat's stock press photo, a sexy shot with her hair at its blondest and fullest and her lips as pouty as a plum. There was something hilarious about the incongruity of the stock shot with this story. The caption might as well have been "My nanny just died, but I'd love to get laid."

It appeared from perusing the papers that there hadn't been any major developments in the story since I'd left Cat's yesterday afternoon. If there had been, the press hadn't been privy to them—and neither had I.

I'd gotten home at about five the night before, after a

long walk through the East Village. I felt edgy from all the coffee I'd drunk and suddenly in desperate need of company. But after fifteen minutes of calling, it was clear I wasn't going to dredge up anyone on such short notice. Even my regular crisis manager, Landon, my seventy-year-old gay next-door neighbor, was MIA. Usually I have advance plans for Sunday nights, but I'd stupidly left this one open, hoping that K.C. would wake up Sunday morning and refuse to leave my side. As I sat holding my phone, I imagined him moored on Long Island Sound, boinking some girl on the deck of his sailboat as the sun began to sink.

Since I couldn't dredge up anyone to join me for dinner, I had to find another way to stop those vomit-crusted sea foam towels from snaking around my brain. I'd once asked a Dallas homicide detective how she managed to cope with the horrors she saw, and she'd told me she surrounded herself with "things of beauty." I was dubious that that approach would do much to help me, but I gave it a stab anyway. I put on some Mozart and ate a salad with a glass of Cabernet. Then I took a lavender-scented bath, soaking for an hour, with the light on low and my head back against a folded towel.

The longer I soaked, though, the worse I felt. First of all my emotions, which had gone into some kind of insta-freeze that morning, had finally thawed and I was over-whelmed by sadness over Heidi's death. She had died so young, all alone in that apartment, with no one around to help her. My thoughts also kept coming back to Cat and Jeff. Was everything *okay* with them? I wondered. Sure, her job made plenty of demands, but for her to skip a weekend trip to their country home in Litchfield, Connecticut, in order to review plans for a film festival was a little like telling a guy you couldn't go out on Saturday night because you had to defuzz your sweaters. Jeff had been comforting to her when he'd arrived, but as time wore on he'd seemed to grow more and more detached. Cat was certainly going to need Jeff now. If Heidi had died from a drug overdose, they would face some ugly press scrutiny.

After my bath, I phoned Cat. I doubted the police would have shared much with her at this point, but I was anxious for any scrap of info I could get. Her machine picked up—she and Jeff were obviously screening calls. I tried reading for a while in my living room. As I'd told K.C., I'd ended up with the apartment two years ago, after the demise of my eighteen-month-old marriage. It was just a one-bedroom with a large walk-in closet that I had converted into an office, but it had the terrace and the great view of Village rooftops, and it was my sanctuary. People were always surprised that, considering New York real estate prices, my ex had let me keep it, but he'd had other things on his mind, namely getting out of town in the wake of his gambling debts.

I tried Cat again at nine and one last time at ten-fifteen, but I continued to get the machine. I felt annoyed that she wasn't returning my calls. I'd hauled myself out of bed at an ungodly hour for her, and now I was getting boxed out. But it wasn't totally unexpected. This whole Heidi thing was most likely turning into a PR crisis, a work situation, and I was never called in to deal with those matters. That's why God created butt kickers like Leslie. Or maybe Cat was just totally spent.

At around midnight, I'd climbed into bed with my

book and tried to will myself into drowsiness. Ever since my divorce I'd suffered from a torturous case of insomnia, often in the form of what's called "early final awakening." I'd fall asleep okay but then I'd wake at two or three A.M. and never be able to drift back. I ended up putting on the TV and watching a documentary on mudslides that wasn't as mind-numbing as I hoped. The last time I glanced at the clock on my nightstand, it said 2:22.

Done reading the media spin on Heidi's death, I was anxious to talk to Cat this morning, but I felt I'd left enough messages. Besides, she'd have to make contact at some point, at the very least to tell me how to deal if I got any calls from the press. In the meantime I decided to make an attempt to get some work done. I pulled out several files from my tote bag, along with a composition book. Though I've focused mainly on crime dramas the last few years, I still take on a straight human-interest story if it has enough mystery and intrigue to it. My latest story, the one due in four weeks, fell into that category. It involved a lower-middle-class family of five near Olean, New York, who suspected that their home was being haunted by a poltergeist. They would leave a room for a few minutes and discover upon their return that furniture had been scooted across the floor, or pillows tossed from a bed, or, in one instance, wallpaper peeled from the walls. On several occasions, so they claimed, objects had been hurled through the air by some, quote, invisible hand.

I'd gotten wind of the story from a small newspaper clip that a friend in the western part of the state had sent me (I have a whole network of friends and relatives around the country who regularly pass along intriguing stuff to me). No one lay dead with purple ligature marks around the neck or had vanished without a trace, yet my curiosity was piqued, and when I pitched the idea at *Gloss,* Cat said yes immediately.

I had driven my Jeep out there several weeks ago and spent two days with the Case family. I certainly didn't come away believing the house was haunted, but on the other hand, I couldn't tell who was creating the commotion—the parents themselves or one of the kids. On my second day there, a stuffed animal had gone flying by my head. Several people, including the twelve-year-old daughter, Marky, were in the room, but I couldn't determine who was responsible.

Early last week I'd done a phone interview with a "parapsychologist" who had been consulted by the family. His conclusion: not a poltergeist at all. Rather, everything was being caused by "telekinetic energy" emitted from the somber, sometimes sullen, little Marky.

"In ninety-nine percent of these cases there's a child, usually a girl, going through puberty or under tremendous stress," he'd explained, feigning patience with me. "Endocrine changes create electricomatic energy. And then, you see, the girl throws her energy in a spiral trajectory without realizing what is happening. And *that* is what makes things move and spill and fly."

I spent about forty-five minutes going through the transcript of the interview, which I'd gotten on Friday. I still had more people to interview, including a professor of child psychology from Georgetown who was here in New York this month, preparing to teach at NYU for the summer. He considered parapsychologists to be buffoons and had a different theory on what made things go bump in the night.

After an hour of work, my brain stalled. I couldn't stop thinking about Heidi. I picked up my phone and punched Cat's extension. Her assistant, Audrey, answered. Cat, she explained, was not in and wasn't expected.

Next, I flipped through my Rolodex and found the work number for Dr. Paul Petrocelli, head of the ER at a small hospital outside of Boston. I'd interviewed him once because he'd treated a rape victim I was writing about. Since then he'd allowed me to badger him for info for other stories. I tried the number, and when they said he was too busy to talk, I left a message.

Grabbing a clean coffee mug from my shelf, I decided to head down the hall toward the *Gloss* coffee station. The fashion department was almost directly across the hall from my office, and as I stepped out of my office I found the raven-haired fashion editor, Sasha, standing by her door, wearing low-riding brown pants, a pink tank top, and a tiara, and holding an orange stiletto. She was overseeing several prepubescent-looking assistants and interns packing trunks full of fall clothes.

"Traveling this week?" I asked, stopping in front of the door. I barely knew anyone in the department—they all had names like Tara and Tanya and Tamara—but since our offices were so close, Sasha and I occasionally engaged in borderline moronic chitchat.

"We're shooting near Palm Springs," Sasha said, all happy. Her lips seemed fuller than the last time I'd seen her, as if she'd either had collagen shots or been stung on the mouth by a hornet.

"In the desert?"

"Yes. The light is *so, so* beautiful there," she said, tossing the shoe into one of the open trunks.

I strolled down the hall toward the coffee machine, passing offices where at this hour editors usually could be found talking on the phone, staring at their computer screens, or licking the froth off their lattes. But today their offices were mostly empty. As I filled my coffee mug, someone called my name and I turned to see the executive editor, Polly Davenport, hurrying in my direction. Though Polly was the person I reported to at *Gloss*, that had not gotten in the way of us becoming pals, grabbing sandwiches or sushi together, and commiserating about being thirtysomething divorcées in New York City.

"Morning," I said. "Where *is* everyone?"

"They're all in the pit, yakking about what happened. You know, right?"

"Yeah. Why don't we talk in my humble abode."

We walked back to my office and I shut the door most of the way. Polly had her long, reddish blond hair in a braid today and was wearing a knee-length black jumper-style dress over a white T-shirt, calculated to minimize her hips, the bane of her existence. Polly had tried almost every diet imaginable, even "the stewardess diet" she'd found in a twenty-five-year-old copy of *Gloss*, and she was still thirty pounds overweight.

"How much do you know about what's going on?" she asked, taking a seat in the extra chair.

"Well, I'm incommunicado today, but I was up there yesterday. I was the one who found the body."

"God, you're kidding me. What exactly happened?"

"I'm not sure. Cat called and asked me to come up because Heidi wasn't answering her door. She was worried, and I got to be the one who went in there. Her body was on the floor, in that little apartment they have for her. She'd thrown up all over the place—so something made her sick. The obvious thing is drugs, but—"

"That's what the paper implied. You think she was using heroin?"

"I have no idea. I didn't see any sign of drugs, but then the police didn't allow me to do a search of the room, either."

"Was it awful, to find her like that?"

"Yeah, it *was*. I didn't really know her, of course, but it's sickening when someone so young dies regardless of whether you know her or not."

"Where *is* Cat, by the way?" she asked irritably.

"Home, I guess. According to Audrey she may not be in today."

"Well, I've tried to reach her all morning. We're shipping the ovarian cancer story. It's totally late and it's got to go today. I know she's got a lot on her mind, but she insisted she wanted to read the final."

"How'd you hear the news?" I asked.

"On the eleven o'clock news last night. But, of course, I'm used to hearing my news about *Gloss* secondhand."

It never ceased to annoy Polly that though she shared the second line on the masthead with Leslie, it was Leslie who was Cat's confidante. Yet in my opinion Polly was the more valuable asset. A lot of people could do what Leslie did, but Polly was enormously talented, a terrific line editor, and a brilliant title and cover-line writer. Cat might be the visionary of the magazine, the one with great instincts and a Rolodex jammed with writers and contacts, but Polly did the top edit on most of what ran in the magazine and wrote the titillating cover lines that helped sell so many copies—lines like "Why I Date Your Husband," "Perfectly Normal Women Obsessed with Having Pelvic Exams," and "Seven Sex Tricks So Hot His Thighs Will Go Up in Flames."

"If it's any consolation, I'd be lost without you," I said, smiling.

"Thanks. . . . Leslie is a no-show today. Do you think she's in the thick of things?"

"Yeah, she got called in to deal with the press. She's probably up there shooing away reporters."

"Well, I'm pleased for her. Leslie is happiest when she's kissing Cat's ass." With that Polly pushed herself out of the chair and stepped toward the door. "I've got to go rewrite some really bad captions. I'll stop by again later. How's your poltergeist piece, by the way?"

"It's getting there."

"You know it's in September now, right?"

"Yeah, no problem," I said.

As she went out the door, the phone rang, and she paused midstep, obviously thinking it might be Cat. I answered and gave Polly a shake of the head, indicating that it wasn't Cat. But it was.

"Hi," I said as Polly hurried down the hall. I figured Cat might be trying to keep a low profile and wouldn't want anyone to know she was calling in. "You okay?"

"No, I feel like shit," she said.

"What did I miss yesterday afternoon?"

"Just more misery. Look, I know you tried to call me last night, but things just got nuttier and nuttier. The police were here for what seemed like hours. They interviewed Jeff—all by himself like they did you and me.

And then the press descended like wild dogs. Jeff went out and got Tyler at around seven, and I took some Excedrin PM and crashed."

"The police didn't share any theories with you about what they think happened?"

"No, nothing. Totally tight-lipped."

"Did you reach Heidi's family?"

"Jeff talked to them. They didn't sound all that bothered by the news, though Jeff thought they'd get more excited if there was a chance they could sue someone. We're sending the body back, but not till the police release it."

"There'll be an autopsy, right?"

"Yes, today, I think. I'm hoping to hear something in the next few hours. That's why I'm not coming in. Plus, there may still be some stalkarazzi lurking around and I'd prefer not to let them take my picture."

"Can I help in any way?"

"Actually, yes," she said. "I have this bad, bad feeling this whole thing is going to explode somehow. And I need to know more about what was going on in Heidi's life. I need you to snoop around for me."

"Snoop?" I said. "You mean go through her things?"

"Maybe. But first I want you to talk to people she knew. She had this one good friend, another nanny. And there's Jody, her ex-boyfriend."

"But, Cat," I said, "wouldn't it make sense to wait till you find out how she died?"

"I don't want any surprises." A pause. "Bailey, I need you. I really do."

"Of course I'll help," I said. Heidi's death was eating at me, and I preferred to be in on the action rather than off on the sidelines. "There are a couple of things I want to ask you about anyway."

She suggested that I come to her place, where we could talk, but that it might be best to first see if I could connect with the friend and the ex. She told me to get in a cab and call her from my cell phone for the info—this way we'd save time. I told her I was on my way.

As I was packing up my tote bag, Dr. Petrocelli returned my call. I launched into my gruesome discovery yesterday.

"Not a very nice way to spend a Sunday," he said.

"That's for sure. Can you hazard a guess about cause of death?"

"How old was she—and when was the last time someone saw her alive?"

"Just twenty-two. And her boss talked to her Saturday afternoon."

"God, she was young for sudden death. The first thing I'd wanna know is whether or not there was any sign of trauma."

"Not that *I* could see. There was no blood or obvious bruising. She was on the floor, but it looked almost as if she'd slipped off the couch."

"Any underlying medical conditions?"

"Not that I know of."

"It sounds like you're probably looking at a toxicology case."

"You mean drugs?" I asked. "That's what jumped to my mind, of course."

"Yeah, drugs. Heroin can make you vomit copiously. Or alcohol. Or some kind of combination of both. The patient vomits and then chokes or aspirates the vomitus. If you're drunk or stoned, your gag reflex is depressed and your airways end up getting blocked. We see it all the time."

"The only thing is I didn't notice any signs around the apartment that she'd been drinking or doing drugs."

"She could have— Hold on a second." He turned to give some kind of order to someone. "Okay, where was I? She could have done it someplace else. I'd also consider Ecstasy—that can make you vomit. Or a date rape drug—GHB or rohypnol. Someone could have slipped it to her at a bar or party without her knowing it."

"I suppose that's a possibility," I said. "But she'd said she was staying in. What about food poisoning—salmonella or botulism?"

"That's not sudden death. It usually takes three or four days to die from something like that. There are some other possibilities. An aneurysm or a fatal pulmonary embolism. They can both trigger vomiting before they kill you. But those don't usually occur in someone so young. I'd say it's a tox case. Something she took—or maybe foul play."

When he said the words *foul play,* I got an instant case of goose bumps.

"Thanks, this helps," I told him. Though I actually felt even more confused—and concerned—than I had before.

CHAPTER 5

I TOLD THE cabdriver to head up Central Park West, then cut through the park, and that I'd provide him with the exact destination in just a sec. As we sped around Columbus Circle I called Cat on my cell phone and she gave me the info on the two people she wanted me to try to see this morning.

The other nanny was named Janice and she had apparently been Heidi's closest friend, her only friend, in fact, as far as Cat knew. Like Heidi, Janice was American, something that according to Cat was fairly unusual in the New York City nanny world. Cat had seen Janice on only a couple of occasions, knew practically nothing about her, and had her number only because it had been offered up by the housekeeper, Carlotta.

The other person to contact was the ex-boyfriend, name of Jody Ransom (or possibly Radson). He worked at a Starbucks on Third Avenue at 90th Street, but Cat had no idea where he lived. She believed he had begun dating Heidi sometime early last fall and had gotten the boot after the first of the year, though he had turned up sporadically in the new role of "friend." In fact, according to Carlotta, he had stopped by Thursday evening when Cat was giving a party for former *Gloss* editor in chief Dolores Wilder.

"When they were dating, did this Jody guy sleep over?" I inquired. "I mean, were they shacking up?"

"On the weekends, I think," Cat said. "We're usually gone then, you know, but Carlotta comes in once in a while on the weekends and I believe she got a shot of his bare ass once."

"Was that against the house rules?" I asked.

"No. I mean, I certainly didn't want guys traipsing in and out, and she knew better than to have anyone over during the work week. But on the weekends it was okay, as long as I didn't have to have it shoved in my face."

I told her I'd make an attempt to connect with both of them and then swing by her house. I'd finally have the chance to ask her about the things that had been bugging me.

As soon as I signed off, I called the number Cat had given me for Janice and she answered the phone herself. I explained that I was a friend of Cat's and that she had asked me to get in touch. Yes, she had heard about what had happened and was in her words "totally freaked," particularly because she had been unable to get through to the house for details.

"Well, that's why I'm calling," I said. "Cat wanted me to talk to you about some things. I was hoping I could drop by this morning."

Yes, she said, come by. She was going to be home until after lunch, and I told her I'd be there within the next hour or so.

After I'd tossed my cell phone back into my purse, I leaned back against the seat of the taxi, closed my eyes, and summoned the memory of the first time I'd laid eyes on Heidi. It was late last summer in Cat's garden at a dinner party she'd given in honor of someone who'd done something of note, but I couldn't remember who or what. As we were sitting down to eat, Heidi brought Tyler into the backyard to say good night to his parents. Cat looked mildly annoyed at the intrusion—probably because the delay was going to take the chill out of the gazpacho—but everyone else sat there in awe. Heidi, who had just started the week before, was stunning to behold. She was about five feet seven and curvy in only the right places. She had long blond hair, with streaks as light as butter, and her eyes were khaki green. I remember thinking that if I were married, I'd never have the nerve to bring someone that gorgeous to live in my home, but then Cat had supreme confidence in her own beauty as well as Jeff's ga-ga-ness over her.

What struck me that night as much as Heidi's stunning good looks was her aloofness. She seemed like an ice princess, the kind of girl who would choose a horse over a guy any day, but it was clear that she connected with men on some imperceptible level, kind of like the way a dog whistle works. A few of the men in the garden got goofy faced at the sight of her, and that included my date (whom, by the way, I later ditched on the corner of 91st and Park, leaping into a cab as he attempted to scrape gum off the bottom of his shoe).

After that night I bumped into Heidi occasionally at the house, and though she was polite, there was always that coolness and we never became friendly. I had no sense at all of what she was really like.

My first stop was Starbucks, where I hoped to hook up with Jody. It was eleven forty-five and the place was almost deserted. In the background some annoying merengue music was playing, all wrong for the mood and the time of day.

"Can I get a large cappuccino to go?" I asked a twentysomething girl in a green apron and black Starbucks cap. As the milk steamed, she stared off into the distance, with the boredom of someone who'd heard that annoying whine a million times before. I waited until she was handing me the change to pop my question.

"Is Jody here today?"

"Is it about a job?" she asked.

"No, it's personal."

"He *was* here. But he had to leave. You a friend of his?"

"Actually a friend of the family his former girlfriend worked for." Her eyes widened and I could tell that she was in the loop about what had happened. "I wanted to see how he was doing."

"Not so good," she said.

"How did he find out?" I asked.

"I think he saw it in the paper."

"Did you know her—Heidi?"

"She used to come in all the time—with that little boy. But not so much lately."

"You don't have an address for Jody, do you? I need to get hold of him to make sure he's okay."

She shrugged her shoulders. "Don't have an address. But I could give you a phone number."

Number in hand, I headed for 93rd and Second Avenue, where Janice lived with the family who employed her. The apartment building turned out to be one of those forty-story-tall condos that had gone up in the 1980s, full of yuppies who, as Cat had once pointed out, could afford the mortgage but didn't have enough equity to snag a more fashionable place west of Lexington Avenue.

The concierge announced my arrival and directed me to go to 31E. It took Janice about a minute to answer the bell. I could hear her hushing a kid, and then the sound of her making her way to the door, her shoes or sandals flip-flopping across the floor. Her looks surprised me. Probably because of Heidi, I had expected Janice to be pretty, too, but she was short and plump, and her long, brassy blond hair was styled in a bad version of Farrah Fawcett's *Charlie's Angels* do. She was squeezed into a pair of jeans and a black CK T-shirt—about three sizes too small.

"Hi, Janice, I'm Bailey," I said, sticking out my hand. "Thanks so much for seeing me. I'm sure this must be hard for you, since you and Heidi were so close."

As soon as I said Heidi's name, tears began to fall, depositing streaks of mascara as they slid down her face.

"I'm so upset," she said. "I've been calling the house over and over to see if someone would, like, talk to me, but I keep getting the stupid machine."

"Well, the press is pestering the family—because of Miss Jones's job. May I come in?"

"Oh yeah, sorry."

The apartments in these kinds of New York City build-

ings all look pretty much the same—rectangular rooms
without any ornamentation, parquet floors, tiny
kitchens—so I was surprised by the place as I got my first
full glimpse of it. The owners must have totally gutted the
existing apartment—several apartments, for that matter—and had created a loftlike space with a large open
kitchen, dining, and living area. The furniture was mostly
contemporary, and though the space was decorated de-
cently, there was stuff piled on every possible surface—
shrink-wrapped packages of Pampers, tubs of baby
wipes, Blockbuster videotapes, magazines, mail, cata-
logs, unfolded laundry, a six-pack of vanilla pudding. In
the living area was a huge TV screen, practically the size
of ones they use in football stadiums to show the replays.
Parked in front of it in a baby walker was a nearly bald
baby, probably just over a year old. He was gumming a
bagel to death and watching a show or videotape featur-
ing a giant blue-spotted dog.

Janice flip-flopped her way in a pair of black mules to
the dining room table and plopped down in one of the
chairs. On the placemat in front of her was a can of Diet
Coke and a plate of half-eaten French fries, the kind with
ridges that you buy frozen and heat up in the oven. I sat
down at the spot directly across from her, with a stunning,
unbroken view to the East River and Queens.

"You wanna soda?" Janice asked, pushing aside the
plate of fries and picking up her own can. Her inch-and-
a-half-long nails were painted purple and had little flower
decals on them.

"No thanks, I'll just drink my cappuccino," I replied.
As I took a sip, Janice glanced over at the baby. He was

bouncing up and down giddily in his walker, watching the blue-spotted dog roll in a puddle.

"What happened to Barney?" I asked. "Do kids still like him?"

"Barney is *sooo* over," Janice said, giving her head a shake of disgust. "And I'm glad, too. He makes me sick."

"Did you and Heidi meet as nannies?"

"Yeah, at Gymboree," she said. "We were, like, the only two nannies who weren't from the Islands."

"Gymboree's a place for kids?"

"Yeah, it's like these classes where you hold the kid and help him go down a slide or you bounce him on a trampoline and sing that song, you know, 'Three Little Monkeys Jumping on the Bed'?"

"How did you hear that Heidi was dead?" I asked.

"A friend called—she heard it on the news." Tears began to roll down her face again, and she wiped them gingerly with the pads of each index finger, careful not to lance a cornea with her nails. "But I don't get it. How do you get sick and die in a day?"

"They don't have any idea right now. It's a complete mystery. They'll do an autopsy and some tests. When was the last time you spoke to Heidi?"

"On Saturday. I talked to her on the phone."

"About what time?"

She thought for a moment, twirling one of her hair wings. "It was like one o'clock or so. I tried to talk her into going out with me that night, but she didn't want to."

"She had other plans?"

"No, she just said she didn't want to go out. She never wanted to go out at night anymore. We used to go to this place on Third Avenue all the time—the Caboose. She loved it. Guys there thought she was awesome. But lately she'd become like this homebody." She walked two fingers on nail tips toward the plate of cold fries and picked up one of them, holding it as if she were dangling a night crawler.

"Did she give any indication she wasn't feeling well?" I asked.

"No, she just said she felt like staying in."

"Was she depressed, down in the dumps?"

"No, I don't think so. She said she just wanted to read—and listen to music."

"What kind of music?" I asked, remembering what she'd had playing in the apartment.

"Jazz. She'd gotten a thing for jazz lately. Go figure." She folded the cold French fry into her mouth.

"When was the last time you saw Heidi in person?" I asked.

"On Friday. Wait—I mean Thursday. We took T and G out and had a coffee together."

"T and G?"

"Oh, that's what we call Tyler and George for short."

"When the two of you used to go out at night together, did Heidi ever have too much to drink?"

Janice snorted. "No—I mean, once in a billion years she'd have a glass of white wine, but she didn't like to drink. Seltzer was her drink of choice."

"And what about drugs?"

"*Drugs?* Is someone saying she did drugs?"

"No, no. It's just I wondered—because she was sick. There's a chance someone might suggest it."

"Heidi wouldn't take any drugs," Janice said, shaking

her head. "Don't take this the wrong way, but she thought that sort of thing was beneath her."

Little G had begun to fuss in his walker, maybe because the blue dog had vanished from the screen.

"You want a bobbie, G?" Janice called to him. He gave a grunt of approval, and she got up and went to the refrigerator, grabbing a short bottle already filled with milk. As she walked toward him, both arms shot straight up to take it from her. I wondered if there was anything wrong with me because at such moments I wasn't overwhelmed with baby lust.

"He's way too old for a bottle if you ask me," said Janice, rolling her eyes as she sat down again. "But his mother lets him have them. She doesn't know how to say no to him."

"Did you know Heidi's boyfriend—Jody?"

"God, that relationship was *sooo* over. But yeah, I've met him. He's an annoying person."

"In what way?"

"He made Heidi think he was much more important than he was. He told her he was like the manager of that Starbucks but he's really just the assistant manager. He told her his family in Colorado was rich, but that's not true, either. After she broke up with him, he kept calling her, bothering her."

"Was he still annoying her?"

"I think he finally took the hint, if you know what I mean."

"Was she seeing anyone else yet?"

A long pause.

"I don't know," she said finally. "Heidi told me she

was taking a break from guys. She wanted to, like, take
some time to herself. But . . ."

Janice leaned back in her chair and lowered her head,
her hands in her lap. Her blond hair cascaded down in
front of her face.

"But what?"

"Heidi claimed she didn't want another boyfriend, but
I can't picture Heidi without a guy," she said, glancing up
through a fringe of hair. "I almost got the feeling . . ."

"Yes?" I urged delicately, not wanting to look as if I
were pouncing.

"I almost wonder if she was seeing some guy but
didn't want to introduce me to him. Like . . . like she was
embarrassed of me or something."

Her plump lower lip began to tremble and a tear
squeezed out from behind each eye.

"If only I'd talked Heidi into going out with me Saturday night, she might be alive," she wailed. "I would have
seen her getting sick and I could have helped her."

"Janice, you shouldn't feel that way," I said. "We don't
know yet how she died. There's probably nothing you
could have done."

Little George chose this moment to hurl his bobbie
across the large square coffee table, overturning an empty
liter bottle of Diet Dr Pepper, which then skidded onto
the floor. It seemed like a good time to exit.

"Look, Janice," I said, standing, "I better let you get
back to work. Let me give you my number, and if you've
got any questions, call me at *Gloss*—I work with Ms.
Jones—and just leave a message." I handed her a card
with my phone numbers, and she gave me her cell phone
number on a scrap of paper.

"What were you going to tell me, though?" she asked as she walked me to the door. "You said Mrs. Jones wanted you to get in touch."

"We just wanted to be sure you were all right. We know what good friends you and Heidi were."

"Oh, yeah," she said.

"I don't know anything about the funeral," I said, stopping by the door. "I assume it will be held in the town where Heidi's relatives live. Did you know anything about her family? Did she ever talk about them?"

"Her parents were dead. She had this aunt she hated. She didn't want to talk about her—she said she was a witch."

She bit her lip then, as if she were deliberating about saying something. I stood very, very still, waiting.

"Look, there's one thing I need to mention," she said finally. "I loaned Heidi a pair of earrings about a month ago and she kept forgetting to give them back. Do you think I'm going to be able to get them? They cost like forty dollars."

"Of course. I can ask Carlotta to look for them."

She described the earrings—dangly gold with a pearl on each end—and I said good-bye. Once outside I flagged down a cab, and as it headed toward Cat's I pulled out my notebook and began jotting down notes from my conversation.

I hadn't gathered a ton of info, but what I had was interesting. Point A: According to Janice, Heidi didn't drink or do drugs, which, if accurate, put the kibosh on the idea that her death might have resulted from an overdose. Of course, she could have ingested too much of something without knowing it. As Paul had said, she may have been slipped a date rape drug.

Point B: Heidi had told Janice that she wasn't interested in dating right now, but, like Janice, I was dubious about this. Twenty-two-year-old girls don't take sabbaticals from boys and booty—at least intentionally. It sounded as though something were cooking, something that Heidi hadn't wanted Janice to know about. Interestingly, Cat had remarked yesterday that Heidi had seemed detached lately.

But if she had a new guy, why wasn't she with him Saturday night? Maybe he was out of town or unavailable for some reason. Maybe she *had* been with him and hadn't wanted to tell Janice about her plans. She could have lied to Janice and gone out on a date, though there seemed to be no reason she would have also lied to Cat, telling her she was staying in. Maybe the mystery man came to *her* place that night. Did he know anything about what had made Heidi fatally ill?

Point C: And why, if there really was a new man in her life, keep it a secret? Sure, there was the chance she was embarrassed to introduce him to Janice, but Cat hadn't been in the loop, either. Maybe *he* wanted it kept a secret. He was older and didn't want anyone knowing he was dating someone who was practically jail bait. Or he was married. That would certainly explain the need to keep it under wraps. And not only would he want discretion because of his situation, but Heidi would want it, too, knowing that Cat would have no tolerance for the situation. This could also explain why Heidi was apparently alone Saturday night.

A married man. New York was overrun with them.

Heidi could have met one while she was out pushing Tyler in the stroller. She could have met one at a bar, his wedding band stuffed in his pocket. She could even have met one at Cat's house, at one of her many shindigs.

As I neared the corner of Park and 91st Street, I froze on the sidewalk. What if she *had* fallen for a married guy she'd met at Cat's house? What if it was the married guy in residence, the one who belonged to Cat?

CHAPTER 6

I SHOOK THE thought of a Heidi/Jeff liaison out of my head for the time being because (1) it seemed fairly preposterous; and (2) what I needed to focus on now was dodging any press lurking outside of Cat's. As the cab sped down the block, however, I saw that it was deserted in front of the town house. I paid the driver, and before springing up the stoop, I paused to stare at Heidi's apartment. A strip of yellow police tape was stretched across the iron gate.

I climbed the stoop and rang the doorbell. It was answered by Carlotta, Cat's housekeeper from Guatemala, a woman of around fifty who wasn't a hair over five feet tall. She kept the chain on the door until she saw who it was.

"The reporters aren't here anymore, Carlotta?" I asked as she let me in.

"No more, Miss Bailey. They go already. Yesterday it was not berry nice."

"Is Cat here? She asked me to drop by."

"She know. She ask you go to her office. You know, the third floor?"

I'd been in the upper part of the house only a couple of times in the four years Cat had owned it. On the third floor were a large master bedroom and bath and a small study for Cat. On the fourth and top floor were Tyler's room, a guest bedroom, and a darkroom/office for Jeff, though as far as I knew he did all of his work in his studio downtown.

As I stepped onto the third floor landing, I spotted Cat standing in her study, with her ear to a cordless phone. She was wearing a pair of flat-front khaki pants in some sort of stretchy-looking fabric and an orange top with an off-center zipper in the front. How was it that she could carry off orange so well? The few times I'd tried it, I'd looked like a crossing guard. She also had on a pair of faux cheetah-print heels. Cat was a notorious shoe slut, and she especially liked the kind that showed off what she called "toe cleavage," which this pair certainly did.

I fell into the kilim-covered armchair and glanced around the room. The walls were a hunter green, and the color, combined with the dark shutters on the windows and the wooden overhead fan, could make you feel as if you were in a novel by Somerset Maugham. Cat hadn't said a word into the phone since I'd entered the room, and it was clear from her expression that she was growing impatient with whoever was yapping into her ear on the other end. Finally she cut the person off.

"So she refuses to wear leather. We'll put her in something pretty by Dolce and Gabbana. Or Versace. Let's just get the date nailed down."

She listened for a minute, simultaneously gesturing for me to pick up the newspapers on the desk behind me. I started to mouth that I'd seen them, but suddenly she was riveted to what she was hearing.

"What?" she yelled. "She thinks silkworms are mistreated?" A pause. "You've got to be fucking kidding me. Forget it. I'm not going to get into any kind of dance with a nut like that. Her last two movies were dogs, and she should consider herself lucky if we asked her to model the Cheryl Tiegs Kmart collection. We're going to have to find someone else."

The person at the other end was obviously Rachel Kaplan, the *Gloss* entertainment editor, who apparently was now making a stab at getting Cat to reconsider her decision to cancel some petulant, PETA-sympathizing star's shot at a cover.

"Tough," Cat said. "She sounds like a lunatic, and I know just what would happen. We'd go along and get to the shoot and find out she won't put on cotton because—because it's bad for boll weevils or something. I'm not taking any chances. Who else has a movie in October?"

Long pause. "No—she's death on a newsstand."

Another long pause. "She could work, though she's got that heinous publicist who never gives us anybody. Before you try, have Peter call in some paparazzi shots of her. We need to do a chubby check. I've gotta go." She put the phone down without bothering with good-bye.

"I thought you'd never get here," she said, flopping down in the other armchair. "You want anything to drink—or eat?"

"In a minute, maybe, after we talk."

"Did you find out anything about Heidi?"

"A bit. I didn't hook up with Jody yet, but I spoke with Janice. She said Heidi rarely drank and didn't do drugs. She was pretty adamant. How did you find Heidi, anyway?" I asked. "Did you get her through an agency?"

"No, it was a word-of-mouth kind of thing," she replied. "She'd been working up in Westchester and she wanted to get out, to find a gig in the city."

"You said Heidi and Jody hadn't been going out for a while. Do you think she'd hooked up with someone else?"

"Not that I know of." She had paused just a beat before answering.

"Heidi always spent weekends here, even if you guys were up in Litchfield?"

"For the most part. Though she came up with us a few times this spring. We didn't expect her to work weekends, so she'd do her own thing, go off on a bike for the day. Why?"

"I'm just wondering what she may have been up to. Janice told me that Heidi hadn't wanted to spend as much time with her lately. She'd become kind of secretive, too."

"That's the kind of thing I need you to look into," she said, leaning forward. "Like I said, I don't want any weird surprises. Did you see what the *Post* did with this already? They said she died in my basement. They're making it sound like the JonBenet Ramsey case."

"I'm happy to help, Cat, but if Janice doesn't know anything and Jody's not likely to, that doesn't give me much to go on."

"Why don't you take a look at some of her things and see if you can find anything out from that? I should do it myself, but I can't bear to."

"But are the police finished with the room? Surely they don't want people traipsing around yet."

"They spent a whole day there and they're done. I called last night and they said it was okay to use the room—though I can't imagine who'd want to."

"Well, I can look around down there, but I assume if there was anything interesting, the police took it with them."

"They told me they took her address book and purse. But there may be other stuff that you'd recognize as significant and they wouldn't. I just want to make sure she wasn't into anything weird."

"Fine. I'll poke around. There are a few things I need to clarify with you first, though."

"Okay, shoot."

This wasn't going to be easy. For all the confidences that Cat had shared with me, she loathed being questioned directly about her private life.

"Was there a reason you were worried about Heidi that you didn't want to share with me?"

"What do you mean?" she asked. "I'm not following you."

"Well, it's just that you were so anxious over the simple fact she wasn't answering the door, and as it turned out your fears were totally justifiable. Did you have some concern that you weren't sharing with me?"

"Was I holding something back? No, not at all. It was eight in the morning, she was supposed to be home, her lights were on, and she wasn't answering the door. It seemed like reason enough to worry."

"On the phone you didn't mention the lights being on, did you?"

"I don't remember *what* I said," she replied impatiently. "I was alarmed, I called you for help. I think most people would say my gut instincts are on the mark."

"Point taken. Another thing. You said you wanted to meet with Heidi to talk about Tyler. Was something the matter?"

"Why do you ask that?" I saw her body tense slightly as she spoke.

"Well, it just sounds a little odd—you scheduling an appointment with her on her day off."

"Okay, there *was* something the matter," she said, running her hand through her hair. "Lately, Heidi hadn't been totally into her job. Like I said, she'd been distracted. I was worried that she might not be giving Tyler her full attention. I wanted to talk to her about it. She gets up early, so there was no reason not to do it then. I didn't want it hanging over my head the whole day."

"But why on Sunday, her day off?"

"Honestly? Because Jeff wouldn't be around. He says we've had too much nanny turnover, and he thinks I'm partly to blame—that I'm overly critical. Since he had to be up in Connecticut and I had to be here, it seemed like a good time to do it."

"I didn't think you and Jeff spent weekends apart." If asking about Heidi was awkward, drilling her about Jeff was a hundred times worse. As she took in my comment, her face remained placid and her eyes held mine, but her butt shifted a millimeter in the chair.

"We don't usually. But this weekend I finally had a chance to do this film festival meeting and Jeff had to keep an appointment with the landscape artist up in Litchfield. It was unavoidable. Why the third degree, Bailey?"

"I just wanted to make sense of everything." Her explanations sounded reasonable enough, and I was relieved to be able to halt the inquisition.

"So do you want to look through Heidi's stuff or not?" she asked, sounding suddenly peevish.

"Sure, I'll do it. Though you mentioned food earlier. I'm famished."

"Carlotta's got stuff set out in the kitchen. Do you need me to come down with you?"

"No, make calls, do what you have to do," I told her. "I'll get something to eat and then I'll go down to the apartment. You're not expecting anyone, are you?"

"I'm making people come up to the house for a planning meeting—but that's not for over an hour."

As I walked out to the hall, I heard Tyler's sweet, squeaky voice from the top floor. I glanced up and saw him sitting in the doorway of his room, his pale blond hair falling forward as he scooted a toy truck back and forth. I turned back to Cat and she answered my question before I had a chance to ask it.

"Carlotta's cousin is taking care of him for now—while an agency tries to get me someone else."

I went down to the kitchen and helped myself to a Caesar salad and a white bean dish that were sitting on the counter, both in beautiful ceramic bowls, next to a plate of chocolate brownies, one of Cat's biggest weaknesses. There was a pitcher of iced tea, too, with a metal cylinder for ice in the middle to keep it cold. And pale yellow cloth napkins, perfectly pressed and fanned out beside everything. When I'd been married I'd begun to fantasize about leading the good life like this, filling my life with little luxuries. But since my divorce I'd let that go for now. I had a neat apartment and a good career, and over the past two years I'd focused just on trying to feel sane again.

While I ate I checked my voice mail at work. The child psychologist I was supposed to meet on Thursday had called to confirm his appointment. As I heard his voice for a second time, I realized that he might be younger than I'd first imagined, maybe mid-thirties. The only other calls were from Leslie's assistant, telling me that my expense reports were two months behind schedule— in the same frantic tone someone would use to announce there'd been a breakout of the Ebola virus in the building—and my friend Landon, who'd read the news about Heidi and was dying for details, unaware of the role I'd played. What wasn't on my voice mail was an "I read the *Post* and I hope you're *okay*" message from my Saturday night date. Maybe he'd fallen overboard while attempting stand-up sex on the bow of his boat.

After a helping of food and a glass of iced tea, I managed to steel myself for a return trip to Heidi's apartment. I grabbed my steno pad from my purse in the hallway and headed downstairs.

The bookcase door was partially open, and as I slipped through into the hallway I discovered that the putrid smell from yesterday had abated but not disappeared, like a headache that's gone from sledgehammer strength to a dull, steady throb. There were no lights on. I reached blindly into the bathroom, fumbled around for the switch, and flooded that room with light. It seemed as good a place as any to start.

The room was tiny, with a shower stall rather than a tub. The pile of sea foam green towels that had haunted me last night had been removed, obviously bagged by the police, and it was clear at a glance that the only spot likely to cough up anything of interest would be the medicine chest. I'd searched my fair share in my day, and I knew that they could sometimes contain nasty surprises—like when you discover a strip of Zovirax tablets and realize your date has herpes. Heidi's was stuffed with cosmetics and toiletries, all high-end stuff—Calvin Klein, Estée Lauder, Shiseido, Chanel—and I was surprised by the selection until I realized that they were products Cat would have brought her from the *Gloss* beauty closet.

The other products were all within the realm of normal: a bottle of Aleve, an extra toothbrush, dental floss, mouthwash, echinacea. No birth control, though, or anything else to suggest she'd been doing the dirty deed lately.

Right across from the bathroom was the Pullman kitchen: just a sink, refrigerator, half-size stove, a few cabinets, and a foot of counter space. Opening the cupboards revealed that Heidi had not been a regular viewer of the Food Network. Other than a box of granola and a few cans of lentil soup, her cupboards were bare. The fridge was just as pathetic. There was a solitary container of peach yogurt, past its prime, a bag of carrots, a carton of grapefruit juice, and about five bottles of salad dressing—Caesar, ranch, strawberry vinaigrette, French—all low-fat or no-fat. No wonder Heidi had pinched the box of chocolates.

It was time now for the main room, and my heart took off at a gallop as I floundered around looking for a light. My hand finally hit a switch on the wall that worked the floor lamp by the couch.

The space was even smaller than I'd realized in the dimness yesterday. There wasn't much in the way of furniture: the convertible couch, the trunk used for a coffee table, and a small armchair, all in the center of the room; a dresser and a pine wardrobe along the wall to my right; a small TV on a stand and a waist-high bookcase on the left; and a small table and chair between the windows in the front. Though the room was tastefully done—the walls were yellow and the fabric on the couch a pretty blue-and-yellow check—it was obvious Cat had done it on the cheap. For a moment I just stood motionless in the middle of the room. A homicide cop I'd profiled told me that the first thing he did when he walked into a crime scene, before he'd even looked at the body, was to attempt to get a feeling for the room. I closed my eyes and tried to do that now. What I sensed was emptiness, confusion, and fear—but I had no idea if it had to do with Heidi or my own reaction to everything that had occurred in the last twenty-four hours.

There wasn't much in the way of knickknacks or possessions lying around on the surfaces. The chocolates and water bottle, which had been sitting on the trunk, had been removed. I lifted up the lid: Inside was a blanket and two bed pillows with light blue cotton pillowcases.

The table by the window had been set up like a desk, and I moved over there. There was a phone, a round wicker pencil holder stuffed with pens, a box of blue notecards, and a saucer filled with paper clips and stamps.

Saving the dresser and wardrobe for last, I took a look through the bookcase next. There were a few thrillers—by John Grisham, Nicci French, and Sandra Brown—and an odd selection of new age stuff—a guide to creative visualization, two books on astrology, and a book called *Celtic Symbols*, with a black spiral design on the front. Most of the shelf space had been used for storing magazines—*Cosmo*, *Vogue*, and *InStyle*—and she had them stacked in piles by name, like a little reference library. On the top of the bookcase was her radio/CD player as well as a stack of CDs: Faith Hill, Destiny's Child, 'NSync, and Madonna—all of which you might expect for her—and five or six jazz CDs, which you wouldn't. I recalled how the radio yesterday had been set to a jazz station and what Janice had said about Heidi's newfound interest in that kind of music. There were also two photos of Heidi in cheap brass frames. In one she was posed on the dock of the Circle Line cruise—that's a boat trip around the island of Manhattan—with another girl. It was obvious from their clothes it was summertime, and her hair was only to her shoulders. Most likely the shot had been taken just after her arrival in New York late last summer. In the other photo she stood in front of a thick cluster of trees—in the countryside, perhaps, or maybe even in Central Park. The picture seemed more recent, taken perhaps within the last several months: Her hair was longer and she wore jeans and an oversize yellow crewneck sweater, the kind of clothes you'd put on for a late winter or early spring day. She seemed positively kittenish—leaning forward from the waist, tugging down on the bottom edges of the sweater with both hands, biting her lower lip.

So far, I'd kept my feelings in check as I'd been paw-
ing over Heidi's things, but when I opened the pine
wardrobe I felt a rush of sadness. Maybe it was from seeing her clothes hung so neatly, ready and waiting to be
worn again, or maybe it was because she had so few of
them. There was a red parka, a full-length black wool
coat, a yellow windbreaker, several dresses—one a sun-
dress with a halter that hung clumsily on its hanger—four
or five pairs of pants, and on the bottom a few pairs of
shoes and boots. Had she simply not wanted to come to
New York laden down with loads of things, or was this all
she had in the world? On top of the dresser were a few
stuffed bears and a tray of costume jewelry, mostly earrings. I spotted the pair Janice had mentioned, and as I
scooped them up I noticed that one was missing a pearl
on the dangly part.

The selection in the dresser was just as paltry as the
wardrobe. There were eight or nine T-shirts and tank tops,
three sweaters, a few halters, panties, thongs, bras
(34C)—stuffed in haphazardly, probably because the police had looked through everything. In the bottom drawer
I found what appeared to be the jeans she'd worn in the
photo by the trees, but there was no yellow sweater anywhere. Not surprising, since it had been far too big for
her. Had it been borrowed from the photographer she was
looking at with such mischief in her eyes?

I reopened the top drawer and reached with my hand
carefully under the piles of clothes. Beneath the T-shirts I
found a square turquoise Tiffany box. Carefully I wiggled
off the top. Inside were a pair of diamond stud earrings,
about three-quarters of a carat each, and a gold bangle
bracelet inset with six diamonds. Yowzer. The earrings

and bracelet together were probably worth ten grand minimum. Heidi certainly hadn't bought these herself. They were most likely from a guy with money to burn. The question was: Were they gifts from a former lover or a new one—namely, the mystery man?

I went back through each drawer then, reaching underneath the clothes. Beneath the jeans I could feel another box, this one bigger and longer. I tugged it out. It was a box of Trojan-ENZ "ultrathins."

As I was tucking it back under the clothes, I heard a shuffling sound behind me. I spun around to find Carlotta standing behind me.

"Jesus, Carlotta, I almost had a stroke," I burst out.

"Sorry, sorry, Miss Bailey. But Miss Jones wants you upstairs right now. The detective, he called, and he's coming over, right now."

"Oh shit," I said. "How long ago did he call?"

"Just this minute."

"Okay, I'll be right up."

I had a little time, I figured, so I took a moment to scribble down a few notes.

As I was about to flick off the light in the kitchenette, I stopped, remembering something a cop had once taught me. I snapped open the freezer compartment of the refrigerator. Lying on its side, all by its lonesome, a full bottle of Stoli, sealed.

Heidi supposedly didn't drink, but someone who came calling apparently did. Who was it? Jeff, to my recollection, drank beer and bourbon, like a good southern boy. Had this mystery man/vodka lover been around this past weekend? Had he been aware that Heidi was getting sick? Or had he done something to make her that way?

CHAPTER 7

As I REACHED the top of the stairs, I discovered Cat in the living room, draining a glass of iced tea.

"What's going on—why's he coming?" I asked, breathless from having taken the stairs two at a time.

"Not sure," she said, turning her attention to me. "He just called and announced that he needed to come by—he's got other questions he wants to ask me."

"Maybe something turned up in the autopsy," I said. "I should scram, don't you think? He's not going to love having me here."

"Don't go, Bailey," she pleaded. "I don't want to be alone with him when he starts asking his questions. Besides, don't you want to see what he's wearing? He'll probably have on a pair of Haggar slacks or something nifty like that."

"Do you think Jeff should be here, too? Or what about a lawyer? Have you got a lawyer in the loop on all this?"

"Yes, we talked to him yesterday, and he said that for now it was better to handle the police alone, unless they sounded at all accusatory. Please just hang around, will you? I'm still having a tough time coping with all of this."

My arm needed no twisting, and I agreed, taking a seat across from her in a creamy white armchair. I was anxious to hear anything Detective Farley had to say.

"Okay, so what did you find downstairs?" Cat asked. "Talk fast."

"Well, there wasn't exactly a lot to go through. Heidi didn't have much in the way of earthly possessions, did she?"

"You mean clothes?"

"Clothes, books, knickknacks. You've been in her room at some point, haven't you? I can't imagine you not sneaking a peek at her setup. And don't be coy, Cat. I know you."

"The most I did was poke my head in occasionally. And I had Carlotta clean in there once a week. Our last nanny was such a pig, we got mice."

"Well, like I said, there wasn't much to look through, but I did get a vibe that there was a new man on the scene."

"Why?" she asked, her face expressionless.

"Couple reasons. She had some new jazz CDs, and since she appears to have had pretty mainstream music taste, my guess is that some guy gave her the CDs or she bought them to be knowledgeable—for a guy's sake. There was also a bottle of vodka down there, in the freezer, and if we're to believe Janice, that Heidi wasn't a drinker, she obviously had the stuff stocked for someone. And there was a box of condoms in her drawer—though it's possible they were left over from her Jody days. Last, but not least, she had a

Tiffany box with a very expensive bracelet and diamond studs."

"Really?" she said, half question, half statement. Her voice was even, but her eyes widened slightly.

"I doubt very much that Jody gave them to her. Any idea where they came from? She didn't pinch *those* from you, did she?"

"No and no." But I could sense the wheels turning in her head as she processed the info, obviously trying to see if it added up to anything—or anyone. I wondered if Jeff's name had flashed across her mind as it had briefly mine.

"Well, it seems pretty likely—"

At that moment the front doorbell rang.

"God, he's here," she said. "Let's finish this later," as if I'd even consider describing my amateur detective exploits in front of Detective Farley.

Farley was all alone this time, and as Carlotta led him into the room, Cat and I both stood up at attention. He was in navy blue today, this suit too tight just like the other one. He'd either gained weight since he'd been clothes shopping or he bought them on the tight side because he liked the snugness, the feeling of having everything contained and controlled.

"Thanks for taking the time to see me on short notice," he announced. He glanced over in my direction and gave me a knowing look and a nod. "Miss Weggins."

"Please sit down, Detective," said Cat. "Can I get you a glass of iced tea?"

"No, thank you." As he lowered himself into an armchair, he brushed imaginary lint off the taut pant fabric on his thighs.

"Do you know anything yet?" Cat asked, sitting back

down again as I followed suit. "Do you have any idea what happened to Heidi?"

"In a minute I'll explain where we are in the investigation, but I need to ask you a few questions first."

He reached inside his suit coat pocket and pulled out a notepad, flipping through until he found a blank page.

"You mentioned to me yesterday that Heidi and Mr. Radson—Jody Radson—had stopped dating," he said, looking directly at Cat. "Do you have any idea which one of them decided to call it off?"

He got my full attention with the first question. If he was wondering who dumped whom, it meant that something fishy was up.

"Well, she never told me," Cat said. "But if I had to guess, I'd say her."

"And why is that?"

"Because she didn't look that upset when she told me about it. Of course, it could have been mutual—but it so rarely is, is it?"

"Mr. Radson—we spoke to him yesterday evening— said they had stopped seeing each other in January. Does that jibe with what you know?"

"January?" she said, wrinkling her nose. "That sounds about right. Carlotta, my housekeeper, might know for sure."

"Have you seen him around lately?"

"Yes, he came by the house sometimes. It was just a friendly thing now. He was here the other night, in fact, according to my housekeeper."

"Which night was that?"

"Thursday. Why are you asking this? What's going on?"

What exactly, I wondered, did they suspect Jody of?

Could he have stopped by Saturday night while Heidi was home? Could he have done something to harm her?

"We're trying to determine if he might have given her a box of chocolates. Maybe in an attempt to win her back. Do you know where she could have gotten a box of chocolates?"

I flashed back on the gold box of Godiva chocolates that had lain just a few feet from Heidi's lifeless body, and I felt the hair on the back of my neck go up.

"Not Godiva chocolates?" Cat asked.

"Actually, yes. That's right."

"Well, if you're talking about a box of Godiva chocolates, they were mine. Why? . . . Did Heidi get sick from the chocolates?"

"So *you* gave her these chocolates?" he asked, ignoring her question.

"No, she seems to have snitched them. They were a gift to me—someone brought them to a party I gave Thursday night here at the house. People know I've got a thing for chocolate. Heidi, I guess, took them downstairs with her at some point during the evening."

"Who were they a gift from?"

"I don't know. They'd been left on the hall table by one of the guests. Why, what's wrong with the chocolates?"

"Miss Jones, I get to ask the questions right now," he said, not in a snippy tone, but one that told her to cool her jets for a minute. "How do you know Heidi, as you say, snitched them?"

"Well, when I went to open the chocolates later, they were gone. I thought the caterers might have put them away someplace, but I couldn't find them anywhere. Then Bailey told me she had seen them in Heidi's apartment."

He snapped his head over in my direction. "When did you see the chocolates in the apartment?" he asked.

"When I found the body. I'd never been in the apartment before then," I added defensively.

"Why would you mention them to Miss Jones?"

"It just came up," I explained. "We were talking about Heidi while we waited for the ambulance. Because she'd thrown up, we discussed what kinds of food she ate, and Cat said she sometimes snuck food out of the fridge and I mentioned the chocolates. That's all."

He jotted a few notes. I was dying to know what was going on. Had the chocolates been doctored somehow? If they *had* been, it would mean *Cat* was the intended victim, not Heidi. Cat looked superagitated, but she took a deep breath and I realized that since she'd found her pestering had proved ineffectual, she was about to try another tack. She lived by the principle that there was more than one way to skin a cat.

"Look, Detective," she said with her best sugar lips, "I'm relieved that someone of your caliber is on this case and I don't mean to be a nudge. But it's obvious you have some concerns about the chocolates, and since they were left for me, I need to know what the problem is."

"I'm going to explain everything to you, Miss Jones," he said. "But first I need a few more facts. Can you describe the box you saw on the hall table?"

"It was the usual gold Godiva box. Except that instead of just some gold elastic around it, it had an artificial flower on it as decoration—like they sometimes do around a holiday. The flower was pink, I think. A pale pink."

"And you feel strongly that Heidi took the chocolates?"

"It's just too big of a coincidence otherwise," Cat said.

"Someone brings me a box of chocolates. The box mysteriously disappears off the hall table. A short time later a box of truffles turns up in Heidi's apartment. Heidi, who can't afford to buy such things on her own and has a habit of pilfering sweets from us all the time."

"Was Heidi around that night?"

"Yes, she was working. I needed her to watch my son, Tyler, while I gave the party."

"I actually saw her in the hallway," I interjected. "I saw her get Tyler's jacket. In fact, she looked a little odd and I couldn't figure out why. Maybe it was because she thought I'd caught her."

"Please," Cat pleaded. "I can't stand this. What is going *on?*"

"All right," said Farley. "There seems to be a problem with the chocolates. Most of the box had been consumed. We took the ones that hadn't been eaten in to examine, and we think they may be tainted in some way."

"Tainted?" Cat said. "You mean *spoiled?* That's pretty hard to imagine with Godiva."

"The chocolates in the box weren't actually Godiva chocolates," Farley explained. "They're truffles, but not the kind made by Godiva. It looks as if they're homemade and that someone took out whatever candies were in the box and substituted these."

Oh boy. This was bad. Someone had wanted to kill Cat, and Heidi had died because of it. But I could tell Cat hadn't fully grasped it yet.

"But what exactly do you mean by *tainted?"* Cat asked. The sugar lips were gone now and she was speaking in the clipped, irritated way she used with someone who was pitching an article idea but had failed in the first twenty seconds to make it sound sexy as hell. Underneath, though, I could detect a swelling panic.

"We don't have the final autopsy report—or the tox reports—but we believe there was something in the chocolates that killed Heidi. It may have been some kind of poison."

A look of astonishment began to form on Cat's face.

"Wait a minute," she said finally. "Are you telling me that my nanny died because she ate a box of poison chocolates that were meant for *me?*"

"I don't want us to draw any conclusions right now—not until we get the autopsy report back and the tox reports. But it does appear that the box was tampered with and that the chocolates may have caused her death."

"This is incredible," Cat exclaimed, using her hand to comb through the top of her thick blond hair. "It can't be real—it's like a movie." She stood up and took a few steps aimlessly around the room. "What do I *do?*" The last question seemed intended more for the gods than for either of us. Farley just sat there watching her pace, his lips pressed hard together.

"Detective," I said, leaning forward, trying not to sound as freaked as I felt, "when are you going to know for sure? How long do all the tests take?"

"It's a frustrating process in New York City because there's a backlog," he said. "We'll get the autopsy report soon, but the tox reports can take weeks."

"Weeks?" Cat screeched. "So for weeks I'm in limbo?"

"No, we're proceeding with this situation as if it's highly suspicious. We've already begun investigating. And of course, with what you've just told me, we'll start down a new line of inquiry—that if the candies were doctored in some way, you may have been the intended victim, not your nanny. Tell me about this party that you had—you said it was Thursday night."

"It was a boring book party—for a woman named Dolores Wilder," Cat said, not hiding her agitation. "She was the editor of *Gloss* before me. She edited a collection of short stories from the magazine, and I got stuck giving her a party."

"Is there anyone who could have been in a position to see who brought the chocolates? Your housekeeper, for instance."

"I know Carlotta didn't see anything. When I asked her later if she'd put the box someplace she said she hadn't and she told me she had no idea who brought them."

"I want a list of everyone who attended the party—and I need it today. You can have someone fax it over to me. Have you had any threats against you?"

"No. At least nothing out of the ordinary. People sometimes say they hate me, but that's—that comes with the territory." I had thought for a split second that she was going to say, "But that's always been the case."

He told her to think about it, that something might come to her over the next day. She should consider, he said, whether anyone had ever threatened her even in a veiled way, or if anyone at the party might have a grudge of some kind against her. He also said that since the apartment was most likely a crime scene, the police would come back and examine it again.

"Don't let the housekeeper go in and clean up," he told Cat. "We need to keep it totally off limits."

I wanted to shoot Cat a look, but Farley would have caught it.

He rose to leave and I thought Cat was going to dive to the floor and grab him around the ankle with both hands.

"You're going? What about my situation? Am I in danger?"

He launched into his little mantra again about not jumping to conclusions, but he suggested that she keep a fairly low profile—and he promised that he would be in touch. He also handed each of us a business card with his phone and fax numbers and told us to contact him immediately if we had any thoughts, information, or concerns.

Wondering if there was anything he'd say or ask me out of Cat's earshot, I volunteered to see him to the door. The only tidbit he offered was that since the case was starting to look like a homicide and he was a general precinct detective, he would now be working with detectives in the homicide division. I felt my blood curdle at the word *homicide*. As he stepped out onto the stoop, he reminded me to get the party list over to him as soon as possible. I didn't dare tell him what I'd noticed in Heidi's apartment. He'd kill me for having gone down there, and besides, if the police hadn't yet done a thorough search, they would now.

When I got back to the living room, Cat was lying on the couch, eyes closed, with a bag of frozen peas on her head, obviously riding the first wave of one of her legendary migraines. As much as Cat had angered people over the years with her abruptness and bitchiness, it was hard to believe she'd inspired someone to decide to kill her. I wanted to reassure her, to comfort her, but I felt at a loss. I was anxious and scared and just plain dumbfounded by the fact that a murderer had been at the party that night.

"Cat, tell me," I said, sitting at the end of the couch by her bare, pedicured feet and trying to keep my voice calm, "is there *anyone* you can think of who might want to harm you?"

"Are you wondering why I didn't offer up Dolores's name on a silver platter?" she asked plaintively from under the picture of the Jolly Green Giant. "Because, after all, we both know how much she despises me."

"Well, she certainly jumps to *my* mind. Why didn't you mention her to Farley?"

She lifted the bag from her head. Her eye makeup had begun to smear and she looked both worried and wiped out. "Because the timing seems all wrong," she said. "When I got the *Gloss* job, maybe, but why now, so many years later? Besides, it's hard to picture her in an apron with a candy thermometer. The only reason Dolores ever goes into a kitchen is to find the martini olives."

"Well, I think you need to discuss the situation with Farley. Let him be the judge. Can you think of anything else? Is there anyone really pissed at you?"

"People are always pissed at me, but there's a difference between pissed and murderous rage. I don't know anyone who feels *that* way toward me.... You know what this means, Bailey? I'm the reason Heidi is dead." Her eyes watered as she spoke, something you didn't see every day.

"That's not your fault, Cat. There's no possible way you could have prevented this. Look," I said, switching gears, "we've got to be proactive about the situation."

"Please don't say 'proactive.' You know I hate that word."

"Who was the caterer you used for the party?"

"It's a small company I use all the time. Why? You don't think *they* had something to do with this?"

"No, but you need to double-check and make sure that

they didn't take the box of truffles from the hallway and stick it away somewhere. We need to be sure there's only *one* box in this picture."

"Okay, okay," she said, bag on head again.

"And I think you need some security."

"You mean like a bodyguard?"

"Maybe."

"What I need is a food taster. But they went out about five hundred years ago."

"Why don't I call that guy who heads corporate security—Eddie something or other."

"Oh, he'd be a help. The most exciting thing he's ever done is catch someone smoking in their office."

"He might have some ideas, though. I'll call him, and I'll call Audrey for the party list. When are people supposed to be here for the planning meeting? We should try to cancel that."

Tossing the bag of peas on the coffee table, she glanced at her gold Cartier panther watch.

"In two minutes," she said.

"Can you handle it? Can you act normal? Because for now it's probably best if they not know a thing. Maybe I should just intercept them when they get here and say you have a migraine."

"No," she said. "I need to do this meeting. We should have started planning October a week ago—and I've got to stay busy. If I don't, I'll go out of my mind."

"Okay, but not a word to anybody," I told her. "Now, what about Jeff? We have to get hold of him. Is he at the studio?"

There was a pause, that funny beat like earlier.

"Yes, I think so," she said. "I need to call him."

"Are things okay with you two?" I asked.

"Yes, of course," she said. She held my eyes as she spoke, something liars rarely do, but Cat was a good liar and I couldn't tell if what she said was true or false. Maybe everything was just dandy with the two of them. Or maybe it wasn't and she just felt uncomfortable telling me. When she and Jeff had been dating, she'd shared their ups and downs with me, the roller-coaster ride of their romance, but once they'd married and their life had settled down, she'd been more private, protective. I had been the same way about my husband. At some moment I might need to press her to be more forthcoming, but this didn't seem like the time.

I asked if I could use her office since I wanted Audrey to fax me the party guest list, and she said yes, retreating under the peas again. "One more thing," I said. "Why would you let me search Heidi's room when it was clearly still off limits?"

"I didn't know it was, I *swear.* I called the precinct last night to ask if it was okay to arrange to have it cleaned, and the guy on the desk said okay."

It sounded like one of Cat's convenient misunderstandings. I left her lying there and, my adrenaline pumping, took the stairs to the third floor two at a time.

Audrey was at her desk and I explained quickly that I was with Cat, who was nursing an orca-size migraine, and that we had just learned there might have been some "irregularities" at the party Thursday night. We needed the guest list right away. It turned out that not only could she provide a list of the RSVPs but because she had been at the party supervising—as she did whenever Cat threw an event—she knew who had actually showed and who hadn't. I asked her to fax one copy to the number that Detective Farley had given me and another to Cat's house.

While I waited anxiously for the fax to come through, I gave the corporate security guy, Eddie, a buzz. He was out of the office, his secretary told me, but she volunteered his cell phone number, and he answered on the third ring. Describing myself as Cat's right-hand person, hyperbole that seemed warranted if I was going to capture his attention, I explained the situation in broad strokes and said Cat needed to be provided with as much security as possible.

"Are you saying someone tried to poison her?" he asked, sounding stupefied.

"Yes, possibly," I confirmed. "The police are on the case, but we need your help, too."

"We're not the Secret Service over here," he said.

"I know, I know, but the guys in the lobby have to be told to be extra cautious, and someone should walk the floor from time to time. Can you think about what's in your department's capabilities and give Miss Jones a call at home?"

I sensed he was clearly torn between wanting to horn in on the excitement and not wanting to move his butt one inch more than he had to, but he said he would get back to Cat soon.

I heard the doorbell ring below, and as I scurried down the stairs with the two fax sheets, I saw the senior *Gloss* staffers being greeted tepidly in the hallway by Cat, who had found a moment to freshen her makeup. The group included Leslie, of course, in a navy pin-striped sleeveless dress (obviously selected for its slimming effects) and a quilted leather Chanel bag the size of Yankee Stadium; Polly, looking overheated and beleaguered in the blazer she'd thrown over her jumper; and Kip, who was wearing the same scowl he'd sported earlier. There was Rachel Kaplan, too, the entertainment editor whom Cat had been bullying on the phone earlier. People liked to comment on how she worked at being a Cat clone, and today it was especially true: her blond hair was cascading down her shoulders, and she had on a straight knee-length skirt, a strapless lavender top with a matching sweater around her shoulders—and lots of toe cleavage.

The group had obviously traveled by cab together, and they looked ornery, like people on a group tour who had just learned that the bus's air-conditioning was not going to be repaired in their lifetime. They also appeared surprised as hell to see me dashing down Cat's stairs, but she offered them no explanation. As they filed into the dining room, I pulled Cat aside. I told her in a near whisper that since she had the meeting to attend to, I was leaving, but that the police had the invitation list and Eddie would be calling her. I suggested that she get Jeff to come home as soon as possible and that she inform her boss, Harry, the owner of the company, about everything that was going on. Listening distractedly, she slid closed the two pocket doors to the dining room.

"Bailey, I'm terrified," she said, turning back to me. "You've got to help me. You're the only person I can really trust."

"You know I'll help," I told her. "Call me immediately if you feel anxious or scared or if you get any sudden revelations about who might have done this."

"I need more than that. You've got to help find out who's trying to hurt me."

"But now that we're almost sure it's foul play, it's something for the police to handle, Cat."

"I want you to look around, too," she said. "This is your specialty, Bailey. You're a crime writer."

"I *write* about crimes, Cat. I don't *solve* them."

"But you always manage to see things from a different angle from everyone else. You notice what no one else does. . . . Please."

"Okay, let's get together tomorrow—early—and we'll make a plan," I told her. "It's probably best if it's out of the office—call me and let me know what's good for you." I told her I had a copy of the guest list, which I'd look over tonight, and suggested she have Audrey dig out the résumés of everyone on staff who had come to the party, and we'd review them together. "Until then, please be careful—get Jeff to come home, and both of you just stay put."

I gave her arms a squeeze and said good-bye. Outside, the street was bustling with private-school kids—but no press. As I hurried toward Park Avenue to hail a cab, my heart pounding and my stomach churned up, I thought about how everything had shifted in a matter of moments. I'd spent half the day focusing on Heidi, trying to unravel the secrets in her life and what might have led to her death. But it turned out that her life and her secrets didn't matter a damn in the new scheme of things. It was Cat who was the center of the story and *her* life that needed to be scrutinized. Someone had come to the party armed to kill her. Why? A grudge, a vendetta, jealousy? And would that person, having failed, try again? I had the guest list, and I'd pore over it as soon as I had the chance, seeing if anything jumped out at me.

As I climbed in a cab, a very scary thought occurred to me. I had just left Cat alone with four staffers—all of whom had been at the party Thursday night. I grabbed my cell phone from my purse and hit Cat's number.

"Carlotta's still there, right?" I asked when she answered.

"Yes, why?" she asked impatiently.

"Just checking," I said. "That's all. And look, be careful. Promise me you'll be careful."

CHAPTER 8

I GOT THE first hang-up call at six-thirty P.M. that night—though I didn't think anything of it at the time. The phone was ringing as I flung open the door, and—you'll find this pathetic—I nearly broke my neck racing for it, thinking it might be K.C. Yeah, right. I answered, could sense someone on the other end listening, ignoring my two hellos—and then click. My caller ID said "Number blocked."

I hadn't gone directly home from Cat's. That's because as soon as I was settled in a cab, I'd phoned the office from my cell and found that the page proofs for a story I had in the July issue was almost ready, and since the piece was due to ship this week, I needed to read it ASAP. I returned to *Gloss* and hung out in my office for about half an hour. What I was dying to do was review the guest list, but this wasn't the time or the place—I'd save that for later, at home. I used the time to return the call to my friend and next-door neighbor, Landon. I explained I had lots to share and asked if he was free for dinner. He not only said yes, he offered to cook.

At around four I dragged my butt over to the pit, hoping that if I loitered, it would encourage the production people to make my piece a priority. The atmosphere was totally nutty out there, kind of like *Lord of the Flies*—maybe because the senior players were off premises. There were a dozen buff male models milling around, all with barbed-wire tattoos on their biceps; the art director was squabbling with his number two; and the photo editor was screaming at someone over the phone. He'd apparently rented a herd of buffalo for a September fashion shoot out west and now they were missing in action. Maybe what was making it so strange for me was that in the midst of such silliness I was holding on to a terrifying secret: Someone had tried to kill Cat.

When the copier finally rolled out the proof of my piece, I took it back to my office to read and cut the thirty-line overrun. The article was about a twenty-eight-year-old Georgia woman who had been arrested for stalking and harassing a female co-worker—everything from mailing her photos of double-D girls from the pages of *Jugs* to setting fire to her garage.

After two days in Atlanta, I found I loved the stalker—she was funny and smart, though horrified by the idea of facing a trial—whereas the victim gave me the creeps. Within two days I had a theory and two small, tentative pieces of evidence to back it up: The alleged stalker hadn't done any stalking at all; the victim had set everything up to make it *look* as though she had. I went to the police with what I'd found, which had fueled growing doubts of their own, and the charges had eventually been dropped. Turning over a few extra stones had been enough to make me see the truth. I wondered if I'd be so lucky in Cat's situation. As soon as I had signed off on the proof, I sprinted for the door.

By the time I had navigated the subway, unlocked the door of my apartment, and dashed for the hang-up call, I felt fried. After stripping down to my underpants and washing off, I slipped on a sleeveless cotton dress and lit a few eucalyptus candles. Now I was ready for the party list. This was a job that called for expansive thinking, so I set myself up on the pine dining room table at the far end of my living room.

From a glance at the check marks on the sheet of paper Audrey had faxed, it appeared as if fifty to sixty people had actually attended the party. Not exactly a crushing crowd, but because of the layout of Cat's house—the living room and dining room on one floor, the library on another—there had been lots of movement, and it had seemed bustling that night. The point of the party had been to generate buzz for Dolores's book. Titled *Love at Any Cost,* it was a collection of love stories, by a variety of writers, that had run in *Gloss* during what Dolores called the glory days—*her* reign. Cat, by the way, would never have given the party if her boss, Harry, hadn't pleaded with her to do it.

Audrey had set up the list by category: press, the book publishing company staffers, fiction writers featured in the book, *Gloss* staffers, miscellaneous editors from other magazines. I decided I'd cross a line through anyone who couldn't possibly be a suspect and star any names that demanded more scrutiny.

I started with the book publishing company, a small house that specialized in fiction. A gaggle of their employees had apparently attended—the editorial director, the sales and marketing director, the editor and her assistant, and what appeared to be the entire publicity department. Publishing companies rarely threw book parties anymore because of the expense, and this group had obviously been thrilled to get out and gobble up some red potatoes stuffed with crème fraîche and caviar. I distinctly recalled Cat saying before the party that she had never met a soul from the company—or in her words, "This is the first and hopefully the last time I'll ever set eyes on any of them." I put a pencil line through each of their names.

Next there was press. I'd heard it had been as tough to round up anyone as it is to get a grease stain out of rayon pants, but in the end a little arm-twisting on the part of *Gloss*'s PR agency had produced a few bodies, including a reporter from *People,* one from the AP, and a producer for *The View.* As far as I knew, Cat had never met any of them. I put a line through their names. Also in attendance was one of the gossip columnists for the *Post*—a guy who sometimes ran bitchy items about Cat with headlines like CAT IN A SPAT and PURRRFECTLY AWFUL. Cat despised him, but I couldn't picture *him* with a motive for killing *her.*

The biggest group of all at the party were the *Gloss* staffers. The magazine business could be cruel, and editors often took a psycho delight in gossiping about each other, but it was hard to imagine anyone actually being a murderer. They gave out kill fees, they didn't kill. Yet the murderer could easily be someone from *Gloss.*

All the senior staff from *Gloss,* plus Audrey, had been invited, though not everyone had showed. The photo editor and art director, for instance, had wiggled out of going, and so had the beauty editor, who was on maternity leave. Leslie, Polly, Rachel, and Kip had come, as had Sasha, the fashion editor, who was now in Palm Springs with those orange stilettos. I thought for a second about each of them. None had displayed any hostility toward Cat recently, at least not that I'd witnessed. Earlier in the day, though, Cat had been extremely curt to Rachel on the phone. Worth checking out.

The *Gloss* copy editor and his associate also had attended, which had surprised me that night, since neither was on what you'd call Cat's A list, until I remembered that both had worked at the magazine under Dolores and she had undoubtedly invited them. They were practically the only ones left from her era. Cat had followed a scorched-earth strategy when she was hired at *Gloss,* with special emphasis on leveling the fashion and beauty areas, and also the food department, where they had still been creating recipes for crown roasts and Swedish meatballs. When possible, rather than out-and-out fire people, she had relied on her intimidation skills. The two members of the copy department had survived in part because they were good, in part because they wouldn't get in Cat's way of re-creating the magazine. Were they bitter? I wondered. Though I didn't know either especially well, the only thing they ever seemed annoyed with was working late during closing.

At the last minute, because of a mediocre response from the press, an additional dozen *Gloss* staffers had been invited, in order to pad the room. I could see their names as add-ons at the bottom of the list. They were mainly senior editors in fashion, beauty, and articles. Could one of them have an ax to grind? Cat was a demanding boss, frequently abrupt, generally on the far side of tactful in her comments. She liked talent in people and she encouraged it, but that meant she often had pets, which left some people feeling excluded. There was no one in this group I felt 100 percent comfortable eliminating because I didn't have enough info at this time.

There were also two spouses on the list: Kip's wife, Jane, who was slurring her words by seven-thirty, and Leslie's husband, Clyde, the zillionaire, whom I'd found myself smushed up next to in the library at one point. He was a moody guy, though attractive in a Heathcliff kind of way, with curly black hair, black eyes, and skin as smooth and white as candle wax. Trying to make conversation, I'd asked him for some investment advice.

"It would be a disservice to offer you simplistic tips over cocktails," he said, snootily. "Surely, you're too smart for that." His tone suggested he thought I had all my money in a passbook savings account. I put a pencil line through both his name and Kip's wife's because I couldn't imagine either having a motive.

Also on the list were about a dozen editors from other magazines, mostly women, who had worked with Dolores at *Gloss* over the years. A few, I knew, had been fired by Cat. Was one still holding a grudge? I would have to run their names by Cat.

I was almost done. The last "group" were four of the authors whose romantic short stories were featured in the book and who had been nauseatingly toasted that night by Dolores as "women who knew how to tell a love story in

a way that could make your legs turn to jelly and your
heart swell." Three of them, all over fifty, didn't even
write short stories any longer. I put a pencil line through
each of their names. The last one, however, a fortyish
woman named Nancy Hicky, who for obvious reasons
wrote under the pen name Nancy Highland, was still
churning out romance novels and seemed to have a chip
on her shoulder. I'd had the misfortune of being cornered
by her early in the evening. "You're with the *new*
crowd?" she'd asked bitingly, and then demanded I tell
her "why in God's name you've decided to drop fiction."
I suggested she pose that question to Cat, who had made
the decision, and scampered off in search of another
drink. As angry as she was, however, it was hard to imagine it would propel her to murder.

Last, but certainly not least, there was Dolores, who
had been displaced by Cat and apparently never hidden
the fact that she loathed her. To set the record straight, her
being kicked to the curb by the owners of *Gloss* was
hardly Cat's fault. She was around sixty-three at the time,
and the magazine, the least up-to-date of all the "Seven
Sisters," had been on a slide for at least the final seven
years of her twenty-two-year reign. She'd grown out of
touch with both the times and her readers and had been
running the magazine on automatic pilot. Some of her
last issues carried endless pages of instructions for ugly
craft projects, and her household hints columnist had
once suggested using a tampon if the wine cork had been
tossed accidentally. One of her last covers had featured
the cover line "Our Pasta Cookbook: Need We Say
More?"—which suggested she'd been hard-pressed to
summon, in her lifetime, one more fun and fetching

phrase about fettuccine. She'd earned her termination (and was damn lucky to have been given a phantom job as company consultant), but Cat, I must say, had rubbed Dolores's nose in it, bad-mouthing the old *Gloss* whenever she got the chance. She was fond of referring to Dolores's era as the *"Gross* magazine" days. Dolores, in turn, never passed up an opportunity to complain publicly that *Gloss* today was "rude, crude, and lewd." She certainly deserved to be on the short list of suspects.

Interestingly, Dolores's husband had been missing in action. I vaguely remembered hearing someone say a slipped disk had laid him up.

Speaking of husbands, there was someone at the party who wasn't on the list: Jeff. I'd noticed him shortly before I left, though he may have been there earlier. At really hotsy-totsy parties Cat gave, those with big names and celebrities, Jeff would play co-host, but at an event like this he might make only a brief appearance or not even bother. He'd seemed slightly bored that night—I'd caught him once wrinkling his nose in distaste as a waiter passed a tray of toast points with seared foie gras.

I was back to what I'd been mulling over earlier. Was everything really okay with Jeff and Cat? And a far scarier question: Was there a reason he wanted her out of the picture? Though I was no longer focusing on Heidi, it did appear that she'd been seeing someone secretively. Could that person have been Jeff, and could he have tried to eliminate Cat so he could be with Heidi? It was hard to believe—certainly on Sunday he hadn't looked like a man who had accidentally poisoned the love of his life— but nonetheless I needed to find a way to lift the lid on Cat and Jeff's relationship.

I had now crossed off the names of the people who appeared to have no reason in the world to eliminate Cat Jones from the planet—and I still had a pretty long list. I thought back on the party, trying to remember if anything seemed odd or suspicious. Nothing stood out. I obviously wasn't going to make much headway until I went over the list with Cat the next day.

At seven I tucked the fax sheets into my purse and headed over to Landon's apartment with a bottle of good California Cabernet. As I knocked on his door I got a whiff of the wonderful aromas emanating from within and realized that I hadn't eaten a decent meal since Saturday night.

"You are very sweet to do this," I said to Landon as he swung open the door. "I need your food and I need your wisdom."

"Well, darling, you didn't give me much time, so it's just roast chicken," he announced in his deep, sexy voice. "There's only so much magic I can do with just a few hours' notice." Five feet nine, trim, with light brown eyes and closely-cropped curly silver hair, Landon was more youthful looking than any seventy-year-old I'd ever laid eyes on. He ran a company that designed and renovated building lobbies, but somehow he managed to stay tan as a walnut most of the year. He was dressed tonight in his typical casual but dapper fashion—tight blue jeans and an off-white cotton boatneck sweater. For an apron he'd tucked a waffled green-and-white-striped dish towel in the front of his pants.

"Well, it smells fab, especially considering what I've been smelling the last few days."

"Do I want to know?" he asked, leading me into the

kitchen, where he poured me a glass of champagne from a just opened bottle.

"Cat's nanny? I was the one who found the body. It was pretty gruesome."

"My God," he said, eyes wide in surprise. "I had no idea you were involved. What in the world happened?"

"Well, there's lots to tell, and I could use your advice, but I'd love to just relax and chow down first. I feel I need a little time away from all of it."

"Fine, fine. Take your champagne into the living room and we'll just chat for a bit. Besides, I'm dying to ask you about that handsome young stud I spotted you with in the street early Saturday evening as I was driving off."

"Oh, *him,*" I said sardonically, falling into an armchair.

"Not Mister Right, then?"

"I don't know *what* he is," I said. "Correction: I know he's great in the rack, but I don't know what else. Thinking about him makes my cheeks flush and I may have a crush. What I've begun to suspect, unfortunately, is that he's Mister I'll Never Commit, maybe even a cad. Which is too bad, because for the first time in two years my heart doesn't feel as vestigial as my appendix."

"Well, I'm not a psychotherapist, but maybe you're not as ready as you think."

"What do you mean?"

"Well, maybe you're attracted to him because he *is* a bit of a cad and you know he'll never want a relationship."

"Oh, God, who knows? I thought you were supposed to be recovered from a divorce in two years. Sometimes I feel I'm just flopping around, like a big tuna that's been hooked and hauled onto the deck of a boat. Let's talk about you. What's happening with that guy Mitchell?"

"We had a lovely dinner, and he said he'd call—but nothing. I left a message on his machine and haven't heard a thing."

"Well, don't call again."

"I know, I know. I should be more of a *Rules* girl, but I can't help myself. Usually when I don't hear from someone I do something totally insane—like send clippings of articles I think they'll be interested in."

"Well, then I suggest you stop your home delivery of the *Times* for a few weeks," I said, smiling.

He excused himself and retreated to the kitchen to check on the chicken and I had a few quiet moments to sip my champagne. I always loved being in his place. It was a two-bedroom, originally similar in layout to mine, but he had gutted it, breaking through the dining area into the extra bedroom to create a large, loftlike living space, with pale gray walls, pickled gray parquet floors, and gray sofas and chairs. The other furniture, all antiques, was dark wood, a striking contrast. He had beautiful drawings on the wall, including one by Mary Cassatt that his mother had left him.

Though we had lived side by side through the eighteen months of my flash fire of a marriage, I hadn't known him then, except to exchange small talk in the hallway. When the marriage was over, when I'd come up for air and stopped contemplating a header off my terrace, one of our hellos turned into a glass of wine, and soon after we were hanging around the Village together. I had more in common with my friends from Brown and people I had met at *Get* and *Gloss,* but due to sheer proximity, Landon had become one of my closest pals.

The meal that night was to die for—despite Landon's protestations that he'd been hindered by a shortage of time. Besides the chicken, there were roast potatoes with rosemary, green beans, and carrots cooked with pecans and brown sugar. We ate with the door to the terrace open, and though it had grown cooler, the spring air felt wonderful. Afterward, instead of dessert he served a selection of cheeses. It was the perfect excuse to have a third glass of Cabernet.

It was also time to tell him the story. I shared the whole terrible tale—from discovering Heidi's body to the latest realization that the truffles had been meant for Cat. His reaction was a mix of shock and total fascination, and of course I couldn't blame him.

"I hate to say it," he said, "but Cat's sort of brought it all on herself."

"What do you mean by that?" I asked, stuffing another slice of baguette with double-crème Brie into my mouth.

"You live by the sword, you die by the sword. She's used some people, stepped on others, and now she's made someone very, very mad."

"I think you're overstating it," I said. "She's been bitchy at times and not always superconsiderate, but I've never seen her be *ruthless.*"

"If you didn't work with her, would you still be her friend?" he asked, pouring us each a cup of coffee from the pot he'd set on the table.

"Sure," I replied. "At least I think so. She's smart and charming and funny—at least when she's not dealing with a death in her house."

"Sometimes, though, it seems like she gets more out of the relationship than you do."

"Oh, I don't know if it's all that lopsided," I said defensively. "First of all, I'm flattered someone in her position relies on me. Second, she's been my mentor in a very loose sort of way—my setup at *Gloss* is great." As I spoke, though, I felt a tiny twinge in my stomach, because there were times when I did worry that things were slightly out of balance.

"Do you have *any* idea who might have wanted to kill her?" he asked, leaning forward, palms against his chest.

"No—but she wants me to try to figure it out."

"What's wrong with the police?"

"Nothing. But it's Cat's style to double team. I've seen her give the same assignment to two different writers. That guarantees she gets what she wants."

"Wouldn't it just be smarter for you to stay out of it?" he said.

"But how can I? Someone tried to kill Cat, and they might easily try again. If there's any possible way for me to help her, I've got to do it. I know the players at *Gloss*, and maybe, just maybe, I'll see something the cops don't. Besides, you know this is the kind of story that makes my pulse race. Plus, in so many of the cases I cover, I'm forced to work around the periphery. This time I get to be smack in the middle. This may turn out to be the most exciting story I've ever been involved in."

"It's just that I worry about you," he said, looking worried. "I could barely think straight when you went off to spend the day in Ohio with the husband whose wife had disappeared."

"Him?" I laughed. "You know, in ninety percent of

cases where the wife has disappeared, the husband's guilty. He's bashed her head in with a chipping hammer and dumped her body in a lake. But I'm pretty sure that guy was innocent."

"Well, just watch what you eat, okay?"

"I'll just have to take all my meals here."

It was close to midnight when I finally let myself back into my apartment. According to my answering machine, not one single person had attempted to make contact this evening. Doing a quick calculation, I figured it was just about dawn in Italy, where my mother was traipsing around, enjoying her retirement, and I fought off a momentary urge to call her. Why worry her needlessly?

I slipped into a pair of cotton jammies and headed out to the couch, where I pulled a chenille throw over me. Three glasses of Cabernet had done nothing to quell my state of agitation or make me feel sleepy, but there was a chance the couch would do the trick. Because my brain associated my bed with *not* sleeping, I occasionally had luck in other locations. That was the only worthwhile advice I'd gotten from the shrinks and sleep specialists I'd seen. What they all loved to tell me was that my insomnia had to do with my divorce, that I had yet to work through everything, and until I did I'd be doomed to toss and turn for hours and be jolted awake at three A.M. I had a slightly different theory—though it also related to my marriage. My husband, the perfectly normal-seeming attorney, had turned out to be a compulsive gambler and had run through most of our savings. I believed that sleeping often eluded me because my unconscious wanted me to be vigilant, something I hadn't been when my hard-earned dough was being used to cover his bad bets on football games.

Just as my thoughts were breaking up into nonsense, the phone rang. It startled me and I knocked over a framed photograph on the end table as I fumbled for the phone and said hello.

"Bailey, were you sleeping?" It was a woman's voice, but I couldn't place it in my groggy state.

"Who's this?" I asked.

"Oh, sorry, it's Leslie. Did I wake you?"

Well, this was a first, getting a call from Leslie at home, let alone at some ungodly hour. There was often a secret agenda with Leslie, and I wondered what it might be this time. "No, I was just reading," I lied.

"Sorry to call so late, but I know you're a night owl. Cat told me the latest, and I thought we should chat. How does she seem to you? When I spoke to her, I practically needed to talk her off the ledge."

It figured that Cat would ultimately feel the need to confide in Leslie. How many other people had she blabbed to? Leslie probably was calling just to make sure I knew she was squarely in the midst of things. God forbid I have an exclusive on something to do with Cat.

"Yeah, she seems freaked, but that's to be expected," I said. "I hope she's keeping this under wraps for now." As I talked I found the lamp switch in the dark and turned it on.

"Yes, of course. But you wouldn't expect her not to tell *me?* And she's got to call Harry on this, too. It's a company matter. Her life's in apparent danger, but so is everyone else's when you think about it."

"What do you mean?"

"Whoever did this killed someone other than who he or she had planned to. They're careless or stupid, and that puts me and you and everyone else in potential jeopardy." Leave it to Leslie to immediately start thinking about the ramifications for her.

"Do you have any ideas about who might be responsible?" I asked. "Anyone particularly upset with Cat these days?"

"There's no one who jumps to the top of the list. But I'm still thinking. It's got to be someone who knew her fairly well, who was aware that if they showed up with a box of Godiva chocolates, she'd devour them as soon as she got the chance."

"Do you remember seeing the box on the hall table?" I asked.

"Yes, I do. I'm not sure if it was there when I came in, but I saw it when I went to the powder room. I remember joking to someone standing next to me that I didn't know that I was supposed to bring a hostess gift."

"What about later? Did you notice at some point that the box was missing?"

"No. It might have been there when I left or it might not have been. I just don't recall."

"Does your husband recall seeing anything?"

"Pardon me?"

"Your husband. He was there that night."

"I'll have to ask him. He's out tonight, and I haven't even filled him in on the latest developments. You know this is going to be a press nightmare, don't you? Especially after the first person links it to Tucker Bobb's death."

"What?" I'd started to zone out as she spoke about her

husband, but this remark yanked me back with all the force of someone grabbing me by my hair. Tucker Bobb, editor in chief of *Best House,* another one of what used to be called the Seven Sister magazines, had died last fall. "What are you talking about?"

"Tucker Bobb."

"But what about him?" I asked. "I thought he had some kind of internal bleeding problem."

"He died of kidney failure. But they thought it might have resulted from eating poison mushrooms. Did Cat not mention it to you? She and I talked about it earlier tonight. She wondered if there was a connection."

"How did Tucker Bobb happen to eat poison mush-rooms?"

"It was a hobby of his—hunting for mushrooms—and they assumed he picked the wrong one to eat. I'm not sure of all the details. I was on vacation then, in Spain. But that's what I heard, and people are going to wonder."

"Gosh, I'd never heard that," I said.

"You have to wonder." She sounded momentarily dis-tracted. "Look," she said, "I think my husband just got in. I've got to go." She hung up while I was still saying good-bye.

I lay back against the arm of the couch, amazed at what I'd heard. Could there really be a connection be-tween the two deaths? Could someone be trying to knock off the editors of women's magazines?

The phone rang again and I assumed it was Leslie, calling back with some additional observation or ques-tion.

"Yeah," I said.

Nothing from the other end, just breathing. I hung up

and sprinted down to my office to check the caller ID box. A blocked number, just like earlier. Once could have been a wrong number. Twice was something else. An old boyfriend or ex-husband, perhaps, calling just to hear my voice? Or was someone doing it to rattle me?

Could it be the *killer*? People knew I was tight with Cat and if the killer had gotten wind of the fact that I was helping her, the calls might be a way to keep tabs on me—or give me a scare.

If so, they'd more than succeeded.

CHAPTER 9

I WOKE AROUND seven-thirty on Tuesday morning, my back achy from having slept on the couch, but at least I'd managed to make it through the night without once waking up. After putting on the teakettle, I padded down to my office and pulled out a spanking new black-and-white composition book.

Whenever I take on an assignment for an article, the first thing I do is get out a composition book and write the working title of the article at the top of the first page. As I begin researching and interviewing people (I use a steno pad and tape recorder for that), I scribble in the composition book my initial observations, highlights from interviews, angles worth pursuing, tidbits I'm not yet sure what to do with, and eventually a rough outline. It's through this process that I begin to get a sense of how the article should take shape. Though I write the actual story on the computer, it takes longhand, with a number 2 pencil, to kick-start my thinking. And it's while I'm scribbling in the composition book that I sometimes begin to see something in a whole new way. I suppose if I had a specialty as a writer, that would be it. I'm only an okay interviewer, always slightly anxious about putting my finger in the open wound of someone's suffering, but I'm good at seeing things overlooked by everyone else.

Though I wasn't on an official writing assignment with Heidi's death, I was going to handle things as if I were. I cracked open the composition book and wrote at the top of the first page, "Death of a Nanny." Not sure why I chose that—it's just the first thing that came to me. Then I went back to my bedroom, threw on some jeans and a T-shirt, and made myself coffee. I took my cup back to my office and picked up my pencil. For the next forty-five minutes I jotted down everything I knew about the Cat crisis so far, including the main questions I'd been toying with.

At around nine, I called Cat to determine where and when we would meet. She suggested we have lunch together at a little restaurant on Madison Avenue. She sounded *very* edgy.

After I hung up I dug my Filofax out of my purse and called an acquaintance, Megan Fox, who was a deputy editor at *Best House*. We'd met on several occasions at the apartment of a mutual friend, and though we weren't close, we liked each other and I figured she'd be willing to cough up what she knew about her boss's death. Ever since Leslie had dropped the bomb last night about Tucker Bobb I'd been racking my brain for someone to pump, and she was the only one I could come up with. I got her voice mail and left a message saying that I needed to talk to her.

I also used the morning to check out several Web sites devoted to mushrooms. When I'd first started reporting stories, I'd had to spend big chunks of time at the library digging up info, but these days I could find almost everything I needed on the Web. Except court records, which still involve dragging one's butt to the courthouse and making nice to fat, sullen civil servants who move at the speed of drying paint.

It turned out there's a whole slew of poisonous mushrooms in the United States. You could get sick just from reading some of the names: devil's tongue, deadly conocybe, poison puffball, brain mushroom, and my personal favorite, sweat-causing clitocybe.

A little after eleven I shut off my computer and changed into black pants and a yellow cotton sweater. Before heading out the door, I checked my office voice mail—yes, in the ridiculous hope that K.C. had phoned there, but no such luck. In my mind I heard a line a friend of mine once said: "They don't call and they don't call—and then you begin to love them."

Because I had plenty of time to get to the restaurant, I opted for the subway, jumping onto the Lex at Astor Place, just two blocks from my apartment building. The restaurant turned out to be a block from Cat's, on Madison at 90th. There's something almost European about that stretch of Madison Avenue: Most of the buildings are just four stories high, with shops and galleries and restaurants on the ground floor, many of them sporting colorful awnings—yellow or blue or red-and-white stripes.

I sauntered into the restaurant exactly one minute

early. It was a small place with a French/Middle Eastern theme. A waiter, yammering on the phone, indicated with a wave of his hand that I could sit anywhere I wanted because the restaurant was nearly empty.

After allowing me a few minutes to admire my surroundings, the waiter finally strolled over, handed me a menu, and asked what I wanted to drink. I explained there'd be two of us and ordered an iced tea.

Cat was twenty minutes late. I spotted her first through the restaurant window, dashing across the corner of 90th and Madison. Since she lived around the corner, it was only reasonable that she would have walked, but it was a shock nonetheless to see her on foot—a gossip columnist had once pointed out that she was rarely more than ten feet away from a town car. As she pushed open the door, the customers who had arrived while I'd waited all turned to stare. She was wearing a tobacco-colored sleeveless dress, and in addition to a brown leather tote bag, she carried an itty-bitty Louis Vuitton purse, the size Barbie might use. Her shoes were slingbacks in a brown-and-black leopard print, cut on the top to reveal huge amounts of toe cleavage. Two ladies-who-lunch types at a nearby table checked out her bare legs—Cat wore hose only during the three coldest months of the year, and then only if the temperature was subzero.

Sliding into the chair across from me, she pulled off her sunglasses, flung them on the table, and gestured for the waiter.

"You know what you want?" she said, more a statement than a question. I guess she figured since I'd sat there long enough, I ought to have memorized the menu.

As soon as the waiter walked over, we ordered; me a salad Niçoise and Cat the lamb stew.

"Any update on things?" I asked.

"I had Carlotta chuck all the food in the house and buy new stuff. And Farley called this morning—went over all the names on the list with me. Wanted to know who was who."

"What about the caterer?" I asked. "Did you call and ask about the candy?"

"Yeah, I spoke to Maverick, the owner, who was at the party herself," she said. "She remembered the box on the hall table. She remembered that it said truffles on it and that it had a flower on top."

"And she didn't put the box away anyplace?"

"No. And I had Carlotta check every place, just to be sure."

"So that pretty much confirms it. The candy was meant for *you.*"

"Here's a fun little tidbit," she said sarcastically. "Maverick said one of her helpers had wondered if they should put the candy out on a plate in the living room. She thought someone had brought them to be served at the party. But she double-checked with Audrey, and Audrey told her no way. Can you imagine if she'd put those truffles out? Half the room might be dead. And what if Tyler had gotten into them? I get sick just thinking about it."

"One thing that's curious is that Heidi took the box of chocolates on Thursday night but obviously didn't eat them until the weekend."

"Maybe she stashed the candy away—for a time when

she felt ravenous. Look," she said, shifting gears, "are you aware of how Tucker Bobb died?"

"I talked to Leslie about it last night. She didn't seem to know if the poison mushroom thing was just rumor or fact."

"But what if it's true? What if it's all connected? This could be some kind of plot."

I pushed my straw around my iced tea a minute as I mulled over what she'd said.

"It *is* odd," I told her, "and you have to tell the police about it, okay? I'll ask around, see what I can find out. But, you know, it doesn't change the fact that whoever's involved in Heidi's death was at your house Thursday night. And we have to give everyone who was there consideration."

"I've got that stuff you wanted, by the way. People's résumés. Audrey messengered them over to me." She pulled a large manila envelope out of her tote bag and slid it across the table to me.

"Is this everybody?" I asked, sticking the envelope into my own bag.

"Everybody except one guy in production whose file we can't find. But I've never said boo to the guy."

"Maybe he's been hoping to get a boo."

"That's the damn problem, isn't it?" she snapped. "People expect me to coddle them and not complain when they turn in crappy layouts or articles that read like the instructions to a Japanese VCR."

"So let's talk about people," I said. "You said that you couldn't think of anyone who was especially antagonistic toward you, other than Dolores. But let's go through people one by one. Tell me what's going on with everybody."

She started with the inner circle, going in no particular order. Things with Audrey seemed "absolutely fine," she stressed. Audrey was a forty-two-year-old prematurely gray executive secretary who ran Cat's life brilliantly. She left every day shortly after six and went home to her dog, Muchi, and her book club and didn't seem to give *Gloss* another thought until she was back at her desk the next day. Cat reported that her relationship with Audrey was without trouble, except for a minor tiff a week ago over a misplaced message.

"And you don't see any significance in the fact that she told the caterer not to put the chocolates out—to keep them for you?" I asked.

"No, no. She was just looking out for me," Cat said with a dismissive wave of her hand.

Sasha, the fashion director. She'd been at the magazine for two years, beating the record for a *Gloss* fashion director by about thirteen months. Sasha, Cat said, was one of the first fashion editors to seem to value her opinion, and Cat showed her appreciation by giving Sasha lots of autonomy. Around the first of the year there had been one blowup over Sasha's disregard for the budget, predicated by the revelation that at one shoot the catered lunch had included chateaubriand carved tableside, but they'd patched things up.

Then there was Rachel. As I'd suspected, there was definitely tension between them, Cat said. She had heard from two different sources that Rachel had finagled a lunch with Harry, the company owner. Cat felt that Rachel would love to position herself as Cat's replacement, especially since for the first time since Cat had come to the magazine, newsstand sales were soft.

"She thinks she could run *Gloss* better than you?" I asked.

"Oh, sure," Cat snickered. "She's been criticizing some of my cover choices lately, and I caught her smirking at a meeting the other day. I let her have it later in my office. She thinks she's so damn smart. Up until I hired her, her biggest coup had been discovering that Jennifer Aniston hadn't eaten a potato or slice of bread in three years, and now she thinks she's Tina Brown."

"Why not just fire her, then?" I asked.

"Because as a wrangler she's not that bad. You know what a rat race this celebrity thing is, and she gets us people."

They brought our lunch and we let go of the conversation for a minute as we dealt with our food. My salad had the air of someone who'd been sitting around all night waiting for a date to show, and I dug in without much enthusiasm. Cat poked at her stew before taking a bite. It would be a long time, I realized, before she stopped being nervous about the food she ate.

"Okay, let's keep going," I said after a few bites. "Polly. Everything basically okay with you two?"

"I guess," she said, giving up on the stew and spearing a green bean.

"What does 'I guess' mean?" I asked.

"You know Polly," she said, rolling her eyes. "She's not exactly a happy person. If she unloaded twenty-five pounds and resisted the urge to register for fish forks the moment she met a decent guy, things might change for her."

"Forget that for a sec," I said, trying to hide my irritation. "Is everything basically okay between the two of you?"

A pause.

"Not completely," she said finally. "I think she's still a little pissed over something that happened."

"Well, don't make me drag it out of you, Cat," I said. Placing my fork along the edge of the salad bowl, I leaned back into my chair.

"All right." She sighed. "A couple of months ago, Harry decided to start a gardening magazine, and Polly got wind of it and threw herself in as a candidate for editor in chief. I didn't exactly champion her cause, and somehow that fact got back to her. I heard through human resources that she was livid—but she never said anything directly to me."

"Why didn't you think she'd be right for the job? It sounds like a good fit."

"I know you adore Polly and I'm the first to admit she's extremely talented. But being editor in chief takes more than knowing how to line edit and write cover lines. You need to have a vision and you need to know how to make that vision a reality. Personally, I just don't think Polly could handle a number one job."

"Has the position been filled?"

"Yes, and Polly knows that. But it's not going to be announced for a few weeks. The editor's coming from England."

The waiter slunk over to clear the plates and take our coffee order, and as he shuffled around the table, I remained quiet. Frankly, I was stunned by Cat's revelation. Working for Cat had been a springboard for plenty of people's careers, and though she was always furious when they jumped ship, she also seemed to bask in her reputation as someone who groomed talent. This was the first time I'd ever heard of her squashing someone's chances for success. Did she honestly think Polly wouldn't be able to cut it as editor in chief—or, I wondered, was she scared to lose her, especially at a time when newsstand sales were less than stellar?

"Okay, Leslie," I said finally. I figured this one would be easy. To my surprise, Cat just sat there, nibbling on the tip of a fingernail, saying nothing.

"What?" I asked.

"You know, of course, that Leslie and I have a great working relationship. A lot of the staff find her tough to take, but I could never have gotten *Gloss* off the ground again without her."

"Yeah, and . . . ?"

"Well, I remembered something last night. There was a kind of weird incident a few months ago. Nothing major, but I've been trying to think of *everything.* She and her husband, Clyde, have a house not far from our place in Litchfield. We see them sometimes—for dinner, at parties. One day after a party, Leslie called and accused me of flirting with Clyde. I couldn't believe it."

"Had you been?"

"What? No, of course not. Okay, I'm not above flirting or even a little dirty flirting, but I swear, in this case, I was just being friendly. He's a kind of morose guy and at that particular moment didn't have anyone else to talk to. You know what they say? No good deed goes unpunished."

"Did Leslie seem very upset?"

"Yeah, but just momentarily. I was tempted to tell her

she was out of her mind, but I defused the whole thing. Just said I was sorry, had only been trying to be friendly, and so on. After that, everything seemed to go back to normal. I'm sure it's nothing, but I thought I should mention it."

"What about some of the other people at the party?" I inquired. "Was there anyone who might be angry with you? Leave Dolores out of it for a minute. But let's consider the authors or the reporters or any of those editors from other magazines. Any reason to suspect one of them?"

"I didn't even know most of those people."

"What about the lower-level *Gloss* staffers—particularly the ones left over from the Dolores days? Could somebody have a grudge?"

"No, no, no. I mean, I banned microwave popcorn in the office lately because I can't stand the stench, but I don't think someone would try to kill me because of *that.*"

"So the only person we know for sure totally *despises* you is Dolores."

"Yeah, but like I said yesterday, why would she try something *now?* It's been over four years since she got the boot, and though she can't stand me, things have generally calmed down with her. She's got her stupid book and she's focused on that these days."

"But think about it," I pointed out. "There's all the more reason to do it now, when people would be less likely to suspect her. I'm cooking up an excuse to talk to her so I can get a read on her."

The cappuccinos came and I stirred mine a few times, mixing the foam into the espresso.

"Let's go back to Tucker for a minute," I said. "You knew him, right? Did you have much to do with him?"

"Oh, please. I couldn't bear him. He took me to lunch at the Four Seasons when I got the *Gloss* job, and he treated me as if I were his niece from Idaho on her first trip to the big city. I thought he was going to tell people he introduced me to that I sewed my own clothes."

"Did you cross paths often? Were you on committees together, for instance?"

"Not if I could help it. I saw him at industry functions, but that's it."

"What about the editors of the other women's magazines? Do you have much to do with them?"

"No. You know I've tried to make *Gloss* different, and I hated being lumped with them."

"But despite that, could someone have lumped you together in their own mind? Seen you as part of something—or responsible for something that didn't please them?"

"There is one thing, but I'm sure it's barking up the wrong tree. Abortion. I believe all the editors in chief are pro-choice and sometimes I get letters from right-to-lifers who notice that. They see it as some sort of a cabal."

"Hmmm," I said. "It seems pretty farfetched that it could be related to that. Of course, some of those pro-life people are nut cases and they kill. But they use bombs and shotguns, not truffles."

I took a sip of my cappuccino and then licked the froth off my top lip.

"Okay, for starters, I'm going to concentrate on two areas," I explained. "One is people at *Gloss*. I'll go over the résumés and maybe something will jump out. I'll look to see if anybody ever worked for Tucker at *Best House*. In the meantime, I want you to think back over the last few weeks and ask yourself if any of the more junior staff has acted pissy, upset, or just weird. Second, I'm going to check into Dolores. Do you think there's some reason she could have hated Tucker as much as you?"

"Not that I know of. Though I assume it irked her that she was run out of her job and he wasn't."

Cat flagged down the waiter for the check, which she paid, and we collected our things and walked outside. It was bustling along Madison Avenue now—private-school girls in skirts so short that you could practically see their butt cracks, older women in Chanel suits, little kids riding silver scooters, mothers who six months ago were managing $20 million hedge funds and were now pushing strollers—and looking as if they preferred it. There was a town car idling along the curb, and when I saw Cat catch the driver's eye I realized that he was waiting for her.

"You want a ride?" she asked, sliding her sunglasses onto her face.

"Nah, I'm going to walk around for a bit. I'll call you if I find anything on the résumés. And be careful."

"The problem is, I'm not even sure what I'm supposed to be careful of. Do you know I even tossed the damn toothpaste? God, this is surreal, isn't it? If I think too much about it, I feel like I'm about to sob."

"You going into *Gloss* today?"

"No. I was going to go right after lunch, but I'm not feeling up to it. I have some things to take care of, and then I think I'm going to work from home one more day."

The driver jumped out at this point, as if he had picked

up some infinitesimal signal from Cat that it was time to open the door. As she slid into the backseat, a thought suddenly occurred to me.

"Hey, one more question," I said, leaning in through the open window. "I never asked about Kip. Anything to report there?"

Much to my astonishment, she blushed—not on her face, but on the delicate white skin of her neck. It was faint but swift, like a Cabernet seeping through a white cloth napkin.

"No, nothing," she said. "I'm happy with his work, we get along."

"I've heard people complain that he's arrogant."

"Not to me. Like I told you, he's doing his job well. There's really nothing to say."

The driver must have sensed that this was one of those "I've said all I'm gonna say" moments because he put the car in drive. I gave Cat a quick "See ya" as the driver pulled the car seamlessly into the traffic on Madison Avenue.

It was one-thirty and I headed east, in the general direction of the Lex line but in no big hurry. My goal was to wander and think. I had come to lunch hoping to make progress, to discover that Cat had recalled something of significance. What I'd gotten was not at all what I'd been expecting. First there was her betrayal of Polly. Polly must be furious at Cat, but she hadn't breathed a word about it to me. Was she angry enough to want to poison Cat? I *did* adore Polly, and it troubled me to think that she could ever be a suspect. And Leslie. That was a freaky little story Cat had shared. Was there more to it than she had let on? And last but not least, what was up with Kip? I don't think Cat was aware that she'd blushed or that I suspected any disingenuousness on her part, but it was clear that her statement "There's nothing to say" was a big fib. Was something going on between her and Kip? And if the answer was yes, had Jeff gotten wind of it?

Finding myself suddenly at the corner of Lex and 88th, I realized I was only a couple of blocks from the Starbucks where Jody worked. Heidi was no longer the center of the story, but in the interest of some closure, I decided I'd pop in and see if I could talk to him.

He was there this time, a good-looking and very buff guy in his late twenties, wearing the black baseball cap and green apron and sliding chairs back under empty tables. I introduced myself, and it was clear that he'd been told I'd dropped by before. He suggested we go outside, and I followed him out to an area on the sidewalk near the side entrance, a few feet away from a Dumpster.

He turned out to be one of those guys who's better looking from ten feet away. He had a monobrow that up close made his hazel eyes appear slightly cross-eyed and surly. As we talked I saw that he had an annoying habit of flicking his brown bangs off his forehead every few seconds.

"This must be awfully hard for you," I said as he leaned against the wall of the building.

"Yeah, that's an understatement. And I can't get any information."

"What do you need to know? Maybe I can help," I said.

"What happened?" he said testily. "I just want to know what happened."

"No one really knows right now. It looks like Heidi

might have died from something she ingested. Have the police talked to you yet?" Farley had said they had but I was playing dumb.

"Yeah, and they came by here Sunday—which was real sweet of them."

"What were they interested in knowing?"

"Did Heidi do drugs, that kind of thing—or was she depressed. They were all over the map. I told them that she barely touched alcohol. And I have no clue whether she was depressed that weekend. I had the weekend off and was out of town. Besides, Heidi and I were over—I hardly even saw her anymore."

"Where'd you go last weekend?"

A flick of the bangs. "New Jersey. A bike race. And yeah, I got proof."

"When was the last time you *did* see Heidi?" I asked.

"I dropped by the house last week. It was the night Cat Jones had one of her big parties going. But Heidi was busy and I never said more than hi to her."

He glanced at his watch, then into the store. "I gotta get back," he said. "What did you say your name was again?"

"It's Bailey. Bailey Weggins." I pulled a business card from my wallet, offered it to him, and told him to call if he needed anything, though he seemed as interested in staying in touch as he did in eating a tongue sandwich for lunch.

As I walked toward the subway stop, thoughts of Heidi that I'd pushed from my mind came rushing back again. The hair crusted with vomit, her faded eyes, the sea foam green towels. She'd snitched those truffles and had died an awful death, all by herself, because of it.

There were so many questions about the case, but one thing in particular had been bugging me ever since my discussion with Cat at lunch. Hadn't the murderer taken an awfully big chance leaving the candy on the hall table? It was obviously a hostess gift, so the killer could be reasonably sure that at the end of the evening it would be waiting there, beckoning Cat. But the killer also must have known there was a possibility something unpredictable could happen to the box. Cat could have opened it and passed the candy around at the party (not likely, because she didn't like to share, but as Cat had informed me, the caterers had *almost* done that). Or someone in the household could have opened the box and eaten the candy before Cat got her paws on it (exactly what *had* happened).

Of course, maybe that didn't totally matter to the killer. Maybe he or she had factored that in and was happy to settle for wreaking havoc in Cat's life. In some ways, that was an even scarier scenario. It was one thing to long to take down your nemesis, quite another to kill innocent bystanders. The situation seemed more dangerous than I'd even realized. And I was now smack in the middle of it.

CHAPTER 10

As soon as I returned to my apartment, I made a pot of coffee and spread the forty-seven résumés from the envelope on top of my dining table. For the next hour I pored over each one of them, looking for anything the teeniest bit weird, focusing on individuals who'd attended the party but reading the others as well. Funny what you don't know about people. One of the fashion editors, for instance, who I'd always assumed was as dumb as a sponge, turned out to be a Harvard grad; the associate book editor had spent two years as a masseuse, specializing in hot stone massage; and good old Kip, who referred ceaselessly to his years at Princeton, had started out there but ended up graduating from the University of New Mexico. But beyond that there was nothing that made me go, "Oh boy."

I also didn't come up with anything that suggested a connection between the attempt on Cat's life and Tucker

Bobb's death. Two junior people on staff had worked at both *Gloss* and *Best House,* but neither had attended the party.

Since the résumé exercise proved to be a bust, I turned my attention to the other item at the top of my to-do list: talking to Dolores. On the subway ride home I'd come up with a good strategy. I'd call Dolores and tell her that I was putting together an anthology of my articles (true, of course) and since she had done such a brilliant job editing *her* recent anthology, *Love at Any Cost,* I'd be grateful for her advice (ridiculous lie). After finding her number in the company directory I kept at home, I placed the call. An assistant answered, a woman who sounded old enough to have worked for Clare Boothe Luce during *her* magazine days. I explained my request, and after putting me on hold for about ten minutes, she offered me either tomorrow afternoon or next Monday. Needless to say, I opted for tomorrow.

I also made a call to Polly and suggested, as casually as I could, that we get together for lunch or a drink. She was crazy busy because of the July close, she told me, and said maybe we could grab a drink after work on Friday or sometime over the weekend. That was the best I was going to do.

Though I'd made tentative plans to see a movie that night with an old friend from *Get,* I begged off. Instead I took a load of clothes to the dry cleaners, hit the gym, ordered a deep-dish pizza to be delivered at home, and spent another half hour going back over the résumés, concentrating this time on just the people who had been at the party. Nothing jumped out at me. The rest of my evening couldn't have been more of a bore. No crank calls. No calls, in fact, from anyone. I went to bed around midnight, fell asleep just after one. Up again at 2:44. Last clock sighting before morning: 4:10.

On Wednesday I was at *Gloss* early. I wanted to be on the premises to observe whatever I could, and I also needed to get some work out of the way. The final of my stalking story would be coming through midday, so I had the morning to concentrate on Marky and the poltergeist.

Around ten-thirty I headed down to Cat's office, taking the long way so I could check things out. Polly was on the phone with her door partially closed; Rachel, according to her assistant, had not yet returned from breakfast with a publicist; Leslie was holding her weekly production meeting at the conference table in the pit; and Kip was nowhere in sight. As I got closer to Cat's office, I could see her through the glass wall, sitting at her sleek black desk, reading with a frown on her face. I tapped on the glass before entering. The first thing Cat did was thrust a copy of the day's *New York Post* toward me, with her thumb on an item reporting that Cat Jones's nanny had most likely been murdered and Cat was probably the intended victim.

Who would have planted that? she demanded. As far as I knew, Jeff, Leslie, and I were the only ones in the loop, and I certainly hadn't been blabbing. I pointed out that the reporter may also have gotten it from contacts in the Nineteenth Precinct. Cat went off on a tear about how the police didn't seem to give a damn about her safety. I let her rant for a minute, and when she calmed down she admitted that they had called with one piece of news: The autopsy had seemed to confirm a death by poison, though the toxicology reports, as Farley had said, wouldn't be in for days. Had the police been interviewing people? I asked. They'd talked to Carlotta, the caterers, and Jeff once more, but that's all she knew of.

"I thought I'd feel better being here, having something to do," she said, wringing her hands. "But I'm scared. I may call Jeff later and have him pick me up."

I mentioned my upcoming meeting with Dolores and left her office with an assurance that I was delving into things, as promised. The fact that other reporters were digging around gave me an added sense of urgency.

Just after I returned to my office, the phone rang. It was Megan Fox from *Best House*.

"Sorry not to call back yesterday," she said. "I was jammed up."

"No problem. I know we vowed to have lunch soon, but I was actually calling for another reason. I need some info on Tucker."

"Well, first and foremost, he's dead."

"You're funny," I said, flipping open my steno pad so I could take notes. "Was it in October? Is that when he died?"

"That's right. Why so curious?"

"I can't explain right now, but I'll fill you in later. Someone told me lately that he died from eating poison mushrooms. Is that really true?"

"Now what little bird told you that?"

"A little bird who sounded awfully sure of itself," I said.

"I didn't realize that theory was circulating out there. As far as I knew, it had been kept under wraps."

"So it's true?"

"I don't really know." She sighed. "What I *do* know is

that it's not just some urban legend. It was a theory that apparently was proposed by one of the doctors."

"What was the party line, though?"

"Kidney failure, but it was all kind of mysterious. He had what seemed like a nasty stomach flu, but it got worse fast and he died within a couple of days."

"Did it happen here in the city?"

"No, out in Bucks County, Pennsylvania, where he had a farm. But it started here—he got sick one Wednesday or Thursday afternoon before going there for a long weekend. By that night he was in the hospital out there. His kidneys and liver shut down and he ended up dying two days later. It was later that one of the PA doctors said that his symptoms were similar to what happens if you eat bad mushrooms."

"So how did he eat a poison mushroom in New York City?"

"Now, Bailey, you're putting words in my mouth. I don't really know if he *did* eat any poison mushrooms. But mushrooms were a hobby of his. He belonged to this club that looks for morels and stuff in Central Park. He was always rooting around there—at lunchtime or after work. So maybe he went out at lunch that day, picked the wrong kind, and took a few bites on the way back to the office."

"But were there any tests—to show whether he'd eaten bad mushrooms?"

"Apparently it's not easy to detect that sort of thing."

"Did anyone ever talk to his wife about it? He had a wife, right?"

"Yeah, Darma," she said dismissively. "Wife number two. One of our former food editors, in fact."

"Oh, gosh. I think I knew that once, but I'd completely forgotten. Did he ditch number one for her?"

"Yeah, but it wasn't such a crime. The first one looked like the sister of Jabba the Hutt. And she was just as evil."

"So did this Darma ever volunteer whether she believed the mushroom theory?"

"No, she was pretty buttoned up, if you'll excuse the expression. We saw her at the funeral and that was it. Didn't even return calls. She had some professional movers clear out his office. Apparently she also sold their Manhattan place and is ensconced full-time out in Bucks County."

"Interesting. Well, look, I appreciate all the info."

"This doesn't have anything to do with *your* boss, does it? I read that her nanny had died somehow."

"No, no," I said. "Just curious."

I hustled her off the phone with a promise to set up a lunch date in a few weeks.

At one I ran out to get lunch, a take-out order of California rolls from the Japanese restaurant down the street. On the way back to my office, I made a loop through the corridors, looking again for the senior staffers. Polly, Rachel, and Kip weren't at their desks, Leslie had her door closed. Next I walked through the pit, just to measure the mood. It was like a beehive that had been knocked to the ground by a baseball—phones jangling, people buzzing and shouting. The pit residents were always hyper during final closing week, but I was sure today's nuttiness was the result of word spreading about that nasty item in the *Post*.

Back in my office, I devoured a California roll, read the finals of my girl stalker story, and then, with my door closed, formulated some questions to ask Dolores. Shortly before two-thirty, I started to pack up my things, figuring I'd go straight home from my interview. As I was separating some files to toss in my tote bag, Leslie sashayed into my office with a look on her face that suggested she'd been combing through my expense report and discovered I'd overtipped a chambermaid while out of town on my last story. I was eager to talk to her, but I wasn't in the mood for getting chewed out. When she spoke, though, she was friendly enough—for Leslie.

"I just read the final of your stalker story. It's good."

"Thanks. You holding up okay?"

"Well, as you can imagine, after that item in the *Post* today, people are in a total tizzy."

"Do you think the guilty person *is* here?" I asked. I watched her intently as she answered.

"Well, we certainly can't kid ourselves. Someone at that party did it, and half the people who were *there* work *here*. I've had the refrigerator emptied, and I'm going to discourage anyone from leaving food around. What do *you* think?"

"That sounds reasonable," I said. "Of course, it gives people something else to buzz about, but on the other hand, you don't want to take any chances, either."

"No, I mean what do you think about the situation as a whole? Do you believe the person who did it works here?"

"Leslie, I'm as baffled as anyone," I said. I had no interest in sharing any of my ruminations with her. What I *was* still interested in was the story Cat had told me about Leslie's jealous snit, but nothing about her demeanor suggested anything antagonistic toward Cat.

"But I thought you were helping Cat," she said. "Surely you must have some ideas."

"Nothing—at least nothing at this point. Cat has more confidence in my ability to help than I do."

She just stared at me, kidney-bean nostrils flared, and I could tell she thought I was holding back.

"Well, I've got stuff to do, and you do, too," she said finally, with a trace of snippiness. "By the way, I hate to tell you this, but that adoption story we had scheduled for August isn't going to happen. We need your poltergeist piece."

"You're not serious. That means it was due a week ago. And I haven't even started writing yet."

"Cat wants it. We can crash it, so you've still got a *little* time. You'll have to finish it in the next week. I'm sure it's inconvenient, but life will be crazy here for the next few weeks because of what's happened and we'll all have to make some sacrifices."

I resisted the urge to throttle her from behind as she strutted out of my office. Did Leslie enjoy making me miserable when she had the chance, or did she just give that impression?

This new development was going to force me to shift into high gear with my article, though I wouldn't be ready to write until I talked to the child psychologist tomorrow at lunch and got his perspective. Doing a quick calculation in my head, I figured I could hole up at my place tomorrow afternoon to do the outline and then try to write as much of the piece as possible on Friday and over the weekend. Somehow I would also have to manage to make room for helping Cat.

It was time finally for my interview with Dolores. I

had thought she might want to meet in the "consultant" office she kept on the second floor of our building, but her assistant had told me to show at Dolores's apartment on Lexington Avenue at 70th Street. As I bounced along in a taxi, I suddenly realized that I felt mildly anxious about the prospect of being in the same room with her. I had that sensation you get in your stomach that makes you wonder if you somehow managed to swallow a peach pit when you weren't paying attention.

For starters, she was supposed to be a real pit bull. Even the people who had worked with her for years had a tough time summoning any affection. According to one legendary story that had made the rounds at *Gloss* after Cat assumed command, Dolores had emerged from the office ladies' room one day with the back of her dress tucked into her panty hose and no one had bothered to tell her.

In addition to being fierce, she apparently had the attention span of a three-day-old rhesus monkey. Her staff, at least the ones who'd wanted to get ideas green-lighted by her, had learned to boil down their idea pitches to one minute or less.

And last but hardly least, I was also disconcerted by the idea of sitting in the same room with the woman who was up at the top of my suspect list. Would I be all alone with her in her apartment? What if she saw through my lie and realized what I was up to?

The answer to the first question turned out to be no. A housekeeper opened the door, a woman of about sixty-five wearing a half apron covered with faded cherries. She informed me that Mrs. Wilder would be with me shortly and led me down a narrow corridor to the living room. As soon as she'd shuffled out of the room, I surveyed my surroundings. Dolores had run *Gloss* in the days when editors had plenty of prestige but not the power salaries they do now, and though Dolores's place was roomy for New York, it didn't come close to Cat's town house. Considering the number of doorways I'd counted off the hallway, it was probably no more than a two-bedroom with a maid's room.

The living room appeared to have last been decorated in 1964. It was filled with about four hundred yards of faded chintz—on couches, chairs, pillows, windows, even as little curtains on the windowed doors of a mahogany hutch. There were several mirrors on the wall, but practically no art, except for a large oil portrait of Dolores holding a cocker spaniel, who I suspected, based on the old-dog smell permeating the apartment, was still hanging on by a hair somewhere on the premises.

I cooled my heels for about fifteen minutes, leafing through a two-week-old copy of *Time* on the coffee table. Finally, there was a gun burst of conversation down the corridor and a minute later Dolores blew into the room. I jumped from my seat and stuck out my hand to greet her. She was a short, stocky woman, no more than five feet one, which contributed to her pit bull persona, and she was wearing a fairly ridiculous getup today—red slacks and an orangy blouse with a big loopy bow—that only exaggerated the lack of height. She'd let her short-cropped hair go totally gray, the flat, drab shade of a highway guardrail, and her skin was heavily wrinkled and waffled under the eyes, like the skin of a chicken. And the mouth—well, that was legendary Dolores. Due to either deteriorating eyesight or the disappearance of her lip line with age or just pure orneriness, she always wore a big undefined smear of fire engine red lipstick, as if someone had rubbed a thumb hard across her mouth after she'd applied it.

"Dolores, I so appreciate your seeing me," I said as she plunked down on the sofa in the middle of the room and placed a hand on each knee. I quickly took a seat across from her in an armchair.

"You're a staff writer?" she asked before I had a chance to get in a question. "I'm surprised they have staff writers over there anymore. That's something everybody's getting rid of these days."

"It's not actually a staff position," I explained. "I'm a contributing writer. They keep a little office for me, and I write some of the human-interest stories and—"

"Those are the only things I bother to read in the magazine anymore. Did you write the story on the clitoridectomies they're doing in Africa?"

"Clitoridectomies? I don't believe *Gloss* ran an article on that subject. It might have been *Marie Claire* that—"

"It's a terrible thing. And they showed the pictures— of girls being held down. Africa's a hellhole. And it's never going to change." She flung her arm across the back of the sofa, craned her neck around, and barked: "Madge? . . . Madge?" I assumed she was summoning the woman who had answered the door, but it could just as easily have been the dog.

"Actually, I do a lot of crime stories, and they're going to be collected in a book," I explained as she turned back around again. "You did such a great job with your anthology—I thought you might have a few words of wisdom for me."

"On what kinds of stories to write?"

"No, no, I've already written them. There are about a dozen altogether, most of them crime stories. I thought you might have some suggestions on packaging and marketing them. Anthologies can be tough to sell."

"Stick the word *love* in the title." She craned her head around toward the door again. "Madge, I need you . . . For God's sake, where is that woman?"

"You've got 'love' in the title of your book, of course. Do you think it's helped?"

"How would I know? It just came out two weeks ago. Of course, you work at the 'newer, fresher, more *rel-e-vant Gloss,*' so you might want to put the word *sex* in the title. What is it with her and sex? Is she *obsessed* with it?" I had heard from several people that Dolores never ever used Cat's name when discussing her.

"Gee, I don't know," I said with a little laugh. "But speaking of *Gloss,* do you think having the book party was helpful in terms of getting press? Should I try to get someone to do that for me?" It was a non sequitur, but I was pretty confident she wouldn't notice.

"Oh, please, Billy. The only reason she had that damn party is that Harry forced her. And press? The dead nanny's ended up with all the press this week."

It seemed pointless to tell her she had my name wrong. I was just happy that in less than a minute she'd ricocheted over in the direction where I wanted to be.

"Well, that's not Cat's fault, of course."

She let out a half snort, half laugh. "Oh, really? I wouldn't put it past her, would you? Deep-six the nanny to deflect attention away from me?"

Had she not seen the press today about Cat being the

intended victim? Or was she just making me think she was in the dark?

"It was a terrible thing, though, wasn't it?" I said. "To have someone so young die such an awful death."

"The police were around *here,* you know? Asking all sorts of questions about the party. I take it they think someone from the party may have seen something suspicious that night. I told them I didn't know the girl personally and I didn't see a damn thing."

"I think they're going to be questioning lots of people."

"Well, they certainly didn't clue me in on their game plan," she said. She paused and pursed her lips so that the top part stuck out like a duckbill. "With girls like that nanny, there's usually lots of people who'd like to see them pay for their sins. She went around asking for trouble and she finally found it."

"What do you mean?" I asked, baffled about how she'd know anything about Heidi.

"She was what in my day we called a tart. One of my short story writers knew her. She once worked for her as a nanny up in Westchester."

"One of the writers at the party?" I asked, incredulous.

"Yes, of course. Nancy Highland."

"I wasn't aware of that," I said.

She reached over to a pewter bowl on the coffee table to pluck out a cellophane-wrapped lemon ball and then jerked her head back in my direction.

"Well, *she* didn't kill the girl, for God's sake, if that's what you're thinking. But she told me that nanny was a snake. Nancy remarried a year or two ago and had this baby late—she's forty-two, forty-three—and Hildy was her nanny for about the first six months. Nancy has a son from another marriage, he's about eighteen, and Hildy or Heidi or whatever her name is got involved with him. Then she dumped him and he was ready to put a gun to his head."

"Did Nancy see Heidi at the party?"

"She got a glimpse of her, and the girl got all flustered. Nancy knew she worked there, you see. She went to New York directly from the job in Scarsdale. Nancy didn't find out about the damage the girl had done, though, until after she'd left."

All of this info about Heidi was intriguing, but I needed to drive the conversation back to Cat.

"I take it you haven't heard," I said, "but apparently *Cat* was the intended victim. Heidi ate some chocolates that were left off for Cat the night of your party, and it appears that the chocolates contained poison."

It took about three seconds for what I said to register with her, because she'd gotten preoccupied trying to scrape a stubborn piece of cellophane off the lemon ball, but when it did her head shot up and she appeared completely stunned. She was either the world's best actress or it really was all news to her.

"What? Who told you that?" she demanded.

"Well, it's been in the paper. I know it from Cat, too."

"The cops kept asking—they don't know who did it?"

"No, but it was obviously someone who attended the party."

Her brain went into overdrive, but I couldn't tell from looking at her what was going on in there. She asked me bluntly if I had any more questions about my book.

"I'm struggling with my intro a bit. A book editor once

told me that when people pick up an anthology in a bookstore, they skim the introduction, and if it's tantalizing enough, they buy it. Did your editor give you any guidance on the intro? Is there any advice you'd offer me?"

She looked at me stupefied, as if I'd just asked something completely inane, like did she believe in the existence of an Antichrist or what was the cup size of her bra. Then she shook her head in irritation.

"Do you want to talk to my editor? Is that it? You don't have an editor yet?"

"No, no, I have an editor, but I thought you— Look, this is obviously a busy time for you. Why don't I get going. If I have other questions, I can give you a call."

I stood up from the sofa, but she just sat there, brain still racing. At that moment Madge finally materialized through the doorway, carrying a small wooden tray with two cups of what appeared to be Sanka.

"For God's sake, Madge, where were you? Look, I forgot to tell you, Herb isn't going to be home for dinner tonight so you can make me the halibut. And I'm going to need a taxi in ten minutes. Let them know downstairs."

Where was she heading off to all of a sudden? I couldn't tell whether I'd triggered some kind of tizzy or this was the way she was naturally. I'm sure it had occurred to her that if someone had attempted to kill Cat, she would be a very obvious suspect.

"You think it's the husband?" she asked, still on the sofa.

At first I wasn't sure whether she was talking to me or making some final point to Madge, who was clearing room for the Sanka on the coffee table. I volleyed back an "Excuse me?"

"Mr. Jones. Do you think he might be responsible?"

"I can't imagine that," I said, trying to look aghast. "They have a very nice life together."

"He didn't seem very happy to be there that night, if you ask me."

"No couple's perfect," I said. "But overall Jeff and Cat seem to have something special." I'd obviously just developed a rare form of Tourette's syndrome that involved verbally hurling out saccharine clichés rather than obscenities.

"Most people don't even try these days," she snapped. She stood up finally and edged her way out from behind the coffee table.

"You know, I invented togetherness," she said.

"The expression?" I asked, mystified.

"No, the whole thing. The idea of it. I did the first articles on it. In 1971. In those days magazines had power. They shaped how people thought, how they acted."

"That's not true anymore?"

"Not on your life. People don't respect the magazines that are published today."

Seemed like a good time to be making my getaway. I said as pleasant a good-bye as I could manage, and she told me that Madge would see me out. Then she steamed across the room and out a doorway on the other side.

Rather than hop on a subway home, I walked a few blocks until I found a coffee shop. I wanted the chance to jot down verbatim as much of my conversation with Dolores as possible—which would be tough, considering it had been like dialogue from a play by Ionesco.

I asked for a cappuccino, and then, realizing I was ravenous, I ordered my dinner—a cheeseburger and a glass of red wine. Once I'd re-created as much of the conversation as possible, I sat back and considered the significance of it all, particularly the moment at which I had told Dolores that Cat was the intended victim. Could she have been faking her shock at that news? I didn't think so. She had honestly appeared flabbergasted. Besides, my read on Dolores was that she'd been so busy bulldozing her way through life that she'd never learned the art of camouflaging what she wanted or the way she felt.

And if she didn't know Cat was supposed to die, then she could hardly be the demon candy maker. That meant I needed to concentrate on all those magazine people at the party—and also figure out what was going on with Cat and Jeff.

I flipped back a few pages in my steno pad to the notes I'd taken down about Tucker Bobb. If he really had died from poisonous mushrooms and someone had tried to kill Cat with some type of poison, then there definitely might be a connection. Maybe someone had a vendetta against women's magazines and was attempting to systematically off the editors. Other editors' lives might be in danger as well.

It was about six-thirty when I finished my meal and a second cup of cappuccino. As I stuffed my pad into my tote bag, I realized to my complete dismay that I had left several research files for my Marky story at the office— I could suddenly picture them on my side chair, where I'd set them just as Leslie had dropped by, demonstrating all the charm of a blowtorch. Since it was essential for me to begin crash writing my piece at home tomorrow, I'd have to make a trip back to *Gloss* tonight. Major bummer.

Subwaywise, there was no easy route from the coffee

shop back. I decided I'd hop a cab to the office but then
subway home. It would be almost seven by the time I got
to *Gloss,* but since it was a closing night, I figured there'd
still be plenty of people around.

But there weren't. As I walked into the pit I spotted
only one person, a guy in the production department, and
he was busy buckling his knapsack. His only acknowl-
edgment to me was a nod of the head, and then he swung
his knapsack over his shoulder, flipped a baseball cap on
his head, and strode away. Maybe there was a company
softball game tonight. Or maybe people didn't want to
stick around because they were just too damned freaked
out about everything that had happened.

I hurried through the empty pit and turned left onto the
main corridor. Polly's office was dark; so were Kip's and
Leslie's. The only sound was the buzzing of the exit sign
over the stairwell door. As I neared the turnoff to my corridor, I heard something just around the corner, the sound,
I thought, of someone stepping on the pedal of the water
fountain. But three seconds later, as I swung around the
corner, I saw that the corridor was empty. Except for the
mannequin nicknamed Fat Ass, which was standing in
front of the darkened fashion department, wearing a
shaggy burgundy sweater without any pants. I glanced
behind me. Nothing, no one. I was starting to get a bad
case of the creeps.

I walked the length of the short corridor to my office.
To my surprise, my office door was closed. I never closed
it. Maybe one of the cleaning people had been by and
shut it by mistake. I pushed open the door and hit the light
switch. My trash basket was still full, and the space
hadn't been tidied up. Weird. My forgotten files, how-

ever, were sitting right there on the extra chair, just as I had pictured them in my mind. As I shoved them into my tote bag, something caught my eye from the left. I spun my head around. Sitting smack in the center of my desk, all by its lonesome, was a silver-wrapped Hershey's Kiss.

CHAPTER 11

THE SIGHT OF the Kiss made me catch my breath. It was just a little piece of chocolate wrapped in foil, yet it delivered a big, ugly message. I backed clumsily out of my office and shot a glance up and down the corridor. No one. Nothing. Part of me wanted to tear out of there, but the other part of me, the part that was more pissed than scared, wanted to find out whatever I could. I dug around in my purse for a tissue, stepped back into my office, my heart beating hard, and carefully picked up the Kiss with the tissue. As soon as I'd tucked it in my purse, I cautiously retraced my steps to the main corridor. Still empty. I heard a rumble from the pit and froze, waiting. A cleaning lady, not a day under sixty, rounded the corner pushing a large cart with a trash bag and a slew of cleaning products.

"Excuse me. Have you seen anyone else on the floor?"

She looked at me seemingly without comprehension,

and I wondered if she spoke English. I gave it one more shot.

"Have you—"

"I just got off the elevator. I didn't see anyone."

I overlooked her rudeness because frankly I was glad for the company. Before heading back toward the pit, I walked the length of the main corridor in the opposite direction, toward the coffee station and a short back hallway with offices for the articles editors and copy editing department. Not a soul in sight.

There was one more thing worth inspecting: the sign-out log in the lobby. I took the back way to the elevator bank and headed down to the main floor. As I signed my own name into the book, I glanced over the rows of names. Most of the people I knew at *Gloss*, including Kip, Polly, and Leslie, had signed out between six and six-fifteen. Nothing unusual jumped out at me.

The subway home was packed, but I hardly noticed. I was too busy concentrating on the evil Kiss that was now resting in the zipper compartment of my bag.

There was only one reasonable explanation for it. Heidi's killer had put it there. Sure, staffers at *Gloss* sometimes left treats on my desk, but no one would make that kind of gesture these days in light of everything that had happened. Surely the killer knew there was no chance I'd eat it. It had been placed there obviously to scare my pants off, to intimidate me. Clearly word was out that I was helping Cat, and this was a message that said "You better mind your own beeswax." I would now bet that the hang-ups were part of the same scare tactics.

From the Kiss on the desk it wouldn't be a big leap to conclude that the killer worked at *Gloss*. And I certainly had names to consider: Polly, who Cat had enraged; Leslie, who she'd infuriated; Rachel, who she'd dressed down; and Kip, who she'd possibly seduced. And the staff might include other walking wounded I didn't know about.

Yet there was also a chance someone from the outside had gotten onto the floor. There was no receptionist by the elevator bank, and though visitors were supposed to sign in at the guard's desk on the ground floor of the building, it was fairly easy to slip by, especially at busy hours and if you looked the part.

My heart was still beating faster than it should have when I stepped off the subway. As soon as I got home I phoned Cat. Her machine picked up. Then I checked my own machine. Only one call, Landon saying hi. No K.C. It was Wednesday night, and this meant he was not interested in guaranteeing himself a position on the weekend dance card. How had I been so blind early on to what a commitment-phobe he was? Stay calm, I told myself. Resist the urge to scream.

What I should have done next was throw some laundry into the machine down the hall, because the only clean underwear I had was a pair of granny briefs from a three-pack I'd bought in a Texas Wal-Mart when I was delayed doing a story down there. But I had no interest in leaving the security of my apartment. I still felt rattled from the damn Kiss. I decided that first thing the next morning I'd call Detective Farley and ask him what he wanted me to do with it. I'd also try to reach Cat again and fill her in on my meeting with Dolores as well as the nasty treat I'd been left. Plus, there was a piece of information I wanted to extract from her. I had remembered, too late to check the log, that Jeff was supposed to come by to pick her up at work. What time had he arrived? And had he gone upstairs to her office or waited in the lobby? Last, but not least, I was going to begin finding out what I could about Tucker Bobb's death.

After throwing on a T-shirt for bed, I splashed some of the Courvoisier usually reserved for company into a brandy snifter. Maybe that would take the edge off my anxiety. I'd just fallen into my bed and was channel surfing with the TV remote when the phone rang. I picked it up, figuring it was probably Landon. There was just breathing—about four seconds' worth—and then a click. I checked the caller ID box in my office, but I knew what it would say: number blocked. I felt the same flood of fear and anger that I'd experienced in my *Gloss* office earlier. I added one more thing to my list for the next day: Call the phone company and see what recourse I had in dealing with the hang-ups.

When I woke the next morning (time I fell to sleep: roughly midnight; number of awakenings: two), my bed was in a pool of sunlight and I felt better, less frazzled—though there was an annoying pounding above my left eye, probably from the brandy. I stepped out onto my terrace and scanned the dozens of apartment buildings I could see to the west. Somewhere out there was a killer, a killer who now was toying with me.

As soon as I'd wolfed down a toasted English muffin, I called Detective Farley. He wasn't due in, they said, until the afternoon, so I left a message. I didn't have any luck with Cat, either. At the town house I got only the machine, and at work her voice mail. I left messages both places, asking her to call ASAP.

Next I called the phone company, and after a Kafkaesque experience with voice mail, I hooked up with a human actually eager to help with hang-ups. Unfortunately, she said, there was no way to unblock the number and see who had been harassing me. But what the phone company *did* offer these days was a service that allowed calls from blocked numbers to be intercepted. The person would be asked for their name and if they didn't give one, they would be disconnected. It worked not only with stalkers, but also for telemarketers—I would never again have to listen to a pitch for a new credit card. But I passed. Right now I was reluctant to shut out my mystery caller using this kind of tactic. Doing so might aggravate him or her, prompting more aggressive behavior. Besides, just as he was keeping tabs on me with the calls, I was able, in a way, to use the calls to keep tabs on him.

Finally, I set about trying to get the number for the Merry Widow Bobb—without having to call my *Best House* contact back. It turned out to be a breeze. A bio of Bobb on the Web gave the town in Bucks County where his farm was located, and he was still listed with directory assistance.

Darma Bobb sounded breathless when she answered, as if she'd just hurried in from outside, and she was curt as could be when I identified myself as an editor at *Gloss*. I explained to her that I was calling on behalf of Cat Jones and had something of the utmost urgency to discuss with her. Would it be possible for me to drive out tomorrow and talk with her? She pressed me to tell her why. I was afraid if I did, she'd find a reason to dodge a visit from me, so I kept insisting that what I needed to say was too sensitive to get into over the phone. Her curiosity edged ahead of her irritation, and she relented. We agreed on two P.M. Landon's weekend home was in Bucks County, too, in a town called Carversville, and as soon as I hung up, I left a message on his machine, asking if I could bunk down there Friday night. It would spare me a second two-hour drive in one day. I also called Polly and suggested we meet Sunday night rather than Friday because I had to go out of town.

I spent the rest of the morning organizing all my notes and files so I could begin my Marky outline in the afternoon. If I was going to make my new deadline, I was going to have to write at light speed.

Finally it was time for lunch with Dr. Jack Herlihy, child psychologist and poltergeist exposer. I hate doing interviews over a lunch because it always entails a messy, awkward routine of eating, writing, and napkin dabbing, but he'd seemed to be pushing for a meal. Maybe the food stipend for visiting professors left a lot to be desired. "Pick a spot," he'd said. "You know the Village." There'd been a slightly bossy quality to his tone, typical of a lot of shrinks I'd interviewed.

I had suggested we meet at a little café on East 9th Street with an outdoor courtyard. I changed out of my sweats and T-shirt into a short denim skirt I hadn't worn since last August and a pair of red slingbacks. I know this sounds very un-PC, but cute clothes do wonders in interviews with male members of the species.

As I hurried out of my apartment building, I glanced up and down the street. Nothing ominous. Just the usual Village types. I was two minutes late, and I was relieved to see that the shrink was late, too. Or, at least I thought he was. There was one solo person in the courtyard, a guy in jeans, a white T-shirt, and an unstructured navy blazer who hardly looked the part. But when he glanced up from his *New York Times* and spotted me, he raised his hand in a greeting. I couldn't believe it was him—though obviously he'd gotten a brilliant read on me over the phone.

Whereas I'd expected someone bearded, possibly balding, rumpily professorial, and over forty, he was clean-shaven, sophisticated, no more than thirty-four or thirty-five, and extremely good-looking, if your preference is the non-rugged-looking type with high cheekbones and smooth skin, which isn't exactly *my* type, but I can appreciate what works about it.

"Hi," he said, standing as I walked toward the table. "Jack Herlihy." He was at least six feet two.

"Bailey Weggins," I said. "I see you found the place okay."

"It's not what I expected over here," he said as we both sat down. "I'd always heard the East Village was this fringe area with lots of very strange street people."

"I think it was that way in the sixties, but now it's charming in its own way," I said. "I live right on the border of the East and West Village, so I've got to be loyal to both. You said you were on Mercer?"

"Yeah, they've got me in a furnished sublet in some university-owned housing. It's not bad—from what I hear, I'd be paying way over two thousand a month for a one-bedroom place down here, so I shouldn't complain—but the furniture looks like something out of an Adirondack lodge, circa 1940. I feel like I should get a CD of loon calls to play as a backdrop."

"You don't have a moose head over the bed, do you?"

"Not that bad." He laughed, brushing his hand through

his sandy brown hair. "But at least forty percent of the furniture seems to be made of birch bark."

Personalitywise he wasn't what I'd imagined, either. On the phone he had sounded cerebral and no-nonsense, more than anxious to give me a piece of his mind about the so-called science of parapsychology. I felt slightly discombobulated by his easygoingness. I suggested we order first, which we did, and then I quickly fished out my tape recorder from my bag, explaining that I liked to use a tape recorder and take notes as backup. When I pressed down the play and record buttons, he leaned back in his chair with his arms against his chest and watched me with a slightly bemused look in his eyes.

"As I mentioned to you on the phone," I said, trying not to sound as awkward as I felt from having those blue eyes on me so intently, "I'm doing a piece about a family who's had some crazy things happen in their house. A lot of people have suggested they have a poltergeist. From reading the two papers you did, I take it you don't believe that it could be a ghost or spirit."

"You know as well as I do," he said, "or at least I assume you do, that there's no such thing as ghosts or evil spirits. Though I'll confess that I saw *The Exorcist* on a sleep-over when I was twelve and it scared the hell out of me. I think I slept on the floor of my parents' bedroom for six months after that."

"I interviewed a couple of parapsychologists for the story," I explained. "Though these guys, by definition, believe in the paranormal, they don't think there's anything supernatural going on in this particular case. They say it's Marky's telekinetic energy that's creating all the commotion." No question. I just let the comment hang there.

"Does that make sense to you?" he asked.

"I'm interviewing *you.*"

"Okay," he said, smiling. He put his hands together like a steeple in front of his face and pressed them into his lips, holding them like that for a few seconds before speaking.

"I know all about these Ghostbuster-type guys. They sound scientific. And in these kinds of cases—the ones involving adolescents—they sound like the voice of reason, because everybody else is yelling poltergeist and they come in saying, 'No, no, don't be ridiculous, there's not a poltergeist. It's this troubled child's energy run amok.' But the idea that a kinetic force can be emitted from a child's brain is preposterous."

"Then who's creating all the havoc?"

"Who do you think?"

"Stop that. I'm asking you."

He smiled again, staring at me intently. I realized something fascinating at that moment about his looks. The whole was greater than the sum of the parts. His pale blue eyes were nice but not amazing (and his eyebrows were so pale that you almost couldn't see the outer ends); his mouth was full enough but not anything you'd melt over; and his nose was just okay, straight and proportional but a little on the large side. There was not a single drop-dead gorgeous feature, yet it all came together to form one drop-dead gorgeous face. No wonder he'd decided to focus in his practice on kids. He was too good-looking to be the kind of shrink who counseled adults—half of his patients would have ended up stalking him.

"It's the kids themselves who do the dirty work," he said finally.

"But how?" I asked. "I know that's what you found in the cases you observed, but in this instance I can't see how this girl, Marky, could have pulled everything off— or why she's going to all the trouble."

"Well, first, let me talk about the kids for a second. In almost all of these cases the child is an adolescent—or a preadolescent. Generally it's a girl. And they're always either very angry or troubled. In some cases she's been adopted or there's been some terrible disruption in her life. She fakes the phenomena in order to get the attention she craves—or it's a passive-aggressive expression of anger."

I told him a little bit then about Marky. The criteria fit, most definitely. Though it seemed that Marky's family cared about her, she was not actually the parents' natural daughter, but rather their niece. The wife's sister, the town tramp, had given birth to Marky illegitimately and had died of ovarian cancer when Marky was four.

The waiter arrived with a large bottle of Pellegrino and two goblets that he carried with the stems through the fingers of one hand. He poured us each a glass and set the bottle on the table.

"It's just hard for me to imagine that Marky's capable of *all* the mischief that's gone on up there," I said. "Some of the furniture that's been moved has been heavy."

"These kids have their ways. Even if you're not strong, you can move a big piece of furniture across the floor if you get the right momentum. I videotaped a kid doing that when he thought no one was looking. And some kids are even more sophisticated. They're like little magicians."

I asked him if there was a chance anyone else could be doing it—like the parents, in an attempt to turn Marky into a minor celebrity, or one of the brothers, in an attempt to create problems for her. He said that anything was possible, but he would put his money on Marky.

Our sandwiches arrived and it seemed an okay moment to take a break and eat. The day was exquisite, one of those afternoons when the air feels like a soft cloth against your neck and you want it never to end. In spite of everything that had been happening, I felt oddly relaxed.

As we fumbled with our food, I inquired about his background. After college, he explained, he'd gotten his doctorate and counseled kids for a couple of years before deciding that he'd prefer to teach, though he said he occasionally consulted in special cases. He liked his job at Georgetown but had accepted the summer gig at NYU because he was toying with the idea of relocating one day.

"How did you get interested in poltergeists?" I asked.

"A graduate supervisor of mine asked me to look into a case involving a ten-year-old kid whose mother had run off with a guy and left him behind with the grandmother. Everybody thought their house was haunted by the ghost of a farmer who had been bludgeoned to death there years before."

"I take it you didn't suspect a ghost?"

"I didn't know what to think at first, but I kept a low

profile and spotted the kid making a chandelier swing with a ruler."

When we were done with our sandwiches, we ordered coffee and he asked for a tiramisu.

"Two forks?" he asked, glancing toward me.

"Oh, yeah, sure," I said, flustered. God, what a date-y thing for him to do. What was his situation? I wondered. He didn't seem gay. He wasn't wearing a ring, and it was sort of clear from the way he talked earlier that he was living alone. There was probably some chick pining hard back in D.C., counting the days until his return in September and totally wigged out over the fact that he was flirting with the idea of relocating.

"Will you be going back to Washington on the weekends?" I asked.

"Not really. Maybe once or twice to check on my place. That's a town that really shuts down in the summer. I've got friends coming up here, though."

He glanced at his watch, and I realized I'd better hustle things along. I waved for the check. He tried to wrestle me for the bill, but I insisted, explaining that it was against journalistic ethics for me to allow him to pay.

We said good-bye on the sidewalk and then experienced that awkward moment that occurs when you discover you're going the same way and must restart a conversation you've just wrapped up.

As we walked west, he asked me about my job, about how I'd gotten started as a writer and what kind of pieces I liked to work on and what a typical day was like for me. His questions were thoughtful, and it was delicious to have a guy be so curious—though I chalked it up to his shrink training. All of a sudden he grew slightly distracted, as if he were trying to converse and simultaneously handle some minor mental task, like recall where he'd left his passport. I felt a weird urge to engage his attention fully again. I blurted out the story of Heidi's murder.

"How chilling," he said. "Do the police have any suspects?"

"Not that I know of. Cat seems to have annoyed lots of people over the years, and it may take a while to sort through all of them."

"The thing about premeditated murder—and I don't know a heck of a lot about it, but I do know this—is that it almost always involves some pretty intense self-interest and emotion. No one is ever going to plot your demise because you gave a boring dinner party. There's got to be something very intense behind it—like jealousy or greed or revenge. And then there's thwarted love—always a biggie."

He stopped suddenly, in the middle of the sidewalk on Broadway and 9th, and I realized that it was because he was about to turn south, back toward NYU.

"Well, look," I said, sticking out my hand, "I can't thank you enough for all your insight about Marky. It's been very helpful."

"I'm glad I could help," he said, smiling. "Call me if you've got any other question—and don't talk to any more parapsychologists. They'll start making telekinetic energy shoot out of *your* brain."

I laughed. "I probably will need to ask you a few more questions over the phone once I've gone over my notes. Thanks again."

He strode off, south on Broadway, the back of his

jacket flipping up as he walked, headed toward his office or his Adirondack cabin in the sky, to prepare a lesson plan or find his passport or call his girlfriend in D.C. and demand that she shuttle up this weekend and satisfy the desire surging through his loins. Why was I thinking these things? I wondered. Lookswise, he was not really my type, and I couldn't imagine dating a shrink.

My apartment house was only thirty feet away, but instead of going into the building, I headed west on 9th Street. My body was craving more caffeine, and I also wanted to sit in the fresh air and think through how I would work the information Jack Herlihy had given me into my article. I'd bought everything he said, but I wasn't sure yet how to weave it in. I could be straight with the reader up front or make the story more of a mystery.

On University Avenue I picked up a double cappuccino to go and walked over to Washington Square Park. It was packed, with people pushing strollers, Rollerblading, or just lolling about in the sun. I found an empty bench near the bocci court and parked myself on it.

With my cell phone, I checked my voice mail at work. Two messages. My editor at *Travels* had called to say she was faxing over more background material for my trip to England and Scotland in July, and my friend Mitch had left a message reminding me that his sister would be singing in a club on the Upper West Side tonight and I'd better show. I'd forgotten all about it.

Next I tried home, hoping Detective Farley and Cat would have made contact. No messages in the two hours I'd been away. But two hang-ups. My heart jumped, as if someone had come up from behind and given it a shove.

Tossing the cell phone back into my bag, I pulled my legs up onto the bench, careful not to give the entire park a view of my granny panties. As several mangy squirrels scampered around me, I took a careful sip of cappuccino and tried to concentrate on my article.

But it was tough. With no gorgeous Dr. Herlihy around to distract me, my mind kept coming back to the Kiss, to all the hang-ups. Right now the killer was only sending me messages, but what if he—or she—suddenly turned up the heat? It was clear to me that he wasn't simply a person who had hated enough to kill. He was frighteningly reckless—after all, he had left the truffles for Cat without really caring if someone else ate them—so I had every reason to be worried. Landon was right, that the smartest thing for me to do was back off. But I couldn't see myself curling up in a ball and whimpering. I was too concerned about Cat's safety, too angry over Heidi's senseless death, too pissed as hell that someone was threatening me, and, yes, too excited about being in the middle of it. Besides, at this point there'd be no way to signal to the killer: "Hey, leave me alone, I'm not playing junior detective anymore." So tomorrow, as planned, I'd go out to Bucks County and see if I could discover if there was really a connection between the two incidents, and if I couldn't find one, I'd come back to New York and continue to dig things up. I'd talk to the *Gloss* staffers, find out what I could about the people from other magazines who'd attended the party. And I'd watch my back at all times.

What I needed to do right this minute, however, was start my Marky piece. Maybe I'd have more luck on the computer. I pushed off the bench, tossed my cup in a trash container, and hurried through the park. As I crossed under the marble arch at the north end of the park where Fifth Avenue starts, I turned quickly and looked behind me. I had the weirdest sense someone was following me. Yet when I turned no one was there.

CHAPTER 12

I WAS ON the road to Bucks County, Pennsylvania—I-78, to be exact—by nine the next morning, and I couldn't wait to put a hundred-plus miles between me and Manhattan. Not only had I ended up with two more hang-ups the night before, but I'd done something supremely stupid in the K.C. department.

I wish I could at least plead intoxication as the reason for my dumb-ass behavior, but the entire evening I'd drunk only two Amstel Lites—well, and part of a third. In fact, the throbbing headache I was experiencing as my Jeep sped along the highway was not the hangover kind. It was due to a high-octane blend of fatigue, the heebie-jeebies, and a splash of self-loathing.

Much to my surprise, K.C. had called late Thursday afternoon as I sat nose to the grindstone in my home office, finished with the outline for Marky and two pages into the first draft. For me the secret has always been generating the first paragraph of an article, because everything flows from that. I'd nailed it pretty early this time, using something Jack Herlihy had said, Jack of the pale blue eyes and beguiling butt. For a guy who wasn't my type, I was having a hard time keeping him from my thoughts.

When the phone rang, I was sure it would be Cat or Detective Farley, since neither had yet returned my call. I could barely contain my surprise when I heard K.C.'s voice. We exchanged how-are-yous, he briefly described a deal he was winding up (was that supposed to explain why he'd been incommunicado?), and I told him about finding Heidi dead, which both surprised and shocked him (I guess he didn't peruse the *Post* on a daily basis). He asked a few questions, and I offered some broad answers, not bothering to get into much detail on the phone. Then, out of the blue, he changed direction, bringing up our mutual friend Mitch and his sister Trudy's singing gig that night. Was I going? he wanted to know. Fumbling for the right answer, I ended up with the brilliantly precise, "Maybe—but I'm not sure." He made a flip comment about Trudy's singing talent and sounded suddenly distracted (did I have some sort of *deficit,* I wondered, when it came to holding a man's attention?). Then, to my absolute stupefaction, he announced, "Well, then maybe I'll see you there. I think I'm going." And he signed off.

I was tempted to hurl the phone off the terrace in fury. What was that call all about? Had he simply wanted to check in, say hello? Had he intended to ask me out but done a 180 when I'd failed to sound cute enough on the phone? Or was he trying to arrange to meet up with me without having to lay out any cash? Let him go, I told myself. Cut the rope and turn your back as he drifts out to sea.

There was no point in returning to my piece after that. Three-hour stretches of writing are about my maximum, and I'd hit the wall. I made myself a cup of coffee and tried Cat again. Carlotta answered and passed the phone to her.

"Where've you been?" I asked, slightly irritated. "I tried you earlier."

"In bed. With the kind of migraine that only comes around once in a century. I could barely lift my head earlier."

"Sorry to hear that. Look, I've got some news."

I filled her in on my conversation with Dolores, finding the Kiss, and my plans for the Bucks County trip. Rather than peppering me with questions, she just listened and offered a few huh-huhs. Either the migraine medication had dulled her brain or she was unraveling from all the stress she was under. I was relieved when she said that she and Jeff were going to Litchfield for the weekend. I gave her Landon's number and told her to get in touch if she had any trouble.

I'd no sooner put down the phone than Farley called. I started to thank him for returning my call. "What's the deal?" he asked, cutting me off, and I blurted out the story of the Kiss and a description of the hang-ups. He didn't say anything at first—the infamous dead silence that cops love—and then the questions started. What time did this happen? Was anyone around? Where was the candy now? When I told him I had the Kiss, he said he wanted me to drop it off and be careful not to touch it directly. Yet he didn't sound overly concerned. I wondered if he thought I was just being paranoid or was PMSed. Then things got worse. He ended the conversation with a lecture on not meddling in police business. I hung up feeling both annoyed and agitated.

I was too wired to stay in for the evening, waiting for the next hang-up, so I decided I'd drag myself out to hear Trudy sing. Yeah, K.C. would be there, but I'd just ignore him and flirt with any good-looking guy who crossed my path. My attire: the tiniest skirt I owned and a tank top that squeezed my breasts so tight that I almost needed an inhaler.

I headed out about nine, superconscious, as I hailed a cab, of who was around me. I had the driver first take me to the Nineteenth Precinct on the East Side and wait two minutes while I dropped the Kiss off in a shoebox with Farley's name on it. From there we headed to the hole-in-the-wall on the West Side where Trudy was doing her gig.

There were loads of couples there, married friends of Trudy's, and only a few single pals of Mitch's, most of whom I'd met before. No K.C. During a break, a ridiculous guy with a large head and hair as thick as roof thatch started chatting me up. In the six weeks since I'd met K.C., I'd let every other romantic prospect fall by the wayside, so I had no one but myself to blame for the fact that I was forced to spend part of a night talking to a man who could easily have been the son of Howdy Doody.

K.C. snuck in around ten, and after offering him a perfunctory hello, I proceeded to give him the cold shoulder. But later, as I was pulling my jacket off the hook in the back corridor, he cornered me and laid on the charm real thick. I was feeling slightly sorry for myself right then, so I let him buy me a drink at the bar and gape at my Sluts

R Us outfit for a while. The longer I sat there and the more he told me how fantastic I looked, the more I could feel my defenses caving. By midnight, I'm sorry to say, I was doing the mattress mambo at his place in the West 80s. I have no good explanation for my stupidity. Maybe my undeniable physical attraction to K.C. and my fears over the fact that I was being stalked by the killer formed a speedball of pure horniness. I bolted at six the next morning in a weak attempt to regain an air of mystery. K.C. was probably waking up right now, struggling for a second to remember who had made the indent on the other side of the bed.

For the time being, though, I could leave all that behind me. I was on my way out of town, to a place two states away. There was just enough traffic on the road to keep my mind temporarily off both my K.C. follies and the hang-ups I'd discovered on my machine when I returned home—the last at close to midnight.

I'd been out to Bucks County a couple of times before, always to visit Landon. The county covers an area north of Philadelphia, and though some suburban sprawl is pushing its way in, much of the region is still rural and charming, with old stone houses from the 1700s, rambling stone fences, and covered bridges. The drive out takes you first past Newark Airport and through the stinky, industrial part of New Jersey, but there's a spot on I-78 where that suddenly all falls away and you see your first red barn and silo and the world becomes both sylvan and serene. I hit that spot just after ten and my headache began to recede to something the size of a tiny, tiny ding.

I had two interviews arranged for the day. There was Darma, of course, and late yesterday afternoon I'd also managed to arrange an appointment with Dr. Kate Tressler, a doctor with the Doylestown Hospital ER, where, according to his obit, Tucker Bobb had expired. I'd been bounced around on the phone to about ten different people at the hospital before I found her, and when I did I proceeded cautiously. If you're trying to arrange an interview with an M.D., the worst thing you can do is trigger the statement "I think you need to go through the PR people." If you're dealing with anything the least bit controversial, the PR people will shut you down. So I told Dr. Tressler that this wasn't for a story, that I wasn't interested in quoting her, that I was helping an editor whom someone might have attempted to poison and I desperately needed background info. She let her guard down and agreed to meet with me. Our appointment was set for three-thirty, about an hour after I should be done with Darma.

I got off I-78 at Exit 7 in New Jersey, drove into Pennsylvania, and then picked up smaller roads that eventually took me to the small, quaint town of Carversville. Landon's place was a charming Victorian-style house, a few blocks from the main street, with a wraparound porch and an in-ground swimming pool. Being his houseguest was as close to paradise as you could get. He'd originally planned to come out this morning, too, but had left a note under my apartment door saying that due to a client crisis he wouldn't be arriving until around nine that night.

I pulled up to his house just before eleven. The azalea bushes in his front yard were on fire with color, and there were flowers in pinks and reds and purples bursting out of the windowboxes and the border gardens along the front of the house. As I let myself in with the key he'd loaned me, I wondered if it would be weird to be in Landon's house without Landon. And it was. There was no crackling fire, no Mozart, no votive candles twinkling on every surface, no aroma of cassoulet from the kitchen. It was almost as if I had mistakenly entered the wrong home.

After dropping my bag in one of the upstairs guest rooms, I opened a can of soup for lunch. The house was totally silent, except for the drip of the faucet. Once I'd cleaned up, I changed into a yellow cotton dress, a yellow cardigan, and a pair of slingbacks. I left early for Darma's, allowing myself plenty of time to get lost on the twisty backcountry roads of Bucks County.

I did get lost, too, maddeningly so, for about twenty minutes. Darma lived on Old Hollow Road, but I had to find Beaver Road first, and it wasn't where she'd said it would be. After a while I even suspected that she had sent me on a wild goose chase and was snickering in her living room at this very moment. Finally I pulled over and asked directions from a guy getting into his pickup truck, and he sent me back and around. Just when I was about to lose my mind, I found Old Hollow, coming in north of where I was supposed to. The driveway to her place was a road itself, and it wound for about a quarter mile through maples and oaks and fir trees, past the well-tended ruins of two stone outbuildings, down into a hollow that seemed a million miles away from anywhere.

The main house was amazing. All stone and easily over two hundred years old, long and rambling with two-feet-deep windows cut into the stone walls. I parked the car in a courtyard by a large wooden barn that appeared to serve as a garage. There were two other smaller barns off the courtyard, and I caught the edge of a man, in a denim shirt and jeans, slipping into one of them just as I climbed out of my Jeep. Walking round the side of the barn, I almost had a heart attack. A peacock, neck stretched and feathers dragging on the ground, stood ten feet in front of me. Tucker Bobb had certainly been playing the role of lord of the manor before he died. He'd come from a rich southern family, I'd once read, which put him in a different bracket from Dolores's.

By parking at the barn, I was near the back of the house, so I walked around to the front on a brick path bordered on both sides by spring flowers. It took two rings of the bell and several knocks before I heard the crack of the door opening. And there was Darma. She was beautiful and striking, in a trophy wife sort of way—pale skin, long blond hair in zillions of Raphaelite waves, a slim figure with major boob action. Her clothes were maximum country squiress: a man-style white shirt, tan jodhpurs, black riding boots, all tied up in a pink *pashmina.*

"I thought we said one o'clock," she said, sounding as if I'd just wrecked her day.

"I'm sorry, I ended up getting lost."

"Well, come in," she said. Wow, this was going to be fun.

She led me silently through a series of rooms, and as we walked I discovered the main drawback of this beautiful old house. It was as dark as a church on a January day. The windows were partly to blame, so small and deep, and blocked on the outside by those big maples. We ended up in a sunroom at the far end of the house, a big open room with floor-to-ceiling windows and walls the color of raw silk. But it was dark as well, just not as dark as the rest of the house.

I sat down gingerly in a small yellow armchair with at least three throw pillows wedged into the back. There was a silver tea service perched on the coffee table, but Darma ignored it as she sank into the sofa, and it became clear very quickly that no refreshments would be offered. This experience was going to be as far as you could get from one of those General Foods International Coffee's moments.

"Your home is so lovely," I said, trying to break the ice. "Did you decorate it yourself?"

"Mostly. Though of course I had someone I worked with." She shook her massive mane of hair off her collar, as if she were imitating the movement of a horse. In the brighter light of the sunroom, she appeared five years older than she had in the doorway. I put her age somewhere between forty-five and fifty. I also noticed that despite the *pashmina* and pearls, there was something slightly cheap about her. Even though she'd had a career in magazines, she brought to mind hat check girls who married millionaires after a six-week courtship.

"You're living out here full-time?"

"Yes," she said, "there's really no reason for me to be in New York anymore. And you—you're out just for the day?"

"Actually, I'm staying at a friend's in Carversville."

"Perhaps I know her."

"It's a man, an older man, named Landon Hayes. He's got a busy social life out here, so your paths may have crossed."

"I don't know the name. We always socialized with a close circle of friends."

"I'm so sorry about your husband," I said. "I only met him briefly at a few industry events, but of course I know what a great reputation he had."

"*We've* never met before, have we?"

"No, I don't think so. But I'm sure we've worked with some of the same people over time."

"Leslie Stone's at *Gloss*, isn't she?" she asked. "I worked with her at *Food and Entertaining*. And I know Dolores, of course. She and Tucker were friends. They were both horrified, of course, when they saw what Cat Jones was doing to *Gloss.*"

"It's not everyone's thing. But readers seem to like it."

"As they say," she said with a sniff, "there's no accounting for taste. Now what is it that you needed to talk to me about so urgently?"

"Well, first of all, thank you for seeing me, because it's really pretty important. You probably wouldn't have heard this news out here, but Cat Jones's nanny died on Sunday and apparently she was poisoned. It seems the intended victim was actually Cat herself. I wondered if there was any chance her death could be linked to your husband's."

With her emerald green eyes, she offered me a stare so cold and hard that I had to resist the urge to squirm in my chair.

"This is why you wanted to see me?" she said, barely containing her anger. "This is the reason that you insisted on coming out here?"

Oops.

"Yes, I thought you could help us," I said quickly. "I'd

heard there was some speculation that your husband died from eating bad mushrooms. Two incidents like this six months apart—it seems awfully strange, perhaps more than coincidental."

"So the poison mushroom myth is still floating around out there," she said cryptically.

"That's not what happened, then?"

"They really have no idea what caused Tucker's death. And there's not one shred of evidence it had anything to do with mushrooms. One of the doctors at the hospital suggested that without any proof whatsoever."

"Your husband liked to hunt for mushrooms?"

"Yes. And he liked to eat them, too. I suppose there's a chance he might have eaten the wrong one. The whole thing sounded more like ass covering on the part of the hospital, if you ask me."

"He got sick at work?"

"Yes."

"In the middle of the week?"

"It was a Thursday. He didn't feel quite right after lunch. He had planned to drive out for a long weekend— I was already out here—but he felt bad enough that he ended up taking a car service. By the time he got out here he was seriously ill and I took him right to the hospital. He was nearly seventy. These things happen at that age, unfortunately."

"He never said anything about eating mushrooms?"

"No, he did not," she snapped. "And frankly, what difference does it make now?"

"Well, as I said, since it appears that someone tried to kill an editor in chief of another woman's magazine, I wondered if his death might be the result of foul play."

She paused and turned her profile to me as she stared vacantly out the windows. The tip of her nose had an odd little round ball at the end that you couldn't see when you looked at her straight on.

"Oh, now I see," she said sarcastically. "Kind of like *Someone Is Killing the Great Chefs of Europe.*"

"Well, I never read the book, so I wouldn't know. But it does seem as if there could be a connection between the two deaths, that someone might have a grudge against the editors of women's magazines and could try again."

"Oh, is that right?"

"At the very least, I think someone should mention it to the police."

Her face hardened. "As far as I'm concerned, it all sounds preposterous—and I'm not in the mood for it. My husband is dead and it doesn't matter one iota to me what's going on back in Manhattan."

"I can understand that," I said. "I just have one more question. Had your husband had problems with any employees before he died? Had anyone made any threats against him?"

"People *adored* my husband. If you had known him, you wouldn't be asking outrageous questions like that."

"Well, I'm sorry I didn't know him," I said. "Why don't I head out now and not take up any more of your afternoon." Maybe, I thought, what killed Tucker Bobb was the sheer terror that resulted from pondering what would happen if he ever stepped out of line with this babe.

Instead of leading me back through the house, Darma rose and crossed the room to a large glass door that opened onto a patio. It bounced on its track from the force she used as she slid it open.

"This way," she said, dismissing me. "The garage is over there."

"Thank you for taking the time to see me," I said, sticking out my hand. She shook it limply and dropped it almost instantly. I was barely out onto the patio before she rammed the glass door shut again.

I hurried across the lawn to my Jeep, wondering if she was about to detonate it with a remote-control device or at the very least set a pair of Dobermans on my heels. It took three tries to fire up the engine. Finally it caught and I headed out the gravel drive.

But I hadn't gone two minutes before the road narrowed and turned from gravel to dirt, and I realized I'd taken the wrong way out. I was on some sort of logging or hiking road. There was no easy spot to turn around, and I'd be damned if I was going to continue through the woods to find one—the day had enough of a *Blair Witch* feeling to it already. So I backed out, a laborious, jerky process.

No, she was *not* waiting for me with a shotgun on her shoulder when I pulled back into the courtyard. I put the Jeep in drive and crept forward, looking for the right way out. It was behind the biggest barn, which I should have remembered, but I guess I'd been too hell-bent on getting out of there. As I drove off, I glanced in my rearview mirror. The Marlboro Man in the denim shirt was heading up the path to the house.

Despite my agitation I managed to find my way easily to Route 611. The time was exactly two P.M. Since the interview had been so brief, I had over an hour to kill before my appointment with Dr. Tressler. Halfway to Doylestown I pulled into Sammy's, one of those roadside food stands where they sell hot dogs and ice cream and buckets of fries and you have to give your order through a window with a screen that they lift up when they take your money. I ordered a black-and-white milk shake and took it back to the Jeep.

I pulled out my steno pad and jotted down what I could remember from my conversation—if you could call it that—with Darma. I hadn't wanted to take notes in the house for fear of spooking her, which was ironic considering I was the one who'd ended up spooked. I was tempted to immediately do a mental postmortem on the experience, to try to figure out why her ass had gotten so chapped from my questions, but that would be putting the cart before the horse. It was essential to get down her comments and my impressions before I drew any conclusions.

When I'd finished, I started the Jeep and got back on my way. The hospital, Landon had told me, was right off Route 611 and there'd be signs along the way.

Sure enough, I spotted the big white *H* on the blue sign by an exit ramp just as I came toward the city and I swung in that direction. The hospital was less than two minutes from there.

The ER reception area was a study in Danish modern. When I explained to the woman behind the information desk that I had an appointment with Dr. Tressler, she told me to have a seat and she'd page her. There were only a few people in the waiting room—a fiftysomething couple (she for some reason in boat-size blue bedroom slippers) and a mother with a little boy who was hitting her on the head with a rubber cow. It was impossible to tell with either twosome who the patient was. I'd only perched my butt on the edge of a seat for a minute before a woman wearing a white doctor coat over pants pushed open a door at the far end of the room and strode purposefully in my direction. She was about thirty-eight, thirty-nine, attractive in a mannish sort of way, and she appeared to be in a hurry.

"Bailey Wagon?" she asked before she was even halfway toward me. I started to rise and explain the mistake with my name, when she held up both hands in a stop position, as if she were helping me back out of a tight parking spot.

"Look, don't get up," she announced. "I've got a patient and I'm going to be at least twenty to thirty minutes. Sorry, but I can't predict these things."

"That's not a problem. I appreciate your taking the time."

"It might be easier for you to wait in the cafeteria. You could grab a coffee and I'll run over when I'm done."

"Sounds good," I said.

"You just take the yellow hallway there," she said, pointing behind me. "Follow the signs." Then she turned and strode away.

I found my way to the cafeteria and bought a cup of coffee, which tasted like a liquefied rubber band. I had nothing to read, so my only choice was to sit there, taking tiny sips so I wouldn't gag. Thoughts of the previous night began pushing into the front of my brain. It was clearer than ever that K.C. was interested in nothing more than a fling and I'd be smart to just back off before I got burned somehow. He'd probably never call again, anyway.

I was halfway through my coffee when Dr. Tressler

flopped down in the next chair and thrust her legs straight out in front of her. She had brown eyes, with two small beauty marks in the lower lashes of her right one, a strong nose, and a long mouth that seemed to run across the entire length of her face. No makeup. Earlier I'd thought she had short hair, but now I saw it was actually long and pulled back in a French braid. Under her lab coat she was wearing tan pants and a navy turtleneck, and she had a pair of brown clogs on her feet.

"Sorry about the delay," she said. "This ten-year-old kid had an altercation with a skateboard ramp. He needed twenty-seven stitches."

"I guess you see all sorts of disasters once the warm weather comes."

"Oh, yeah." She'd brought her own coffee in a Styrofoam cup and used her thumb to pop off the lid. "So you work for *Gloss*? You don't have anything to do with those sex articles, do you? Wow, I took a look at a copy last night. That's pretty graphic stuff."

"No, they don't let me near that material," I said with a laugh. "I work on the news stories. But I'm also a good friend of the editor, and that's why I'm here. As I mentioned on the phone, it appears that someone tried to poison her. Tucker Bobb was in the same industry, and I wondered if there could be a link."

She cocked her head to the side. "How so?"

"I'd heard there was some thinking he might have died from poison mushrooms."

"Mushroom."

"Excuse me?"

"Just one kind of mushroom—a type called *Amanita*

phalloides, more commonly known as death cap. I'm the one who suspected that might be what killed him."

"Did you treat him yourself?" I said, flipping open my steno pad and beginning to write. "By the way, the notes are just for my personal use."

"No, I was out of town at a medical conference when all of this was happening. But since he was a big shot, I reviewed the chart when I got back."

"The doctors who treated him never suspected?" I asked it casually, not wanting to sound critical.

"Look, you've got to understand," she said, crossing her arms, "death by poison mushroom isn't something you see every day in an ER. And the symptoms can look like a lot of other things. Generally the only reason you'd even know you were dealing with mushrooms is from the patient history. But if the patient doesn't offer it up, it's probably not going to come to mind. And you can't detect it in the blood."

"Why did it come to *your* mind?" Again, casual.

"It's an interest of mine, kind of a minor specialty. I was doing my residency in ER medicine in Ohio. A family of Laotians came in deathly ill, and we realized that they'd all eaten death caps. *Amanita phalloides* looks almost identical, it turns out, to a totally benign mushroom found in Laos. We lost three of them. Two of the youngest we saved with liver transplants."

"Too bad you weren't on duty when Tucker Bobb came in."

"Wouldn't have done any good. He was past the point of no return by then. And because he didn't mention anything about mushrooms, it might not have even occurred to *me.* It was only after I talked to his M.D. out here and heard about the first attack that I really suspected amanita."

"You've lost me."

"Yeah, sorry," she said. "It's a bit confusing. When you eat a death cap, the symptoms generally occur in three stages." As she spoke she peeled off three small pieces of her coffee lid and laid them in a row. She pointed to the first.

"Stage one: About six hours after you consume amanita, you start to get real bad abdominal pain and you start vomiting. Most of the time a person will head to the ER with these symptoms, but sometimes they pass it off as a bad stomach flu and don't get treatment."

She pointed to the second piece of lid. "Then there's this weird period of false recovery. Your symptoms disappear. You think, Okay, I'm all better now. That lasts about four days." She touched the last piece of lid with her index finger. "Then suddenly, around day five, the symptoms come back, *bam*, and it's then that everybody realizes something more serious is going on. The liver and kidneys begin to fail, the heart goes. It's especially deadly for kids, but if adults eat enough, they can die, too. And that's why you can't test for it. Ten days after ingestion there's no trace left in the system."

"And Mr. Bobb had an *earlier* attack?"

"Yeah, that's what I was starting to say," she continued. "I called his M.D. out here to get a bit of background. It's not his regular doctor—his regular guy is in New York—but this is a local doc he goes to when necessary. Well, this guy tells me that Bobb had called the previous weekend complaining of stomach flu. His M.D. suggested he come to the ER—he didn't think it was anything more than flu or food poisoning, but with a guy Bobb's age you worry about dehydration. Bobb told the guy he was waiting for his wife to get back from a horse riding competition or something and would probably go to the ER when she got back. But he didn't. Or at least he didn't come here. Obviously he didn't feel so terrible that he thought he needed medical help. And that's the trouble with stage one."

"Do you remember what day it happened—Saturday or Sunday?"

"It was late Sunday, I believe. If he'd eaten a death cap, it was probably Saturday evening."

"Is there any possible way he could have eaten it earlier in the week and gotten sick on Sunday?"

"Nah, too much of a delay."

"You know mushrooms were his hobby," I said.

"Yeah, which is, of course, another reason amanita fits. Though it's hard to imagine someone with his knowledge cooking up anything with even a *passing* resemblance to a death cap." Pause.

"So then how did he end up eating it?"

"That's the mystery, isn't it? And, of course, if he had *knowingly* eaten mushrooms, why not mention it?" Before I could read her eyes to see how much she was implying, she glanced down at her waistband and I realized her beeper had gone off. Squeezing her chin into her neck, she squinted at the message.

"I got two more minutes. Tell me about the other case. Any similarities?"

"You mean, could she have died from an amanita? It doesn't sound like it. The girl who ate the poison—it was in some chocolates—died within a few hours of eating it, and as far as I know, she didn't have an earlier attack. But look, it's still been very helpful to talk to you. I hope you won't mind if I call you with any other questions that come up."

"That shouldn't be a problem," she said. "Though, just so you know—the New York police are apparently looking into this. I heard they spoke to the director of the hospital, and I think they may be paying us a visit."

So Cat had shared the info with them. I just hoped Farley didn't find out I'd been out here.

We walked out of the cafeteria together, and Dr. Tressler showed me a shorter route to the parking lot. I navigated a maze of corridors, getting lost only once before I came to the front lobby of the hospital. When I pushed through the revolving doors, I saw that the sky had darkened and a light rain was falling. Pulling my sweater over my head, I raced in the general direction of my car. By the time I found it, two rows over, and flung myself into the front seat, I was as damp as a sneaker left out overnight.

I didn't start the car right away. I sat there taking in the full impact of something Dr. Tressler had said: Tucker Bobb's health problems had begun in Pennsylvania, *not* in New York City, as his employees had assumed. If the cause of his death was a mushroom, it had been consumed out here. And if someone had deliberately poisoned him with that mushroom, they'd been in Bucks County that weekend. The likelihood that Heidi's killer, someone who had attended Cat's party, had also done in Tucker Bobb two states away on an earlier date seemed remote to me—though I couldn't give up totally on the idea. Maybe the killer was a magazine editor or writer who had visited Bobb that weekend. Or he or she had a house out here and had managed to slip Bobb the mushroom at some event that weekend.

What a dreadful little thought. For all I knew, the killer might be traipsing around out here this weekend.

CHAPTER 13

DAMP AND TUCKERED out, I headed toward Carversville. Now that I'd gathered what information I could out in Bucks County, I felt anxious to get back to New York, to pursue whatever leads I could there. Yet trying to turn up much on a weekend would most likely prove to be a bust. Besides, I knew Landon was looking forward to having me around, and it would be rude just to bolt.

What I'd do, I decided, was have an early dinner tonight at the inn in Carversville, catch up with Landon later in the evening, and leave sometime on Saturday.

As soon as I got back to Landon's, I peeled off my dress and slipped into pants and a sleeveless shirt. With my laptop set up on the dining room table, I made a sizable dent in the Marky story. At around six-thirty I locked up to go to the inn, taking both my steno pad and composition book with me. The rain had stopped, so I decided to walk instead of drive—it was just a few blocks away.

The intoxicating fragrance of lilacs wafted through the dusk, and as I strolled I felt more relaxed than I had in days. If I bumped into someone from Cat's party at the inn, I'd know to panic, but otherwise I felt out of harm's way.

The inn was practically empty when I strolled in. I opted for a table for two against the wall—with a small lamp that would allow me to read without squinting. I ordered a glass of red wine, and after my first sip, I flipped open my steno pad and read through the notes I'd taken today.

First there was Darma. Testy babe, wasn't she? I'd been expecting someone still shell-shocked by her husband's death. What was that expression people always used when someone was in mourning—prostrate with grief? That's what it seemed like the death of a loved one would do to you: leave you flat-out in despair, head flopped on the arm of the sofa, heavy as a cannonball. But there was nothing flat-out about Darma. Maybe Tucker's death hadn't saddened her all that much. According to the bio of Bobb I'd found on the Web, they'd only been married for four years—but that was enough time, of course, for even the most blissful of relationships to sour.

There was one thing I knew for certain: My questions about his death had seriously pissed her off. Sure, if she *was* grief-stricken, it might be tough to rehash, but on the other hand, wouldn't she be interested in knowing whether Tucker had been the victim of foul play?

And who was the *Lonesome Dove* dude I'd seen slipping into the barn and then later heading into the house? A caretaker? A horse trainer? A boy toy?

The waiter took my order—asparagus vinaigrette to start (I passed on the mushroom tart) and lamb chops—and I moved on to my notes on Dr. Tressler. Her theory seemed credible, especially in light of Bobb's fascination with mushrooms. But as she'd indicated, there was no way to prove it. In hindsight I realized how much better it would have been if my interview with Darma had occurred *after* my appointment with Dr. Tressler. I would have tried to extricate certain details about the weekend before Tucker had died. What he'd eaten on Saturday night. Who'd been around that day. The time Darma had returned Sunday. And why, in the end, he hadn't gone to the ER. Yet Darma probably wouldn't have been forthcoming.

I started to play around in my head with what might have happened to Tucker. Maybe he'd gone mushroom hunting up that dirt road I'd accidentally taken, mistaken death caps for something benign, and later (unbeknownst to Darma) eaten a batch he sautéed nicely in butter. But even if he'd committed that kind of goof, once he began to hurl the insides of his stomach he would surely have made the connection and hightailed it to the hospital. The other possibility, of course, was that someone else had been the bearer of bad mushrooms—either accidentally or on purpose—and Tucker had eaten them unaware. Perhaps he'd sat like a king in the candlelit dining room of his big stone house on Saturday night and been served a beef bourguignonne loaded with carrots and onions and wild mushrooms from the woods—prepared by the fetching former food editor.

An intriguing idea, maybe worth a police investigation of its own. It would also mean, then, that the two deaths were nothing more than a bizarre coincidence. When I returned to New York I'd see if I could turn up the name of the mushroom club that Bobb belonged to. Maybe someone in that group could tell me how likely it would have been for him to mistakenly pop a death cap in his mouth.

My asparagus arrived, so I snapped shut my composition book and turned all my attention to the meal. The dining room had begun to fill up, mostly with couples—either alone or in pairs—and as I devoured my food I watched surreptitiously as they interacted. There was such a distinguishable difference between the newly besotted, in the throes of a chat fest, and those together long enough to have run out of things to say. Several people glanced in my direction occasionally. I'm sure they wondered what I was doing eating alone at a country inn on Friday night.

When I was first married I had cajoled my husband into taking a few weekend excursions to country inns. They were part of a plot I'd concocted to try to reconnect with him, to recapture the bond that we'd had during the first six months of our relationship but that had then begun to erode, almost imperceptibly at first, and then, since the day of our marriage with terrifying speed. On each of these hapless excursions he'd been restless and wired. He'd paced our room whenever we were in it and sat at dinner stretching his neck as if the collar of his shirt were choking him. My first suspicion, even before the proverbial other woman, was drugs—cocaine, or crack—but searches on my part turned up nothing. Eventually, of course, I came to understand that you squirm and pace like that when you owe a bookie twenty grand.

When would I get the chance to sit in this kind of a

room with a guy again? I wondered. Six months ago I wouldn't have been ready for anything so damn intense, but lately I'd begun to feel a yearning for romance. I certainly wouldn't end up someplace like this with K.C. Besides the fact that things were going nowhere fast with us, anything this romantic would terrify him. This was more for guys like the handsome and suave Dr. Herlihy. Where was he tonight? I wondered. Maybe showing off his Village pad to his Washington girlfriend, up for the weekend. The thought, oddly enough, irritated me.

For the rest of my meal I tried just to concentrate on the food and allow my mind to idle. By the time I'd had coffee and paid the bill, the dining room was packed and so, I saw as I departed, was the barroom, people jammed around the bar and others eating below a fog of smoke at small tables that had been set up with white tablecloths along the wall. In the hallway the hostess had her head in the reservation book, obviously searching for the name given by two couples who had just arrived. My exit went unnoticed.

Stepping outside onto the long, narrow porch, I was startled to find how cool it had gotten. It was also pitch dark out. I felt like an idiot for not having brought the Jeep. Though the walk to Landon's was short, the thought of doing it in the cold and darkness held absolutely *nada* appeal.

I took a seat on one of the porch's old rocking chairs and punched Landon's number on my cell. Surely he was there by now. And being one of those fabulous old-fashioned guys, he would think there was nothing wimpy about my calling to request that he drive over and rescue me. His machine picked up. Odd. It was past when he said he'd be there, and he was punctual to a fault. I hoped nothing had happened to him on the road.

I got up from the rocker, buttoned my sweater, and stepped off the porch, headed right on Main Street. There were street lamps on ahead of me, and a light was falling from the second floor of a little antiques shop. As I walked I could hear the sounds of the inn falling away behind me: a cacophony of chattering voices as the front door opened, a car door slamming in the front parking lot. I passed the small general store, the "Closed" sign dangling on the door, and the antiques shop, where through the second-floor window I could see a woman moving about, probably the owner who lived above the store. The house was similar to the one my mother had moved to four years ago, with a white picket fence all around it.

Thinking of my mother made me flash onto something she had once shared with me about so-called bizarre coincidences. She believed that at least half the events we dismiss as coincidence really aren't. They're related, though not necessarily in a direct way, and if you go back far enough or look closely enough, you'll spot the connection. She informed me of this the night my two sisters-in-law, who had been invited over to my mother's house for dinner with my brothers, each arrived with a homemade lemon tart. I was home for the weekend, and later, while loading the dishwasher, I noted to my mother what a coincidence the twofer tart situation had been. Perhaps, my mother remarked, it *wasn't* such a coincidence after all. Maybe, she said, there had recently been a recipe for a lemon tart in *Martha Stewart Living* and both girls had clipped it. Or maybe, she mused, Amy had mentioned to Sydney a week or two before that she planned to make a tart for the dinner, and Sydney, listening absentmindedly, had filed away the idea (but not where it came from) and in a burst of supposed originality had baked one herself. Or—and here was an evil thought—Sydney might have learned of Amy's plans and then decided to trump her and arrive with the tastier tart (and indeed it had been).

I wondered what insight my mother could offer now. If I told her about Tucker's possible poisoning and the failed attempt on Cat's life and suggested they were a bizarre coincidence, she would say no, not necessarily, or not totally. She'd note that both Tucker and Cat were the kind of difficult people who might infuriate someone, so the likelihood of each being poisoned was greater than the average person's. Or maybe, she'd say, the person who tried to kill Cat had heard the poison mushroom rumors surrounding Tucker's death and been inspired, consciously or unconsciously. Or maybe the person who had tried to kill Cat had used poison so that Cat's death would *seem* related to Tucker's. Two editors poisoned. It would point toward the idea of someone in the industry with a grudge against editors or against women's magazines, someone who'd managed to poison Tucker Bobb one afternoon and then brought a deadly package to Cat's place. And it would point away from people in Cat's personal life and inner work circle.

If this *were* the case, the murderer was very clever. He had thought out his plan carefully. It would also mean that he must be fairly entrenched in the magazine business to be aware of the theories floating around about how Tucker Bobb had died. The only hitch: He hadn't been aware that Bobb's poisoning had occurred in Bucks

County, making the plot-against-editors idea less probable.

I reached Pear Street, the street where Landon lived, and before I turned right to travel the two blocks to his house, I stopped and checked behind me. The sidewalk was empty, and so was the street. The only sound was the heavy swish of the wind in the tree leaves, a sound that seemed more like fall than late spring. As I stood there, the light above the antiques shop blinked out.

I moved faster now, heading up the slight hill of Pear Street. There were fewer street lamps in this area, and though lights were on in some of the houses, others were totally dark—everyone gone to bed or out for the night. The wind died down for a split second, as if someone had shut it off with a switch, and then picked up again hard, shaking the tree leaves so that they shimmered in the light of the slivered moon. I couldn't see Landon's house yet, but it was just around the bend. There was a scraping sound suddenly ahead of me, near a parked car, and before I could be afraid, I watched as a possum scurried out from underneath it, over the sidewalk, and into someone's backyard.

Finally I could see Landon's house just ahead—and he was there. I'd left only the front parlor lamp on, but a light was now burning in his bedroom and the front porch light was on as well. Relieved, I broke into a jog for the rest of the way up the street.

"Hello there," I called after I'd unlocked the front door and swung it open. "It's just me, Kato Kaelin, your favorite houseguest."

Silence. I figured he was in his bedroom or bathroom with the door shut. I climbed the stairs, stuck my head in the open doorway of his bedroom, and called out his name two more times. Nothing. His bathroom door was open, the room dark. Pulling aside the gauze curtain on one of his bedroom windows, I glanced down toward the back of the driveway, which I'd failed to check out earlier. No car. As I let the curtain settle back into place, my eye fell on his bedside table and I spotted the little box next to the lamp. It was on a timer. And the porch light was probably rigged to a light sensor. He wasn't even here. I looked down at my watch: 9:17. I turned off the bedroom light and trooped back down the stairs.

While I was turning on lights downstairs my eye caught the pulsing red light of the answering machine. It was probably my call from the restaurant, but I hit the play button just in case there was a message from my missing host. There was.

"Darling, are you there? No? You must forgive me. Just got out of the world's most dreadful meeting. It's nine and I'm nervous about driving. I'm not exactly a narcoleptic—or a necrophiliac, for that matter—but lately I've developed the very bad habit of dozing at the wheel if I'm driving too late. If you won't hate me too much, I'll set out first thing in the morning. Don't eat breakfast. I'll make you scrambled eggs with caviar."

Great. Besides the fact that Landon didn't have cable and his video collection was devoid of a single film made after 1964, the thought of sleeping all alone in his house gave me the creeps. I considered just jumping into the Jeep and making the trip back to New York. I'd had two glasses of wine at dinner, though. Not a smart idea.

I made a check of the doors and windows. I recalled Landon saying once that he hadn't bothered getting a se-

curity alarm system because the town was safe and his
neighbors close enough. That lack of concern was reflected in his locks. Though the front door had a fairly
sturdy dead bolt, the windowed back door in the kitchen
had nothing more than a button in the handle that you
pushed to lock. The windows appeared to be more re-
spectable. They all had latches, and all were locked—except the second to the last one I checked, a big
double-paned window in the dining room. I discovered,
to my dismay, that the latch had been painted into the unlocked position—four or five coats ago.

I prodded it, cursing out loud as it refused to budge.
There was nothing I could do but try to keep myself from
wigging out. But already I could feel a low dose of dread
starting to run through me. I would have to keep reminding myself that, as Landon had said, the town was safe.

I poured a glass of seltzer and took it upstairs, where I
filled the tub in the guest bathroom with steaming hot
water, adding a big glob of scented gel. I soaked for about
half an hour, leafing through old magazines stuffed in a
nearby basket, listening to the house creak and settle.
When I'd run through all the available hot water, I got out
and changed into my pajamas. I went back downstairs to
the study, turning on Landon's ancient TV in order to
catch the end of a ten o'clock Philadelphia news show.

There were only sheer white curtains on the windows,
and I wasn't crazy about sitting down there alone in my
pj's, so exposed. Before the show was even over, I
trudged back upstairs, leaving a lamp burning in the main
parlor. I had my book, and I planned to read in bed until
I felt sleepy, which at the rate I was going wouldn't be till
dawn. Though it was cool out, the guest bedroom was

stuffy, and I opened the window nearest the bed just a crack. No one, I figured, would be coming by with a ladder. After crawling under the covers, I picked up my book, a biography of Anne Boleyn that I'd been inspired to read for my upcoming trip to the United Kingdom. Reading about all that connivery and death so many centuries ago relaxed me. I'd devoured four chapters when I found, to my surprise, sleep taking over. I switched off the bedside lamp and relaxed my head onto the supersoft pillowcase. Landon bought only the highest thread count.

When I woke with a jolt, I had no idea where I was. I lay in pitch darkness for at least ten seconds, straining to see my surroundings, before it came to me. Landon's. Bucks County. I squinted at the Day-Glo numbers on my watch: 2:15. Usually my nocturnal wakenings occurred a little deeper into the night. Had a dream rattled me awake? I wondered.

And then I heard it. A crunching sound from outside, like a foot coming down on gravel or twigs. My heart threw itself against my rib cage. I remembered the possum I'd seen earlier. Maybe he'd worked his way in this direction. I lay there completely motionless, waiting, listening. There it was again. It was definitely a footstep, right below the open window, someone trying to move slowly and quietly. Could it be Landon, having changed his mind about driving out tonight? But even if he hadn't left till ten, he would have arrived ages ago.

There was another footstep, but no longer directly below my window. I slid quietly out of bed, dropped to my knees, and crawled over to the window. I lifted my head cautiously and glanced to the left, where the footsteps had seemed to be headed. As dark as it was outside, the parlor lamp was casting light through the side window and I made out the form of someone—a man, I thought—moving along the edge of the driveway toward the back of the house. He stopped suddenly and I ducked my head in case he turned back in my direction. When I peeked out again he was gone, blended in with the darkness. I couldn't tell if he was still along the side of the house somewhere or if he'd rounded the corner and was now in the backyard.

Shit, I needed a phone. There was one in Landon's bedroom, I was almost positive. I jumped up and hurried in the darkness to his room, ramming my thigh hard into the edge of a hall bookshelf along the way. The phone, I figured, would be on one of the bedside tables, and after fumbling frantically in the dark, I found it. The numbers glowed green in the dark, and I punched in 911.

An operator answered after three rings. "There's a prowler," I blurted out. In my panic, it took me a second to remember Landon's address. As I listened to her assurance that she would send someone quickly, I inched toward one of the windows and peered out at the backyard. I could make nothing out in the darkness except the faint glow of the flagstone around the pool.

The operator said she'd stay on the line, but I needed to figure out where the prowler was now. Dropping the phone, I crept out to the hallway and edged my way to the top of the stairs. A new sound now. Someone was turning the handle of the back door, little turns back and forth, back and forth, impeded each time by the lock. It might be ten minutes before the police came. I had to do something.

My eyes had begun to adjust to the dark, and I could

see the wicker stand of walking sticks Landon kept at the top of the stairs. I reached out, grabbed the first one I touched, and yanked it out. My heart thudding so hard that I could feel it in my ears, I started downstairs. The rattling of the door had ceased now, and my mind flashed to the dining room window that had stubbornly refused to lock.

At the bottom of the steps I stopped. Down the hall toward the back was the kitchen. Silent now, in total darkness. Off the hallway to my left was the parlor, the lamp casting a small patch of light onto the hallway floor. To my right was Landon's study, in total darkness, and behind that the dining room. I inched my way through the study and into the dining room.

It was empty, the window still closed. I waited in the shadows, straining to see outside, gripping the walking stick, silently urging the police. *Please, please, hurry,* I pleaded in my mind.

Suddenly there was a sound. Behind me. I spun around, facing the doorway to the kitchen. The noise had come from there, and as my eyes frantically swept the kitchen, I saw the form of someone, a man, standing only a few feet away through the doorway, his back to me. He started to turn, as if he'd suddenly picked up my scent, and I took two steps forward, raised the walking stick, and brought it down on him as hard as I could.

It glanced off his head and hit his shoulder with a crack. He yelped, knees buckling. I raised the stick once more, ready to strike again, but as he rose he staggered to the right and when I lowered the stick this time it whacked the edge of the kitchen table instead. I blundered backward a step, as the man straightened and turned fully around. He had on a ski mask, beady dark eyes looking as if they'd burned through the fabric. He lunged at me.

Instinctively I took a step backward and to the side, and though he rammed into me, I didn't get the full force of his body. I staggered back, my butt hitting the edge of the dining room table. He came at me again, stinking of sweat, and this time I raised the walking stick and slapped it across the side of his head. He cursed in pain and caught the stick in a gloved hand, then hurled it to the far side of the dining room, where it shattered something made of glass.

"I called the police," I blurted out, breathless. "They're coming." I'd backed away from the table and was turning, trying to run. He caught my arm and shoved me hard, sending me sprawling onto the floor. I frantically grabbed a breath and rolled onto my back, ready to kick. But when my eyes focused I saw that he had turned on his heels and was scrambling back toward the kitchen. I heard the screen door fling open and slam shut and the clop-clop of his footsteps on the back stairs. I hoisted myself to my feet and inched into the kitchen. Through the open back door I could hear him crashing through bushes in the backyard. At the far end of the yard a beam of light broke through the darkness, a flashlight. The beam bounced a few times and disappeared. It was totally silent for about thirty seconds, and then from the street behind Landon's I heard the sound of a car engine roaring to life.

I slammed the kitchen door, flipped on the overhead light, and dragged the small breakfast table quickly across the floor, heaving it against the door since obviously the lock had proved useless. As soon as I took my hands from the table, they began to tremble. The shaking seemed disconnected from me, as if I were holding an injured bird that was straining to get free. I took deep breaths, willing myself to calm down.

From the front of the house I heard the sound of a car tearing up the street. For one frantic moment I thought it was him again, driving right up to the house. I raced through the center hallway and glanced out the window. It was a state police car. No siren, but the blue light was dancing on top of the car.

Two uniformed guys jumped out and jogged up the porch steps, hands on their holsters. I must have looked pretty shaken because as soon as they stepped inside, one of them, cute and twentysomething, laid his hand on my shoulder and asked me worriedly if I was all right.

"Yeah, I'm okay, just a little shaky." As proof, my voice actually shook as I spoke.

"Was he in the house?"

"Yeah, I think he got in through the kitchen door, though I know I locked it. I hit him with a walking stick, and he ran out."

"Which way did he go?"

I flung my arm in the direction of the back door. "Through the backyard. I heard a car start on the street behind us. It might have been him."

"Stay here," the cute cop said, and he and his pudgy partner took off, hands on holsters again. I heard the table being dragged away from the door and one of them say something over a radio about an attempted burglary. Once they were gone I flipped on some more lights and snuck back out into the kitchen. The door was partially ajar, and without touching it I took a closer look. There

were no signs that anyone had tampered with the lock.
The glass in the window was totally intact. I glanced
around, looking for anything the prowler might have left
behind. Nothing. Unless you counted the total terror I
was still feeling.

I could see and hear the two cops moving around the
backyard, the beams of their own flashlights bouncing
against the darkness. I tried to think straight. The cops
had used the word *burglar*, but I didn't buy it. The one
night I'm in Landon's house alone turns out to be the
night a burglar decides to strike? That would surely fall
under the category of coincidences my mother wouldn't
accept. This was about me. Maybe the killer *did* live out
here and had somehow learned I was here and where I
was staying. Or maybe he had followed me all the way
from Manhattan.

I left the kitchen and sprinted upstairs. After stripping
off my pajamas and pulling on jeans and a T-shirt, I began
flinging my belongings into my overnight bag. The police wouldn't be here forever, and there was no way I was
going to hang around waiting for the intruder to come
back.

As I set my bag down at the bottom of the stairs, the
two cops strode down the hallway from the kitchen, the
pudgy one slightly out of breath.

"You're Mrs. Hayes?" the cute one asked, ushering me
to a chair in the parlor. They must have checked before
they got here who owned the residence. I explained who
I was, where I was from, and the circumstances of my
being in the house alone.

"Tell us what happened." From the cute one again.

"Oh, by the way, I'm Officer Andrews and this is Officer Persky."

I went through the whole story, explaining that the only description I could give of the prowler was that he was on the tall side. When I got to the part about him shoving me, they both looked shocked and wanted to be sure I didn't need medical attention.

"No, no. I'm okay. Just a scrape on my knee. Could you tell how he got in?"

"There's no sign of forced entry," said Andrews, "and since you say you locked the door, my guess is he used a credit card on the back. It's one of those locks you can do it with. Would you know if anything's missing—or maybe that's something your friend will have to determine."

"I doubt he had time to take anything. When I surprised him in the kitchen he must have just gotten in."

"That's your car in the driveway, right?"

"Yes. Why?"

"Well, it's such an obvious sign someone's here. We get burglaries around here, but generally it happens when people are working—or away." He paused. "You don't have any enemies, do you? I mean, it's hard to believe, but I've got to ask."

"Like I said, I'm not even from around here," I said carefully.

"No jilted boyfriend who might have followed you out here?" Andrews asked with a smile.

"No." I smiled wanly. "Not these days, anyway."

"Did you go out tonight? Could someone have seen you and followed you back?"

"I ate at the inn. I did walk back alone. I was paying

attention, but there's a chance someone could have followed me without my being aware of it." This was the moment to reveal what had been going on back in New York, but I let it pass. It seemed too complicated to get into at this moment, with this particular cop. I would get hold of Farley when I got back to New York.

"Well, we'll get someone out here first thing in the morning. We'll see if we can lift any prints."

"He wore gloves."

"Okay then. But he left his footprints out back. They'll take some impressions."

"You'll have to wait till Mr. Hayes gets here tomorrow," I said.

"Where are *you* going to be?"

"I can't stay here. I'm going to head back to New York."

In near unison they both held up their hands in protest. It wasn't a good idea, Andrews said, he didn't like the idea of me on the road at this hour, and I was in no shape to drive. He promised that if I stayed, they'd drive by every fifteen minutes or so. No way, I told them, no way in hell.

Realizing that convincing me was a hopeless cause, they offered to tail me out of town—just to make certain no one followed me. As we stepped outside, I saw that some of the neighbors, wrapped up in bathrobes, had gathered on their porches, and a man from across the street scurried over to inquire if everything was okay. Andrews explained what had happened and asked if he'd seen anything suspicious, and the neighbor said no and explained breathlessly that they'd never had a single problem on the street before.

I shook hands with both cops, unlocked the Jeep, and climbed in, tossing my bag into the backseat. As promised, they followed directly behind as if we were an official motorcade. They stayed with me even after I turned on to Route 611, but after about ten minutes, they flashed their lights, indicating my escort was over.

I was on my own now. The road was lined mainly with commercial buildings, all with security lights on the edges of their roofs, which cast an eerie glow into empty parking lots. I checked my rearview mirror every minute, making sure I wasn't being followed, but there was no one in sight, and just a couple of cars passed me going the other way. Eventually I had to leave Route 611 and wind along rural roads on my way to I-78. My hands trembled as they gripped the steering wheel. The houses I passed were dark, deserted looking, except for one that had electric candlelights in every window. I had been on this route five or six times, but never in the dead of night, and I was worried I'd get lost. As it turned out, I found my way without trouble and saw only one car on the entire fifteen-minute stretch, a souped-up sports car coming the other way, probably full of Friday night revelers. The worst thing that happened: I picked up the smell of a skunk, which seemed to stay with the car forever.

I felt better when I finally merged onto I-78, though the driving there was hardly a day at the beach. Trucks and more trucks barreled along beside me as I stayed meekly in the middle lane. I stuck in a CD of Maria Callas's Puccini arias, opened a bottle of Poland Spring water that I kept in the Jeep, and chugged half of it down in one gulp. Should I have been more forthcoming with the two state police guys? I kept asking myself. It had just seemed like too much to get into with two patrol cops who wouldn't know what to do with the info. Farley was the one to share everything with. Though he might kill me when I told him.

In the sky directly ahead of me, the gray light of dawn began to seep though the blackness and the first flames of sunrise reached over the horizon. It should have been comforting, but my hands would not stop shaking.

CHAPTER 14

I PULLED INTO the parking garage just before five-thirty A.M. and rushed home the half block to my apartment building. The lecherous night porter was still on duty in the lobby, wearing a doorman cap three sizes too big that he'd obviously borrowed from one of the day guys. He gave me a disgusting "Hey baby, big night, huh?" smirk and I brushed past him with a look that I hoped revealed that I considered him the most absurd-looking turd ever to appear on the planet. Once in my apartment with the door closed and the lights on, I was overwhelmed with a sense of relief. I overrode my temptation to wake Landon and pour out the story and instead wrote him a note saying that I was home and not to leave without talking to me, and slipped it under his door. All of a sudden I felt nailed by fatigue. Afraid of not hearing the doorbell, I flopped down on my couch instead of the bed, pulling a chenille throw over my shoulders.

I'd slept for just two hours when Landon rang my bell. My note had thrown him into a tizzy, which quickly escalated into shock when I described the break-in. Before he had a chance to assume "burglar," I relayed my theory that the episode was connected somehow to my involvement in Cat's situation rather than to someone's interest in his sterling silver. Regardless, I told him, I didn't like the idea of him being alone in his house that night. He explained that he had other houseguests arriving later in the day, so he'd have plenty of company. His biggest concern seemed to be leaving me on *my* own, possibly in the throes of post-traumatic stress syndrome. I insisted I'd be fine and sent him on his way with the info on the two police officers so he could follow up with them—and a strong urging that he improve his lock situation immediately.

After he left I trudged down to my bedroom, tore off my clothes, and fell into the kind of deep sleep I hadn't experienced in years. I awoke groggy, with a headache, feeling as if I'd just gotten off a seventeen-hour flight across the Pacific.

A shower helped a little, as did two cups of coffee. I knew I needed food and decided to walk over to the small restaurant where I'd eaten lunch with Jack Herlihy. Before I left I finally remembered to check my messages. A couple of calls from friends and one from my brother Cam. A long-winded message from the Howdy Doody progeny I'd met Thursday night at the bar, who must have wrestled my phone number from someone there. And interestingly: not a single hang-up. It was as if my phone stalker had known I was going out of town this weekend.

As I left my apartment building, I glanced up and down 9th Street a few times. Nothing ominous: just people on their way shopping or errand running or Rollerblading or dog walking or perhaps heading over to Washington Square Park to just loll around in the sun. It was another gorgeous day, and people were dressed in capris and shorts. A few had even abandoned regulation Village black for pastels.

At the restaurant, I ordered a Caesar salad and a glass of iced tea. When my order came, I nibbled on a few croutons, but they had all the appeal of mulch. I still felt incredibly wigged out from the night before. Yet in the last hours, as I'd thought more and more about what had happened, I'd begun to make sense of it. And I no longer believed that the attack on me the previous night had anything to do, at least directly, with Cat's situation.

That's because as I'd combed my memory I'd realized that there was no way anyone who'd been at Cat's party could have known I would be at Landon's house last night. Cat was the only one who knew I was going out to Pennsylvania, and though I'd given her a contact number for me, I'd never said who I was staying with, so she couldn't have inadvertently passed on the info to the killer. And I was nearly positive I hadn't been followed. I recalled glancing in my rearview mirror on those rural stretches between I-78 and Landon's house, just out of habit. There'd been times when not a single car had been behind me.

One person, however, *had* learned where I was staying: Darma. She'd asked and I'd given her Landon's name and the town he lived in. He was listed, so she could have easily found the street address. Prickly, agitated Darma. In her living room I had appeared to hit a nerve with my questions about Tucker's death. Maybe something fishy *had* gone on, maybe she really *had* snuck death caps into his food and wasn't at all happy with the fact that I was poking my nose into things. That certainly hadn't been *her* in the kitchen, her curls stuffed inside a ski mask. But maybe it had been the *Lonesome Dove* dude, sent on a mission to scare me out of town.

There was something else. The prowler's gloves. They'd been made of heavy cotton, maybe denim, the material that work gloves are made of. The kind people use outdoors, in yards and barnyards. The kind the *Lonesome Dove* dude might easily wear. I didn't have enough proof to go running to the police with it, but it made sense to me.

All very interesting and troubling. Something I needed to consider sharing with the police out there. But I couldn't let myself get distracted by it. I needed to focus on Cat's case. For the time being I was going to assume that Bobb's death and Heidi's *weren't* related, that no one had a vendetta against women's magazines. That meant reconsidering who on the guest list, excluding Dolores, had a reason to want Cat (and just Cat) out of the picture.

As I sat at the same restaurant where I'd gone with Jack Herlihy, my conversation with him about Heidi's murder bubbled to the surface of my mind. He'd said that when people planned a murder, they did it not because they had a hair up their butt about some minor insult or infraction, but because they were in a frenzy of emotion—they felt jealous as hell or totally betrayed or rabid with rage. And that, I realized, was what I had to keep in mind as I considered the partygoers. No pussyfooting around with anyone who had minor grievances. I needed to concentrate on people who might be tasting their own bile because of something Cat Jones had done to them.

I felt pretty comfortable knocking Leslie's name off the list, at least for now. Though she might have been miffed at Cat for allegedly flirting with her husband, that was ages ago, and she exhibited no sign of holding a grudge. I also mentally crossed off Rachel. If she wanted Cat's job, she'd know that eliminating Cat would never guarantee she'd get it.

Apparently, however, there were people who *might* be in a big enough frenzy to want to murder. Polly for one. I felt so seditious just thinking her name, but she had every reason to be running over with rage. Cat, who owed Polly big-time, had thwarted her chance to finally be an editor in chief. Jeff. Something was definitely amiss on the Cat and Jeff love landscape. Had Cat been unfaithful? I could still see the pink flush on her neck when I asked about Kip. If she *had* been a bad girl, maybe Jeff suspected. Maybe it made his blood boil. Or perhaps there was some other reason he might want her dead. The money? Cat not only made more than Jeff, but had come into some family money in the last couple of years. Kip. Though it was hard for me to imagine Cat feeling the slightest attraction to Kip, a guy who not only worked for her, but seemed to be suffering from near toxic levels of testosterone, there was definitely something going on—I could feel it. And an affair, or even just a fling, could have generated strong feelings in Kip: jealousy, anger, regret.

Three people. Or actually four, because I wanted to add Person X. That covered anyone stewing big-time over something that I had no clue about, perhaps an editor from one of the other magazines who had attended the party or a *Gloss* staffer who'd found a secret reason to hate Cat big-time. I'd have to keep my eyes open. But until I had other info, I was going to concentrate on the first three. I was due to see Polly Sunday night for dinner, but maybe I could move it up to tonight. Jeff and Cat were out in Litchfield for the weekend, but I might be able to arrange to see them Sunday evening and have a better chance of talking to Jeff than I did the day Heidi died. Kip would have to wait until Monday.

I paid the bill and started home. As soon as I got into my apartment I left a message for Polly, asking her if we could move up our date. I also tried Cat's place up in Litchfield. No answer, so I left a message. As for Detective Farley, there seemed to be no need to call him now. I didn't think the Friday night prowler had any connection with Cat, so why would he need to know? And since he was apparently heading out to Bucks County to pursue the Tucker Bobb angle, he could draw whatever conclusions he liked about Bobb's death.

Finally I set to work on my Marky story. I'd actually made plenty of progress on it over the past couple of days and was just about finished with the first draft. Though my passion now was for magazine writing, I'd benefited from my years of working on newspapers. With a daily deadline that could never be ignored, I learned how to crank it out regardless of how much commotion was going on around me in the newsroom or how much chaos existed at a given moment in my personal life.

There was, however, one aspect of the Marky story that I was going to have to resolve before I could finish it. Since my interview with Jack Herlihy, I'd reviewed my notes on the various "poltergeist" incidents, and though I could guess how Marky might have managed to pull off most of them, a few still mystified me.

What I needed to do, I decided, was talk to Jack Herlihy again. I felt a nervous kick in my stomach just thinking his name, not the kind you get before an interview with a hotshot, but the kind you get when the phone rings and it's a guy you've taken to imagining naked. I doubted he'd be home on a Saturday afternoon, and I was right. I left word on his answering machine asking that he give me a call.

At five Polly phoned on her cell from a movie line, saying that dinner tonight wouldn't work but she could do lunch tomorrow. The rest of the night was pure pathos. I ate dinner at the restaurant/coffee shop in my building, along with two glasses of cheap red wine, took all my summer shoes out of shoeboxes from the back of my closet and replaced them with winter pairs, and watched *Sense and Sensibility*. I crawled into bed at midnight and woke once during the night from a nightmare of someone holding my head underwater.

Sunday I was up at eight, feeling better, less tense, less as though my blood were low on oxygen. Polly and I had agreed to meet at twelve-thirty in Chelsea, her neighborhood, and I used the morning to start editing the draft of my Marky article. At around ten, just as I was pouring myself a cup of coffee, Cat finally made contact.

"Hey," I said. "How are you doing?"

"I've been better. It helps to be up here, out of the city, but I'm still pretty much a wreck. Have you found anything out?"

I'd already decided not to share the prowler incident with her, at least not at this time.

"Yeah, I talked to both Darma and one of the doctors at the hospital where Tucker died, and I found out some in-

teresting stuff. Tucker *may* have eaten a killer mushroom—there's no way to know for sure—but even if he
did, it doesn't seem very likely that his death had anything
to do with your situation. There's—"

"How can you be so sure?" she asked.

"It had to do with the timing of him getting sick. People in New York always assumed he came down with
something in his office midweek," I explained. "But that
probably was a relapse."

"I'm not following this at all." She turned away from
the phone for a second and said something quietly to
someone else in the room, something I couldn't make out.
"Look, we're trying to pack up and get out of here. Jeff
has to edit some film in the studio this afternoon. Can we
get together first thing tomorrow? I need to hear more
about this. And I need to fill you in on stuff."

"What about tonight?" I asked.

"Tonight's not good," she said vaguely, so I told her
fine, my Monday morning was clear. She'd be at a photo
shoot, she explained, and suggested that I meet her at the
studio in the West 20s.

I was about to hop into the shower when Polly phoned.

"Can I ask a favor?" she said. Damn, I thought, she's
going to reschedule. But what she wanted was for me to
skip lunch and just walk with her.

"I've lost three pounds, and I know if I sit down in a
restaurant, I'll eat everything but the menus."

"Sure, that's fine with me," I said, lying. "Where do
you want to meet?"

"I'll ring your bell in, like, one hour—and we'll just
see where the wind takes us."

My appetite was back, and I'd had my heart set on

something like penne puttanesca, eaten at an outdoor café, and now I was going to be forced to scrounge around my refrigerator, praying for a miracle. The best I came up with was a puckered slab of duck liver mousse pâté that Landon had sent me home with when I'd eaten dinner at his place. I sniffed it. Probably okay. After showering and getting dressed, I ate it on my terrace with crackers and a glass of instant iced tea and was just putting the dishes in the sink when Polly buzzed.

Her appearance nearly knocked me over. She looked not only lovely, but positively carefree. Instead of the perennial Pippi Longstocking braid, she was wearing her hair loose and flowing, though she had some of the wispy front pieces pinned back with colored bobby pins. Her skin was glowing, and she'd dabbed on a hint of pink lip gloss. It was hard to imagine the heart of darkness was beating away inside her.

We decided to head south on Broadway, figuring it would be less crowded in that direction. It was obvious by the first block that she had no interest in attaining a maximum fat-blasting pace—you'd burn more calories shaving your legs than you would at the speed we were walking. But that was okay. I wanted to concentrate on Polly, her mood, her attitude about everything that had happened.

"So what happened to your weekend plans?" she asked as soon as we were in gear.

"They just kind of unraveled," I told her. Right now I had no intention of sharing what had happened with her. "But tell me, what's going on at work?"

"Friday was *insane*. I just wish you could have been there to experience it."

"What do you mean?" I asked.

"Did you see the *Post* on Friday?"

"No, I left town early that morning."

"Well, they ran an item, a story actually, saying that Tucker Bobb may have been poisoned, too, and his case and Cat's case could be connected. Maybe there's a disgruntled employee who worked for both of them and or even some kind of psychopath who hates women's magazines and wants to knock off the editors one by one. It's like something out of a movie."

"So everyone was buzzing about it?"

"Too mild a word. Cat left for the country at about eleven, and after that all hell broke loose. People were running around flapping their lips about it, speculating ridiculously, making things up. The phones were ringing like crazy. Leslie sent out a snippy memo telling people that if they talked to the press, they'd be fired. And you know that ridiculous beauty assistant, the one I told you once said she wished she had a stalker because if you have a stalker it means you're pretty? She resigned and left that day."

"Oh, my God," was all I could manage.

"Wait—it gets worse," she said. "Detectives came by. There were two of them, and they wanted to talk to as many people as possible who were at the party that night. We're all freakin' suspects, I guess."

"Did they talk to you?"

"Oh yeah. And I was terrible. I was just so nervous. It's like going through customs. You know how when they open your bag and all you can think about is that they're going to find a kilo of cocaine."

"Do you have any reason to believe they suspect you?"

"No, no. Their questions were more like 'Did you notice anything funny?' 'Had you seen a box of candy on the hall table?' 'Did lots of people at the office know that Cat was a chocoholic?' Plus, I think they could tell just by looking at me that I'm too much of a nervous Nellie to off anyone."

Did I believe that? I wanted to. But the jury was still out.

"How were other people acting?" I asked. "I'm sure they were nervous, too."

"Hard to tell, because things got real quiet once the cops arrived and pretty much everyone who was questioned kept to themselves after that. Kip didn't say a word—I believe it's the first time in recorded history he didn't have a sarcastic comment to offer up. Rachel peeled out of there early. Let's see, who else? Oh, Leslie shut her door and didn't open it again. I'm sure she was blabbing with Cat on the phone. Oh, wait, this is a hoot. Our brilliant fashion editor Sasha comes down to my office, practically hysterical, asking if I think the police are going to want to go through expense account records as part of the investigation. She's probably afraid someone'll find out she charges all of her personal dry cleaning to the company."

We had reached Houston Street by now, and we stopped to confer about what direction to go from there, deciding on south to Canal Street, then west for a few blocks before heading back toward the Village.

"Poor Cat, what a mess she's in," I said as we continued. I just let the statement hang there, waiting to see how Polly would respond.

"If you say so," she said. "It's Heidi I feel sorry for. Getting too close to Cat has been a liability for an awful lot of people, but as far as I know, this is the first time someone has actually ended up in rigor mortis from it. Wait, correction. Second time. I heard once that a guy who was obsessed with her in college committed suicide."

"Is that how you feel—that being involved with Cat has been a liability?" I asked.

"Yes . . . and no. I mean, working for her magazine has given me a certain amount of professional clout. But she hasn't done me any favors, either."

"She thinks you're fantastic at what you do," I said. "I've just never understood why she has such a hard time acknowledging that publicly."

"You know, I can live with that. A lot of powerful bosses hog the credit, and you accept that and know that you can at least get to ride their tailwind someplace good. And, of course, Cat's Cat. From the moment you meet her, you know she's not the one you call if you need a bone marrow donor. But she did me dirt lately. A great position opened up in the company and I wanted it and she made darn sure I didn't get it."

"You're kidding," I said, attempting to sound surprised. "What was the job?"

"You know what," she said, coming to a complete stop on the sidewalk and turning to me. "It doesn't matter anymore. Look, I've been dying to tell you this, but it's got to be a secret. In about five weeks, I'm going to hand in my resignation. I'm leaving *Gloss*."

I let out a little gasp. I'd been so preoccupied lately, I hadn't spotted any signs that she was finally going to act on her discontent.

"Geez, Polly, I'm speechless. And I'm thrilled for you. Though I'm awfully sad for me."

"Don't be. I see this as the beginning of a great friendship between the two of us," she said. "Working together, with me top editing you, has always been just a tiny bit awkward. Now we can be buddies, pure and simple."

"Well, like I said, I'm thrilled for you," I said, giving her a hug. "I know you've been pretty miserable this last year."

"And it's not just because of Cat," she explained, starting to walk again. "The work has begun to bore me. If I could deal with your pieces all day, it would be one thing, but editing stuff like the beauty and fashion copy has become mind numbing. One of the beauty editors used the term *buttne* in some copy the other day. Do you know what buttne supposedly means? It's acne you get on your butt. When I tried to explain to her that it was stupid to use a word like that, she looked at me as if *I* were the moron. And another thing—I just don't fit in with the staff these days. They're all so young and hip. You're thirty-three and you get it, but I'm almost forty and I don't. A few of the girls in articles were talking the other day about something called booty calls. I asked them what the term meant. I thought they were going to say it's when a construction worker yells out a comment about your ass or something like that, but it turns out it's when you want to get laid and you call a guy you used to go out with or know casually and you go to his place just for sex. Or maybe he calls you. Not only had I never heard of it, but no one has ever made a booty call to me in my entire life."

"So you're just going to quit?" I asked. "Will you freelance?"

"No, no, I've got a job. I'm going to be helping to run that theater group I volunteer with—the Chelsea Players.

They've figured out a way to swing having someone handle PR and marketing and that sort of thing. It doesn't pay great, but I've got some money left from the divorce settlement, and I'm going to do what I want for a change. It doesn't actually start for a few more weeks, so I figured I'd keep working at *Gloss* and sock away what I could. I would have told you sooner, but it's been up in the air for the past two months and I didn't want to jinx it."

We had reached the West Village and I suggested we grab a cappuccino. We stopped at an outdoor café on Bleecker, and as we sat in the sunshine talking about her plans, I could see how truly happy and exhilarated she was. And seeing that happiness made it almost impossible for me to believe she had tried to kill Cat. From what she was saying, the possibility of the position with the theater group had begun to materialize right around the time she had lost out on the job with the gardening magazine. Rather than nurse a hatred for Cat, it appeared she had quickly begun to focus on a new opportunity. It sounded as if Cat had stopped mattering to her then, one way or another. Of course, she could have fancied a turn of the screw as she went out the door, but I didn't think so. Polly seemed completely checked out from *Gloss* and not the least bit invested in the idea of revenge. I felt relieved.

After we paid the bill, I offered to walk her back to Chelsea. Swearing her secret was safe with me, I hugged her in front of her apartment building and wished her good luck. I started home at a much brisker pace than we'd walked earlier, zigzagging south and east.

When I reached Sixth Avenue and 18th, it hit me that I was not far from Jeff's studio, though I couldn't remember the exact address. I'd been there once in the famous courtship days—Cat had asked me to tag along while she popped in to tantalize him in a dress the size and sheerness of a gauze bandage. I used my cell phone to call directory assistance and found that his studio was on 19th Street between Fifth and Sixth. Cat had said he'd be working this afternoon; and if I went by his studio and found him there, it would be an opportunity to spend time alone with him. I wanted to hear him talk about Cat and the murder and see what leaked out. I walked back north a block and then headed down 19th Street until I found his building.

The block, like others in the neighborhood, is filled with studios and residential lofts that were once small factories. There's a cavernous feel to the neighborhood. The wide, ten-story buildings are layered with soot and do a good job of blocking the sun.

Jeff's building was about three-quarters of the way toward Fifth, a dingy-looking place with a photo lab in the ground-floor space. The sidewalk in front was littered with trash and old newspapers. I opened the first door, stepped into the vestibule, and scanned the intercom for the buzzer to his studio. He was on the sixth floor, along with a company called New Century Video.

I felt uncomfortable ambushing him this way, but I also knew that caught off guard, he might give more away. I pressed the buzzer and waited. Nothing. I tried again. Still no reply. I was about to turn on my heel when a voice, unrecognizable because of the crackling, came over the intercom. It was male and I thought he said, "Who is it?"

"Jeff? Hi, it's Bailey. I was in the neighborhood and wanted to talk for a minute—if you have a minute." Brilliant.

There was a pause, and I wondered if he hadn't heard

me or maybe the person who'd answered wasn't Jeff. Suddenly the buzzer on the door went off and I pushed through the vestibule into a dusty gray lobby.

It took a few minutes for the elevator to show up on the ground floor. I could hear it grinding above me somewhere, obviously moving between floors, and when it finally settled on the ground floor I expected someone to step out, but it was empty. I rode up to six, the elevator clanging as we passed each floor.

As I walked in the dim light of the corridor toward Jeff's studio, I saw that the door was ajar an inch, with the dead bolt released so that it wouldn't slam shut. I pushed it all the way open and stepped into the studio.

It was smaller than I remembered, about 1,500 square feet, with the front end set up like a small reception area and the middle area a big open space filled with studio lights and tripods and a large roll of backdrop paper mounted on the left-hand wall. There were windows along the long wall to the right, covered with city grime. It was absolutely silent, as if someone had turned off the sound. No sign of Jeff, though a gooseneck lamp on the desk had been switched on and there was another light in the small office that he had built into the space at the back.

"Jeff?" I called. "Anyone here?"

He stepped out of the office silently, pulling the door closed. He was wearing an olive green T-shirt, baggy khakis hanging low on his hips, and no socks or shoes. As he walked toward me, he let his hands swing at his sides. Jeff was the kind of guy who never nervously touched his face or his hair.

"To what do I owe this honor?" he asked. There was an edge to how he said it, and he didn't appear delighted to see me, though when he reached me he leaned forward and brushed my cheek with his lips. They felt chapped, the kind of chapped you get from a weekend on a sailboat.

"I hope I didn't pull you out of the darkroom or anything," I said. "I had lunch with a friend nearby and ended up on this street and thought I'd just pop in. Cat had mentioned you were working today."

"I've got film to edit," he told me. "Not the most fun way to spend a day like today. You're here to rescue me, then?"

Hmmm. Not sure what to say to that.

"There's something I wanted to ask you about, actually."

"Sit," he said, pointing to a black leather sofa against the wall. "Want anything to drink? I may have a beer myself."

"Sure, that'd be good," I said.

As Jeff sauntered back toward the end of the loft, to an area with a small counter and refrigerator, I walked over and perched on the edge of the leather couch, avoiding the slash in the cushion with the stuffing coming out. My desire for a beer at this hour was about as intense as my urge to clean out my wallet, but I figured sharing a drink might diminish the awkwardness.

As he kicked the refrigerator door closed and turned around, he glanced back toward the office for a split second. Was there someone *in* there? I wondered. It had seemed odd earlier when he'd pulled the door shut.

He walked back toward me carrying two Coronas by their necks, stopped at the desk, where he patted some papers until he located a bottle opener beneath them, and popped off the tops. He handed a bottle to me and plopped down on the couch. After taking a long swig of his beer, he leaned into the sofa, draping one arm across the back. His biceps actually strained the sleeves of his T-shirt, and it was clear he'd been working out lately in a serious way.

"What kind of work are you doing these days?" I asked after taking a half sip from my beer bottle. "Still concentrating on fashion?" The studio had the look and feel of a vacant lot.

"A mix," he said. Another swig of beer.

"I don't want to keep you. But I've been so worried about Cat lately and I thought it would help to talk to you."

"What help could I possibly be?"

"Well, for starters, have you got any ideas whatsoever about who might want to harm Cat?"

"Well, we both know she's ticked off a fair number of people in her day. But no one specific rushes to mind."

"You've never gotten any weird phone calls at home or anything like that?"

"Nope. Not that I know of, at least. Maybe you ought to ask Carlotta."

He seemed peevish, annoyed, but I couldn't tell if it was from my barging in on him or from something else entirely.

"I was away for a few days," I said, "but I heard the papers had a story linking the case to Tucker Bobb's death."

His beer bottle was halfway to his mouth, but he paused and shot a glance in my direction.

"Cat told me you'd been out to Pennsylvania and didn't think there was a connection."

"I'm not a hundred percent positive," I said quickly. "But there doesn't *appear* to be a link."

He smiled a bad-boy smile. "That puts me back on the suspect list, then, doesn't it?"

"The police aren't treating you that way, are they?" I asked.

"No. Not yet, anyway. Though they spent a lot of time with me one day this week, asking all sorts of questions. Maybe I ought to tell them that I'm the one person who knows that Cat actually prefers Maison du Chocolate. Or at least I've always assumed I was."

"What do you mean?"

"Nothing. Making a joke."

"Did you get the feeling the police had formed any ideas about who might have done it?"

Again the sly smile. "They didn't seem interested in sharing any of their thinking with me. Though I will say they couldn't disguise the fact that they viewed me more as the resident boy toy than king of the castle."

I decided to go down another road entirely and see what happened.

"I keep forgetting the fact that you guys aren't just dealing with the threat against Cat, but with Heidi's death, too. You must feel awful about that."

"Of course," he said, staring into the Corona bottle. "And guilty."

"Guilty? Because Heidi ate what was meant for Cat?"

"Yeah," he said. "And because if Cat had been there, like she was supposed to be that weekend, maybe Heidi would have had someone to turn to when she got sick."

"What do you mean, like she was supposed to be? I thought she had to go to East Hampton."

"When Tyler and I left for the country, it was because she needed us out of her hair so she could work," he said.

"The next thing I know, she's calling from Long Island. But then you know as well as I do that it's tough to keep up with Cat." It was said with bemusement, but there was a soupçon of bitterness underneath.

He took a big sip of beer and wiped his bottom lip with the edge of his hand. Then he slid down into the sofa and stretched out his legs in front of him. His feet, I noticed, were very tanned. I also saw that the second toe on each foot was slightly longer than the big one. I had read somewhere, probably in *Gloss,* that it was supposed to indicate something about a man—that he had a need for control, maybe. Or that he told lies easily. Or maybe it was that his penis was unnaturally long.

"This must all be very scary," I said quietly.

"You bet. Having Heidi die, having someone leave a box of poison in your home, that's pretty serious stuff. And the worst part of this whole thing is Tyler. What if he'd somehow gotten those chocolates off the table? We drove him up to Cat's mother's in Massachusetts yesterday, and he's going to stay there until things chill here. If they ever do."

There was an uncomfortable silence, and I pondered where I should go with the conversation next. Buying time, I started to take another swig of beer when Jeff leaned slowly in my direction, his right hand extended. For one terrifying instant I suspected he was going to pull me toward him and kiss me. Instead he tore a ragged piece of foil off the neck of my beer bottle.

"We don't want you to cut your lip," he said, flicking it onto the floor.

I was barely halfway through my beer, but it was

clearly time to beat it—before things went from bad to worse.

"Well, look, I appreciate you talking to me about this," I said, rising. "If there's any way I can help, will you let me know?"

He stared at me without offering a reply but lifted himself up from the sofa. When I looked around for a place to set my beer bottle, he pulled it gently from my hands, glancing at how much was left.

"Remind me next time to offer you an Evian water."

"Sorry—beer makes me sleepy if I have it in the middle of the afternoon," I said.

"Well, we wouldn't want that, would we?"

He walked me toward the door, and as he opened it with his right hand, his left grasped my shoulder and he leaned down and kissed me on the cheek again, the chapped lips prickly on my skin.

As we stood there, I noticed for the first time that there was a coat tree behind the door, with a turquoise coat, nylon or rayon, hanging on it.

"Stop by again," he said as he closed the door on me. He didn't sound as though he meant it.

Out in the hallway, it was so silent it seemed as if someone had turned off the sound. As I waited for the elevator, I considered the turquoise coat. It might have been left behind by a model or stylist one day or even by Cat. Or maybe it belonged to someone who'd been sitting in the little office, someone waiting silently and patiently for me to get the hell out of the studio.

CHAPTER 15

BOOTY CALLS. I hadn't wanted to admit this to Polly, but not only did I know what a booty call was, I'd also been on my share of them over the years. In fact, as I sat on my terrace just before dusk Sunday evening, sipping a glass of Saratoga water and watching a sprawling, five-alarm sunset, I realized that my plans for the rest of the evening could more or less be defined that way.

It's not how I'd planned for the night to unfold. I'd left Jeff's studio in a state of agitation, preoccupied with the many questions that had been churned up from my clumsy encounter with the man with the too long second toe. For starters, I couldn't shake the idea that someone had been sitting in the back office, waiting for Jeff to come padding back in his bare feet, and if that was the case, who the hell was it? A model or stylist he was shagging from time to time when the mood struck? Or someone he had more serious designs on? Was there any chance it'd been Cat, laying low so she could hear the reason for my mystery visit? That didn't seem likely, considering the snippiness in Jeff's tone when he had discussed her.

And what exactly was going on with him and Cat? The hint of disenchantment and "boy toy" comment had startled me. I also didn't like what he'd said about Cat's mad dash to the Hamptons last weekend. To me she'd made it sound like a prearranged business trip, but that wasn't the version Jeff was presenting. Maybe Cat really *was* having an affair.

Other questions: What was up with Jeff's work? Did he even *have* any? What had happened to his reportedly red-hot career?

And the most important question of all: Was there a problem big enough in the marriage that could have propelled Jeff to try to murder Cat? Had the size of her success compared to his galled him into doing it? Or maybe another woman was the motivation. A divorce would mean kissing good-bye the comfy lifestyle he'd grown accustomed to, but killing Cat and making it appear like a plot against editors would allow him to have his cake and eat it, too. The thought made me shiver.

On the way home I stopped off at a gourmet food store on University Avenue and bought ingredients for penne puttanesca—ever since my plan to have it for lunch had been derailed, I'd felt a craving too big to ignore. I dropped the bag in the kitchen and then checked my answering machine. Four messages—a record for me on a Sunday. The first was from Landon, calling just before he left Bucks County for New York to say he was alive and unharmed and would try again later. Jack Herlihy had returned my call, and my mother had left a brief hello from abroad. And one hang-up, number blocked. My phone stalker had taken most of the weekend off but was now back on duty. The call had been made *since* the time I'd left Jeff's studio.

Before I could let myself get freaked out about the hang-up, I dialed Dr. Jack back. He sounded awfully chipper and not at all annoyed that I was calling for more of his expertise.

"I've looked at all my notes on Marky and there are a few things I can't make fit with what you said," I explained. "If you have any time early in the week, I'd love to ask you some more questions—and we could easily do it on the phone."

"Tell you what," he said. "I'm happy to help, but why don't you let me buy you dinner. This way you can introduce me to another place in the Village."

Ahhhh. So he *had* been interested at lunch. I'd suspected as much when he'd requested the double forks, but his distraction later on had left me doubtful. Now what? My life was too crazy these days for another romantic dalliance. I needed to help Cat. I needed time to get K.C. out of my system. I didn't like guys with such smooth skin. I couldn't imagine dating a shrink. But before I could form an excuse, I heard myself saying yes. Was I nuts? We agreed on seven the next night, and I told him I'd come up with a restaurant choice and leave a message on his machine tomorrow.

I'd just set the phone down when it rang, startling me. Wondering if it was a hang-up, I picked it up and just listened, not saying hello. To my total shock, K.C. was on the other end.

"Bailey?" he asked. "You screening your calls?"

"Hi. No. I've just been getting a lot of hang-ups lately. I didn't expect anyone to be there."

"I swear it's not me doing it," he said in mock defense.

"I believe you."

"So tell me, was it something I said?" he asked. "If your cologne hadn't been on the pillow, I would have sworn I'd imagined the whole thing."

Was he just feigning being hurt? I almost felt guilty. "I was leaving town," I said. "I had to pick up my Jeep at the garage really early."

"Too bad. I'd been planning to make you a fabulous breakfast."

"Right. I looked in your refrigerator. There was a six-pack of beer and a bottle of Tabasco sauce."

"Buy. *Buy* you a fabulous breakfast."

"Well, I guess I'll have to take a rain check, then."

"How about tomorrow morning?"

I laughed out loud. "Great, where should I meet you?"

"Well, it's kind of a twofer. I buy you dinner tonight, as well."

And that's how I came to find myself sitting on my terrace pondering booty calls. I'd said yes, just as I'd said yes to Jack Herlihy—though I was clearer on the reason. I was still infatuated with K.C. And maybe I'd underestimated him. He'd sounded troubled by the fact that I'd run off Thursday night. Maybe he was more interested in a relationship than I'd sensed he was, and maybe he just hated the game playing—the kind that involved calling for a date six nights in advance. And one more thing: By saying yes, I'd be able to forgo a night at the Hotel Insomnia, dwelling on Heidi and the Hershey's Kiss and the man who'd come to Landon's to scare me to death.

He arrived fifteen minutes late, looking especially roguish (tan pants, white button-down shirt, yellow cotton crewneck sweater tied haphazardly around his shoulders, the top of his nose peeling from a sunburn). I'd changed into black slacks and a black halter top, and as he kissed me hello in my living room, he untied the back of the halter, laughing, and let it fall to my waist.

"I'm sorry," he said. "If you'd told me you were thinking of wearing this, I would have warned you. There's no way I can resist this through an entire evening."

He leaned forward but instead of kissing me, he ran his tongue around the edge of my lips. At the same time he began to caress my breasts, his hands still cool from the outside. I was caught off guard by this turn of events. I'd been expecting hello, are you ready to go? not this seduction in the middle of my living room, lights on, blinds up, half of the West Village able to rubberneck. But when he began kissing me deeply, his tongue full in my mouth, I just let go, feeling my nipples harden in his hands. There was something both tender and urgent in his touch, as if he wanted me bad but was going to take his damn sweet time. He dropped one hand from my breast and slid it down my legs, over my black lycra pants. When he ran it between my legs, I got so wobbly with desire I could barely stand.

"Hungry?" he asked, pausing.

"That depends on what you mean."

Forty-eight seconds later we were in bed—and we never even made it out to a restaurant. At about nine we took a break and I whipped up the penne puttanesca, which seemed appropriate. Doesn't it mean whore's pasta?

He was up at six A.M. because, he said, he had a seven A.M. business meeting—the promise of breakfast had apparently been a bold-faced lie—and as soon as I'd let him out I felt my free-floating anxiety returning again. My appointment with Cat wasn't until ten, so I threw on some sweats and ran over to the gym, where I jumped on the treadmill for thirty minutes. Back home I showered and drank two cups of coffee. At nine forty-five I flagged down a cab on Broadway.

As the taxi wound its way toward the most western block of 26th Street, I realized that I had no clue what the photography session was for. The only shoots for the magazine that I knew Cat dropped in on were the celebrity cover shoots when they were done in New York, but she certainly would have mentioned it if I were going to be seeing some famous actress getting her hair blown out and throwing a hissy fit about the clothes.

The studio was on the ground floor of a three-story building, and after being buzzed in through a doorway, I found myself in the middle of a truck-loading area that I had to walk through in order to get to the studio space. A girl with short choppy black hair and white skin opened the door.

"You're with *Gloss*?" she asked before I could say a word. She had the slight lisp you get when you've recently had a tongue stud put in. I could see the flash of silver in her mouth.

When I answered affirmatively she gave a little nod of her head, and as I stepped inside she raced off to pick up a ringing phone. I found myself in a huge studio, with superhigh ceilings and exposed brick walls. The space up front had been sectioned off as an office area—there was a large Parsons table that served as a desk, filing cabinets, and a refrigerator, a sink, and a table spread with platters of breakfast food. It seemed a far cry from Jeff's studio. Over to my left was a counter with mirrors and makeup lights, where a guy dressed in black jeans and a Rolling Stones tongue T-shirt sat on a stool reading *Interview*. All the action was going on in the back of the studio, where the photographer was snapping away at someone who was standing on gray seamless paper and couldn't be seen from this angle. A fairly large crowd was buzzing around like bees back there—a couple of assistants, a makeup person, a hairdresser with a spray bottle of water wedged into his back pocket. I also recognized Josh, a stylist from *Gloss*'s fashion department. But no Cat anywhere in sight.

"I love it when you lift your chin like that," I heard the photographer say. "Let's do one more roll like that." As he took a step away from the tripod, I saw that the subject of all the attention was Cat herself.

Oh great, I thought. This could be all morning. I dropped my tote bag on the floor, scooped up a miniature bagel with salmon and cream cheese from the food table, and walked over to the makeup counter.

"Is this for an ad campaign, do you know?" I asked the guy in the tongue shirt, whose eyes slid over toward me as I sat on a nearby stool. Cat had mentioned a while back that she might be featured in an ad campaign for *Gloss*.

"Don't think so," he said in a British accent. "I believe it's for that page where the editor says what she thinks about everything."

"They're shooting a picture for the 'Letter from the Editor' page?" I exclaimed, having a hard time containing my stupefaction.

"Yes, right. I believe that's it."

Cat had a murder investigation swirling around her, but she'd decided to take time to update her head shot. It was the sort of thing that redefined the notion of fiddling while Rome burned.

I'd taken only a couple of bites from my bagel when the action on the set came to a standstill. After a brief confab with the photographer, Cat trounced over in my direction, towing the makeup person and Josh behind her. Her hair was superfull, cascading around her shoulders, and she was wearing globs of makeup. Her lips, in fact, had so much gloss that you could almost see your reflection, but underneath it all she looked exhausted.

"How long have you been here?" she asked as a greeting when she spotted me.

"Just a few minutes." I said hi to Josh, who was sporting a sailor shirt and a pair of nuthuggers, pants so tight that the only thing left to the imagination was genital skin tone. "So what's the plan here?" I said, turning back to Cat.

"I'm done, I guess. I don't think I can change clothes one more time."

"You're not going to wear the *Dolce?*" Josh gasped. He looked at her as if she'd just announced she was about to drown a litter of newborn kitties.

"I can't. I can't do this one more minute," she said. "Will you tell everybody I said we've got enough.

"Besides," she added, dropping into one of the

makeup chairs and swiveling around to face the mirror, "I look like hell."

The makeup artist walked over to a position directly behind her and rested the fingertips of each hand on Cat's cheeks. "You know what I'm seeing?" she said. "I'm seeing a lot of stagnant toxins in your face. They're not draining because of stress. Have you ever considered face reflexology? I could do a little right now."

Cat stared at her without answering, as if she'd just been told something in Portuguese and didn't understand a word. Then she stood up and announced she was going off to change her clothes. In the reflection of the mirror, I saw the makeup chick shoot a look to the guy in the tongue shirt. It was a look that said, "Have you ever met a bigger bitch in your life?"

A few minutes later Cat emerged in a fuchsia-and-white tie-dyed skirt and matching short-sleeved jacket. She suggested we go to the corner and look for a place to have coffee, and to my surprise she even suggested we walk, which we did, with the town car moving slowly alongside us, the way the Secret Service cars trail a president when he jogs. We found a place on Tenth Avenue calling itself a deli/café, with an overhead fan and the smell of overripe bananas, like something out of a third world country. We got two coffees at the counter and an ice water for Cat, then took them back to a small, round table. As soon as we sat down, Cat burst into tears.

"Oh, Cat," I said, squeezing her arm. "This must all be so awful for you." In the background a radio played salsa music, oblivious to her mood.

"Everything in my life is total shit," she said, sniffling. "Tyler's gone to stay at my mother's, Carlotta looks like she's ready to quit any second, I've got a billion pa-paparazzi around my house, and I'm going to lose my freakin' job if I'm not careful." She took a paper napkin from the table, balled it up, and dabbed at her eyes with it.

"What do you mean you're going to lose your job?" I asked.

"Newsstand sales stink. They've been moderately awful for months, and then this morning this guy from circulation, the one who loves to pull wings off flies, called me at eight-thirty and gleefully told me that April is going to be a huge bomb."

"A bomb? What constitutes a bomb?"

"Try nothing alive within five miles of the epicenter." She began to cry again. "Harry's already on my ass about that, but this murder stuff has him apoplectic. I thought he'd be sympathetic or at least like the press coverage. The guy lives for a mention in Liz Smith. But he thinks advertisers are going to run for the hills."

"I know it must be hard for you to be at work these days and try to concentrate, but the more you can do to demonstrate you're in full control, the better," I suggested, trying not to sound too nudgy.

"It *scares* me to be there. I feel so exposed."

"Are the police making any progress? I hear they talked to people at *Gloss* on Friday."

"Who the hell knows? And you know what Farley told me? Even when the tox reports come back, which apparently is going to be in the next century, we may still never know what killed her. There are lots of poisons they don't test for—including natural stuff. That's what makes me keep wondering about Tucker Bobb. Why are you so sure there's not a connection?"

"Well, there actually *may* be a connection—but not a direct one," I said.

"What do you mean?"

"Okay, let me explain," I said. "Like I mentioned yesterday, there's a chance Tucker died from eating poisonous mushrooms. But based on the timing of his illness, he would have had to consume them in Pennsylvania, not New York. That means if someone used the mushrooms to kill him, they fed them to him out in Pennsylvania. Of course, someone who was at your party could have visited him out there. But it seems awfully unlikely."

"So you're saying the two incidents *aren't* related."

"Yes and no."

"Bailey, you're going to have to move this explanation along before I go insane."

"Okay, sorry. Here's the connection. I think the person who tried to poison you knew about Tucker's situation and the mushroom theory and decided to make it *appear* that they were related."

"Why would they do that?"

"Probably to create confusion about the motive. If it appeared that someone was trying to kill more than one editor, it would suggest a person who had a gripe against women's magazines for some reason—or women's magazine editors. The police would concentrate on that angle and might ignore something of significance related to you personally."

"So the person who tried to kill me hated me and only me."

"Right. And so we have to focus. We know the person

was at the party. And it's not someone who feels a little hatred for you. It's a big hatred. Or a big need to see you out of the picture. Who could that person be?"

She rubbed the tips of her fingers on her forehead and rested her head into her hand. "Other than Dolores—and you've ruled her out—I can't think of anyone at *Gloss* who could feel that level of rage toward me."

"This isn't easy," I said, summoning my nerve, "but I've got to ask it. What about you and Jeff? Things seem off between the two of you."

Her head nearly snapped back. "*Jeff?* You can't be serious. You think *Jeff* tried to poison me?"

"Cat, lower your voice, okay? We have no idea what tabloid types are stalking you these days. Look, I know it's not pleasant, but you have to consider it. Someone at that party tried to kill you. Chances are it's not someone on the periphery of your life, but someone closer, someone close enough to be really upset about something to do with you. Does Jeff have any reason to be upset with you? Things seem a little funny with the two of you these days."

She took a long sip of water before speaking.

"We've had some ups and downs lately. But nothing that would make him want to kill me, for God's sake."

"What kinds of ups and downs?"

"I hate to even get into this."

"If I'm going to—"

"Okay, okay. Around the first of the year he started pressuring me to let him shoot fashion stories for *Gloss*. I said no. And he wasn't very happy about my answer."

"What made it such a bad idea—his working for *Gloss*?" I asked.

"Well, for starters, it would be incredibly awkward for the art department, being forced to give assignments to my spouse and trying not to step on anyone's toes. Second, he's not ready for *Gloss* yet. We're using people with far more fashion experience. But his request really had nothing to do with him wanting to make a contribution to *Gloss*. He wanted me to bail him out of a problem. He was going through a slump. That's okay, that sort of thing happens, but I think my helping him would only make matters *worse*. I'm not obsessed about the age gap between us, but it *is* something I think about, and I don't ever want to play the role of mommy with him."

"And he was pissed when you said no?"

"Yes. But then it blew over. He got a new agent, and just lately he started to get more work again. Things got back to normal." She glanced away for a second, making a quick scan of the diner. Could have been restlessness, but it read more as an attempt to avoid eye contact at that moment.

"Besides," she said, looking back at me, "if Jeff wanted me dead, he wouldn't mess around with a few little truffles. He'd snap my neck in two or hold my head underwater with one hand."

Yes, I thought, if he didn't care who knew. But what if he wanted to get away with it?

She began to make movements to go, scrunching her napkin into her coffee cup, checking her reflection in a hand mirror.

"I've got one more question," I said. "What's going on with Kip?"

She flushed, just as she'd done when I brought up his name several days ago.

"What do you mean?"

"Cat, if you want me to help," I said, leaning forward, almost whispering, "you've got to clue me in. You can't tell me some things and leave me in the dark about others. I'll never be able to find anything out if you send me down the wrong track."

She let out a long sigh before speaking, one that seemed half exasperation, half regret. "We rolled around on a sofa together one afternoon a few months ago. It never amounted to anything because it became clear in less than three minutes that we generated about as much heat together as two olives attempting to mate. Fortunately he went as floppy as a wet dishrag and I regained my senses. And don't tell me I was an idiot because I already know it."

"I'm not passing any judgment," I said, though I couldn't resist mentally doing so. Even though I'd considered that she might have had a dalliance with Kip, now that I had confirmation, I was shocked. "I'm just surprised. I never sensed any chemistry between the two of you."

"Well, there wasn't and isn't. It was just one of those things—I was alone and feeling needy, and I'd had about three glasses of Chardonnay, and he shows up, telling me I'm a goddess."

"Was this at your house?" I asked.

"Not in New York. Litchfield. Jeff and I were supposed to stay in town for the weekend because we were going to some gig he needed to be at on Saturday night. We had a huge fight Saturday morning—partly related to this whole idea of him shooting for *Gloss*—so I took off for Litchfield. I don't like being in the house alone, but

Heidi and that girlfriend of hers, Janice, were going to be driving up a little later. I'd told Heidi the week before she could have the house for the weekend. In the end, they didn't come—Heidi had a cold or something, and I was up there by myself. At around four Kip shows. I was flabbergasted. He said he'd found out I was there alone and had wanted to see me, and the next thing you know I've got my shirt bunched up around my neck."

"So you rolled around on the sofa. What happened next?"

"He got in his car and drove away. And about fifteen minutes later I drove back to the city."

"What I meant was, what happened with you and Kip?"

"Absolutely nothing," she said. "Well, that's not exactly true. For three days I'd start to dry heave every time I thought about it. But then I managed to just forget about it. Maybe this will surprise you—or maybe it won't—but I've never cheated on Jeff. Okay, I kissed an old boyfriend in L.A., but that's been it. I hated myself for that little episode in Litchfield. I even had the sofa recovered so I'd never have to be reminded of that day."

"Do you think Kip managed to put it behind him, too? He isn't secretly pining for you, is he—or furious you dumped him?"

"He acts as if it never happened. I have to admit that I was kind of surprised he could be so hot and bothered one minute and so cool the next, but who knows, maybe he's embarrassed over the flubby chubby. I wish I didn't have to work with him, but he does a good job and I certainly couldn't fire him *now*. If he's got anything on his mind, it's the fear that his shrew of a wife would catch him with his pants around his ankles."

"Speaking of spouses, is there any chance Jeff got wind of this?"

"No. Like I said, I drove back to New York, showed up at his gig, and we kissed and made up."

"When did all of this happen, by the way?"

"Back in March. Trust me, it's old news—and I'm sure it has nothing to do with what's happening to me now."

We wriggled out from the table and walked outside, where the town car was idling at the curb.

"Do you need a lift home?" Cat asked. "I'm heading downtown."

"No thanks. I'm going up to *Gloss*." I was tempted to tell her about my *Cape Fear* night in Bucks County, but this didn't seem like the time. "Are you going in today?" I added.

"Later," she said vaguely, sliding into the backseat.

I watched as the car pulled away soundlessly. It was a black Lincoln, shiny and sleek, except for a small ding in the back door.

Had she told me the truth? I wondered. About her and Kip, I thought yes, more or less. Maybe things hadn't stopped at the point she'd said they had—indecent groping—and maybe there'd been a *few* encounters, not just one, but I felt pretty sure that the relationship had been no more than a fling, was now kaput, and she felt nothing more than regret. To some degree, I was letting my personal bias affect my opinion. I couldn't imagine anyone wanting an affair with Kip. With a head that small and that smug face of his, it would be like going to bed with a Boston terrier.

What I didn't know was how *Kip* felt. Maybe he hadn't taken the finale as well as Cat thought. I needed to spend some time with him, calibrate his state of mind.

And then there were Cat's revelations about Jeff. There was definitely something she wasn't telling me. She had a right to be private about her marriage, but unless I knew the extent of any troubles they were having (and how pissed off Jeff was about them), it would be hard to determine how much of a suspect he truly was. I was going to have to figure out a way to get her to loosen up. I was also going to have to get her to talk about what kind of prenup arrangement they might or might not have. If Jeff had flipped for someone else and knew he would walk away from the marriage financially intact, there'd be no incentive to take Cat out of the picture. But if he would be forced to walk away almost empty-handed . . . well, that would be *very* significant.

It was time to hightail it to *Gloss*. Though I dreaded going into my office, I wanted to make contact with Kip. It was starting to sprinkle and I spent the next fifteen minutes with a newspaper over my head, looking for a cab.

By the time I arrived it was after noon and the entire art department was sitting around the pit conference table, eating Thai food from cartons. First stop: my office. I stepped into the room tentatively and flipped on the light. No candy, no leave-behinds of any kind, nothing out of place. I set my bags on the side chair and switched on my computer. After ordering a sandwich and cappuccino on the phone, I moseyed down to Kip's office. The lights were off and it was empty, though his assistant, a snippy brunette, was at her desk in the outer office, drinking a Diet Dr Pepper.

"Kip around?" I asked.

"No—and I'm not sure when he's coming. His cat got wedged behind the refrigerator and he's been trying to get it out." Her voice was dripping with sarcasm, as if she were reporting he'd called to say he was having lunch with Elvis.

On my way back to my office I popped into the ladies' room, and I spun around when I felt someone right on my heels. It was Leslie.

"Got a second?" she asked as I started to push open the door to a stall.

"Sure," I answered. "Do you mind if I pee first?"

"Just drop by my office, okay?"

I assumed she was looking for an update on when I'd be handing in the Marky piece, but when I stepped into her office five minutes later, I discovered she had something else on her mind.

"What's up with Cat?" she asked irritatedly, shoving the door closed. "Have you seen her?"

I took a quick second to ponder whether Cat would want me to spill the beans about our coffee klatch and decided I'd better not.

"Nope—I did talk to her on the phone yesterday. She was up in Litchfield this weekend."

"I *know* that. But she hasn't showed yet this morning—or called. She's got a huge stack of copy in her office."

"What does Audrey have to say?"

"That she's off on some, quote, appointment. Here," she said, clearing off a stack of magazines from the chair in front of her desk, "sit down." She walked around the desk and took a seat on the other side, in the power spot.

Whereas the majority of *Gloss* staffers had made little effort to dress up their work spaces, Leslie had gone to town on hers, decorating it with a small gray love seat, houseplants, several framed museum posters, and about fifteen shots of her and her husband, Clyde, in various vacation spots around the world—as though they'd somehow been chosen Cutest Couple in the Universe. These little touches, however, couldn't help make the room inviting. As everyone knew, if you were called into Leslie's office, there was a good chance you were due for a verbal spanking.

"Leslie, I'd love to chat," I said, perching on the edge of the chair, "but I'm a little pressed for time. I'm trying to wrap up the Marky piece."

"Well, I have some concerns that are bigger than that, concerns involving the entire staff. You can appreciate that, can't you, Bailey, even as a free agent?" Her nostrils flared and she sounded tightly wound. It brought to mind a recent *Gloss* cover line: "Bloated Belly? Bitchy Mood? PMS Solutions That Work Instantly."

"Sure, go ahead."

"I talked to Cat as well this weekend, and she told me you said that this—this thing—doesn't involve Tucker Bobb at all. That it's all a coincidence. That you went out to the Poconos or wherever he lives and talked to people."

"Yeah, Cat asked me to," I told her. Obviously Cat had been giving Leslie updates so there seemed no point in being coy. "From everything I can tell, they're just not related. I don't think someone is systematically trying to knock off magazine editors. I think they wanted to hurt Cat and Cat alone."

She looked at me, not saying a word.

"What exactly are your staff concerns?" I asked, attempting to hurry things along.

"People are starting to panic about everything that's happened. The police were here on Friday, and that terrified everyone. I don't blame Cat at all for not wanting to be here, but her absence makes this feel like a sinking ship."

"I'm sure she'll start coming in again. She's just trying to adjust to it all."

"You're going to continue to help her, aren't you?"

If Cat wanted to share my pursuits with Leslie, that was one thing, but I felt no obligation to give her any sense at all about what my plans were.

"If she wants me to, of course," I said. "But for now I'm going to focus on finishing my poltergeist story."

Again, that fruit bat stare of hers.

"Look," I told her, easing myself out of the chair for my escape, "I'll be working in my office for a while longer. If by any chance I hear from Cat, I'll let you know."

"All right," she said stingily, and I left her office curious about what her agenda had been. Was she genuinely worried about Cat and the magazine? Or was she more concerned that I was in on the action and she wasn't?

I needed to get to my Marky story, to call her parents and ask them to comment on Jack's theory that she was the poltergeist. But before I did, I went on the Internet and ran a search on poisons. There was an endless array and, as Cat had said, many natural ones that could be fatal. I discovered that curare beans, certain flowers like monkshood, and plants like hemlock all produce severe vomiting and diarrhea, as well as paralysis, confusion, and delirium. Death can occur rapidly, within as little as two hours.

Just reading the info brought back the sight of those sea foam green towels and Heidi, crusted in vomit, lying dead on the floor. I shook my head to make the image go away.

For the next two hours I worked on Marky, tinkering with the lead until I felt I had something really compelling. Every so often I'd saunter down toward Kip's office, but as the afternoon wore on, there was still no sign of him, and his assistant started looking at me the way a security guard stares at someone he's sure is about to shoplift.

Around four my brain began begging for caffeine, and I headed down to the coffee station. The sight of it nearly made my eyes bug out. Not only had Leslie, as promised, cleared away all the complimentary food for staffers— the microwave popcorn, the Snackwell cookies, and bags of chips—but the teabags and coffee were gone, too. The only thing left was a box of wooden stirrers.

If anything was going to fuel mass hysteria around *Gloss*, it was a scene like this—all that was missing was a sign that read "Killer on Premises." Of course, I couldn't really blame Leslie for the precaution.

And that brought me back again to what had bugged me about the whole situation—the haphazardness of it. Hadn't the killer been taking a terrible chance leaving the truffles on the hall table? Didn't he—or she—realize that there was no guarantee Cat would eat them? Or hadn't the killer really cared who ate them as long as *somebody* died? If I could only make sense of this, I felt, I would be closer to knowing who the killer was.

CHAPTER 16

AT FIVE O'CLOCK I did one last walkabout in the direction of Kip's office. His assistant, jeans jacket over her shoulders, was stuffing a few magazines into her backpack, preparing to flee.

"So what's the deal—is he coming in?" I asked.

"Guess not."

"Have you talked to him?"

"I called his house about an hour ago and no one answered. If he'd left for the city, he'd be here by now."

"Maybe he's at the animal hospital," I said. As I walked away, I could tell that nimble mind of hers was trying to figure out whether I'd said it sarcastically or not.

There was no point hanging around any longer, so I packed up my stuff. Though I hadn't planned to come into *Gloss* the next morning, I would have to now, because I needed face time with Kip. What was the significance, I wondered, in his vanishing act this afternoon?

Polly had said he'd gotten real quiet after the police had talked to him on Friday, and now he was missing in action. Did he have something to hide? Was he running scared?

When I emerged outside I saw that the skies had cleared, and it was now partly sunny and warmer. I took the subway home; it was refreshingly uncrowded, and after stepping off the elevator on my floor, I went directly to Landon's apartment and rang the bell.

"My poor darling!" he exclaimed as he flung open the door. He was wearing a white polo shirt and a pair of khaki cargo-style shorts, and he was about three shades tanner than when I'd seen him before the weekend. "How are you feeling? I'm just sick about what happened."

"I feel okay, really," I said, stepping inside. "Have you talked to the police?"

"Yes. They're clueless about who broke in. But they say they're going to keep an eye on the house, drive by every so often. I'm wondering if I should have an alarm put in. I was just about to fix a cup of tea, by the way— would you like one?"

"I'd love one, but unfortunately I've got to dash. I'm doing an interview in a little bit. But look, don't get all caught up in the idea of some two-thousand-dollar security system. I'm convinced it was someone trying to give me a scare."

"Do you really think it could be related to that poor girl's murder? Oh dear, I told you you shouldn't be getting involved."

"No, not Heidi's death. I know I said that yesterday, but now I have my doubts. I don't have time to go into it now, but I rattled someone's chains out there and I think she arranged for my chains to be rattled back. And my guess is that it was a one-time thing and you don't have to worry."

"Well, I still don't like the idea of you running all over town playing private *dick*. Something bad could happen."

I poo-pooed his concerns, but as I let myself into my apartment, I played his words over in my mind. Something bad *could* happen. The mystery Kiss had been a warning. But I couldn't turn back. I'd made a commitment to Cat. I wanted to know who'd killed Heidi. And I was angry that someone was trying to scare me off.

There were no messages on my machine, no hang-ups, either. I spent about half an hour getting a few bills cleared off my desk and throwing junk into drawers around my apartment. Before I knew it, it was time to dress for dinner. But *how?* I was feeling kind of weird about the evening. I couldn't deny that I found Jack Herlihy intriguing, and when he'd called I hadn't been able to resist saying yes to his invitation. But that was before my Sunday night carnal carnival with K.C. Since then I'd been feeling that I needed to see where things were going with *him*. Maybe he wasn't as skittish as I'd thought. My life was too freakin' complicated at the moment to get involved with more than one guy, and for now that guy was going to be K.C.

What I needed to do, I decided, was to signal to Jack that I saw this evening not as a date, but as part two of our interview. I decided to go with stretchy beige slacks, black flats, and a black cotton twin set. Attractive enough, but not sexy—the kind of ensemble Laura Petrie might wear around the house.

Earlier in the day I'd left him a voice mail suggesting

a Spanish restaurant on Thompson Street that served paella. The setting was very old-style Village—quaint, but a tad down at the heels. The kind of choice that couldn't possibly send the wrong message.

I'd told him I'd meet him at the restaurant at seven-thirty, and I sauntered over at around seven-fifteen. The sky was the color of dark blue denim. Washington Square Park was packed, and as I walked by I could feel the nutty energy people were experiencing now that spring was in full swing.

He wasn't at the restaurant when I arrived, but they seated me anyway, in the corner by the front window, under a cheap oil painting of a matador. I took out my notebook immediately and laid it on the table—a sign that I was here for business. I was just ordering a glass of Cabernet when he rushed in, running his hand through his sandy brown hair. He was wearing a navy blue sports jacket, more regulation style than the one he'd had on last week, a blue-and-white-striped oxford shirt, and tan slacks, the sort of preppie date look rarely sighted south of 14th Street. I felt that little kick in the tummy again.

"You haven't been here long, have you?" he asked, doing his best to arrange his long legs under the small table and offering that very nice smile of his.

"No, no, just got here," I replied.

"I kept going up and down the street looking for the place and finally realized I was one block over, on Sullivan. I'm determined to know the Village like the back of my hand before the summer's over." As he flicked open his napkin and laid it in his lap, I saw his eyes take in the notebook.

"How was your weekend?" I asked. "Did you go shopping for a pair of parachute pants on Eighth Street or some other fun Village activity?"

"I should have. I need something black at the very least so I don't look like such a tourist. But actually, I ended up going down to Bermuda for the weekend. I left Friday morning and got back about midday yesterday."

Hmmm. Wasn't Bermuda a real couplesy place? Was this his way of hinting that he had a girlfriend and our dinner tonight really *was* about work? Had I been such an egomaniac that I'd misinterpreted his invitation? I should have felt relieved, but I didn't. I felt irritated.

"Just for pleasure?" I asked, trying to sound casual. "Or did you get called down to consult about some rich kid suffering from a terrible problem, like a fear of sand and surf?"

He laughed. "You know, there actually *is* a phobia of waves. It's called kymophobia."

"Really?"

"There are hundreds of phobias—some totally bizarre. There's a fear of fog—homichlophobia. And a fear of puppets—pupaphobia. There's even a fear of the figure eight—octophobia."

"Did you have to memorize all the names in graduate school?"

"No." He laughed. "I did it one day when I was supposed to be doing something else—like studying for finals. You know what my favorite was? Lutraphobia—a fear of otters."

"Otters? I can't imagine that—they're so cute. Oysters, maybe. I've never been able to swallow them."

God, I couldn't believe I'd said that. It was basically like confessing that I gagged easily. He was probably sitting there thinking I also had a fear of performing oral sex.

"Well, maybe what you've really got is blennophobia—fear of slime," he said. "Anything else? Anything that makes you hyperventilate or keeps you up at night?"

Great, he'd known me for less than two hours total and he already could tell I was an insomniac.

"Not that I'd confess to you," I said, laughing. "I've revealed too much already."

The waiter lumbered over with my wine and Jack ordered a glass, too. When we were alone again I tried to get the attention off me, asking him why he'd decided to teach rather than focus mainly on patients. As he talked, I studied his face and that whole-is-greater-than-the-sum-of-the-parts quality to it. I wasn't the only one who appreciated it. Three women eating together at the next table had been gawking at him from the moment he walked in.

I asked a few questions about the special cases he handled, and I could tell by the way he was racing through the answers that he wanted to flip things and ask me about myself, but I didn't give him a chance.

"Look, speaking of troubled kids," I said, "I need to ask you a few more questions about Marky."

"Ahh, the merry little prankster." If he was irritated that I was steering things toward business, he didn't show it.

"What you told me was very helpful. And as I thought back on all the incidents—the ones I heard about and the ones I witnessed myself—I could imagine how she pulled them off. At least most of them. But there are a few things I'm confused about. I'm not sure how she could have done them."

The waiter interrupted us, asking for our order, and at my prompting, Jack went for the paella, too.

"Okay, like what?" he asked as we resumed conversation.

"Well, while I was standing in the room with her and her parents, a stuffed animal went hurtling through the air. And earlier in the day, two cups began to slide across the coffee table. Both times, Marky was standing on the other side of the room."

He turned in his chair so that he was almost perpendicular to the table, crossed his legs, and then picked up his wineglass, twirling it in his hand as he thought for a second.

"When you were a kid, did you ever learn any magic tricks?" he asked.

"I knew a few card tricks—and I could make a quarter disappear from my hand and come out of my ear."

"With the ear trick, you probably relied on what magicians use for practically every trick they do—misdirection. Right?"

"That's when you get the audience to look in the wrong place?"

"Basically, yes. The reason a magician is able to pull off his tricks is that intuitively our eyes want to go where the action is. The magician waves his left hand in the air a few times and we fixate on that, not noticing that his right hand is discreetly pulling off some feat."

"You're a magician in your spare time?"

He laughed. "I wanted to be one—at least at age

eleven. I was obsessed for about two years. I even had my little sister convinced I could make her disappear."

"And this has something to do with Marky?"

"Sort of, yeah. I bet Marky's relying on good old-fashioned misdirection to pull off her tricks. That's what went on with some of the cases *I* looked at. Take the stuffed animal. I assume you were talking to her parents at the time. Marky may not have purposely misdirected you—she just waited for it to happen naturally. And when everyone's attention was absorbed elsewhere, she hurled the toy across the room."

"Maybe," I said. I had flipped open my notebook and was jotting down the gist of what he said. "Yeah, that's a definite possibility. Are you saying she might have studied magic?"

"No, no. I'm sure it's just been something she's discovered through trial and error. There's another interesting thing about misdirection, by the way. It can work with time as well. Often there's a false beginning to a trick. That not only gives the magician more time to pull it off, but it also makes it harder for you to understand how he did it."

"Can you give me an example?"

He thought, pressing the tip of his thumb to his lips. He looked like a guy who had a slow hand in bed. Lots of time for you, lots of attention.

"All right. Let's say the magician does a trick where he changes a blue scarf to a red one. He wads the blue scarf up in his fist and then he places it in a magic box of some sort. He taps the box with his wand or maybe he waves his hand over it, and all the time the audience is looking intently, trying to see how he's doing the trick with the box. But he's already done it. He substituted a red scarf for the blue one before he ever put it in the box. The real trick often begins earlier than you realize. Maybe Marky set something up with the coffee mugs before anyone was in the room. I remember reading once that if you put plates in a small puddle of water, they eventually will float across a table. Could be something like that."

I kept jotting down notes after he was done talking because I hadn't been able to keep perfect pace, plus I added a few questions to myself, things to ruminate on later. What he said was nudging something in my brain, the way someone jostles your shoulder lightly when they're trying to rouse you from a nap on a train, but I wasn't sure what it was. I would have to pull out my Marky notes later at home and see if anything came to me.

The paella arrived and we dug in. He jumped on the chance to ask questions about me, about where I was from, and what brought me to New York, and how I ended up writing the kinds of stories I did. At first I gave brief, superficial answers, trying to keep an interview feeling to the evening. But I gave up eventually because the wine was making me slightly giddy and he was doing such a good job of listening. In describing one point in my career, I mentioned that I'd been married and divorced, which is a wet blanket for a certain percentage of guys, but he seemed unperturbed. Then, to confuse matters even more, a mariachi band emerged from the back of the restaurant and began serenading everyone in the place. They lingered by our table for an entire song. Though I couldn't tell the meaning of the song, they sang the word *amor* around seventy-five times. I felt my cheeks getting hot, and I prayed the place was too dim for Jack to notice.

The waiter asked if we'd like coffee. I said yes, not wanting to be rude. But I felt I needed to clear out of there before things got complicated. I gulped down my coffee and announced, after a shocked look at my watch, that it was time to get home and tackle a bit of work before bed. I offered to contribute to the bill, but he insisted on picking up the entire thing.

"Let me walk you back to your place," he said after we'd left the restaurant and had sauntered down to the corner of Thompson and Washington Square South.

"No, no. That's not necessary," I protested. "It's totally out of your way. I need to make a quick stop at the deli anyway. But thank you. I so appreciate your giving me all this help." I was turning him down, boxing him out. But I didn't feel I had a choice.

He looked at me slightly perplexed, eyes squinted a little, as if he were trying to decide what was going on with me—was I being coy, or was I just plain blowing him off? But it quickly morphed into benign resignation, an expression that said, "So you really *are* giving me the brush-off—well, I'm too polite to act miffed." He reached out to shake my hand.

"Well, thanks for introducing me to more of the Village. The restaurant was great."

Then, as if I were speaking in Pentecostal tongues, I opened my mouth and something flew out that caught me totally by surprise.

"Maybe, if you're around this weekend, I can give you a tour," I announced, chirpy as a bluebird.

"Sure," he said, only half believing me. "Let's talk later in the week."

He turned and headed east on Washington Square South, the back of his jacket flapping up the way it had the other day. Had I lost my brain? What was I doing letting a man like that get away? It seemed that since my divorce my ability to interpret what my heart and libido were really telling me had shriveled up. I felt a brief urge to run after him, grab the tails of that jacket, and suggest a nightcap. But I thought better of it and crossed over to the park.

The night was almost balmy, and though it would have been nice just to stroll, I hightailed it back to my place, stopping for two minutes on University Place to grab a take-out cappuccino. I had the strangest feeling all of a sudden. Partly I was exasperated at myself over being such a moron at love. But mostly it was the sensation I'd had in the restaurant of having my brain jostled. It was as if I'd forgotten something that was now slowly surfacing to consciousness. I was beginning to sense, though, that the feeling had to do with Cat, not Marky. I wanted to get back to my apartment and read through my notes.

No messages waiting on my machine, just two hang-ups, numbers blocked. What was the actual point of them? I wondered. Though the hang-ups were unsettling, they had not gone beyond that—no heavy breathing or threatening words, for instance. Maybe it was less about scaring me than keeping tabs on my whereabouts.

I picked up my notebook from my office and took that and my cappuccino out on the terrace. There was just one light out there, a lantern-style fixture on the wall, but it was enough to read by.

I started at the first page, which I'd titled "Death of a Nanny." Funny I'd chosen that, even when I knew Cat was supposed to be the victim. I went through page after page, but nothing jumped out. The disquietude I felt was growing, like something becoming waterlogged and heavier by the minute. As I thought back over the evening, I realized that I had started to feel the nudging when Jack and I had talked about misdirection. Was it simply because the case appeared to be a study in misdirection? The killer, by using poison, had tried to misdirect everyone into thinking that there was a plot against women's magazine editors when it was only Cat who really mattered.

I closed my notebook and leaned back in the wrought-iron patio chair. The air was crystal clear, and my view tonight had a wonderful fake quality to it, like the painted backdrop for a Broadway show—inky blue black sky; a few faint stars, nothing more than pinpricks; buildings whose lit windows seemed too perfectly random. At eleven I locked up and stuck a tape of *Witness* into the VCR in my bedroom, hoping that because I'd seen it a dozen times, I would fall asleep from sheer boredom. And I did—before Harrison Ford even drove into Lancaster.

Just after three A.M., though, I woke up, my heart racing. It seemed as if a noise had startled me awake, something perhaps from the living room. I got up, turned off the TV, which at this point was offering nothing but a bright blue screen, and made a quick check around the living room, including the door to the terrace. Nothing. As I crawled back into bed, I realized I'd had a dream, a nightmare, really, about Heidi. In the dream I'd walked into her apartment and this time she was alive, standing in the middle of the room with one of the sea foam green towels draped around her neck as if she were planning to head for the beach. I'd started to speak to her, but before I could even say a word she shook her head in annoyance. And that was all I could remember.

I pushed myself up with an elbow and leaned, half sitting, half lying, against the backboard of the bed. I stayed there for a few minutes in the darkness, watching my clock radio jump from 3:16 to 3:17 to 3:18. And suddenly it came to me, along with a rush of fear. I knew what had been bugging me earlier in the evening. And I knew why I'd dreamed of Heidi.

CHAPTER 17

I$_T$ WAS EIGHT-THIRTY A.M. on Tuesday when I finally dragged my butt out of bed. After my nightmare about Heidi, after my middle-of-the-night epiphany, all attempts to get back to sleep had proved futile. I'd tossed around in bed for a while, just to remind myself how damn good I was at it, watched the part of *Witness* I'd missed earlier, and read through almost the entire May issue of *Gloss,* including an item on whether it's safe to tweeze hairs around the nipple (yes!). I'd wanted to fly out of bed early and start checking out the theory that had wiggled its way into my consciousness last night, but when I finally began to feel sleepy around dawn, I shut off my alarm, deciding it was best to grab whatever z's I could. I needed to be at the top of my game.

It was warm out, though slightly overcast again. Since I'd be racing around, I threw on khaki pants, a black T-shirt, and a pair of Merrells. As soon as I'd defrosted a bagel from a package of frozen ones, toasted it, and wolfed it down with coffee, I called Cat's house to tell her I wanted to come up there and go through Heidi's things again. There was something specific I was looking for, and if I found it, everything would change. Carlotta informed me, much to my surprise, that Cat had gone to the office. Maybe she'd finally decided to take the bull by the horns and begin running the magazine again—before it was rudely snatched away from her. I phoned her office at *Gloss,* only to be told by Audrey that Cat was in a meeting. I didn't feel comfortable showing up at the town house without first obtaining Cat's permission, so it looked as though I'd have to hook up with her at *Gloss.* I was planning to go there anyway in order to connect with Kip.

There was a delay of some kind on the R line, and by the time I finally stepped off the elevator at *Gloss* it was almost ten-thirty and things were in full swing. The big surprise: When I rounded the corner from the lobby into the pit, Cat was sitting at the black conference table, holding a meeting of about seven or eight editors, all from the articles department. With her back to me, she didn't notice my presence, but several editors, including Polly, glanced discreetly in my direction.

Cat despised big meetings and therefore rarely held them. She had regular planning meetings with the most senior players—they were a necessary evil—but bigger ones she called only when she was on a tear about something, like she suddenly hated the magazine and wanted to take it in a whole new direction. As a freelancer I was exempt from these meetings and eternally grateful for that: They not only went on forever, but jump-started the jackal in everyone—those who had the weakest ideas or quivered when they spoke were often reduced to a bloody pulp. And if Cat didn't like the direction things were moving in, she was bound to get bitchy. Once, when someone had attempted to stifle a yawn an hour and a half into the meeting, she had asked in mock concern, "Are you *okay?*"

Cat was doing the talking right now—though I caught only the phrase *put the reader in a stupor.* People appeared simultaneously nervous and bored, the kind of look you'd expect if someone were on hold with the Herpes Hot Line. Noting that Kip wasn't among the revelers, I hurried along to my office.

As I was settling down at my desk, something struck me. The red mug that held my pens and sat just to the left of my computer had shifted position to the middle of my desk. Maybe I'd pushed it over and didn't remember. Maybe the cleaning person had moved it. Or hey, maybe Marky had stopped by when I wasn't here. I swung my eyes around the rest of the desk, and then the rest of the room, looking for anything else amiss. Nothing. Next I pulled open the center desk drawer. A take-out menu for Just Soup, which had been lying on top of the mess the last time I looked, was now scrunched off to the side. Someone had been in my office on a reconnaissance mission.

From the hallway I could hear Sasha's voice, and stepping outside, I found her, dressed in a red mini and black tank top, in a tense conversation with the model editor.

"I don't want to use Nadia," Sasha was saying. "This is ten pages. We need a girl who's . . . a girl who's more major."

"I put a hold on Nadia, though," whined the model editor. "What do I tell the agency?"

"I don't know," Sasha said, shrugging. "Say we needed a blonde because of the location and the way Keith wants to shoot it and dit dit dit. Okay?"

The model editor, named something that sounded like toboggan, went off in a snit and Sasha glanced over to me.

"How was Palm Springs?" I asked.

"Okay. But then I come back and everything here is insane."

"Yeah, I know. Look, did you see anyone in my office this morning? Maybe someone waiting for me?"

"No. Well, the door was closed this morning when I got here. I thought you were in there working."

"Yeah, okay, thanks." The door had been open when I arrived.

I went back into my office and looked around again. There were no warning messages this time, like the chocolate Kiss. It appeared as if someone had been snooping around, searching perhaps for files and notes in order to see if I'd left behind any information I'd collected. It felt creepy just to be sitting there.

I picked up my phone, punched Cat's extension, and asked Audrey to give me a time frame for the meeting. This one had just started, she said, and she expected it to go on for at least an hour.

Change in game plan. I needed to go through Heidi's apartment—and it now looked as if I were going to have to do it without official clearance from Cat. I couldn't wait one more minute. Besides, Cat had given me permission to turn over every stone, and Carlotta would be there to supervise.

As for Kip, a talk with him could wait. And if my theory was right, it wouldn't even be necessary.

I took a cab to save time, but when I got to the town house, no one answered the bell. I waited for fifteen minutes near the corner, in view of the house, sitting on a brick ledge that bordered a church and trying to control the ants in my pants. Just when I was wondering if I would have to bag it, Carlotta came down the sidewalk across the street, lugging two shopping bags. Cat didn't make her wear a uniform, but she was dressed nicely, in a long, full navy skirt and white shirt. I lowered my head so she wouldn't see me and gave her a few minutes to unlock the door and get settled before I headed back toward the house.

"Hi, Carlotta," I said a little too perkily as she let me in, having first checked on the intercom who it was. "I'm back. I've got to finish going through Heidi's room."

"Okay," she said, obviously not finding anything suspicious about my request. "I'm in the library, doing the vacuum."

As I trailed her through the living room and down the staircase, I noticed that all the windows were closed. They'd battened down the hatches here on East 91st Street, relying on central air rather than spring breezes to keep them cool.

When we reached the library, Carlotta leaned over to pick up the hose of a small red Electrolux squatting in the center of the room. She was obviously going to leave me to my own devices. I spoke before she had a chance to switch on the machine.

"Carlotta, Cat told me you cleaned Heidi's room every week. Can I ask you a question about that?"

She straightened up and turned back to me, the vacuum hose drooping in her hand. "The policeman, he ask me, did I see drugs over there," she said quickly. "I tell him no, never."

"No, no, not that," I said. "I was wondering what day of the week you worked on her room."

"On Friday. That room I do every Friday."

"Okay, great. By any chance, on the Friday before Heidi died, did you see any kind of shopping bag in her room? Maybe in the trash basket. Someone may have dropped something off for her in it."

She indicated no with a shake of her head.

"It could even have been a *plastic* shopping bag. Or maybe a large envelope."

She looked at me quizzically, without saying a word. Then she turned and walked over to the bookcase, opening one of the cabinets that ran along the bottom. I thought she was returning to her housework, having said all she was going to say, but she lifted a large tan envelope from one of the shelves inside the cabinet, turned, and handed it to me. It was one of those padded Jiffy bags.

"This, this was in Heidi's trash?" I asked, stunned. I had come looking for this, convinced it was a possibility, but now that I was holding it in my hands, I could barely believe it.

"Yes, I save it to use again."

"Do the police know about this?"

She looked all nervous suddenly. "No. They don't ask me about Friday."

"That's okay," I said reassuringly. "You didn't do anything wrong."

I had accepted the Jiffy bag, but I knew it wasn't smart to be getting my fingerprints on it. I set it down on the antique walnut desk behind me. After tugging two tissues from a faux tortoiseshell holder on top of the desk, I picked it up again with the tissues as a barrier to my fingertips.

Though there was nothing written on either side, it obviously had been used to hold or deliver something and then opened, because there was a row of pulled staples at the long end. Whoever had opened it, Heidi most likely, had ignored the little zip tab along the side you're supposed to pull. By pressing with my hands on each side, I puckered the end open and glanced inside. Nothing. Next I turned it upside down over the desk and tapped the side a couple of times. There was a sound as something hit the desk, the sound of something as small as a pebble. I shifted the Jiffy bag to the left. Lying on the desk was a small white petal from a silk flower—broken off, I was almost sure, from the arrangement that had been on the gold Godiva box. The sight of it almost took my breath away.

"Okay, thanks, Carlotta," I said as casually as I could, as I used a tissue to scoot the petal back inside the Jiffy bag.

I tried to recall Cat's words. "It was pale pink, I think," she'd said. But white could have appeared pale pink in the dim hallway.

"Let's put this envelope back in the cabinet," I told Carlotta. "There's a chance the police might want to see it, so don't pick it up again, okay? Don't tell anyone about it. I'll tell Cat that it's here."

She watched expressionless as I opened the cabinet myself and laid the envelope back in the spot where she'd retrieved it.

I had gotten what I'd come for, but as long as I was here, it made sense to make another inspection of Heidi's room. Something might strike me differently now that I had a new perspective.

"Carlotta, I'll let you get back to work," I explained. "I'm just going to look in Heidi's room for a minute, okay? Cat wants me to help her," I added, protesting too much.

I opened the bookcase door to the nanny apartment, and as I flipped on the light switch in the hall, the vacuum roared to life obnoxiously behind me. I closed the door most of the way to lessen the intrusion of the noise. The first thing I noticed was that the smell from hell had finally been vanquished. The second was that someone, Carlotta most likely, had been busy down here. About ten new cardboard boxes stood around the room, four by the dresser and two by the bookcase already loaded with Heidi's possessions and the rest sitting empty and expectant, flaps up, in the middle of the room.

I glanced into each of the packed boxes of clothes. It was all the stuff I'd seen earlier in the dresser and wardrobe, folded carefully as if it would soon be worn again, like clothes going off to camp or college. On the top of the box were two Ziploc freezer bags filled with Heidi's costume jewelry, but the Tiffany bracelet and earrings were nowhere in sight. Most likely Cat had come down and retrieved them after I'd told her about them. I'd want to double-check that.

The two boxes by the bookcase were packed with Heidi's meager collection of books, CDs, and tchotchkes, and I poked through them both. There was nothing I hadn't seen before. From behind the door to the library I heard the vacuum cleaner go dead.

The only objects from the bookcase that hadn't been packed yet were the two photographs of Heidi, which lay on several sheets of newspaper, waiting to be wrapped. I picked up the Circle Line souvenir photo and stared at it. The other girl in the picture was *Janice,* I realized suddenly, though a Janice at least fifteen pounds thinner than she was today and with chestnut-colored hair, not blond. And I realized something else with a start: Heidi was wearing a long turquoise raincoat, something I hadn't remembered from looking at the photo before. It could easily have been the same raincoat that I'd seen hanging in Jeff's studio.

I walked over to the small writing table between the windows. Nothing had been packed yet from this area. Beneath the table I spotted the trash basket where Carlotta had obviously found the Jiffy bag. Taking a seat at the table, I tried to imagine exactly how everything had unfolded. I knew the truth now—I just didn't know the details.

"What are you doing here?"

I jumped so high and so fast that I almost bit off my tongue. Scraping the chair across the floor, I turned awkwardly toward the voice at the far end of the room. For a split second I almost didn't recognize him. But then I saw that it was Jeff, his long hair sopping wet and slicked back from a shower. He was bare chested and barefoot, wearing just a pair of unbelted jeans, a relaxed, "down on the farm" style. But the expression on his face said he was anything but relaxed. In fact, he looked really, really ticked.

"Oh, hi," I said in a squeaky voice that sounded like something coming from a mouse who's just figured out it's made full-body contact with a glue trap. "I didn't realize you were home." He must have been in the shower when I'd buzzed earlier and hadn't heard me.

"What are you doing here?"

"Well, as you know, I've been helping Cat with everything that's going on." I was doing the world's most pathetic job of stalling, trying to light on a good enough lie to tell.

"How did you get in?"

"Carlotta. She let me in."

"What does Heidi's room have to do with helping Cat?"

"Nothing directly," I said, getting up slowly, my heart still racing. "I've just been trying to put it all together in my mind. The candy. Cat. Heidi's death. I thought maybe if I just sat here and thought back on finding the body, it would spark an idea."

"And did it—spark an idea?" Said sarcastically, not with any real curiosity.

"Maybe. But why don't I just get out of here. Cat asked me to help, but I certainly don't want to cause any problems."

"Look, Bailey," he said in a softer tone, taking a couple of steps toward me, "I don't mean to be a hard-ass. But Cat never said anything about you coming by today.

A girl died in this room a week ago, and the next thing you know I hear someone prowling around down here. All I could think of was that one of those lousy paparazzi had broken in."

"Understood. Like I said, I didn't realize you were home or I would have asked Carlotta to let you know I was here. Can I get out from down here? So I don't have to traipse through the house?"

"Yeah," he said, thinking for a second. "If the extra key to the gate is still around. Let's see." He was charming Jeff now, a southern boy with good manners. I followed his tanned back to the small foyer off the room, where he found the light switch with his hand without having to look. It was a small, windowless space, with a hall mirror, a small table, and an empty coat tree, a space I hadn't gotten a chance to inspect before.

"Here we go," he said, pulling a key from a hook by the door. He flipped open the lock to the door and we stepped into the small vestibule under the stoop of the house, enclosed by the wrought-iron gate. He used the key to open the gate and then swung it open.

"Going back to the office?" he asked with a smile.

"Yeah, probably."

Before I could take a step outside, he laid one hand on my shoulder and leaned over and kissed me on the cheek.

"No hard feelings, okay?" he asked. He was so close that I could feel the dampness of his chest hair.

"Of course not," I said, stepping quickly out into the courtyard. "Take care." It was a goofy-sounding farewell in light of the circumstances, but it was the best I could come up with, considering how rattled I felt.

I quickly walked the half block to Madison Avenue

and wandered a block or two until I found a patisserie. It was right out of France, with Provence-style tablecloths covering tiny wrought-iron tables and a big glass case of pastries. The clientele were mainly rich stay-at-home mothers, some with toddlers, some solo and just back from a run in their spandex jogging shorts. I snagged the one empty table in the rear and ordered a double cappuccino and a croissant.

I felt completely perturbed, but not just from my contretemps with not-so-nice, half-naked Jeff. It was from now knowing what had *really* happened the night of Cat's party: Someone had brought those toxic truffles to kill *Heidi,* not Cat. Last night this had been only a half-formed thought that slithered through my dream, then roused me from sleep. But the Jiffy bag and the flower petal clarified everything.

Sipping my cappuccino, I thought about how my conversation with Jack Herlihy had teased my thought process in this direction. The idea that things weren't always what they seemed. That the magician sometimes pulled off his trick in a different spot from where you were looking or at a different time.

Well, there'd been misdirection at Cat's house, too. The truffles, which had appeared to be for Cat, had been intended for Heidi all along. Someone had left them on the hall table to make it appear as if they were a hostess gift, then taken them away and delivered them to Heidi in the Jiffy bag. Or, maybe, I thought suddenly, Heidi had been given her own set of truffles (poison ones) in the Jiffy bag and those on the hall table were a perfectly harmless decoy set, placed there to flub up everyone's thinking. What had bugged me all along was the idea that the killer, by leaving the candy unattended on the hallway table, had taken such a big chance. What if the box had been opened and the candy eaten by someone other than the intended victim? But now I was certain that the box of truffles on the hall table couldn't have killed anyone.

I tried to imagine how it might have been done. The killer arrives at Cat's house the night of the party with the box of candy and slides it out of a briefcase or tote bag onto the hall table when no one is looking. It sits there long enough for people to notice it, for Cat to notice. Before things begin to wind down, when no one is looking, it gets slipped back into a bag. Later, the box of poisoned truffles, tucked inside the Jiffy bag, is dropped off at Heidi's. Slipped between the bars of the gate, perhaps? Why not? It could be done easily, without a trace. No one but Heidi would see them. There wouldn't have been a note because the note would be proof to the police that they weren't the same truffles as the ones in the hall. Heidi would simply assume they were a surprise, a mystery gift from an admirer. Heidi had apparently opened the package Friday but may have waited to eat the candy when she felt the full force of a craving.

The only possible hitch to the plan? If the decoy candy was opened at the party or put away before the killer was able to take it back. But that wouldn't have been the end of the world. There would have been no exposure. The only downside would be that the murderer would be forced to come up with a plan B.

But why have such an elaborate plan to begin with? Why not just leave the candy for Heidi? Well, clearly to throw everyone off. If it was obvious that Heidi was the intended victim all along, that would put Heidi's life under a spotlight. And with that spotlight shining, it would be hard for the killer to slip into the shadows.

At this moment, I had absolutely no idea who the killer might be. There were three things, however, I was sure of: Heidi's killer 1) had been in Cat's house the night of the party; 2) knew Cat loved chocolate; and 3) knew Heidi had a proclivity for pilfering food.

I gulped down the last of my cappuccino, paid the bill, and squeezed out past the tables of women on their second or third lattes. Out on the sidewalk I dug out the slip of paper with Janice's number and tried her on my cell phone. Though Janice had claimed to be in the dark about the intricacies of Heidi's social life, there was always the chance she hadn't been telling me all she knew—or she knew more than she realized—and I wanted another chat with her. The family's answering machine picked up. I had her cell number, too, so I tried that. She answered from what sounded like a wind tunnel.

"Janice, hi, this is Bailey Weggins."

"Who?"

"Bailey, Cat Jones's friend. We talked at the apartment last week."

"Oh, yeah." She sounded less than thrilled to hear from me.

"Look, I've got your earrings. Remember you asked me to find them. Can I bring them over?"

That pumped her up. "You're kidding. You found them? The thing is, I'm not home right now. I'm in the park with George."

"No problem. I'm uptown, just a block from the park, so tell me where you are and I can just meet you."

She explained that it wasn't Central Park, but Carl

Schurz, a park that ran along the East River in the 80s. I could find her in the playground, she said, but George was already whiny so I'd better hurry. I told her to hold tight, that I'd be there in ten minutes.

As I headed east in a cab, I flashed back on Cat's party for Dolores, trying to see it from a new angle. Someone on the premises that night had come to kill Heidi. Jody, of course, was a prime suspect. He hadn't been invited, but he'd popped in to "say hi."

Other possibilities? It was a book party, with guests who on the surface were totally unconnected to Heidi. Yet there could be a connection somewhere. And if so, there was a good chance it was a connection based on those old standbys—love and lust. A connection that had been intense, perhaps secretive, and then had unraveled. As Jack Herlihy had said, murder is motivated by big emotions. It wasn't hard to imagine a few that could have been churned up by a girl who looked like Heidi: jealousy, perhaps, or rage over having been rejected or betrayed.

Jeff came quickly into my line of sight. It was now clear from looking at the Circle Line photo that Heidi may have been a visitor at Jeff's studio. Maybe she'd simply been dropping off something or stopping by with Tyler, but there was also a chance that Jeff had been knocking boots with Heidi behind Cat's back. A year ago it would have been hard to imagine, but if his assignments had evaporated and he was feeling frustrated, and disenfranchised, a randy romp with a twenty-two-year-old who probably perceived him as Fashion Photo God would do a lot to make his ego swell again. But, of course, if Cat found out, all hell would break loose. Yesterday I'd considered whether Jeff, in the throes of an affair, had tried to murder Cat so he could escape the marriage without losing any of the perks. But maybe he didn't want out of his life with Cat. He could have killed Heidi so that Cat would never learn the truth. This morning I'd gotten just a taste of how angry he could get.

But I also couldn't lose sight of the mystery man, the one who had introduced Heidi to jazz and diamond-studded jewelry but apparently preferred to fly below the radar. I didn't think he and Jeff were one and the same. Maybe he'd been at the party. Maybe he had a reason to want Heidi dead.

Another thought to consider: the writer Nancy Highland. According to Dolores, Heidi had apparently pulverized her son's heart and then skipped town. Had his mother decided to exact revenge on his behalf? Was he there himself? No, he couldn't have been. His name wasn't on the guest list and I didn't recall seeing a guy that young.

It took more than fifteen minutes to get to Carl Schurz, a park that abuts the East River. I dashed in through the entrance at the south end, past the hot dog cart, taking one wrong turn before I remembered where the playground was. I was nearly out of breath by the time I found Janice listlessly pushing George in one of those baby swings that's basically a leather bucket with holes for the legs. She had her cut-offs on today and a too tight Planet Hollywood T-shirt.

"I can't stay much longer," she announced as she spotted me. "He's, like, ready to blow."

"Mainly, I just wanted to give you these," I said, fishing the earrings out of my purse and handing them to her.

"I appreciate that, I really do," she said. She stopped

pushing George and spread open the tissue I'd wrapped the earrings in. Her nose wrinkled as she saw that the fake pearl was missing.

"They were like that when I found them in her drawer," I told her before she could say anything. "The pearl must have fallen off while Heidi was wearing them. Maybe that's why she hadn't returned them. She was nervous about telling you."

"That's so typical," she said, shaking her head. "I hate to speak evil of the dead or whatever that expression is, but Heidi could be so freakin' selfish sometimes. These cost me like forty bucks." Janice no longer appeared to be deeply entrenched in a state of mourning.

"Look," I said, pulling my wallet out of my purse and extracting two twenties, "I know Cat would want you to have this."

"Wow," she said, taking the money without the slightest hesitation and stuffing it along with the earrings into the pocket of her cut-offs. From the other pocket she wiggled out a nearly crushed pack of Marlboro Lights and a butane lighter and fired up. As she exhaled a long stream of smoke, George let out something between a grunt and a whine because the swing was wobbling to a stop.

"*Okay, okay,*" Janice said irritably, and began pushing him with one hand.

"Have you heard about what's going on?" I asked.

"Sort of. Jody told me that the papers said there was something wrong with some candy Heidi ate, and that now it looks like it was supposed to be for Mrs. Jones. But he doesn't know more than that. The whole thing is major nasty."

"Jody? You talked to Jody?"

"Well, I went by Starbucks. He's really an okay guy, you know. And I think Heidi made up some of that stuff about him lying to her. It's like she was afraid I wouldn't respect her for dumping him, so she made him look bad."

"And you definitely don't have any idea who she was dumping him for?"

"No," she said, taking a drag from her cigarette. "But there must have been *someone*. The way she didn't have any time for me anymore. Besides, that's just Heidi. She would never be without a guy."

"Could it have been someone who had anything to do with *Gloss*?" I was thinking of the party, of course.

She wrinkled her nose. "Well, I don't think she liked going there. A few months ago she had to take something there for Mrs. Jones and she made me go with her so I could bring it upstairs. She just didn't want to go near that office."

"But she never said why?"

"No."

"Did she ever tell you anything about a guy she was involved with when she worked in Westchester?"

"Oh yeah, Mr. Westchester. There was some dude up there who was loco over her. But I didn't get any of the details—just that she once said she would have gotten in trouble if anyone found out."

"Do you know if she still had any contact with him?"

"Don't think so. She never really liked him all that much. It was just for the challenge, the thrill. Like I said—Heidi always had to have a guy. She wasn't happy if all the guys weren't in a lather about her."

George let out a howl and we turned to see him flailing in his swing. No amount of pushing was going to ameliorate the situation.

"I'll let you get back to your job," I said.

"Yeah, thanks," she said sarcastically. She crushed out her cigarette with the tip of her black mule and lifted the wailing, writhing George from the swing and into his stroller. "Why all this interest in Heidi?" she said as she fought to fasten the seat belt around George, who in protest was arching his back like a bow. "I mean, I thought someone was trying to kill Mrs. Jones."

"I'm just trying to get a sense of Heidi's life. One more question, okay? When did Heidi stop wanting to spend as much time with you?"

She thought for a second.

"'Round January or February, I think," she said. "Yeah, that's right. I remember 'cause my birthday is on February fourth and she didn't even go out with me that night."

"But according to Cat, Heidi invited you up to their house in Litchfield for a whole weekend in March, right?"

Janice stared at me, uncomprehending. "No, she didn't invite me to Litchfield for a weekend," she said finally. "She didn't invite me anywhere for a weekend. Look, I gotta go."

She took off with the stroller, half running. And I just stood there, my mind racing.

CHAPTER 18

I THOUGHT AN ice-cream bar, something chocolate coated, would get my brain working at maximum capacity. I bought one at the entrance of the park and headed over to the river promenade. I started walking north, along the length of it. There were very few people around, just a few speed walkers in Lycra and people with dogs—pugs, dachshunds, corgis. It was so quiet, you could hear the sound of the river being pulled toward the harbor. A tiny red tugboat suddenly appeared from the north, silently leading a black nameless barge down the river. As I walked I considered the significance of Heidi's lie.

She had told Cat that she wanted to take her friend Janice to the house in Litchfield for the weekend, but according to Janice she hadn't been invited. I would bet money on the fact that her intended houseguest had actually been a guy. That's why she had canceled when Cat told her she'd be coming up, too. Jeff was totally off the hook on this one. He was tied up with an event in the city that weekend and Jody had been dumped by that time. More than likely, it was the mystery man.

Who could it be? There might be a clue in the fact that Heidi had wanted to shack up in Litchfield that weekend. Of course, she simply may have wanted to show off the place and play princess for two days. But it *could* mean that on a weekend that Cat planned to be in the city, Heidi felt uncomfortable having this particular guy coming in and out of the nanny apartment. And for some reason they couldn't use *his* place. I was back to where I was a week ago: Everything about this guy spelled married. Heidi must have been pissed about having to cancel her tryst at the last minute, about having to call the guy, and—

But what if Heidi couldn't call his house because his wife was there, or maybe she tried but his wife picked up the phone, or maybe she knew he'd already left by the time Cat so rudely wrecked her plans. Omigod. *That* was why Kip had shown up in Litchfield. Not to bed Cat, whom he'd never shown one ounce of interest in, but *Heidi*.

I know this sounds mean, but I started to laugh. In fact, it made me want to howl, just picturing Kip discovering Cat on the other side of the door and, in a desperate attempt to save his ass from the shredder, confessing that he had a yearning in his loins for her. And better yet was Cat buying it, so blinded by her belief in herself as the hottest girl in any room that she never considered another possibility. No wonder he'd had an iffy stiffy. He'd come within a hair, so to speak, of being exposed as the shagger of the family nanny and had been forced to complicate things further by taking his boss to bed. Ugly as hell, but hilarious.

Yet I was the only one who would find it funny. Kip must have been crazy with worry since then that he'd be found out, that Cat might learn about his affair with Heidi and thus realize the true reason he'd taken his lust on the road to Litchfield. If Cat discovered the truth, there'd be no limit to her rage. As we knew, if there was one thing she hated—more than untantalizing story titles, more than people who spoke in squeaky voices at meetings, more than wimpy men—it was being humiliated. Though she couldn't fire Kip for personal reasons, she'd find a way to do it, that's for sure, and she might even make certain that his wife learned the sorry details of his adulterous spree with Heidi. There would be a big price to pay. Maybe Kip had taken precautions to make sure that his relationship with Heidi would never be exposed. He'd had that weird scowl on his face the morning after Heidi's death. He'd used that pathetically lame puddycat excuse to avoid coming to work. It didn't smell good.

And how ironic. This morning, as I'd seen everything about the case shifting, I'd decided Kip was irrelevant, but now he was smack on the suspect list again. Was *he* the vodka-drinking jazz lover who had bought the Tiffany jewelry? I had to find a way to talk to him. He hadn't been at the meeting today and that meant he wasn't on the premises. I used my cell phone to call his delightful assistant and suss out what was going on. She sounded thrilled to hear from me again (God, I hope she didn't think *I* was having an affair with him) and explained curtly that Kip had a personal matter to handle, and though he was coming in, it wouldn't be till later in the day. This time there wasn't any mention of the kitty.

Before she had a chance to hang up on me, I asked to be transferred to Cat. I needed to do whatever damage control I could before she spoke to Jeff about my unauthorized visit to the town house. I also wanted to take her up to speed on where my thinking was now. What I wasn't going to do was reveal to her that she'd taken part in a comedy of sexual errors at her country house. The truth would be utterly embarrassing. Beyond that, she might go flying off the handle at Kip before I had a chance to talk to him.

Audrey put me through to her right away.

"That looked like a pretty big meeting you were having," I said. "Productive?"

"There wasn't any real point to it. I was taking your advice. Trying to show I'm still in control. Where are you, anyway? The connection is bad."

"I'm up near your house, and I need to give you a heads-up on something."

"Is everything okay? Did you find something out?"

"Yes and yes. But I had a little bit of an awkward situation. I had Carlotta let me in to your town house because I wanted to look at Heidi's room again. I didn't realize Jeff was home, and he seemed pretty annoyed when he found me there."

One of her famous long pauses. Then finally, "I don't get it. Why would you be in Heidi's room?" The connection started to break up as she spoke, so I stood up from the bench and walked along the promenade to see if I could find a better spot to talk from.

"Well, that's what I wanted to tell you—you're there,

right? The more I look into this thing, the more I think
that Heidi might have been the one the poison was meant
for all along."

Silence. Had I lost her—or was she sitting there at her
black granite desk stunned by what I'd said?

"Look, let me shut the door," she said finally. I heard
her set down the phone, and it was thirty seconds before
she came on again.

"What are you talking about?" she snapped.

"I think someone wanted Heidi to die, not you. The
candy was meant for her all along."

"It makes no sense. How could anyone be sure that
Heidi would take the candy?"

"But it didn't work like that. I'm losing you again. Can
you hear me? Look, I'm coming in and I'll explain it in
person." She was gone. I tried three more times to get
through—but without success.

As I headed across the park, I made a game plan for
myself. I would go back to *Gloss* and not only explain
things to Cat, but make a few phone calls. Somehow, and
I dreaded this, I was going to have to tell Detective Farley about what I'd found. But before I called him, I
needed to go by a Godiva store and be absolutely certain
that the flower petal I'd found in the Jiffy bag could have
come from a box of their chocolates—though in my own
mind I had no doubts. I also wanted to make contact with
Nancy Highland, the writer. And of course Kip. I'd have
to hang around until he got there, and hopefully, unlike
yesterday, he'd eventually surface.

But before any of that, I was going to drop by Starbucks and have another chat with Jody.

On East End Avenue, which the park borders, there

wasn't a cab in sight, so I decided to walk, which took longer than I expected. By the time I got to Starbucks I was hot and sweaty and my feet were burning. It wasn't all for nothing, because Jody was on duty behind the counter, working up a head of foam in a silver pitcher of milk. He didn't look overjoyed to see me, but when I indicated with a hand gesture that I'd like to talk to him, he nodded and gave me the five-minute signal. I took a seat at a table that was sprinkled with grains of sugar.

Since it was midday, the place was bustling, predominantly with freelance-looking types like myself. It was ten minutes before Jody finally headed my way, and as he got close to the table he cocked his head, meaning that we should go outside. I followed him to the same spot on the sidewalk where we had spoken before.

"This isn't a good time for me to talk, you know," he said. He was about two shades away from belligerent.

"I'm sorry, I should have called first. But I was up at Cat's this morning and I thought I'd just drop by, see how you were doing."

"Why would you care how *I'm* doing?"

"I know you were close to Heidi at one point, and I'm sure this is hard for you," I said. "It's not really any of my business, but on the other hand, I accidentally ended up in the middle of this thing."

He relaxed his stance a little, leaned back against the wall. His hair was shorter than it was the last time I saw him, no longer flopping in his eyes, yet out of habit he jerked his head to get it off his forehead, a kind of phantom-limb reaction.

"So all this stuff in the paper—that it was Cat Jones who was supposed to die. Is that legit?"

"That's what they're saying," I said, avoiding the truth, "but I don't know any specifics. Have the police been back to talk to you?"

"No. That first week I thought they might be looking at *me,* thinking I'd decided to off Heidi 'cause she ditched me. I guess now, though, they're on to who hated Cat Jones." I figured he was more than relieved at the latest turn of events.

"Where did you and Heidi meet, anyway?"

"Here," he said. "She came in one day last fall, with that friend of hers, Janice."

"What was Heidi really like? I met her, but I never got a chance to know her."

"A knockout, but then I guess you know that. At first I thought she was Swedish or German, you know, on account of her being a nanny and the way she looked. You'd walk down the street with her or into a bar and people would just go bug-eyed."

"What kind of person was she?"

"God, I don't know. Overall, she was nice, I guess."

"Why just overall?"

"Heidi's primo concern in life was Heidi. I don't blame her, really—she had such a messed-up life growing up. But she could get crabby if things weren't going her way. And she used people. You know, to get what she wanted. Like Janice. All she was to Heidi was somebody to hang with when she didn't want to go someplace alone."

Another flick of the imaginary bangs.

"And what about you?" I asked. "Did you feel used?"

"What makes you so interested?"

"Just curious."

"Yeah, I guess you could say she used me. She didn't have any dough, really, and she was new to New York, and I became the guy who showed her around, bought her dinner. And I bet I gave her and Janice five hundred free lattes between the two of them."

"Why did she call things off with you?" I asked.

"Didn't say. Well, what she said was she thought we should, quote, take a break."

"Another guy?"

"Who knows? Probably. A million guys wanted to get in her pants." He glanced into the store to check out what was going on. "But like I said, all she told me was that she needed a break, meaning I didn't do it for her anymore. Heidi had big plans for her life. Someone who works at Starbucks didn't really fit with those plans."

"What kind of plans?" I asked.

"Well, she didn't want to be a nanny for long, that's for sure. She thought about modeling. That guy, Cat's husband, took some pictures of her, and she took them around to some modeling agencies. The problem was her height. She's—she was like five seven, but they told her that to be a model you kind of have to be an Amazon—five nine, at least."

"That was nice of Jeff to do," I said evenly, careful not to let on that this latest piece of info had raised a huge red flag in my mind.

"Yeah, I guess. I mean, that's what the dude does for a living."

"Was Heidi thinking of quitting her job with Cat?" I asked.

"Yeah—when the time was right. She needed something like modeling to happen for her before she could quit. But like I said, I really hadn't seen much of her lately, so I don't know what her schedule was."

"But you dropped by the night of the party?"

"You wanna know why?" he said, pushing himself off the wall. "She owed me three hundred dollars. She'd borrowed it, here and there. I may be moving back out west, and I wanted to make one more attempt at getting it back."

He glanced into the store again. "I gotta go," he said, turning back to me. "We're packed."

"Just one more question," I said. "Did you ever buy Heidi a Tiffany bracelet?"

He looked puzzled by the question. "Why—d'you find something like that?" he asked.

"Yeah. I thought maybe you'd given it to her as a gift."

"Yeah, right. I've never even *been* in Tiffany's."

He strode back into the store, busing a table on his way across the room, and I walked over to Park Avenue, where I flagged down a cab to go back to *Gloss*.

I was unsure of what to make of Jody. He looked like an Eagle Scout, but didn't *seem* like one. He could have decided to kill Heidi in a state of jealousy and rage over being dumped. Though he clearly wasn't the sharpest knife in the drawer, he'd spent time around the 91st Street household and might easily know about Cat's passion for chocolate and Heidi's penchant for pinching food. It was hard to imagine him planting the Kiss in my office, however.

What was really disturbing me was what Jody had said about the photo session with Jeff. Maybe it had been done with Cat's blessing (and it could explain what Heidi's coat was doing in Jeff's studio). But something told me that Cat wasn't in the loop on Jeff's attempt at star making. I couldn't imagine Cat liking the idea of Heidi prancing around on seamless paper with Jeff's Nikon trained on her. Besides, why would Cat want to do anything to encourage any more nanny turnover in her life?

I'd learned a heck of a lot more about Heidi today. In the brief time I'd known her, she'd appeared cool and inaccessible, but now I could see she was also needy, ambitious, and perfectly willing to use people to get what she wanted—and then move on. Eve Harrington with an Aprica stroller.

What was fascinating, I thought as the cab sped down Central Park West, was how Heidi had worked her way up the food chain in the months before she died, setting her sights higher each time. She'd left Indiana for a nanny job in Westchester County, but as soon as an opportunity in New York City presented itself, she'd snared that. She'd immediately gotten involved with Jody, who'd been eager to provide small loans and hot drinks. When that wasn't enough, she'd looked elsewhere. Kip, apparently, was one of her next conquests. He was older and more successful than Jody, though I wasn't sure what specifically he'd had to offer. Maybe just the thrill of the conquest or of doing something naughty. As Janice had pointed out, Heidi liked it when all the boys were in a lather for her. It was clear what Jeff had to offer her. He'd helped her pursue the fantasy of a modeling career. But what I didn't yet know was whether sex had been part of the equation or if he'd simply snapped the photos as a favor to a young woman in his family's employ.

I wondered where those photos were now. And I wondered if Kip really was the mystery man or if there was yet another guy—and if so, where he belonged on the food chain.

When I got to *Gloss* I swung through the pit on my way to Cat's office, but when I was halfway there, I saw that the lights were off in her office and Audrey was not at her desk. I walked down the corridor toward Kip's office, on the off chance he'd come in earlier than planned. His assistant was on the phone and gave me a shake of the head as I walked by, indicating, "Noooo, he isn't there." Yesterday she'd been wearing a white tank top and a rayon faux Pucci skirt. Today she had on the same skirt but with no tank, just her jeans jacket buttoned like a shirt. She was doing a lame job at disguising the fact that she hadn't been home to change her clothes in the last twenty-four hours.

Next stop: Polly's office. She was staring at her computer screen with a grin on her face.

"My, don't we look happy this afternoon?" I remarked. As I stepped into her office, she swiveled her chair around so she was facing me.

"You know what I've discovered, Bailey?" she said in mock seriousness. "I can be happy all day long, even during a brain-pulverizing meeting like the one we had this morning, knowing that I've only got a few weeks left."

"Don't remind me. Speaking of brain-pulverizing meetings, is Cat around this afternoon?"

"No. She apparently had a lunch with some advertisers, then a meeting up in corporate. She doesn't seem at all thrilled to be on-site these days. Here—have a seat."

"Nah, I've gotta finish my story. I should have it to you tomorrow, by the way."

"Why the rush?"

"Didn't you hear? Cat moved it from September to August."

"God, nobody tells me anything these days."

"Are things still going to hell in a handbasket here?"

"Pretty much. People are anxious, and they're so busy gossiping and trying to dig up details, they're not getting their work done. According to Miss Leslie, we're about four days behind schedule for August. Did you see 'Page Six' today?"

"No, why?"

"That new guy in art, Jason, resigned at the end of the day yesterday, on top of that dimwit in beauty, and 'Page Six' has this item about rats leaving Cat's sinking ship."

"Who's minding the store around here—not to mix metaphors?"

"Leslie on her end. Me on mine. Since Cat is barely glancing at copy these days, I'm tempted to send through all the outrageous and ridiculous stuff and give the reader something extra for her money. Listen to this." She turned back to her computer screen. "This is *supposedly* from a reader letter. The health editor put it through for her 'Health Q and A.'

"'Sometimes,'" she read, "'I experience *pooper pains*. These sharp pains in my rectum happen suddenly, usually when I'm resting. Is this normal?' I could let this go through, you know, and Cat wouldn't even notice. Have you ever *heard* of pooper pains? I hadn't until four minutes ago. But maybe there are millions of women suffering and we could blow the lid off the problem. To say nothing of introducing some snappy new terminology to the language."

"On that note"—I laughed—"maybe I should go back and get some work done."

I strode back to my office, curious and anxious about what I'd find. The fashion office was completely empty, though the lights were on, and the mannequin Fat Ass was standing in the middle of the room—in nothing but a short white cape. One entire wall of the room was lined with new fall boots—yellow ones, red ones, turquoise ones, all with really pointy toes. Most of them were flopped over on their sides, as though they'd grown tired of waiting around.

I entered my office cautiously, flipped on the light, and glanced around. Nothing seemed out of place.

The first call I made was to order a chicken salad sandwich, and then I checked my e-mail and my voice mail at home and the office. There was a message from someone offering to fix me up with an optometrist named Bob, two calls from friends at other magazines, both asking if I was still alive and suggesting I find a new work site, and a message from my college roommate saying she'd be in town at the end of May and wanted to get together. No booty call from K.C., but of course it was early in the day for that sort of thing. And no call from Jack Herlihy saying he wanted to take me up on my offer for a tour. I felt relieved—and at the same time I felt a pang of disappointment.

Once I'd played all my messages, I called Audrey, who was now back at her desk, and got Nancy Highland's number—she lived in Scarsdale, a hotsy-totsy suburban town about an hour north of New York City. My pretext for calling her, I'd decided, would be the same I had used with Dolores: Help, I'm putting together an anthology of articles and I could use your guidance. A nanny or house-keeper answered and explained that Ms. Highland was in New York City for the next two days working on publicity for *Love at Any Cost*. This woman hadn't the faintest interest in telling me where she was staying. I called Audrey back for the name of the publicist at the book company and managed to reach her on the first try.

"God, we're all just flabbergasted over here about what happened," she said as soon as I identified myself. "Is the one who died that young blond girl who was around the night of the party? I can't believe I actually *saw* her."

"I'm not sure which blond girl you mean, but it was Cat's nanny."

"What happened? How did she die?"

I played dumb and steered the conversation around to that masterpiece *Love at Any Cost*. She confirmed that Nancy was in New York, but it wasn't part of any major publicity plan. She was simply going to be reading one of the two stories of hers from the book—tomorrow afternoon at a small bookstore on Madison Avenue. It was part of a "tea and reading" series. I jotted down the details and signed off.

Last, but hardly least, I called Kip's office and got his voice mail this time. I left a message, asking that he call when he got in.

Over the next couple of hours I worked on my Marky story, reorganizing several sections and filling in some holes. I was close to finishing it, but I could tell I wasn't going to make it by the end of the day. I found myself distracted by the noises outside my office, by everything I'd learned this morning.

At about a quarter to five, I called down to Cat's office to see if she was back. According to Audrey, she would not be returning to the office today. She was in a town car someplace, and no, she did not have her cell phone on.

As soon as I put down the phone I heard a sound behind me and turned to see Kip standing in the doorway. He looked tired and cranky. His clothes—his standard chino pants and Ralph Lauren polo shirt, today in lemon yellow—were totally rumpled and saggy, as if he'd picked them up from the bedroom floor this morning and worn them for a second day in a row. There were so many nicks on his chin that it looked as if he'd shaved on the subway.

"What's up? Stacey said you seemed desperate to see me." There was an edge to his voice that wasn't the least bit pleasant.

"Oh, yeah," I said, trying to sound relaxed. "There's something I wanted to ask you. Is this—"

"Just shoot. What is it?"

"Actually," I said, lowering my voice, "it's kind of private. Would you mind closing the door?"

He looked as if he were going to refuse, but he stepped farther into the room and pushed the door closed with the heel of his hand.

"Here, why don't you sit," I said, pointing to the spare chair. He blew out a big puff of air and did as suggested, making the chair groan with his weight. He was sitting so close to me that I could see every freckle on his face.

With everyone else I'd spoken to, I'd danced around the subject of the murder, but Kip was cagey and I'd decided earlier that I'd have to be more direct with him— otherwise I'd end up with nothing. Yet it scared me.

"I don't know if you're aware of this, but I accidentally got involved in this whole situation with Cat's nanny," I said, plunging in. "She was from the Midwest and she doesn't have any family here. Cat asked if I could help her tie up any loose ends regarding Heidi—you know, see if she had any bills to pay or any unfinished business."

As soon as I said the name Heidi, he tried to freeze his face, to restrict any expression from forming there, but he couldn't keep his blue eyes from doing a jig.

"And your point is . . . ?" he said, crossing one leg over the other and swiping at his pants leg a few times.

"I'm not sure exactly how to say this but . . . I know you were involved with Heidi and I was hoping I could ask you a few questions—in complete confidence."

"What are you talking about?" He was almost snarling, and his skin, except for the freckles, looked whiter than usual, as if he'd had the blood in his face drained. I felt the onset of claustrophobia.

"I promise—I don't intend to say anything to anyone. But there are some things I need to know for my own edification."

"You're crazy. I don't know where you're getting your information." He made a motion as if he were about to launch out of the chair.

"I know about you and Cat, too—the afternoon in Litchfield," I said. "I also know you went up there thinking that Heidi would be there and you had—you got involved with Cat so she wouldn't put two and two together."

"Jesus," he said. He looked over at the door, as if gauging the heft of it, to determine if our conversation could be overheard by anyone outside in the hall. "Have you told Cat this, your little theory?"

"No, and I have no intention of doing so."

"Why not? Aren't you two such good girlfriends, sharing all sorts of little secrets together?"

"What would I accomplish by doing that? It would make a mess for you—and Cat would only be humiliated. Like I said, I just need to know a couple of things about Heidi."

He paused, lips pursed. Then, to my surprise, he morphed into Pooh Bear.

"Look, let's go get a drink someplace, okay?" he said. "I don't want to get into this here."

A moment of panic. I didn't want to go with him anywhere. But I realized that nothing bad could happen to me in the middle of Manhattan—it wasn't as if he could shove me in the trunk of his car and speed off. On the way in the elevator he suggested Trattoria Dell'Arte, a trendy Italian restaurant on Seventh Avenue across from Carnegie Hall, and we walked the three blocks there in silence. The restaurant was starting to get jammed with pretheater diners, but the bar was empty and we took two seats at the end, away from the main part of the restaurant. I ordered a beer, Kip ordered a Jack Daniel's, neat, and lit a cigarette.

"Okay," he said, waving the match until the flame went out, cigarette still in his mouth. "I'll cut to the chase. I did have a little fling with Heidi. But it was no big deal, and it lasted all of a minute."

"How did you even meet her?" I asked.

"I'd seen her around the office, you know, bringing stuff to Cat. At the time I thought she was jail bait, some sixteen-year-old au pair from Europe, and I didn't do anything other than *look*. Then, around the first of the year, Cat had the dinner party for that airline safety guy whose book we excerpted. I was getting bored and drifted into the kitchen, and she was in there, picking at the leftovers. We just started talking. I realized she was like twenty-two, not sixteen."

"And you called her after that?"

"She called me—I swear." He paused to take a sip of his drink. "I don't go around trying to be a bad boy, despite what people think. I had no intention of starting up any pursuit. But, like I said, she called, claiming she needed some advice, and I agreed to meet her. She made it very clear when we met that she wanted more than advice. My marriage has been in the toilet lately and I didn't feel like saying no. You've been married. You know how fucked up things can get and how crazy it can make you."

"Where did all of this take place? In Heidi's apartment?"

"First of all, there's no 'all of this.'" He took a long drag on his cigarette and another sip of bourbon, licking his lips when he was done. "We probably saw each other ten times over the period of a month or so, and no, never at Cat's house. Do you think I'm nuts? I wasn't going to take any chances. I've got a friend who's in Hong Kong, and I use his pad when I stay in the city nights. I was very cautious. The irony is that in the end I nearly got caught bare assed by Cat."

"What did Heidi want to ask you?"

"What?"

"You said when she first called you she was looking for advice."

"She wanted to know how to break into the TV business."

"You'd told her you used to be a producer?"

"Yeah. But I know jack shit about what she wanted to do, which was become a VJ on MTV. Let me tell you, she started to get real frosty when she eventually realized I couldn't help her."

"Were you upset?"

"Relieved, actually," he said. That was tough to buy.

"You didn't mind being blown off by a gorgeous girl like her?"

"I didn't like the fact that she beat me to it. But I'm not bullshitting. I'd begun to wonder how I was going to extricate myself from the whole situation without sustaining any damage. Before I get the chance, she starts to pull away. And that was just fine with me."

"But if she was cooling it, why did she invite you to Litchfield in March?"

A shake of that Boston terrier head. "That wasn't a planned thing. I was in Cat's office one day and I heard her talking to that maid of hers, explaining that Heidi was going to be up at the house with a friend and that she and Jeff had some event in the city. I had a big blowout with my wife on Saturday morning—I must have done something really, really disgusting, like take a shower without the curtain in the tub—and I just decided on a whim to drive up there, see if she'd help me lick my wounds. I nearly freaked when I saw Cat. I didn't know what else to do."

"You couldn't have just said you were in the area and decided to pop in."

"I was carrying flowers and a bottle of Taittinger. If I'd

seemed surprised to see her, she would have realized that I was balling Heidi. My ass would have been grass—and I'm sure she would have made sure my wife found out. But Cat never found out."

"What would your wife do if she knew?"

He stubbed out his cigarette hard in the ashtray. "Besides hack off my nuts, torch my car, and take me to the cleaners in divorce court? I'm not honestly sure. Look, what's the point of the inquisition, anyway? I don't get what your fascination with Heidi is."

"Like I said before, I found the body and got involved early, and now I'm sort of invested and I want to make sure all the loose ends are tied up. Has it been hard for you—her dying?"

It caught him off guard. "Yeah, of course," he said, red eyebrows shooting up. "I'm not a monster. I slept with the chick and I feel lousy about what happened to her, especially after reading that it wasn't supposed to be her."

"Did you ever give her a Tiffany bracelet?"

"What?"

"A gold bracelet—from Tiffany?"

"Sure," he said sarcastically. "I just put it on my personal account at the store."

He glanced at his watch. "I've got to get rolling," he said, and drained the rest of his bourbon.

"One more question. Were you worried that if Heidi somehow found out what happened between you and Cat, she'd tell Cat the real story?"

"No, not a chance. Why would she do that, anyway?"

"Cat was her boss."

"You haven't been listening. Heidi was a total opportunist. She'd be shooting herself in the foot if she told

Cat. She needed her for the job—at least for the time being."

"Right."

"You got this?" he asked, sliding off his stool. "I better fly."

"Yeah, I've got it," I said.

"I can count on you, right? To be discreet. You said I could."

"You haven't been listening. Absolutely."

He tore out of the restaurant while I settled the bill. I didn't know whether to buy his story or not, that his relationship with Heidi had been nothing more than sport fucking. Kip, from what I knew, was a fabulous liar. I'd once heard him tell a freelance writer that a piece she'd written brought to mind Truman Capote and then announce an hour later in a meeting with Cat that reading it was like undergoing bone surgery without anesthesia. Of course, even if it *had* been only a casual fling, he still might have killed her—if she'd threatened to squeal to Cat. Or maybe he'd misrepresented how Heidi felt. She could have been head over heels about Kip and when she sensed she was about to be blown off, she could have gone psycho and announced that she was going to tell his wife about what had been going on. Kip, of course, could easily have left the Kiss on my desk. Or here was an interesting thought: Maybe his wife had done the dirty work. She'd been at the party that night, slurring her words.

There was one thing I *was* sure of. Kip was no dummy, and if he was the killer, he might have guessed by my line of questioning that I was on to the fact that Heidi was the one who was supposed to die. I may have put myself in real danger.

After collecting my change, I checked my voice mail for messages. There were two. First, Leslie's assistant, haranguing me again about expense reports. The second, at five-fifty, was from Cat—and she sounded freaked.

"Bailey, this is urgent. Something bad has happened. Leave your cell phone on—I've got to talk to you."

CHAPTER 19

I STOOD OUTSIDE the restaurant trying to imagine what might be the matter. Cat had sounded borderline hysterical when she'd left her message. Had she stumbled upon a clue about the poisoning? Had something happened with Jeff? Had someone done something to scare her, as they had me?

I tried her house on my cell phone, even though I figured that if she'd been there, she would probably have said so. Carlotta answered and informed me that Cat wasn't home yet and she had no idea where she was or when she going to turn up. When I asked her if everything was okay at the house, she explained that the powder room toilet was leaking again and that she was waiting for a plumber to come and fix it. Something told me that this wasn't the crisis that had Cat in such a tizzy.

Halfway up the block I sat on the edge of a short wall outside an office building, fished out my address book from my purse, and, after finding Cat's cell number, punched the numbers. People streamed by me on their way home, to Carnegie Hall, or to bars and restaurants in the area. From where I sat, I could see the red and yellow and blue neon billboards of Times Square a dozen blocks farther south, pulsing and gyrating. The air felt heavy, spongy, as if it would rain soon. After the fourth ring her voice mail picked up and I left a message saying that my phone was now on and I'd keep it on till I heard from her. I tossed the phone back in my bag and calculated what my next move should be.

Obviously Cat was someplace she couldn't be reached and I'd just have to wait to hear from her. Chances were that she'd arrive back at the town house before long, and I'd end up going *there* to help her tackle whatever trouble had reared its head. Rather than go home to the Village and then have to come all the way back uptown, I decided to head toward the Upper East Side and hang there until I heard from her.

It took me about fifteen minutes to secure a cab, and then it was only because I outsprinted a lawyerly-looking chick wearing the last asexual all navy woman's suit in Manhattan. I had the driver drop me at a bar/restaurant called Martell's on 83rd and Third. It was a bit of a hike from Cat's, but it was the only place that I could think of, since the Upper East Side isn't my usual stomping ground. I slid onto an empty stool at the bar and ordered a draft beer.

As I sipped my beer I kept my eyes focused mainly on the foam at the top of the glass, because the bar area was becoming packed quickly, and all it would take was a slight turn of my head and a nanosecond of eye contact and I'd have some bozo standing next to me asking me something like "Why so sad—did you lose your puppy?"

Out of the corner of my eye I could see that the place was full of guys who reminded me of Kip. Guys who had an air of entitlement that had been swelling like Jiffy Pop since Duke or Dartmouth, the kinds of guys who still got a thrill from pushing someone into a swimming pool with their clothes on. Actually, Kip belonged to a brainy subspecies. He had the sense of entitlement, but his rush came from saying something witty at your expense or dropping a brilliant reference he knew you wouldn't get.

It had been fascinating to see the smugness fall away when I'd had him cornered earlier. Taking another sip of beer, I thought of the drink he'd ordered. Bourbon, neat. And I thought of what he said about making the trip to Litchfield uninvited. That meant Heidi had extended the invitation to someone else. Kip wasn't the mystery man after all.

Then who was? I had to figure out whom Heidi had planned to play the hot little hostess for. If she'd been following her usual MO, it was someone bigger and better than Kip. And there was more than a better chance it was someone who could help hatch her schemes for success. Her modeling dreams hadn't materialized into anything. Nor had her fantasy about a career at MTV. Had she churned up a fresh scheme and then zoomed in on a fellow who could facilitate her plans? Or had she met someone who opened her eyes to a bold new possibility?

Most important of all, was *he* the one who'd killed her?

The din around the bar was so great, I almost didn't

notice my phone ring. I answered it with my head tucked into my chest so I could hear who was on the other end.

"Jesus, Bailey, there you are." Cat Jones at her most direct.

"Hey—are you okay? What's happening?"

"What's *happening?* What's happening is that someone tried to poison Patty Gaylin. There *is* some kind of conspiracy."

"You're kidding!" I exclaimed. The news was so startling, I was at a loss for words.

Patty Gaylin, editor in chief of *Women's Journal*, was a woman in her mid- to late fifties known for being tough, sometimes tyrannical, but not without mercy if you begged hard enough. Cat called her "Crock Pot" Patty because the magazine ran gobs of recipes for one-dish family meals, most of them calling for several pounds of stew meat.

"No, I'm *not* kidding. Someone wants us all dead."

"Are you home now? I'll come by—I'm only a few blocks away."

There were muffled words as she apparently turned to speak to someone in the room with her.

"I just got to Leslie's. We're having dinner here. Jeff left this afternoon for a shoot in Miami tomorrow and I'm in no mood to go home alone right now."

"Is Patty Gaylin okay?"

"As far as I know. But I'm not. I'm sick to death of this whole thing."

"Cat," I said, trying not to sound as discombobulated as I felt, "I need to talk to you. I came up to your neighborhood thinking I'd be able to meet you here. Is there a chance I could come by—to Leslie's?" The idea of joining a Leslie and Cat get-together was about as enticing as a dermapeel, but I didn't have a choice if I wanted to see Cat.

Again she turned away and spoke to someone, presumably Leslie, who was being asked if she would be kind enough to include me in the festivities. How had I found myself in this position, as a supplicant to Leslie? When Cat came back on the phone, her voice was drowned out by the escalating din in the bar and I had to ask her to repeat herself.

"I said fine, come," she told me, sounding short of patience. "You know the address—One Forty Central Park West?" In terms of invitations, it was hardly one of the most inviting I'd ever been given.

"I'll be there in fifteen minutes," I said.

I had to fight my way through a thicket of bond traders who insisted that the fun was just beginning and I was nuts to leave, but I managed to get a taxi the minute I stepped off the curb. I told myself not to jump ahead, not to start hashing things out in my mind until I had all the facts, but I couldn't help myself. Had I been totally off base with my theory about Heidi? Had I just spent the last day and a half sidetracked, pursuing an idea that was completely ridiculous—and then given Cat misleading information? But I couldn't have been wrong. There was the Jiffy bag that had been in Heidi's trash basket, the one with the flower petal that I was convinced came from the Godiva box. There had to be some other explanation for this Patty Gaylin situation.

Traffic was surprisingly light, and I landed at Leslie's apartment building in under fifteen minutes. Once, after a *Gloss* event on the Upper West Side, I'd shared a cab with Leslie and dropped her off at her building, but I'd never stepped foot in the apartment. I had heard plenty about it, however. It was legendary around *Gloss* because it was huge and luxurious and had a breathtaking view of Central Park. Her husband, Clyde, the one who had made the killing in the market and then been smart enough to get out, worked out of the apartment, managing his money and dabbling in a variety of other pursuits.

It was actually Clyde who answered the door of their fifteenth-floor apartment after I'd managed to get through a screening by the doorman that was just shy of a strip search. He greeted me as if we'd never met before. At least he seemed cognizant of the fact that I was expected.

"They're in the kitchen, having something to eat," he indicated. He was dressed as if he'd just come from some kind of meeting—cobalt blue dress shirt, black slacks, and an exquisite black leather belt that looked as if it might be from someplace like Hermès and probably cost as much as a Ford Taurus. I thought of what Cat had told me—about trying to draw him out and being accused of dirty flirting.

"Should I just go through, then?" I asked.

"By all means," he said in a tone that indicated he didn't care one way or the other what I did. "Why don't you take a drink with you. The bar's over here."

The seven sips of beer I'd had already hadn't made a dent in my nerves, and I figured a glass of wine might help. I followed him down a spacious, gallerylike foyer into a large wood-paneled study. Two walls were nothing but floor-to-ceiling bookcases, and on the other two walls, mounted on brackets, were at least thirty gleaming silver swords with ornate handles. They looked as though they might have been used to drive the Turks from Constantinople.

"I'll just take a glass of red wine," I said, pointing to a bottle of Bordeaux that sat half-full on the wet bar.

He seemed to have no interest in chitchat, so I asked for directions to the kitchen and he pointed to a hallway that ran perpendicular to the foyer, explaining that I'd stumble upon it eventually. The apartment was amazingly huge and decorated expensively, but without any warmth, in shades of pale blue and gray. On my way toward the kitchen, I passed a massive living room with just one lamp burning, a dining room in near darkness, and a hallway that appeared to lead to a bunch of bedrooms. Leslie didn't have kids, but maybe she was planning on it one day or she had scads of overnight guests. Though it was hard to imagine anything fun or festive ever taking place here.

Leslie and Cat were both in the kitchen, a huge room with acres of pale wood cabinets, sitting at a center island beneath a dozen copper pots that hung by hooks from a black wrought-iron frame on the ceiling. In front of them on the island was a half-eaten roast chicken carcass, a wooden bowl with the soggy remains of a green salad, and a near empty bottle of white wine. Cat still had on work clothes, a lavender skirt and a tight-fitting black T-shirt, but Leslie had obviously changed—into a brown turtleneck and a pair of khakis with front pleats that made her look pudgy. The mood was somber, and though they both turned when I entered, neither said hello.

"There's plenty of food left," said Leslie as I walked toward the island. "Do you want anything?"

"Not right this sec, thanks," I said. She was being

pleasant enough now, but I knew it would be only a few seconds before she started that boxing-out thing she did whenever she was with Cat and me. In fact, I had that weird feeling you get when you've accidentally blundered into a conversation that you suspect was about you and probably wasn't flattering. "So what happened?"

"We don't have all the details yet," Leslie said, pulling out a stool for me to sit on. "What we've heard is that Patty received a package of chocolate-chip cookies in the mail today. They were wrapped up like a present from a friend, but there was no note. She would never have eaten them, of course—not knowing who they were from. But her secretary was especially suspicious because of what's been going on. Apparently she took a whiff and it was clear that there was something wrong. They smelled bad. She called the police and they're going to run some tests on the cookies."

"Has anyone gotten hold of the detectives investigating Heidi's death?" I asked, turning to Cat.

She just sat there silently, looking as if she were giving a bad mood a chance to build. It was Leslie who answered.

"Yes, Cat called them as soon as she heard." Why, I wondered, was she being so damn friendly?

"Tell me more about the cookies, though," I said, taking a sip of wine and trying to act, at least, like an integral part of the girls gab fest. "When you say they smelled bad, what do you mean? Could they just have been spoiled?"

"*Spoiled?*" Cat said in a near shriek. "For God's sake, why are you having such a tough time getting your arms around the idea that someone is after the editors of women's magazines?" She sounded mad and mean, and though I certainly had heard her use that tone with other people over the years, it had never been discharged at me. When I responded I spoke slowly so I wouldn't give away that I felt as if I'd been slapped.

"Cat, you've said more than once that one of my skills as a writer is that I keep pushing, asking questions. Why would you want me to do otherwise in this case?"

"I'm not suggesting you shouldn't be asking questions," she snapped. "But it might help if you start asking the *right* ones." She'd been looking in my general direction as she spoke but not making perfect eye contact, and now she turned back to her wineglass. I started to say something, a feeble attempt to defend myself. Leslie, however, cut me off.

"Look, we're all a little crazed right now, and justifiably so. But we need to keep our heads. Let's hear what Bailey has to say, okay?" Cat said nothing, only took another swig of wine, but obviously Leslie interpreted this as a sign to forge ahead.

"Bailey, you don't think what happened to Cat—what *almost* happened to Cat—could be part of somebody's plan to harm editors of women's magazines, maybe as revenge—or even as some kind of *statement?"*

"She doesn't think it has anything to do with me period," Cat said angrily. "She thinks it's all about Heidi."

"Heidi?" Leslie exclaimed. "What are you talking about?"

"She called me today to tell me she thinks Heidi was supposed to die all along."

"But why would someone kill Heidi?" Leslie asked, looking thoroughly bewildered.

"Let Bailey tell you," Cat said, at full-blast nasty. "She's the smartest girl in the class, the one with all the answers."

"You know," I said quietly, standing up from my stool, "I think it would be better if I just left." I picked up my purse and tote bag from the floor and strode out of the room.

When I reached the gallery, I could hear someone behind me, but I didn't turn. Then I heard Leslie's voice.

"Bailey, wait a second. Don't just fly out of here."

I stopped and waited for her to catch up to me. As she reached me she glanced toward the study, presumably looking for her husband, but he had apparently roamed off somewhere in the cavernous apartment.

"Cat's coming unhinged because of this whole thing, so you can't take it personally," she said.

"Thanks, Leslie, I appreciate your support." It came out even more sarcastically than I'd planned.

"Bailey, we've never been friends and we're never going to be, but I respect you—more than you realize. You can't let this bother you. Cat's too crazed to be nice right now. Why don't I call you later. I can fill you in on anything we learn about Patty."

"Fine, I'd appreciate that." I couldn't believe I was being so damn cordial to Leslie.

"Do you really think the killer was after *Heidi?* Who would want to harm her? She was such a nonentity."

"I *do* think that. And she *wasn't* such a nonentity. Guys found her incredibly desirable, and one of them may have killed her. I'm going to figure it out."

She smiled. "I'm sorry Cat's not more appreciative of all the effort you're putting in."

She let me out of the apartment, and I found my way down to the lobby on automatic pilot, unable to give full attention to anything other than how extraordinarily pissed I was at Cat. What had I done to make her tear into me like that? Something seemed to be eating her, *beyond* the fact that she didn't think my theory held any weight.

There was a part of me that also felt humiliated from having been dressed down in front of Leslie. It certainly explained why Leslie had been so gracious to me. She'd known I was in the doghouse, and in her state of glee over this development, she'd been able to throw me a bone.

Outside on the sidewalk, I discovered to my delight that it had begun to rain, a nice steady rain that obviously had no intention of stopping anytime soon. A whole bunch of cabs sped up and down Central Park West, all with windshield wipers flicking and their top lights off. There was no convenient subway for me to get home by. I glanced up at the street sign on the corner—74th Street—and considered whom I knew within a two-block radius who might be willing to loan me an umbrella.

A friend of mine from Brown lived on 73rd and Columbus, but the last I knew he was still in Jakarta for his job. A girlfriend from *Get* had a studio on 72nd, but she was almost always at her boyfriend's in Tribeca. And then—surprise, surprise!—there was K.C., not exactly within the preferred radius, but close enough—81st Street. He'd thought nothing of calling me on the spur of the moment; didn't I have the right to do the same? Weren't we ditching all the game playing? Besides, seeing his face would make me less miserable. I stepped back into the lobby and punched his number on my cell.

Chances were heavily in favor of his not being home, anyway.

But he was. Caught off guard, I sputtered something about a fight with my boss and being caught in the rain and could I come by and steal an umbrella. He hesitated for a minute and I thought, Oh God, he's going to blow me off, but then he said yes, come by, he had umbrellas and I could take my pick.

By the time I'd jogged the seven blocks in the rain to his apartment building, my hair was matted down and my clothes were sticking to my skin, and when I glanced in the mirror in his lobby, I saw that I looked remarkably like a muskrat surfacing on a pond. I tried to do some damage control, but it wasn't very effective. It had been a mistake to call, and I realized that the only possible way to begin to undo the damage was to simply take an umbrella and split.

He was wearing a white dress shirt with the sleeves rolled up, over a pair of tartan boxer shorts. Bare feet. His dark hair was slightly damp and slicked down, as if he'd combed it just after I'd called. Funny he'd taken the time for that but hadn't bothered to put on his pants. But then why be coy? He kissed me on the cheek and led me from the foyer (*past* the umbrella stand) to the living room, where paper and folders were strewn about on the brown leather couch, the coffee table, and even on the floor.

"Oh, God, you're in the middle of working—sorry," I said.

"Actually, I'm done. We finished that deal today, and I'm just trying to organize stuff before I haul it back to the office. You want a beer?"

"I shouldn't. You're busy."

"Sit," he said, clearing off the papers from the couch and plunking them down with the stacks on the coffee table. "I'll be right back."

He walked off toward the kitchen and came back in less than a minute with two Coors and a towel, which I used to blot my hair as he relaxed into the far end of the couch from me. He looked very sexy, with that damp hair and his eyes a little bit on the sleepy side and the still perfectly pressed oxford shirt open halfway down his chest. My pulse should have been racing, but I was feeling an odd disconnect. Maybe it was because my anger at Cat was acting like some kind of roadblock to other sensations. Or because I was suddenly feeling slightly woozy despite the fact that during the course of the evening I'd never finished a single drink I'd started. Or maybe it was because K.C. had chosen to sit five feet away from me.

"Did the deal work out in your favor?" I asked, setting the Coors bottle on the Mission-style end table next to me.

"Yeah, we made a killing, actually," he said with a typically roguish laugh. "So what was this fight with your boss? Did you tell her to stop calling you on Sunday mornings at the crack of dawn?"

"No, though I should have, shouldn't I? Actually, she humiliated me in front of this woman we work with. Which doesn't sound so amazing considering her bitchiness has been registered as a lethal weapon, but it's not something she's generally pulled with me. Of course, she's under all this pressure right now—her job sucks and her marriage has been under strain and she's been under the impression for the last week that someone wants her dead, which I guess could make anyone bitchy. But it doesn't make it bother me any less. I suddenly see how stupid it's been for me to think that I'm immune to her annoyance or wrath. It's like raising a puma in captivity and believing it won't ever maul you."

Lengthwise, my ramblings had seemed to come in just short of the Gettysburg Address, and I decided to shut up then.

"It's always dangerous with bosses," he said. "You should never get too close to them, if you ask me."

His eye contact faltered as he said it, and the words just hung there. Was it because beneath the words there was a story, of him getting burned once at work? Or was he sending a message about his general MO in life (Don't *ever* get too close)?

"Any advice?" I asked. "I'm not sure what to do next." I was fumbling for where to go with the conversation.

"I assume you like your situation there."

"Yes. It's perfect for me."

"Then I'd let it blow over."

Typical guy advice, delivered cut-and-dried, without sentiment. I wondered if I should just *leave*. It seemed clunky and awkward with us, and I felt even more miserable than when I'd first walked in the door. As I struggled in my mind for a way to extricate myself, he flashed a smile and leaned toward me on the couch.

"There is one other remedy, though, one I'd highly recommend."

"Oh, yeah, and what would that be?" I asked, trying not to sound as though I had a lump in my throat.

He closed the gap on the couch, and then, holding my face in both hands, kissed me hard on the mouth, catching my lip with his tooth. I felt a rush of desire, as if my libido had gone from zero to one hundred in four seconds, but also relief, because I wasn't leaving, because I was going to spend the night here, where it was warm and dry and safe. We had sex first on the soft Turkish rug, fast and furious, and then again in the bedroom, a languorous hour's worth. Everything about Cat and Heidi fell away. It was around ten-thirty when we finally untangled ourselves to go to sleep, and within minutes I could hear K.C.'s deep, rhythmic breathing next to me.

I'd slept so easily each time I'd spent the night with him, but this was early for me, and I could tell sleep wasn't going to happen anytime soon. My stomach was growling, too. The closest I'd come to any real dinner that night was staring at the chicken carcass on Leslie's counter. I need to scrounge up something to eat.

Tiptoeing into the kitchen in one of K.C.'s T-shirts, I inspected his refrigerator to see if things had improved since my visit last Thursday night. There were a few reinforcements, including a half carton of eggs, so I scrambled two for myself, careful not to make too much racket. I would have loved toast, but I had to settle for a handful of Carr's water crackers. I turned off the light and sat at the small counter beneath the window so I could eat, fourteen stories up, by the glow from the city outside. My thoughts quickly found their way back to Heidi.

Was Cat right? Was I all wrong in my theory? There was, I realized, another possible explanation for the flower petal in the Jiffy bag. It had been swimming through the reeds of my brain, cagey as a trout, for the last several hours. Let's say Heidi had spotted the chocolates and wanted to pilfer them without being seen. She could have grabbed a Jiffy bag from somewhere in the house, maybe from Cat's office on the third floor, taken it to the hallway, and then stuffed the candy inside. Or maybe that wasn't even a Godiva flower in the Jiffy bag. Because of how things had unfolded, I hadn't had time to go by Godiva today, but I would make time to do it tomorrow.

So I might be wrong, but I didn't believe it. I kept coming back to what had bugged me all along about the truffles. Leaving them in the hallway in order to poison Cat was taking too big a chance. Every part of me still believed that Heidi was the one who was meant to die.

As for Crock Pot Patty, until I heard more details, I could only speculate wildly. The cookies, perhaps, were simply the foul-smelling concoction of a friend or reader who didn't know how to follow a recipe. Or maybe Patty's assistant had fallen victim to the power of suggestion: Editors were being poisoned left and right, and now someone was after her boss.

There was a far scarier explanation. The killer, so expert in the art of misdirection, had sent the cookies not because he or she had anything against Patty, but to make certain that the "someone is killing the editors of women's magazines" theory continued to carry weight. And that no one, for a second, focused on Heidi.

It would have been nice to have hashed this all out with Cat tonight. Why was she in such a miserable snit? Why was she so resistant to the idea of Heidi being the killer's real target? It almost appeared, I suddenly thought, as if she were upset because I was directing all the attention away from *her,* because she would no longer be the center of the universe if Heidi turned out to be the intended victim. Her anger at me had been so out of whack, as if I'd crossed a line, dared to say something I shouldn't have.

I felt the hairs on my arms stand at attention as the next thought took form in my mind. What if Cat's anger had been provoked not because I'd removed her from the center of attention, but because I'd placed Heidi there. What if, despite all her requests for my help, Cat had never really wanted me to find my way to where I was now? Was there something she didn't want me to know?

Could Cat have been the one who killed Heidi?

CHAPTER 20

I DISMISSED THE idea of Cat as the killer almost as quickly as it had flashed in my mind. It just couldn't be true. Cat had seemed genuinely shaken the day of Heidi's death, and beyond that, she had given me carte blanche to snoop around Heidi's things, talk to the people she knew. Besides, I didn't have a shred of proof that Jeff and Heidi had ever done the dirty deed—which left Cat, for now, without a motive. For the time being I was going to assume her bitchiness tonight was due either to an extreme case of frazzled nerves or the threat of losing her role as star of the drama.

I set my plate in the sink, padded back to the bedroom, and crawled in beside K.C., who was dead to the world with his back to me. I scooted over as close as I could get and put my arm around him, trying to feel warmer and safer, to concentrate on nothing but the smell of his skin. It was tough going, though. Thoughts of Heidi and Cat

and everything about the case shoved their way around
my brain. It was at least an hour before I managed to fall
asleep.

I woke up cold, with the blankets snaked around my
legs and my head pounding, probably from not having
had a single injection of caffeine the night before. K.C.'s
side of the bed was empty, but from the bathroom I could
hear the faint sound of shower water running. It was just
6:22 and very, very gloomy outside. I climbed out of bed,
retrieved my clothes from where they'd been flung
around the living room, and splashed some cold water on
my face in the kitchen sink. The Mr. Coffee was already
full—four cups—which I took as a sign that I wasn't
going to be tossed out before breakfast.

K.C. was pleasant enough when he emerged from the
bathroom, a brick red towel wrapped around his waist,
but kind of distant and in, he said, "a big fat hurry." He'd
always been a little cool in the A.M., so I opted not to read
too much into his attitude. While he dressed I popped into
the bathroom. It was clear I wasn't being allotted much
time, so I made it quick. As I brushed my teeth with his
toothbrush, my eye caught the edge of something pink
poking out from behind the shower curtain. I pulled the
wet nylon curtain quietly aside. Sitting on the edge of the
tub was one of those pink Daisy razors, the kind for girls
only.

My stomach did a somersault. I hadn't noticed it last
night in the darkness. Had it been there on Thursday? I
didn't think so. We had taken a shower together when we
got back from the bar, because we both felt so grungy,
and I surely would have noticed it. Someone had been
here between now and then, someone who felt familiar

enough to bring her own razor. I was suddenly queasy—
and furious. At myself more than him. How dumb could
I be?

Poker-faced, I went back to the kitchen, where K.C.,
dressed now in a navy suit and Hermès tie, was scarfing
down a cup of coffee. I poured a cup for myself and drank
it sans milk because I'd seen none in the fridge. K.C. announced that he had a car service waiting downstairs and
that the driver could take me to the Village after dropping
him in midtown.

I wanted to just hightail it out of there on my own, but
I knew I'd never find a cab and I couldn't face the
thought of the subway. Outside, it was no more than sixty
degrees and raining, and I nearly froze in my T-shirt. In
the car K.C. made one comment about the weather and
then turned most of his attention to the *Wall Street Journal*, which had been left for him in the lobby. His office
was on Park Avenue in the 50s, and in the light, precrush
traffic, the trip took just over twenty minutes. As the car
rolled up to his building he kissed me lightly on the lips.

"Gosh, you never did get that umbrella, did you?" he
said with a cocky smile.

Before I could even conjure up a glib reply, he was out
of the car and dodging raindrops.

By the time the driver left me at my apartment building,
I was in the world's suckiest mood and I couldn't even
tell which thing was contributing the most to my misery:
the spat with Cat, my worries about Heidi's death, or that
putrid pink razor. Obviously they were all just slow cooking unpleasantly together in that Crock-Pot of my brain.

I checked my messages. No hang-ups. Just someone

thinking he'd reached Marv and a frantic message from Cat moments after she'd called on my cell last night.

I made coffee and showered. While I was toweling off, I called Landon and asked if he wanted to have breakfast with me. I didn't have much to offer, just frozen bagels, but he was game.

As I set cups and plates on the dining room table, I considered what I needed to do today. I was in a real predicament. At Cat's request I had begun looking into the supposed attempt on her life, but now that she was miffed at me and my investigation was going down a whole different road, she might no longer want me involved. Was I just supposed to stop in my tracks? Well, she might want me to, but I'd be damned if I was going to do that. I felt compelled to figure out the truth. Besides, the killer was watching me. I wasn't going to be safe until he—or she—was caught.

I needed to make the final fixes on my Marky piece this morning, and as soon as I was finished, I'd go drop it off at *Gloss*. I could have sent it electronically, but I was looking for an excuse to check out the scene there. Next, I'd visit the Godiva store on Fifth Avenue. Though Godiva chocolates were sold at gourmet food stores in New York, one of their own boutiques would have the biggest selection. I'd also want to make some calls and find out what I could about Patty Gaylin and the chocolate-chip cookies. And there was the reading by Nancy Highland today. It was at three-thirty at a bookstore in the East 70s, and I didn't want to miss it.

The bell rang and I let Landon in. As soon as he saw me, a small frown formed on his face.

"Bailey, dear, you look exhausted."

"That bad, huh?"

"I didn't say *bad*. It's just that you have very *large, dark* circles under your eyes. Of course, on you it looks sexy."

"Good recovery," I said. He took a seat at the table as I went to the kitchen to collect the French press and pop a bagel into the toaster. "You look a little sleepy yourself," I called out. "Hot date last night?"

"I *thought* it was going to be hot, but it quickly turned into a disaster. That guy Edward, the one with the faux British accent I mentioned several weeks ago, called and asked if I wanted to go to a party with him in a loft in Tribeca. Said he knew it was spur of the moment, but it would be lots of fun, et cetera. He hadn't returned a single call of mine, but I thought, Okay, so he's been busy. Well, I pick him up in a cab, which *I* pay for, and when we get there it becomes clear that we are actually *crashing* the party. It was absolutely humiliating."

"Did you get turned away?"

"No, but that would have been the best thing that could have happened. There was someone at the door who tried to get a handle on who had invited us. Edward glances over to the buffet table, announces, 'We're friends of the *ham*,' and struts in. Then he just *dropped* me. He probably invited me because I don't look like a crasher and he thought he'd have an easier time getting in with me. But forget all that. It's just one more crushing blow to my ego, and I'm over it now. Why did you look like you pulled an all-nighter? What's happening with Miss Kit-Kat?"

I stood up to get the bagel and pop another into the toaster, and as I sat down again I proceeded to give him an update, filling him in on my Heidi theory, including the new details I'd found about Heidi's life and, last but not least, Cat's verbal slap.

"My God, my head is spinning," Landon said. "I can't even keep this all straight. Do you have the slightest idea who might have killed this nanny?"

"No," I said. "But someone has been snooping around my office and calling me and hanging up. I figure it's got to be the killer, and he or she's within range."

"I just wish you'd stay out of it," he said. "It's way too dangerous."

"The trouble is," I said, "I wouldn't know how to signal to the killer that I had decided to back off. So I might be in danger regardless of what I do. It's in my interest to keep going, to figure out who did this."

I switched gears and asked him what he thought I should do about Cat.

"Well, don't grovel or act wounded, that's for sure," he said. "It will only bring out the shark in her. If I were you, I'd just lie low, do nothing, stay out of her range for a few days."

"That's exactly what K.C. said last night."

"Oh my, are things heating up there?"

"No. Cooling down. But I can't bear to discuss it right now."

Before he could run through his usual lecture on how I deserved the most wonderful man in the world, there was a knock on the door of my apartment, and it startled both of us. Outside visitors were always announced by the doorman.

I crossed the room and undid the dead bolt but left the

chain on as I opened the door. Cat Jones was standing in the hallway in a cream-colored trench coat.

"Are you going to let me in?" she asked.

"Of course," I said, undoing the chain. "Is the doorman not down there? No one rang up."

"There *was* a guy there," she said, stepping inside. "But he didn't say anything." The doorman had probably assumed by her demeanor that she'd just bought the building.

"Well, come in. You want coffee? I have some made already."

She looked past me, over my shoulder, at Landon, who was starting to rise from the table, and her eyes widened. The first thing that must have crossed her mind was that I was sleeping with a guy close to forty years older than me. I made introductions, not bothering to say that Landon was my next-door neighbor because I thought it would be entertaining to keep her guessing for a while. But as soon as she shook his hand, I saw that she recognized him. I had introduced her to him once at a *Gloss* event I'd dragged him along to.

I could tell Landon was hoping to hang around for the show, but I gave him a look and he got out quick as a bunny, announcing, purely for my amusement, that he had a brisket he needed to marinate.

"You've really changed this place around since I was here last," Cat said, slipping off her trench coat and tossing it onto the couch. "It's nice. Kind of a Santa Fe thing, right?"

"Yeah, sort of," I said, handing her a cup of coffee. She was wearing a tight, tight brown cardigan with a V neckline and a full skirt with what appeared to be purple lip prints on it. "It's kind of a clichéd idea these days, but I like the colors—and, of course, the baskets are cheap to work with. I was just glad to get rid of all that supermodern stuff I had when I was married."

"Are you okay about that now—the divorce, I mean?"

"Yeah. I'm fine, really. More or less."

"Is it hard to live alone in a space that you once shared with someone you were totally in love with?"

Hmmm. Was she referring to me, or was she in the process of making some plan for herself?

"It depends, I guess. If you're still in love, I suppose it would be hard. That wasn't the case for me. Plus, redecorating does wonders."

"Are you still mad at me?" she asked out of nowhere. She had wandered over to the table and was taking a seat in the chair Landon had occupied. I joined her at the table.

"Yeah. Not as mad as I was last night, but I'd be lying if I said I was completely over what happened."

"Well, I've come to apologize. I know there's no excuse for being so bitchy—to you, of all people—but I hope you can understand that I'm not myself these days. I'm going crazy. I don't have Tyler with me and Jeff's out of town and work is awful and this thing with Patty sent me over the edge. I made Carlotta stay over last night, and I woke up in the middle of the night thinking, Oh, my God, what if it's *her?* What if she's standing outside my bedroom with a butcher knife? That's what a mess I am right now. And it suddenly seemed as if you didn't care, that you were going off half-cocked on another idea."

"I'm sorry if it seemed that way," I said. "And I'm also

sorry that I've been so busy running around lately that I probably haven't had a chance to be very empathetic."

"Of course," she said with the slightest degree of peevishness, "you think I have less to worry about than I do. You think we should be focusing on Heidi."

"Cat, do you really want to get into this?" I asked. "That's how you ended up so annoyed with me yesterday."

"I *do* want to get into it. You were right the other night when you said that the reason I asked for your help is that you're brilliant at pushing, and turning over every stone. I need to trust you."

"I don't believe I used the word *brilliant*," I pointed out.

"Come on, Bailey, you know what I mean. If there's something I need to know about Heidi, tell me. I'm ready to hear it now."

She seemed genuine, so I decided to test the waters—carefully.

"I *have* begun to suspect that the candy may have been meant for Heidi, but I'm not a hundred percent sure. There's still one thing I need to check out."

"But I don't get it," she said. "How could someone be certain Heidi would walk off with the candy?"

"I don't think Heidi walked off with the candy," I explained. "I think the killer set a box of candy on the hall table and took it away later, kind of as a decoy. And then later, he—or she—slipped the poison chocolates through the grated door to Heidi's apartment."

"But *why?* Why would someone at my party want to kill Heidi? Wait . . . Jody came by that night. Do you think he could have done it?"

"He's the logical suspect. But we need to consider whether there could be any others. As far as you know, was there anyone at the party who might have known Heidi in more than a passing way?"

"Well, plenty of people from *Gloss* knew her. She's been in the office a few times to pick things up, and of course, people from work come to the house. . . . Are you thinking someone from *Gloss* might have had a *relationship* with her?" She asked it tentatively, as if it were a direction she wasn't thrilled to be going in.

"Maybe. Any ideas?"

"No, nothing. At least nothing that I ever picked up on."

I watched her closely as she was answering, but there was nothing in her expression that indicated she knew about Heidi and Kip or Heidi and anyone else, for that matter. I had no intention of filling her in at this point. And I wasn't going to raise the Jeff issue. I had no proof whatsoever, I'd already asked her about the state of her marriage, and I wasn't interested in doing anything to set her off again.

"What about the jewelry? I take it you or Carlotta came across the Tiffany earrings and bracelet in her drawer. When you saw them, did they ring any bells?"

"No. Like I said before, I have no reason to assume she didn't arrive in New York with them. They certainly couldn't be from Jody. He's the kind of guy who gives a girl car mats as a gift. What do you think I should do with them?"

"Well, don't do anything with them just yet," I told her. "If it turns out I'm right and that Heidi was meant to die all along, then you need to turn the jewelry over to the police. If the pieces are really from Tiffany, they may be able to trace who gave them to her."

"Well, when are you going to get this info you're talking about?"

"Maybe I'll know something today."

"There's nothing you can tell me right now?"

"Nothing that's going to matter, because it may not pan out. But I promise I'll call you later and fill you in as soon as I have the info."

"I've got an idea, then," she said, pushing her chair back in a way that signaled she would soon be on the move. "I'm driving up to Litchfield at about three today—I have to get out of New York again. Maybe this whole thing isn't about me, but as long as the police think it is and until you have the proof that it isn't, I'm not going to feel safe here. Why don't you come up, stay for a few days?"

"You weren't planning to be there alone, were you?"

"No, of course not. Jeff is shooting just for the day in Miami. He'll fly into La Guardia tonight and take a car service from there directly to the house. And this weekend my mother will bring Tyler down—if I feel . . . if I feel safe."

"I appreciate the invitation, but don't you need time to yourself, time with Jeff?"

"The house is big enough. And it will give you and me the chance to talk more."

"I'd love to come, but I have a pretty full plate today."

"If you've got stuff to do today, you can drive up tomorrow."

"All right, I can probably come. But if I do, it will have to be tomorrow—and I'm not sure what time."

"Doesn't matter," she said. "You've got my number up there. Just call me tonight—I should be there by six." She took a lipstick out of the makeup bag in her purse and, using the side of a table knife as a mirror, touched up her lips with a shade that looked like putty. When she was done, when she'd smushed her lips together so that the color distributed evenly, we both stood. She picked her trench coat off the couch, slipped it on, and glanced around the room in this odd way she had of taking stock of her surroundings before she departed. Maybe she was always nervous about leaving behind a glove or an umbrella, but it sometimes had the look of someone checking for snipers.

"You're comfortable being away from *Gloss* so much this week?" I asked, walking her to the door. "I thought Harry was breathing down your neck."

"I've got him off my case for now. He likes it if you grovel a little and act as if you can't live without his advice."

"Is that where you're headed now—to work?"

"In a while. I've got a meeting outside first."

"Before you go, I do have one other question about Heidi, though. I heard she used to work for Nancy Highland in Scarsdale. How exactly did you end up with her?"

"I know that woman thinks I stole her, but that's not how it worked," Cat said, looping the belt of her trench coat into a knot rather than buckling it. "Last summer Audrey had to call up there, about some minor detail to do with the plan for that ridiculous book, and Heidi answered the phone. She explained that she was the nanny, and since mine had just quit, Audrey asked her in passing if she had any friends who might be interested. The next thing we know, Heidi is begging for the job. Why?"

"Just curious."

"Whatever trail you want to follow is fine with me. I still need your help, Bailey. You know that, right?"

"Okay, I'll keep at it," I said.

She looked anxious to leave suddenly, and she opened the door herself. I said good-bye, promising to help, to get in touch when I had info, to let her know what time I'd be arriving in Litchfield tomorrow.

It was now after ten and I was getting a later start than I'd planned. Without even bothering to clear away the breakfast dishes, I turned on my computer and went through my Marky piece one last time, tweaking a few things here and there. Overall, I was satisfied with it, but I couldn't help thinking that it would have been better if I hadn't been forced to slam it together. When I was done, I made calls to several freelance writer friends who'd worked for *Women's Journal* on and off, but only one was in and she hadn't heard about the cookie caper. Unfortunately, I didn't know anyone on staff I could call directly and pump for news.

Now it was noon and I was anxious to get moving. I decided to switch the order of my plan and go to the Godiva store first and then work my way over to *Gloss*. From my terrace door I could see that it was pouring outside, so I threw on my own trench coat and a pair of black rubber rainboots. Not quite the Cat Jones look, but then I wasn't traveling by town car. At the newsstand above the subway station I picked up both the *News* and the *Post* to see if either had a word about Crock Pot Patty, but there was zip. The train was surprisingly mobbed for so late in the morning, and I had an unpleasant ride uptown, wedged against a bunch of hot, wet bodies.

The Godiva boutique, a wood-paneled sliver of a shop on Fifth Avenue and 54th, was empty when I arrived. I figured with Mother's Day behind us and summer looming, it probably wasn't one of their busier seasons. The shelves displayed various sizes of the classic gold box, some simply sporting the traditional gold elastic around them, others with different types of decorative arrangements on top. I decided to start from the front of the store and work my way to the back systematically. I'd been at it for only a minute when a thirtysomething black saleswoman in a dark pantsuit floated in my direction from the back of the store and asked if she could be of help. I told her I wanted to pick up a box of candy for a friend but wasn't sure what my options were. She took me through the store, showing me the selection, and as I glanced over the merchandise, I saw absolutely nothing with a white or pink flower on top. I bought a box of truffles, thinking this would keep the saleswoman in an accommodating mode, and as she rung up my purchase I asked if they offered a simple white or pale pink flower arrangement for the top.

"We just have what's displayed here."

"Are these arrangements standard, or do they sometimes change?"

"They change, from season to season. Are you giving the truffles for a birthday?"

"Actually, I'm curious if a small white flower I have came from one of your boxes."

"It might have. We sometimes do have flowers." She was handing me my change and looking eager to get over to a man who had just entered the store, shaking off his umbrella. "Do you have it with you? I might recognize it."

I told her I didn't but might come back with it. She gave me a wan smile, as if it had just dawned on her I might be a psycho. I left the store, stuffing the little shopping bag she'd given me into my tote bag.

The quickest route to *Gloss* from Fifth and 54th Street was on foot, and I sloshed over, getting wetter and grouchier by the minute. Now what? I wondered. Earlier, I'd been sure the flower petal I'd found in the Jiffy Bag must have come from the Godiva box but I hadn't found the proof I'd hoped for. Of course, all the police would have to do is compare the petal with the flower they had in their possession, but I didn't have that luxury. And I didn't want to create a ruckus about the whole thing if there was a chance I was wrong. Could I get the petal out of Cat's house and return with it to the store?

Things were deadly quiet at *Gloss* when I arrived, not unexpected considering we were now entering that predictable two- or three-day lull following the close of an issue; but these days it was hard to tell how much of the mood at *Gloss* was normal and how much related to the pure freakiness of what was going on. From the foyer by the elevator I peeked around the corner to the pit—it was like a ghost town there—and then followed the back way to my office, hoping to avoid Leslie.

My office appeared untouched, untossed. I wondered how long it would be before I could walk into the room and not feel squeamish. I slipped out of my trench coat, shook off the water, and hung it on the back of the door.

I tossed the boots and the umbrella out in the corridor and slid on a pair of shoes that I had stuffed in my tote bag.

I'd come to the office to hand in my article, and I planned to get that out of the way immediately, resisting any temptation to continue to tweak it. The reading by Nancy Highland was at three-thirty, so I'd have to leave around three. Hopefully I'd get the chance to chat with her and see just how big a path of destruction Heidi had bushwhacked through her life—and from there I might have a sense of whether it made any sense to consider her a suspect.

But then what? I felt anxious to continue to pursue the Heidi theory, but at the same time I still wasn't 100 percent sure I was on the mark with it. The more I thought about it, the more I realized that what I needed to do was move down two parallel roads—simultaneously. Road number one: I had to get whatever proof I could that my Heidi theory was correct. Road number two: Even while I was trying to prove my theory, I had to proceed as if it *was* true, trying to figure out who had murdered Heidi. If the killer had sent the "bad" cookies to Patty Gaylin to confuse matters, it indicated that he or she was feeling pressured, cornered. I didn't like thinking about what their next move might be.

I'd already talked to the obvious people in Heidi's life, snooped around her apartment twice, turned over every stone in sight, and interviewed the two ex-lovers I knew of, Jody and Kip. What I hadn't managed to do was figure out who the mystery man was, the lover of vodka and jazz and the giver of fine jewelry. I'd assumed at first it was Kip, but he'd clearly been replaced by someone else. Something told me that if I figured out who he was, I'd find myself far closer to the truth. But how could I do that?

I walked my Marky article down to Polly's office and left it in her in-box. Neither she nor her assistant was anywhere around. Back in my office I ordered some New England clam chowder and when it arrived devoured it with three bags of those tasteless little crackers they send with it. As I munched on them, I decided on a strategy. First, I was going to take Cat up on her offer and go to Litchfield tomorrow. Maybe, just maybe, I might learn something up there. I'd get maximum exposure to the Cat-Jeff rapport, and I could better evaluate Jeff as a possible suspect. And since Heidi had spent time at the Litchfield house—and had even planned to entertain the mystery man on site—there might be something revealing. Farfetched, I know, but it seemed better than hanging around New York without any obvious leads to run down.

As for today, once I was done with Nancy Highland I was going to go back to the town house. Cat was on her way to Litchfield, Jeff was safely in Miami, but Carlotta would probably be there. I'd take along a Polaroid camera from the art department, shoot a picture of the damn petal, and show it to the saleswoman at Godiva, hoping she could verify that it had once been part of an arrangement used on top of a truffles box.

I left at exactly three for the reading. The bookstore, on Madison at 71st, turned out to be one of those small independent stores that has somehow managed not to be driven out of business by the big superstores. I worked my way to a small open area in the back of the store, where Nancy Highland had already begun her reading. There were about twenty people, all women, sitting on black folding chairs or leaning against bookshelves. A small table had been set up with a plate of Milano cookies, apparently all that was being done to fulfill the "tea" aspect of the event.

According to a poster, the story, a selection from *Love at Any Cost*, was "Afternoon in Algiers," and from what I could tell, having arrived a few minutes late, it was about a middle-aged divorced woman who goes on holiday to northern Africa and falls in love with the younger man leading her tour group. She said each word with the seriousness of purpose you'd bring to a reading of James Joyce's "The Dead." I tried to look riveted, but it was very, very tough.

Though the crowd was small, it was enthusiastic, obviously a collection of friends and fans, and they all seemed to want to speak with Nancy when she was done. I hung back, waiting for each person to finish her questions and comments, but it was clear after about twenty minutes that two women in particular were not going to budge. If I was going to strike, it would have to be now.

"Nancy, hi," I said, stepping forward and extending my hand. "We met at Cat Jones's house a few weeks ago. I really enjoyed your reading."

She looked at me with distaste. She had one of those small, freckled faces that is considered cute as a button until the age of twenty-four, when it starts to shrink, like a week-old peach. She was wearing a hot pink Chanel suit with shiny gold buttons, perhaps in an attempt to overcompensate.

"You're the one from *Gloss*," she said finally. "I can't believe you came to this."

"Well, I'm a writer, too, and I was interested in hearing you. Do you have a minute to talk?"

"Actually, I don't," she said brusquely. "I'm going to dinner with a couple of friends and they're waiting for me."

"It'll only take a second—and it's very important."

"All right," she said with a big sigh. "But please make it quick."

I lowered my voice because the two friends were hovering nearby. "As you may have heard, Cat Jones's nanny, Heidi, died the other night."

"Why, of course I've heard. The police have been all the way to Scarsdale to ask me about the party. As I told them, I know absolutely nothing."

"Cat's concerned about some of the things that have come to light about Heidi. She asked me to find out whatever I could."

"Oh, *that's* amusing," she said. "She's decided to do the background check *now*." As she talked, she cocked her head back and forth, the way you would if you were saying "Tick, tock, tick tock."

"I know Heidi worked for you and that you had some problem with her."

"Who told you that? Dolores?"

"I heard she made trouble, had an affair with your older son," I said, avoiding giving her an answer.

"My *son?*" she said incredulously. "You *have* been talking to Dolores, haven't you? She can't keep a story straight. No, it wasn't my son. Heidi *toyed* with my son. She teased him and tortured him, which I found out only after he went to Chapel Hill last fall and told me on the phone. But she had bigger fish to fry. The one she got *in-*

volved with was my fellow country club member, Mr. Mercedes Dealership with a wife and two kids. It all came out after she left Scarsdale. The wife has chosen to forgive him, but I can't imagine why—he's pathetic."

"Did you see Heidi at the party at Cat's?"

"Briefly. She scurried off like a rat when she spotted me. I still haven't called my son yet to tell him she's dead."

"He's at Chapel Hill, you say?"

"Yes, with a lovely new girlfriend. You know, at the time we were livid when Heidi left so soon, in part because we'd paid her airfare from Indiana. But it turned out to be the best thing in the world. She was nothing but trouble. Cat Jones stole her away and got exactly what she deserved. It must be terrible working for that woman. I hope you never make the mistake of trusting her."

She turned her back to me and sashayed off to join her friends, who both shot me a glance suggesting they thought I must be a stalker/fan. I slunk out of the store. The rain had stopped, finally, but it was rush hour and it seemed pointless to try to hunt down a cab for the twenty-block ride to Cat's house. The bus stop was right in front of the bookstore and as a number 1 lumbered up I hopped on, figuring it would take less than fifteen minutes to make it to 91st Street.

If I was to believe Nancy Highland, she had no good reason to be on my suspect list. Heidi had left her in the lurch, made her son cry briefly, and created an awkward situation at the club, but those weren't very exciting motives for murder. I needed to concentrate all my efforts now on finding out who the mystery man was.

I jumped off at the corner of 91st and Madison, and

when I was several houses away from Cat's, I spotted Carlotta coming down the front steps in a black raincoat.

"Carlotta, hey," I called, jogging toward the stoop. "Has Cat already left for Litchfield?"

"Two hours—at least, Miss Bailey."

"Oh, shoot, I was hoping to catch her," I lied. "Are you done for the night, Carlotta?"

"Yes. I no like staying alone at night anymore."

"Because of what happened to Heidi, you mean?"

"Yes, it scares me. I tell Mrs. Henderson that."

She climbed down the last two steps, an indication that she wanted to get moving. There was no way I was going to try to convince her to go back in the house and let me take a photo. She'd be highly suspicious and probably would find some excuse to refuse. I fell in step beside her as she headed east, probably on her way to the Lex line at 96th Street.

"I don't blame you for being scared," I said. "This must all be very upsetting."

She didn't say anything, just nodded.

"You must have known Heidi pretty well," I said. "Do you miss her?"

She stopped in her tracks and turned to me. "I don't miss her," she said, her dark eyes holding my gaze. "She make a lot of trouble."

"What do you mean, Carlotta?" I urged as she resumed walking.

"She make trouble with Mr. and Mrs. Henderson. It wasn't so good."

"What kind of trouble?"

"Big trouble. But no, I shouldn't say."

"Please, Carlotta," I said. "I only want to help Cat."

"He act berry friendly to her. They have big fights about that girl. Please, I shouldn't say."

Having dropped the bomb at my feet, she hurried away.

CHAPTER 21

CAT HAD LIED to me. Lied to me big-time. She had assured me that things were all better between her and Jeff. And she had told me she hadn't a clue about whether Heidi was involved with someone else. I felt totally jerked around, used. But I also felt something else: a churning in my stomach. Suddenly Cat had a motive for murder.

As thoughts raced through my head, my paced slowed and Carlotta edged away from me. I doubted I could elicit any more info from her, so I let her go. I took a right on Park and decided to make my way toward the subway as well. I'd get on the Lex line at 86th.

I ambled along, thinking, fuming, worrying, paying practically no attention to the people around me, to the puddles on the sidewalk, to the traffic hurtling by. I felt betrayed and angry, but I also felt worried and totally unsure what my next move should be.

And then things went from bad to worse. At 86th Street I absentmindedly crossed to the south side of the street, which I didn't need to do to get on the downtown train. Twenty feet from a French bistro, I froze. K.C. was climbing out of a cab with a woman—no, two women, both twentysomething and as giddy as can be. I quickly took two giant steps to the right, pressed myself against the front wall of the closest building, and lowered my head so he wouldn't recognize me—but not so much that I couldn't see. As the three of them huddled laughing on the sidewalk, a second guy launched himself out of the front seat of the taxi, tucking his wallet into his back pocket. Maybe they were all just pals. But as the other guy draped his arm around one of the girls, K.C. pressed his hand possessively along the back of the other.

I felt a momentary urge to hurl, but I fought it off and backed up toward Park Avenue. I hurried away, south on Park, and finally at 77th Street I spotted a cab going the wrong way and flagged it down.

When I got back to my place that night, I was almost shaking. I kicked off my rubber boots and dumped my bags in my office. I had practically nothing in the house to eat, but I was too hungry and too agitated to wait for take-out, so I chopped the moldy parts off a hunk of cheddar I had in the fridge and made a cheese omelet. I wolfed it down at the dining room table. Afterward, as I was trying to scrape all the egg from the pan with a tattered scouring pad, I started to bawl my eyes out.

It was hard to tell what was contributing the most to my misery—K.C. or Cat or just everything that had happened over the past two weeks. I hadn't been on a real crying jag since two months after my husband moved out (and everything burst out during a tiff with a rude shoe salesman). After about fifteen minutes, when the sobs were down to sniffles, I felt better. But that didn't mean I had any answers—or knew what to do.

As far as K.C. was concerned, I was willing to accept the fact that I had no one but myself to blame. He'd never done anything to indicate that he wanted an exclusive thing with me, and the Daisy razor should have been a warning to me that I was in occupied territory. I'd stupidly been trying to convince myself that our spontaneous couplings reflected a lack of game playing, but what they'd really been was nothing more than a way for him to secure some easy action. Christ, the girl he was with tonight had at least managed to snag a meal from him, something I hadn't done for over two weeks.

Maybe Landon had been right. Maybe I'd become enamored of K.C. because he was ultimately unavailable.

And then there was Cat. She had misled me, but that wasn't the worst of it. She might be the one who had poisoned Heidi.

I pondered her behavior over the past two weeks, especially the things she'd done that had seemed slightly "off." First there was her Sunday morning call to me. She'd been so convinced there was something the matter with Heidi—despite the lack of any overwhelming evidence—and so adamant that I had to fly up to her place. If she'd killed Heidi, she may have thought that arranging for me to find the body distanced her slightly from everything.

There'd also been the weirdness of her plans that weekend—sending Jeff and Tyler to the country because she supposedly needed to work and then heading out to

East Hampton. Had she even *gone* to East Hampton? Her reason for wanting to see Heidi so early on a Sunday had also seemed lame.

Other things suddenly jumped out at me. Cat had told me right away that Heidi pinched food. She'd pointed out that the chocolates Heidi had eaten must have been the ones that had been left for her. She had also brought up the Tucker Bobb connection—I remembered Leslie saying that on the phone.

Last but not least was how testy she'd gotten when I'd told her I thought Heidi was the intended victim.

Yet if she was in a rage about an affair between Jeff and Heidi—and she would be—then why take it out on Heidi and not Jeff? Because she still wanted Jeff? Maybe what had gone on between Heidi and Jeff was more than just a fling. Maybe Jeff, the husband who was six years younger, had fallen hard, and Cat knew that the only way to end the situation was to eliminate Heidi completely.

Of course, if Jeff and Heidi had really been having an affair, Jeff was a suspect, too.

I wondered what I should do about going to Litchfield. I still felt an overwhelming desire to learn what had really happened to Heidi. But would it be dangerous to spend a night in a house with someone who might very well be a murderer—and might suspect I was getting closer to the truth?

I had to go. I had to know the truth. Besides, something in my gut was telling me that it just *couldn't* be Cat. Yes, her behavior had been strange, but there were other explanations for everything. She'd called me that morning because she'd been scared and, as it turned out, justifiably so. She'd brought up Heidi's pilfering because we were talking about her eating habits. She'd mentioned that the box of Godiva truffles was a gift to her because that's exactly what it had appeared to be.

Besides, there were several factors that undercut the notion of her guilt. Why would she intentionally bring so much misery down around herself by killing Heidi and making it look like she, Cat, was the target? Unless she hadn't anticipated the degree of the fallout. Second, why would she deputize me to snoop around, to turn up the ground, if there was a chance I'd find something linking her to the killing? Unless, of course, she'd wanted to have me stumble on any incriminating info before the police did. And why would she send me on a hunt for the truth and then try to scare me off with hang-ups and candy? Unless, of course, she was a total psychopath.

I had to go to Litchfield to reassure myself, to see if I could shake the truth about her marriage out of her. I'd tell her I'd discovered she'd suspected there was something between Jeff and Heidi, and I'd weigh her reaction and her explanation. There was Jeff to consider, of course. There was a chance he was the killer. But I would be careful. And surely he wouldn't pull anything with Cat around.

The rest of the night was pretty much a bust. Thanks to my sob fest, my eyes were all puffy, my brain was pounding to get out of my skull, and it seemed pointless to attempt anything like a run to the movies. A friend from *Get* called around eight to commiserate about how she'd finally gone to bed with this new man in her life and during the night he'd screamed, "You're hogging my blankie!" Was that enough reason, she wondered, to dump him? God, *I* thought so, but I hedged, figuring that as of tonight it was clear I was about as big a moron as there was in the man department. After I hung up I took a bath and leafed through a six-month-old issue of *Gloss* that I'd never gotten around to looking at. As I got to the tip on how to soften coarse pubic hair (apply ordinary hair conditioner), I decided to try bed. I flopped around for an hour, my brain jammed with thoughts about K.C., Cat, and Heidi. I made a stab at some muscle relaxation exercises, flopped some more, and fell asleep around one. It occurred to me, just as I felt sleep overtake me, that I'd gone the whole night without a hang-up.

I was up early on Thursday, just before seven. Though the weather forecast had called for a nice day, it was overcast and cool. I ordered my Jeep from the garage and headed to the gym for forty-five minutes on the treadmill. Back home, I phoned Cat, told her to expect me for lunch, then showered and threw two days of clothes into my overnight bag. I figured I needed to be on the road by ten.

As I was shutting off the lights in my apartment, the phone rang. Leslie. The new, friendlier model.

"I heard you're going to Litchfield today," she said. "Do you need a lift?"

"Thanks," I said. "But I've got a car. You're going up today?"

"Yes, Clyde and I are taking a three-day weekend. I just barely got the July issue out the door and I need a break."

"Well, thanks for the offer," I said, trying to get off. "Maybe I'll see you around up there."

"By the way, I promised to call you if I had an update on Patty Gaylin. But I haven't heard a thing."

"Thanks, me neither."

"I take it you're still helping Cat. Any luck?"

"Maybe," I said. "But look, I've got to dash now. I promised Cat I'd be there for lunch."

I was halfway out the door when I stopped, dropped my bag to the floor, and went back to the phone. I dialed Jack Herlihy's number. His machine picked up and I left a message saying I'd be out of town for the weekend, but back on Sunday if he wanted a tour. I left Cat's number. My voice sounded high and squeaky, as if I'd just sucked on a tank of helium. As soon as I hung up, I felt like an idiot. Watch. Now that I'd gone out on a limb, he wouldn't be interested.

I made good time in the Jeep, reaching Litchfield County in just over two hours. It's not unlike Bucks County up there, but it's been spared the push of the suburbs. The countryside is lush, rolling, with beautiful old houses and horse farms. Even on a gray, overcast day it was breathtaking.

Cat and Jeff's home wasn't one of the biggest houses in the area, but it was charming and roomy, an old white clapboard farmhouse set just off the road, with about twenty acres of fields and woods behind it, a huge red barn, and several smaller outbuildings.

Despite the fact that it was cool today, the front door was open halfway. I peered in through the screen door and, not seeing anyone, rapped on the frame. No answer. I called out hello—twice—but got no reply. Cat's BMW was in the driveway, and so was their pickup truck. They couldn't be far.

I opened the screen door and stepped inside. The scent of lilacs filled the air, but the house was totally silent.

I called out Cat's name a couple of times, and still nothing. Setting down my overnight bag and laptop in the front hallway, I sauntered off to the left, toward the kitchen. The house was long rather than wide, so that you could shout from one end of it and not hear someone at the other. There was no one in the kitchen, but I spotted signs of life: Three places had been set at the farm table by the fireplace. I headed back toward the other end of the house, checking the dining room, living room, screened-in porch, and small, wood-paneled library at the opposite end of the house from the kitchen. No one.

As I walked back toward the hall, I heard voices and footsteps. Cat came down the stairs, barefoot, wearing jeans and a tight spandex-y black turtleneck with short sleeves, no bra. Her blond hair had been pulled up in a high ponytail. Jeff was behind her, at the top of the stairs, and I caught the final motion of him zipping his jeans. Great. Nothing like catching your hosts with their pants nearly around their ankles.

"You scared me for a second," Cat said. "We didn't hear your car, but then I heard sounds in the house."

"I'm not too early, am I?"

"No, we were just getting ready for lunch." She hugged me casually and Jeff said hello as he came down the rest of the stairs. No chapped lips on my cheek today; nothing sinister, either. Just friendly but distant Jeff.

Lunch was take-out salads and cold cuts that Cat had picked up in town earlier. While Jeff went to the basement to grab a bottle of wine, I helped her open the cartons and spoon food onto plates. Though there were still dark circles under her eyes, she seemed relaxed in a way I hadn't seen since before that horrible Sunday. I guess that's what sex before lunch will do for you. Just before we sat down the phone rang, and after a minute I could tell she was talking to Leslie, mostly about work stuff, but I heard her ask, "What time should we be there?" When she got off she announced that Leslie had asked the three of us to dinner tonight. Something not to look forward to.

It was hard for me to generate much enthusiasm for lunch. My stomach was doing a weird dance, from pure nervousness, I was sure, and the mood at the table didn't help. Jeff was friendly, but in a detached way, making a few bland comments about California wine versus French and then getting absorbed in his food. And Cat seemed quiet for Cat. As I watched her tear off a piece of bread from the baguette, I couldn't help but think that those same hands may have made the poison truffles.

"So when is Tyler getting here?" I asked, trying to find a topic. "I bet you're happy beyond belief."

"My mother is driving him down tomorrow," Cat said. "I had thought it was going to be today, and that's all I've been thinking about. But it turns out she'd planned some little outing for him today, and I didn't want to throw her into a tizzy."

"What are you going to do about a nanny?" I felt funny just saying the word.

"Well, the agency hasn't sent anyone for me to interview, and I think it's because of what's been in the papers. So Carlotta's cousin is going to stay on. Right now, I'll take what I can get."

"Will she live in the apartment?"

"No, she doesn't want to do that. But she'll spend the night when we need her to. Jeff," she said, dropping the nanny topic with a thud, "you *must* show Bailey your studio this weekend. Jeff's redone the top floor of the barn into a work space."

"For photography?" I asked.

"Actually, no—I've been doing a little painting," he said. He had to be one of the few people in the world who looked good with a swipe of mayo on his mouth. "It's always been a hobby—I've just been doing more lately. I'm not pretending to be Jackson Pollock out here, but it's a release, a way to unwind."

"You're being too modest," Cat protested. "The stuff you've been doing is fantastic." She was obviously still in the afterglow of a nooner.

We talked for a few minutes about art, then clunkily moved on to real estate in Litchfield County. During coffee Cat began to trace the inside of Jeff's wrist with her fingers in this hypnotic way that would put a cat to sleep if you did it on its head. What was going on? I wondered. Was she putting on some kind of show this morning for my benefit?

When we finished I helped Cat clear and put the few dishes we'd used in the dishwasher. Jeff announced he was taking the pickup truck to collect some furniture they'd bought several weeks ago at an auction, and I got to watch a twenty-second wet kiss before his departure— you'd have thought he was heading off on the *Millennium Falcon.*

Once he was gone, Cat showed me upstairs to the red-and-white guest room. When I asked if this was the room Heidi had slept in, she explained that Heidi had used a small bedroom at the far end of the hall. She looked curious but didn't comment on my question. Instead, she suggested I meet her on the screen porch, saying she'd grab some blankets since it was cool outside. She was already on the porch by the time I showed up there, reading a stack of *Gloss* copy. I'd brought Anne Boleyn with me. I'd managed to read two sentences when Cat, curled in a black wicker armchair across from me, interrupted.

"Are you *okay?* You're not still upset with me, are you?"

"No, of course not. Why?"

"When you called this morning you sounded kind of odd. And you seem—I don't know. Is something bothering you?"

"You mean other than everything that's happened in the last ten days? I'm tired. I've been running all over the place lately."

"Bailey, I know you. And something's eating you. Is it about me?"

My voice sounded squeaky when I responded. "It's nothing. I've got some personal stuff on my mind and that's probably coming through."

"You know what I wondered about at lunch?" Cat said. "That maybe it has something to do with me and Jeff."

"What do you mean?" I asked, setting down my book. I didn't have a good feeling about where this was headed.

"Well, it felt strange at lunch. I wondered if it's hard for you to be alone with a couple—I mean, since your divorce."

"You mean, am I still so traumatized from my divorce that I can't bear to hang around happily married couples? No, I don't *think* so." My voice was dripping in sarcasm as I said it.

"You're taking this the wrong way. I'm saying it with empathy. I mean, that kind of thing used to be hard for *me* after I'd broken up with someone. I just get the feeling being with me and Jeff makes you uncomfortable."

My blood was boiling now. "The only thing that's *uncomfortable* for me," I said, "is being in such a phony baloney situation. You two act all lovey-dovey, but I know that you've had bigger troubles lately than you let on. Troubles over *Heidi.*"

I anticipated the full force of Cat fury, but instead she began to cry. In her turtleneck and jeans she seemed more vulnerable than I'd ever seen her.

"How do you know that? Who told you?" she asked, wiping her tears away with the edge of the blanket.

"I just know."

"Okay, okay," she said, sniffling. "It's true, but I couldn't bring myself to tell you. I was too embarrassed. I love Jeff. He's not perfect, but there's a connection I have with him that I've never had with anyone else. I started to suspect there was something with Heidi, and it made me *insane.* I still don't know for sure if anything really went on between them."

"When did you become suspicious?"

"It was a couple of months ago. I told you how he wanted to shoot for *Gloss* and I wouldn't let him and he was furious. Well, he didn't get over it as quickly as I said. He started to pull away from me. Physically. In this very slow, torturous way. He'd fall asleep while I was washing my face. When we *did* have sex he seemed distracted, underwhelmed. I've never had the kind of sex I have with Jeff with anyone else, and suddenly it was falling apart. I tried to talk to him about it, and he told me

I was imagining things. That's why I did that stupid thing with Kip. I was totally confused."

"And where does Heidi fit into this?"

"I went by his studio one day to surprise him. I was trying to make nice. He wasn't there, but I have a key and I let myself in, thinking he'd be back soon enough. And then I started looking around. I hadn't planned to, but once I started I couldn't stop. And I found these pictures of Heidi—kind of modeling pictures, but they were very, very sexy. I went bananas."

"You confronted him?"

"Yes, and he said he had simply been doing her a favor. That she'd wanted to be a model and had asked him for help. He said he hadn't told me because he was afraid I'd take it the wrong way. When I suggested there might have been more than a photo session, he acted indignant."

"So why didn't you just give her the boot—right that second?"

She pulled out the rubber band from her ponytail as if it had become too tight and swept her fingers like a comb through her hair.

"You mean why didn't I just shove her ass in the street and toss her bags after her, like I'm capable of doing? Because I was afraid to."

"Afraid?" I said. "Cat, I've never seen you afraid of anyone."

"I know, but I was worried about making things even worse. If Jeff *was* having an affair, I might force his hand in some way. I was terrified he'd run off with her. If he *wasn't* having an affair, he might get even more upset with me—for acting paranoid. I also didn't know what *she* would do. If I threw her out, she might blab to the papers. I wanted to bide my time. Figure out the best way to handle it. You want to know the reason I got so upset when you told me Heidi was the real target? I was afraid Jeff would think I'd killed her."

"When you first raised the idea of an affair to Jeff, why didn't he try harder to allay your fears? If you ended up booting him out, wouldn't that put him in a bad situation?"

"You mean financially? There's no prenup—he'd do just dandy. And besides, he knows that I couldn't bear to lose him, that I'd forgive an indiscretion."

"How are things now?"

"Better. Not perfect, but better. He's seemed really worried about me. And it's such a relief not to have Heidi around. I hated the sight of her."

As she said the words, she caught herself. "You don't suspect me in some way, do you?" she asked.

"I didn't say that."

"But you think it, don't you?" she exclaimed. "That's what all this business with Heidi has been about." She started to cry again. "Bailey, you can't for a second think that I'm capable of that. You don't think that, do you?"

"There are some things I wonder about," I said. "Why did you call me that morning? Why not just go into Heidi's apartment yourself?"

"I was scared, just like I told you. I think it was in part because I secretly wanted her gone and I had this terrible sense that I'd willed something bad to happen to her."

"Why were you so quick to bring up the Tucker Bobb connection?"

"I wasn't. As far as I knew, he'd croaked from an oversize ego. Leslie mentioned it, and once I heard the real way he'd died it seemed like an odd coincidence—something worth looking into."

"And why did you *really* arrange to meet Heidi that morning? What was going on?"

She unwrapped the afghan from her body, stood up, and began to pace up and down the porch.

"I'm going to tell you something that I'm ashamed of," she said. "But you have to understand that I was desperate. I finally figured out a way to get Heidi out of my house—without having to confront Jeff again. I called her and told her I needed to talk to her. I'd decided to tell her that I suspected she might be responsible for a bruise on Tyler's arm and that I was giving her the option of resigning instead of having me report her to social services. I didn't suspect her of anything, but I knew if I set it up that way, she'd be too nervous to make a stink. And Jeff wouldn't take her side."

I looked at her, speechless.

"I know it's awful, but I was insane with worry. I had to get her out of my house."

We heard the front door slam several rooms away.

"Bailey, you've got to believe me," she pleaded in a whisper. "I didn't poison Heidi. I don't even know how to cook."

"Okay, I believe you, Cat." But my head was spinning, and in truth I didn't know what I believed.

CHAPTER 22

CAT PUT HER finger to her lips in a *shhh* signal, and announced that she was going out to help Jeff unload their auction loot from the back of the truck. I offered assistance, but she said they could handle it. I decided it might be best to make myself scarce for a while. I got my jacket from my room, went the back way to the barn, and dragged out an old Raleigh three-speed.

For the next two hours I biked up and down backcountry roads, being careful to keep track of my route so I could find my way back later. Though the day was cool, almost raw, it felt good to be on a bike, pumping hard, having the wind tousle my hair. As I rode I couldn't think of anything but my conversation with Cat.

I'd been blown away by her confession. Of course, there was a chance she might have lied to me, created a wild goose chase of a tale to prevent me from figuring out what had really happened. She certainly hadn't hesitated to mislead me earlier about Kip and the state of her marriage. Yet I believed her. As I'd listened to that whole creepy story of her planning to tell Heidi she suspected her of child abuse, it had the ring of truth.

As ugly as the situation was, I was in one sense relieved. I hadn't been able to bear the thought that Cat, my friend of seven years, was Heidi's killer. As I pedaled along, watching for slippery patches on the road, a question formed in my mind: Why *was* I her friend? When it came to any choice, Cat always, *always,* picked what suited *her,* even if someone else might get hurt in the process. What did I really get out of the arrangement? And was it inevitable that she would betray me or just plain ignore me at a time when I desperately needed help? What had the talentless Ms. Highland said? "I hope you never make the mistake of trusting her."

Since I was making the leap and believing Cat's story, it meant that I was now back to my previous list of suspects. There were Jody and Kip, of course. And Jeff. I'd wondered for days if he and Heidi had been getting it on and so, as it turned out, had Cat. But according to Cat, Jeff had little to fear from getting caught or Heidi blabbing. Cat would have forgiven an indiscretion because she couldn't bear the thought of losing Jeff, and he probably had a sense of his emotional hold on her. And if Cat *had* dumped him, he wouldn't have to worry financially because there was no prenup.

Jealousy might be the motive, though. Maybe Jeff had discovered he wasn't the only game in town and had blown a gasket. The mystery man barged into my brain again.

As I pulled up to the house around five, I was surprised to see Cat outside on the porch, dressed now in slacks and a trench coat and pacing back and forth.

"Am I late?" I asked. "What time are we supposed to be there?"

"It's not that," she said. "We have a Tyler emergency."

"Oh, my God, is he okay?" I asked, heaving the bike against the house and scrambling up the front steps.

"Yes, yes, he's okay physically. But my mother called and said he fell apart today. He became hysterical, crying for me and Jeff. We're going to drive up and get him."

"The poor little guy."

"It will take us almost two hours to get there, and my mother won't let us leave without an attempt to force-feed us beef Wellington. We should be back well before eleven, though."

"That's not a problem," I said. "I'll just read, watch a movie."

"No, no, you can still go to Leslie's. She's expecting you. I called and told her the situation, and if you're nervous about getting lost, Clyde will pick you up and bring you back here later."

"Why don't I just bag it," I said. "I don't want to impose, and I'd be perfectly happy staying here."

Jeff came out of the house in his jeans jacket, car keys in hand, and hurried to the BMW, giving me nothing more than a perfunctory nod.

"You can't bag it," Cat said. "She's got this other couple coming and she'll be annoyed if you don't go. It won't be bad, really." She hurried down the steps as if it were a done deal. "Her number's on the table," she yelled as she jumped in the car. "Give her a ring for directions—or if you want a ride."

I called out good luck as the Beemer backed out of the driveway, but they were too distracted to notice.

Entering the house, I found the number where Cat had left it. I hadn't a shred of interest in dining with Leslie, Clyde, and two strangers, and my guess was that Leslie would be delighted to see me drop off the guest list if given the opportunity. I punched the numbers and Leslie herself answered.

"Hi, it's Bailey," I said. "I appreciate your wanting to include me for dinner even without Cat and Jeff, but why don't I take a rain check. I want to be here when they come home and make sure everything's okay."

"Don't worry, it'll be an early night," she said. "It's really just a casual dinner. You'll like this other couple."

"I appreciate it, but it's probably best for me to hang here."

"I've made a ton of chili, and half of it's going to go to waste," she said peevishly. "Besides, I really need to chat with you. Harry called me yesterday, and he's not a happy man. I need your advice on how to get Cat focused again."

I could see there was no way of wiggling out of the evening without pissing her off. And the Harry stuff alarmed me. I told her I'd be there and took down directions.

Since I had Cat's house to myself for a while, I decided to check out the bedroom Heidi had used on the weekends she'd visited. It was a pleasant enough room, but it was small and set apart from the other bedrooms. It also had a forgotten quality, a room used only as backup when the two main guest rooms were occupied. The only furniture was a bed, a bedside table, a small dresser, and a whitewashed rocker. And the only accessories were a small clock, stopped at two-thirty, and a chipped yellow vase, empty of flowers.

I pulled open the dresser drawers. Nothing but extra blankets and sheets, sitting on top of drawer lining paper that looked as if it had been there since the Kennedy administration. Nothing in the musty closet, either, except what appeared to be a garment bag full of Cat's winter clothes. Heidi had slept in this room, but she'd left nothing behind. What had I expected? A love note from Mr. X, signed with his actual name?

As I was shutting the closet door, I heard a sound, like a screen door closing. I took the back stairs down two at a time and hurried to the front hallway. There was no one there. It was probably just one of those sounds old houses make, but all the terror of my night at Landon's came rushing back at me. There was something freakin' Kafkaesque about the way I kept being asked to people's country homes and then left there alone. I took several deep breaths and did a quick scan of the rooms. I was suddenly glad to be going to dinner at a house full of people.

There was an hour to kill before Leslie's, so I retrieved my book from the screen porch and took it to the library, where it was warmer and cozier. Though I'd calmed down, I found myself rereading the same sentences over and over again. Just before seven, I went upstairs to change. Leslie had said dress casually, so I swapped my jeans for black slacks, a black shirt, and a red leather jacket. Cat had forgotten to make any arrangements with me about locking up, so I made sure the back door and screen porch were locked, but I left the front door unlocked—otherwise I wouldn't be able to get in if I returned ahead of them. I also left tons of lights on.

The drive to Leslie's house wasn't overly complicated, though I worried that later I might have trouble finding my way back in the dark. Having seen Leslie and Clyde's apartment, I was prepared for a big spread, and it was: three stories, shingled, with a huge wraparound porch and none of the country charm of Cat's home.

Leslie greeted me with an air kiss, not the sort of thing we generally exchanged, but then we weren't in the habit of getting together socially, either. She was wearing navy pants and a pink tunic-y top, obviously meant to be slimming but without success. Clyde, she mentioned, was upstairs in his office, but he would join us soon. She led me through a large center hallway, past a living room and a paneled study, and into the kitchen, a mammoth room done all in white so that it looked like a dispensary. As she poured me a glass of white wine from the refrigerator, my eye fell on a big pot of chili on the stove.

"I thought we'd just do something casual tonight since my housekeeper is off," she said, catching me looking at the food. "It's with ground turkey, by the way. In case you were worried there's red meat in it."

"Great."

She asked if I wanted a tour of the house. Sure, I said. My calves were starting to ache from the bike ride, but I sensed that no was not an option. I followed behind her from one big, high-ceilinged room to the next, including a small greenhouse on the back, a damp and spongy room with a big drain on the floor. Her tour included a running commentary about the history of the house and the work she and Clyde had done on it, and her voice as she spoke was bright and loud, making me wonder if the glass of wine she was sipping might be her second, even her third. Maybe the call this week from Harry had rattled her. If Cat was forced out of *Gloss,* Leslie would follow.

The tour ended at a room Leslie called the solarium, with three walls of glass windows.

"I thought we'd eat in here since the dining room table is so huge," she said. In the center of the room was a wrought-iron table. I saw that it had been set with only three placemats.

"It's just the three of us?" I asked, not containing my surprise.

"What? Oh, can you believe it? The Bogards called just after I spoke to you. They were coming straight here from Manhattan and their car broke down somewhere near White Plains. They're not going to make it."

"You should have called me. I would have taken a rain check and you two could have had the night together."

"Don't be silly. And besides, Clyde said he was looking forward to getting to know you."

I nearly groaned out loud thinking of the evening ahead. It almost seemed as if Leslie had engineered the whole thing just to get me alone to talk about Cat's work woes. The only consolation was that it would be better than five hours alone in Cat's farmhouse.

Leslie led me back to the study and we settled there, a wood-paneled room that, like their library in New York, had swords in brackets mounted around the room. It had turned dark out, and Leslie lit several lamps, which because their shades were black cast puddles of light around the room. On the coffee table was a large tray of expensive-looking cheeses. I had only picked at my lunch, and I was famished now. I set down my drink glass and helped myself to a cracker smeared with soft blue cheese. I noticed for the first time there was music playing, something instrumental and soothing, so low that I couldn't determine exactly what it was.

"Tell me about the swords—are they something both of you collect?" I asked, wiping my fingers with a cocktail napkin.

"Oh no, not me," Leslie said. "God forbid. It's Clyde. They're his passion."

"Does he just like to look or does he know how to use them?"

"Actually, he's quite a marvelous fencer. Or was. He was nationally ranked in college."

"What are some of *your* passions, Leslie?"

"You mean," she said, "when I'm not, as everyone at *Gloss* likes to say, kicking butt? I love being out here, actually—antiquing, gardening. I'm very proud of what I've done with this place. Clyde and I have a wonderful life here." It was said almost fiercely, defensively, as if I'd challenged her on it.

"I can see that," I said as pleasantly as I could. "So tell me about the call from Harry. What's going on?"

Her eyes registered annoyance, maybe because I'd changed the subject on her. I noticed for the first time that they were such a dark brown, you could hardly see the pupils.

"He's concerned, very concerned," she said, glancing into her wineglass. "Do you blame him?"

"It's hard to know whether I blame him when I don't know the exact reason for his concern. Is it Cat's safety he's worried about?"

"Yes. But he's also worried about the magazine. All the negative publicity lately. It doesn't help that newsstand sales have been bad this year. And Cat's been out of the office lately more than she's been in. He tries to call her, and he's always told she can't be reached."

"Is that what he said?"

"Yes, I just said that."

"But Cat told me she'd smoothed things over with him this week. She told me that yesterday morning. When exactly did you talk to him?"

"Since then."

"Today?"

"Yesterday. *Late* in the day."

She was being evasive, but I wasn't sure why. I wondered for a second if she was making the whole thing up. Or maybe there was something more to the story that she wasn't telling me.

While I considered how to probe further, Clyde strode into the room, drink in hand. He was wearing perfectly draped beige gabardine pants, a white dress shirt, open at the neck, and another expensive-looking belt—this one appeared to have cost the world several anacondas. I rose from the couch and walked across the room to greet him.

"Oh, please don't get up," he said, shaking my hand anyway. "Sorry for the delay." He appeared to be in the same somber mood he'd been in the other night.

"Everything all right, Clyde?" Leslie asked.

"Yes, fine," he said crisply. He walked over to the bar and lifted the lid off a crystal ice bucket.

"You're all set with your drink?" he asked, looking at me as he used a pair of silver tongs to drop two fresh cubes into his drink.

"Yes, all set." I noticed that he hadn't asked the same of Leslie, whose wineglass was nearly empty. Maybe he thought she'd had enough. After swishing the cubes around in the glass, he opened a wood-paneled cabinet and turned up the volume on the stereo receiver. Music flooded the room, and he adjusted the sound down again, but not as low as before.

"I was admiring your collection of swords," I told him as I sat back down again, looking for some way to move the conversation along. "Are they from all different cultures?"

"Some are Asian," he said. "But for the most part they're Celtic—you can see from the markings. My mother is Jewish, but my father was Irish. He started the collection—and I've just kept going with it. They have a power that's quite breathtaking."

I heard what he said on a ten-second delay, because all my attention was focused on the music now that I could hear it better. It was jazz. Not traditional stuff, but the modern stuff that guys like Sun Ra and Ornette Coleman do. I let my eyes slide down to the drink Clyde held in his hands. A short glass of vodka or gin. Fear rushed through my body, warm and liquidy. I forced myself to say something, anything.

"It makes me think of *Braveheart.*"

"Well, that's right. This is exactly the kind of thing they were fighting with."

"Why don't we talk about it over dinner," Leslie suggested, getting up. "Clyde has the most amazing stories about some of the swords."

"Can I use the bathroom first? I just want to wash my hands," I said, overexplaining.

She showed me to a powder room off the main hall
and said they'd meet me in the solarium. After locking
the door, I lowered the toilet seat lid and sat down on it,
my mind racing. The jazz, the vodka, the income big
enough for diamond jewelry. *Clyde* was the mystery man.
I flashed on the book of Celtic symbols in Heidi's apartment. At the time I'd lumped it with the other new age
books, but it hadn't been that at all. It had been a guide
of some kind. Heidi had probably bought it so she could
learn about the symbols on the swords and impress
Clyde, just as she'd been learning about jazz—or maybe
he had given her the book to encourage her appreciation
of his passion. So Heidi had moved up the food chain in
the most impressive way. If she could snag Clyde, she
must have realized, she'd become queen of the castle.

That's why she'd been so secretive—she couldn't let
Cat get wind of what was going on. That's why she had
felt uncomfortable about going to *Gloss*—she didn't want
to bump into Leslie. And that's why she'd wanted to be
alone in the house in Litchfield for the weekend. It would
have been easy for Clyde to sneak off and be with her.
But what had her chances been of ultimately snagging
him all for herself? Maybe they'd been decent. He
looked like a guy in the throes of some midlife turmoil, a
guy ripe for a new life.

Had he killed her? Maybe she had recently found
someone even better and dumped him like the others,
leaving him enraged. Or maybe he had wanted only a
fling and she'd threatened to tell. He had been at the party
that night and could easily have brought the candy along.

Or, oh God, was *Leslie* the killer? She may have discovered the affair and realized that Clyde was in deep and

that throwing a hissy fit was not going to derail his infatuation.

Regardless of which one had done it, the other person obviously didn't suspect—or else how could they be co-existing?

There was something else. I had been urged to come tonight, and I suspected it was because the killer wanted me here for a reason. To harm me? It didn't seem likely. He—or she—wouldn't dare do anything violent in front of the other person. My guess was the killer wanted to get a handle on exactly what I knew and what direction I was headed in. On the phone, Leslie had prodded me to come tonight, refusing to take no for an answer. But she had also mentioned that Clyde was looking forward to getting to know me. Maybe behind the scenes he had been the one pushing for my presence.

I had no idea which one was the murderer. But I was pretty certain that if I played along tonight, I'd know. All it would take was seeing who was the most curious. Maybe the smartest thing would be to tear ass out of this hell house, but that would certainly alert the killer that I was onto something. And if I left, I wouldn't learn the truth.

I had been in the bathroom too long, and I didn't want to arouse any suspicion. As I found my way to the solarium, my legs felt floppy with fear, like two pieces of fabric. Clyde was already seated at one end of the wrought-iron table, opening a bottle of red wine. Leslie was in the process of setting a mixed green salad on each placemat. She told me to take a seat on the long side of the table and lowered herself into a chair at the end opposite Clyde.

"I hope you like cilantro," Leslie said. "I put a lot of it in the dressing."

"I love it," I said. I was so anxious I'd barely gotten the words out. Somehow I was going to have to summon a way to seem normal.

Leslie took the first bite of salad, the hostess indicating it was okay to start, and Clyde and I followed suit. Though I had a tough time swallowing, it was actually tasty. I suddenly thought of what Darma had said—that she and Leslie had worked together at the food magazine. If Leslie knew about cooking, she could have easily made the truffles.

"How did you find the place out here?" I asked, trying to sound casual.

"Clyde found it, didn't you? Tell Bailey the story."

"There's really nothing so special about it," he said dismissively. I was getting a good glimpse of their marriage tonight—and it wasn't very pretty.

"Of course there is," she insisted.

He rushed through a story about attending a party at the house while he was in college and years later being shown it by a real estate agent—to his surprise.

"You went to college in the area?" I asked.

"In the general area. Yale. Did you and Cat meet in college? Leslie tells me you two are old buddies." He said "old buddies" in a kind of negative way, as if he were saying "old biddies."

"No, we met around seven years ago, working at a magazine."

"And you're helping her now? Leslie says you're looking into the death at her home."

Oh boy, here we go. "Well, I've tried to help," I said. "I've made a few inquiries on her behalf."

"And have those inquiries proven fruitful?" he asked, unsmiling.

I took another bite of my salad to give myself time to form an answer. I wanted to keep him talking, but I didn't want to let on that I knew more than I should.

"I'm probably overstating it," I said. "Mostly I've been a shoulder to lean on. This has been very hard for her."

"By this I take it you mean having someone die violently in your home."

"Yes, and having someone die who you cared about."

"Oh, did Cat care about her nanny?" he said, his voice thick with sarcasm. "I'd never heard her say as much."

"Of course she did," Leslie interjected. I'd been watching her out of the corner of my eye, and up until this moment she had been sitting quietly, pushing the baby lettuce leaves around on her plate. "No one's going to kid themselves and suggest that their relationship was all warm and fuzzy, but Cat was concerned about Heidi's welfare when she was living under her roof. And she's sick about what happened—that Heidi died because someone was out to get *her.*"

No mention of my Heidi theory from the other night. Apparently she hadn't shared *that* with Clyde. As I set my fork down, I glanced over at him. He was staring at Leslie, not bothering to comment on her defense of Cat.

"Well," Leslie announced with a faux chirpiness. "Why don't I serve the chili now."

Refusing my offer to help, she cleared our salad plates and set them on a side table against the wall. That's where the chili was, in a large red pot, being kept hot by a Sterno candle. She transferred it over to the table, onto a hot plate, along with small bowls of grated cheese, sour cream, and chopped onions. As we passed our plates to her, she spooned a large helping of chili onto each of them. We took turns passing and added the toppings. Clyde was going along with the program, but he had grown silent as a stone.

"Oh, good," Leslie exclaimed, again taking the first bite. "I was afraid I'd gotten it too spicy, but it's fine. Do you cook, Bailey?"

"Some," I said, breaking off a piece of bread from a loaf in a basket on the table. "But I don't have any special talent for it."

I finally took my first bite. It seemed sweet for chili, if anything not spicy enough. With my second bite I suddenly felt an intense throbbing in my throat, like instant strep, a pain that went all the way back to my ears. A second later the swelling began in my lips and my tongue and my throat. I had eaten peanuts somehow, within the last twenty seconds. I stared at the plate of chili, uncomprehending. Then I jumped out of my seat, knocking my chair backward to the floor.

"What's the matter?" Clyde exclaimed.

"My purse," I gasped. "I need my purse."

I half ran, half staggered out of the room, terrified, as I felt my throat swelling tighter and tighter. My purse was where I'd left it, on the hall chair. Clyde was calling out something to me, but I just kept moving. I grabbed my bag, turned it upside down, and watched everything splatter onto the floor. At first I didn't see it, the "EpiPen," the syringe of epinephrine, but as I frantically pushed stuff aside I discovered it, under my checkbook. I knocked off the top, pulled up my shirt, and jabbed the needle into my stomach.

Closing my eyes, I lay back on the floor, waiting for the epinephrine to work. It felt as if I had a loaf of sopping wet bread stuffed in my throat. I couldn't swallow and could barely catch a breath. Finally, in seconds that seemed like minutes, I felt my heart begin to jump like a pogo stick, as if it had been defibrillated. But the swelling in my throat was beginning to go down. I opened my eyes and saw that Clyde and Leslie were standing over me.

"Are you okay?" Clyde asked. "What should we do?" He looked frantic. Leslie just stared, her face blank.

"Peanuts," I said. My tongue was still thick, and it was hard to talk. "I'm allergic."

"Peanuts?" Clyde exclaimed. "What do you mean?"

"Oh dear," Leslie exclaimed. "There's peanut butter in the chili. It's an old family recipe. I had no idea you were allergic."

But I bet she *did* know. I'd made it known when I first arrived at *Gloss*. And I bet Leslie had urged me to come tonight so she could try to kill me.

"Here, let me help you," Leslie said shrilly, reaching for my hand.

"Don't touch me," I said to her, trying to catch a breath. "Clyde, please, you've got to help me. Don't let her near me."

"What's going on?" Clyde asked me, baffled.

"She killed Heidi," I said. "And she tried to kill me."

He spun around toward Leslie. "*You* killed her?" he exclaimed, in a state of total bewilderment. "*You?*"

Before I could say another word, Leslie dropped to

one knee and, pinning my arms down, grabbed around my neck with both hands. She squeezed as hard as she could and shook my head back and forth like a doll's. I panicked as I fought to get a breath and couldn't and my brain seemed to bulge with blood.

"Shut up," she screamed. "Just shut up!" Her kidney bean nostrils were so close I could see the hairs in them. I pulled up my knee and struggled to knock her off me. Finally, as my head felt ready to explode, Clyde grabbed her by the shoulders and shoved her away. She regained her balance and ran off, down the long center hallway toward the back of the house. I thought suddenly of all those swords mounted on the walls of the study. Clyde stooped down and lifted me into a sitting position.

"You okay?" he barked.

"Yes. No. I need to get to a hospital. The stuff I took only lasts thirty minutes."

"What's going on? Why did you say that—about Leslie and Heidi?"

From far off, on the other side of the house, I heard what I thought was a door slam. I took as big a breath as I could, forcing air into my lungs. "I put two and two together," I said. "Somehow Leslie found out about your affair. She killed Heidi but made it look as though someone wanted to hurt Cat. And she tried to kill me tonight because she thought I was close to figuring it out."

It seemed to take him a second to process what I'd told him and then his face filled with rage. He rose and turned on his heels. He was going after her.

"Don't leave me," I pleaded. "I need your help."

He yelled something as he flew down the hall, but I couldn't make out what it was. If I didn't get medical treatment within the next half hour, the swelling would start again and I could easily suffocate to death. There was no way I was going to call 911 and wait in this house for an ambulance to come after me. I was going to have to try to drive myself to a hospital. Though I had no clue where the nearest one was.

I rolled over onto my knees, grabbed my car keys from the mess on the floor, and scooted my wallet back into my purse. I struggled to my feet. As I tried to steady myself and catch another breath, I heard a door slam in the back of the house and then the sound of footsteps clomping toward the front of the house. It was the sound of a woman. Leslie was coming back for me.

CHAPTER 23

BUT IT WASN'T Leslie. Suddenly, Cat Jones was standing in the middle of the front hallway.

I didn't even think to ask what she was doing there. I blurted out as much of the story as I could—Leslie had killed Heidi, Leslie had tried to kill me—and told her I had to get to an ER. She grabbed my arm to help me and hurried me through the front door of the house. As we raced across the wet lawn to the driveway, Cat told me she'd discovered neither Leslie nor Clyde in the back of the house but that she'd seen a car peeling down the road as she'd approached the house, and she thought it had come from the driveway. I figured it had to be Leslie.

Once in the car, neither of us said much. Cat concentrated on driving like a demon. I felt too shaky to talk. I lay with my head against the door, eyes closed, keeping as still as possible, willing my throat not to swell again. At one point I heard Cat call Jeff on her cell phone. She told him what had happened and warned him not to let Leslie in if she came by the house. The trip seemed interminable, but as we pulled into the entrance of the Sharon ER I saw from my watch that we had made it in less than twenty minutes. I felt a wave of relief just walking through the entrance.

I only had to say, "Peanut allergy," to the triage nurse and I was ushered back to an examining room, leaving Cat to show my insurance card somewhere. A doctor hurried in, looking like a graduate of the Doogie Howser school of medicine. I didn't go into any of the sordid details, just told him I'd eaten chili with peanut butter in it, never imagining it could be an ingredient. He gave me both Benadryl and steroids and told me to lie still for a while. Cat found her way into the room as he was shooting something into my arm. As soon as he left the room, she stepped closer again and squeezed my hand.

"Cat, we need to call the police," I said. "Can you do it?"

"Sure, but I'll have to find a pay phone. You're not supposed to use cell phones in hospitals."

"Don't call the local police, though—at least not yet. I think you should first call Farley and ask him how to proceed. And you better get hold of Clyde. Tell him where we went and to be careful. Who knows what Leslie will do now."

As she stepped away, I reached out and grabbed her arm.

"Wait a sec," I said. "What were you doing at Leslie's tonight?"

"The doctor said you need to rest. I'll tell you later."

"No, tell me now."

"It was something you said this afternoon. You told me that Leslie had said I'd brought up the Tucker Bobb connection. But it was Leslie who had brought it up to *me*. And then tonight—she seemed so adamant about your coming. I started to get a weird feeling. I called Leslie's house once we got to my parents and the machine picked up, which seemed odd. I made Jeff leave right away."

"Is Tyler okay?"

"He had another meltdown when I left him and Jeff off at our house, but two-year-olds forgive you."

"God, Cat. You came to my rescue."

"Well, don't get used to it," she said with a smirk. "You better rest. I'll make the calls."

As she slipped through the door, I closed my eyes. I tried to make my body relax, but it wouldn't obey my command. Everything that had happened during the night kept replaying itself over and over in my head, especially the terror I'd felt in the hallway as my throat began to swell, as Leslie's hands closed around it and squeezed. How lucky that I'd brought the EpiPen. Over the years I'd gotten a little sloppy about carrying it around, but because I'd been going away for the weekend, I'd made a point of tossing it into my bag. If I hadn't, I'd be dead. And I might be dead if Cat hadn't come striding down that hall. Tears began to squeeze out from under my lids.

I dozed off, but I wasn't sure for how long. When I opened my eyes, Cat was sitting in a chair, leafing through a magazine without really reading it.

"You got through?" I asked.

"Yeah. New developments," she said. "I called Clyde first—just to see if there was anything I needed to include for Farley. Leslie was in an accident. She hit a guardrail or something. I'm not sure of all the details because he was fairly incoherent. She's in the hospital. Busted her leg—but she's not serious."

"She's not *here,* is she?"

"No, no. Farther south. She's been admitted. So then I called Farley. He sounded flabbergasted. He wants to talk to you as soon as possible. I told him you weren't well enough to talk tonight, and he said he wants you in New York tomorrow. No excuses."

"Did he give you any indication of what they would do?" I asked.

"He said he'd handle it. It was clear he was going to talk to the police here. And he said that the local guys would probably want a statement from you before you leave tomorrow."

Doogie came back in at this point to check on me. They took my temperature and pulse again and dismissed me. As Cat pulled the BMW out of the hospital parking lot, she called Jeff on her cell phone and told him we were on our way—and that Leslie was no longer roaming the countryside.

"I can't believe any of this," she said, tossing the phone in her bag. "I feel responsible. Clyde met Heidi through me. I should have seen it. There was a time when I could tell just by looking at them if two people were fucking each other, but it seems I've totally lost the knack. How did Leslie find out, do you think?"

"I don't know. Things certainly didn't seem right between them, and she probably suspected *something* was wrong. And you know how people are. They leave clues sometimes, wanting to be caught. Maybe that's what

Clyde did. Or Leslie may have done some snooping when she felt a change in his attitude or behavior."

"I can't believe she *murdered* Heidi, though. There are other ways to deal with infidelity."

"But you can't make a man fall out of love with someone. I have a feeling Heidi wasn't just a fling for him. My guess is that he was nuts over her—just think of the jewelry. I'm sure he was the one who bought those pieces. We also know how obsessed Leslie was over Clyde. Just think of how she reacted when she thought you were flirting with him. If she found out he was in love with Heidi and suspected he was about to dump her to *be* with Heidi, she may have thought her only option was to totally eliminate Heidi from the face of the earth."

"But how did you figure it all out?"

As we drove along dark country roads, I took her through most of it, from the discussion with Jack about misdirection to the petal in the Jiffy bag.

"God, how diabolically clever," Cat acknowledged. "I know Leslie's a control freak, but I never pegged her as creative."

"And the real beauty of her plan is that because she was so close to the action, she could nudge us along in our thinking. She confirmed that the candy box had been in the hall, and if you hadn't remembered, I'm sure she would have volunteered it. She brought up the similarity to Tucker Bobb's death. It was probably her who tipped the *Post* off to the connection."

"Wait, *is* there a connection to Tucker Bobb?"

"No, I just think Leslie used that to throw everyone off. Though there *is* something fishy about his death. And

I'm pretty sure his widow arranged for someone to give me a scare when I was in Buck's County."

"Do you think Leslie really meant to hurt *you*?"

"It was no accident," I said angrily. "She wanted me dead or out of commission. When I started at *Gloss* I made certain people were aware of my problem with peanuts—I'm sure Leslie knew. The thing is, Leslie needed to shut me up because I was getting too close to the truth. First she tried to scare me with hang-ups and that Kiss on my desk. She also tried to monopolize my time by crashing my article into August. I should have suspected something when Polly wasn't aware it was being moved. The other night, at her apartment, I told her I was going to continue pursuing the Heidi theory, that one of Heidi's boyfriends may have killed her. That must be when she decided to do something more decisive. Of course, she would have claimed it was a horrible accident. It also sounds like she's been unraveling lately. For all we know, she's bonkers. I bet *she* sent the cookies to Patty Gaylin—just to keep everyone confused."

When we got back to the farmhouse, we found Tyler conked out on the library couch and Jeff pacing, desperate for details. It was a relief to know he was neither an adulterer (at least as far as I knew) nor a murderer. I talked for a while but eventually told Cat to take over with what I'd shared with her. I felt overwhelmed with exhaustion. I wanted to be in a bed. Cat hugged me good night at the door of the library, a kind of bear hug I rarely got from her.

"You had a call, by the way," Jeff said, handing me a slip of paper as I started to walk from the room. "A friend of yours, Jack. I hope it was okay to mention you were in the ER."

"*Really?* Sure, that was fine," I said.

"He said to call, no matter when you got in."

I trudged up to the red-and-white guest room, feeling like a rag doll, and sank onto the bed. Fighting the urge just to let sleep overwhelm me, I picked up the phone on the bedside table and dialed Jack Herlihy's number. I could have waited until the morning but I had a yearning to hear his voice, to have someone so wise make me feel safe. When he answered it was clear that I'd woken him, but he didn't sound as if he minded.

"Are you okay? What's going on?"

I poured out the story, letting down my guard in a way I hadn't even done with Cat. Once I even started to cry, though I took a breath and calmed myself. I didn't want to come across like a total wuss. He listened, asked questions, said things to comfort me, just as I'd suspected he would.

"Look," he said finally. "When are you coming back?"

"I've got to come in tomorrow to talk to the police. Who knows how long that will take."

"Why don't we get together later then and talk about this some more."

"You aren't going to bill me, are you?"

"We'll see," he said, laughing. "Maybe we can work out a barter arrangement. Should we have dinner then?"

"Okay. That would be good." I really meant it, and this time I'd be in no rush to leave.

By the time I hung up, the urge I'd been fighting to succumb to a catatonic state had dissipated. I lay on the bed, without even pulling down the covers, and let things swirl around my brain. I thought of the magic trick Jack had mentioned, the one with two scarves. I thought about how many things were like that—not what they seemed. Flying objects weren't really hurled by poltergeists. The candy for Cat had really been meant for Heidi. Miss Totally-in-Control Leslie had gone totally out of control. Perfect marriages were never perfect. Cat, who people said couldn't be trusted, had saved my life. And maybe Jack really *was* my type after all.

More
Kate White!

Please turn this page
for a preview of

*A BODY TO
DIE FOR*

available
wherever books are sold.

CHAPTER 1

When I think back on everything terrible that happened last autumn—the murders, the grim discovery I made, the danger I found myself in—I realize I probably could have avoided all of it if my love life hadn't been so sucky. Or let me rephrase that. Nonexistent. Late in the summer I'd been kicked to the curb by a guy I was fairly gaga over, and though my heart no longer felt as raw as a rug burn, my misery had morphed into a sour, man-repellent mood. It was as if I had a sign over my head that said, "Step any closer, and I'm gonna bitch-slap you."

So when I was invited to spend an early-fall weekend free of charge at the Cedar Inn and Spa in Warren, Massachusetts, I grabbed the chance. Trust me, I wasn't expecting to meet anyone there—except maybe a few rich women in pastel sweat suits and fanny packs who thought having their bodies slathered in shea butter would miraculously vaporize their cellulite. I should also admit that I've generally found spa stuff pretty goofy. I once had a complimentary prune-and-pumpkin facial, and when it was over I kept thinking that I should be stationed on a sideboard between a roast turkey and corn bread stuffing.

But I do go nuts for a good massage, and I was hoping that a few of those and a change of scenery would improve my mood as well as jump-start my heart.

Unfortunately, soon after I arrived at the inn, all hell broke loose.

I pulled into Warren, just before seven on Friday night. A reasonable arrival time, but three damn hours later than I'd originally planned. A combination of things had thrown my schedule into a tizzy. I'm a freelance journalist, specializing in human-interest and crime stories, and an interview that I was scheduled to do with a psychologist for an article on mass hysteria got pushed from morning to midafternoon. I would have liked to just blow it off entirely. But the piece was due at the end of next week, and I was feeling under the gun. I didn't hit the road until three-thirty, guaranteeing that I'd have a good chance of getting caught in a rush-hour mess somewhere between Manhattan and Massachusetts—and I did. In addition, I was undone by a smoldering car fire on the southbound side of the New York State Thruway, which caused people on my side to practically crawl by on their haunches so they could get a better look. You would have thought the front half of the *Titanic* had been dredged and deposited along the side of the road.

If I'd arrived on schedule, I would have been welcomed by the owner of the inn, Danielle (a.k.a. Danny) Hubner. She was the one treating me to an all-expenses-paid weekend. An old college friend of my mother's, Danny had been pleading for me to visit the inn since she'd opened it three or four years ago. But I'd always been too crazed with work—or too caught up in the stages of grief that followed the demise of my flash fire of a marriage: heartache; healing; and manic horniness. This fall, because of my snarky mood, I'd finally said yes.

It would be great, I figured, not only to be pampered twenty-four/seven, but also to spend a nice chunk of time with Danny. She was really my friend, too, and she had a slightly offbeat personality that I found absolutely refreshing. I got the sense my visit would also prove beneficial to *her*. My mother had called right before she flew to Athens for a Mediterranean cruise to say that Danny had seemed in a bit of a slump lately, but she didn't know why. My mother was worried she might be having troubles with her second husband, George, whom I'd yet to meet—and my mother didn't seem wild about.

Since I arrived so late, I'd missed Danny. According to the desk clerk she'd driven into town on business she could no longer put off, but she'd left word that she would check in with me later. I was given a brief tour before being shown to my room.

The inn, a rambling, clapboard building probably

erected in the mid-1800s, was really quite smashing, even more so than in the pictures I'd seen. Instead of dripping with the cutesy country charm that you so often find at a restored inn, the decor was elegant, pared down—lots of beige and cream tones and brown-and-white-check fabric. And there wasn't a whirligig, weathervane, or wooden swan in sight.

Since I was late, I figured I'd blown any chance of getting a treatment that night, but my guide explained that Danny had arranged for to me to be squeezed in for a massage at eight—before a late dinner. The inn's spa, which also operated as a day spa for the area, stayed open until ten.

I had about fifteen minutes to catch my breath before the massage. My room was maximum charming, a suite actually with a small living area. It also sported checks but in red and white and paired with several quirky print fabrics. I unpacked the clothes most likely to wrinkle and hung them in the closet. (I'm a contributing writer for *Gloss* magazine, and I read in a recent issue that you should roll your clothes in tissue paper before packing them in order to prevent wrinkles, but I'd no sooner take the time to do that than I would to iron my underpants.) Next I took a quick shower, letting the spray of hot water do a number on muscles achy from a long car ride.

I dried myself off with a thick Egyptian cotton towel. Thanks to a towel warmer, it was as toasty as a baked potato. As I buffed my body with it, I noticed a small earthenware jar on the bathroom countertop. It was filled to the brim with amber-colored bath salts, and a little tag announced that they were available for sale in the spa. They were a blend of sandalwood and sweet orange aromatics with a hint of frankincense, prepared, the tag said, so I could "surrender to a state of total enchantment and emerge with a primitive power." God, just what I needed. Was it actually suggesting I could get *both* in the same weekend? I glanced up, into the mirror above the sink. I'm five-six, with short brownish blond hair, and blue eyes, and I'm considered pretty in a slightly sporty way, but there was no denying that at that moment in time, I looked weary, even burned-out. It was going to take a helluva lot of bath salts to leave me feeling enchanted and empowered.

I arrived downstairs at the spa with just a few minutes to spare. It was actually a large addition to the inn, abutting the eastern edge of the building. The decor was Asian-inspired: beige walls, cracked stone floors, bamboo plants in large putty-colored pots, and hallways lined with sheer beige curtains that poofed outward from the breeze you created walking by them. It was very different from the decor of the inn, but because they both featured such muted tones, it all seemed to work together.

I undressed in a spacious dressing area, then waited for ten minutes in the so-called relaxation room. Haunting Asian music played in the background, water gurgled over stones in a small fountain, and the scent of green tea wafted from two flickering candles. I tried to let go and relish it, but I felt a little silly. It was as if

I'd somehow stumbled into a scene from *Crouching Tiger, Hidden Dragon*.

Fortunately, it was only a few minutes before I was led to a treatment room. I could barely wait for my massage to start, for the chance to have those sore muscles unknotted. My only concern was that it had been so long since I'd had any physical contact with another member of my species that I might begin to whimper at the first touch—like a poor little pound puppy. Unfortunately, on a scale of one to ten, the massage was no more than a seven. My "therapist," a red-haired woman in her thirties, was skilled enough and had plenty of strength in her hands, but she seemed distracted, pausing at odd moments as she worked. It was enough to make me wonder if I had something weird happening on my butt—like a humongous boil—that was forcing her to stop and gape in horror. I was almost relieved when I was finally back in my suite and could totally veg.

After ordering a club sandwich and a glass of Merlot from room service, I unpacked most of the rest of the stuff from my bag, sticking my underwear and shirts in a dresser. In the early days that I'd traveled I used to wonder who actually *used* hotel dressers, but lately, at the ripe old age of thirty-three I'd come to discover that I prefer not having to forage through my suitcase each time I get dressed.

My food arrived within twenty minutes, and, ravenous, I devoured it. Then, after opening the window a crack, I undressed and turned back the thick white duvet on the bed. I was looking forward to reading between sheets that felt as if they exceeded a three-hundred-thread count.

As I lay between said silky sheets, though, I could feel my mind itching to go places it shouldn't. In other words, it was dying to ruminate about my most recent love trouble. Just as I was about to travel this tiresome ground in my mind for the millionth time, the phone rang.

"Bailey, it's Danny. I didn't wake you, did I?"

As she spoke I could see her in my mind's eye. She was in her early sixties, pretty, or rather handsome, I'd say, with blondish gray hair lightly curled. And she was *tiny*—only about five feet tall and as slim as a candlewick.

"No, no, I'm just lying in bed with a book," I said. "Danny, your inn is absolutely gorgeous. You've done an *amazing* job with it."

"Thank you so much, dearest. How has your evening been?"

"Terrific. I had a lovely massage, then a light dinner up here in my room—or should I say my suite fit for a princess."

"Who was your massage therapist, do you recall?"

"A woman. Redhead. Name started with a P, I think."

"Piper. She has wonderful hands, don't you think?"

"Yes, definitely." I wasn't going to get Piper in any kind of trouble by saying her heart hadn't been totally into her work that night.

"By the way, I've set up a meeting for you and Josh,

the spa manager, at four tomorrow—if that's still okay with you."

I write a few travel articles each year—it's a way to see the world free and also a nice break from the crime grind—and Danny was hoping that while I was ensconced at the inn I could provide some ideas on how better to pitch her place to editors and travel writers.

"Of course," I said. "But when do I get to see *you*?"

"How about breakfast together tomorrow morning?" Danny asked. "Would ten work for you?"

"Absolutely—though I still may be in a stupor from my massage."

She laughed lightly, like someone jangling her keys. "Well, you know what I always say—too much of a good thing is wonderful. Just wait till you have some of the other treatments I've booked for you. Have you ever had a massage with hot stones?"

"No—but I'm game for anything as long as it doesn't involve colonics."

"Oh, Bailey, you always make me laugh," she said. "Well, I'm going to turn in now because my head is throbbing for some reason. I'm staying here at the inn tonight, by the way, in case you need to reach me."

"Do you do that to see things from the guests' perspective?"

"Partly. But also George is out of town, and I hate staying alone. Our house isn't far from here, but it's very secluded. Shall we meet in the lobby then?"

"See you then. I can't wait."

And I meant it. I felt a tremendous debt to Danny. She had been so good to me when my father died the year I was twelve, taking me on all sorts of little adventures and day-trips at a time when my mother was struggling so much it was hard for her to comfort me. Danny must have sensed early on my fascination for the macabre because one of our excursions had been to Salem, to learn more about the witch trials. My mother had looked slightly agog at both of us when she'd learned where we'd ended up that day, but it had been pure heaven for me.

My family eventually lost touch with Danny, during a period when she'd lived out West in a bad marriage. But after she moved back to Massachusetts (with a new husband) to open her inn, she and my mother had reconnected. Though I was only now paying a visit to the inn, Danny and I had spoken a few times on the phone, and I'd had lunch with her once in New York when she'd come to the city on business.

I picked up the book I'd taken into bed with me. It was, of all things, a decorating book. Lately I'd been feeling in desperate need of a change in my Greenwich Village apartment. After my divorce, I'd jettisoned all the modern stuff my ex encouraged us to buy and introduced a Sante Fe feeling—with the help of cinnamon-colored walls and some cheap baskets. But it was suddenly boring me, adding to my burned-out feeling. Last week I'd asked the *Gloss* decorating editor for some guidance and been forced to watch him recoil in horror as I described my place to him. You would have thought I'd announced I'd just installed wall-to-wall shag carpet.

"Santa Fe is totally stupid to do east of the Mississippi," he'd said. "The light is all wrong for it. Besides, who wants to see another turquoise coyote with a kerchief around its neck."

He'd suggested I go "minimal" and pulled a book from his shelf for me to consult.

I'd gone through four or five chapters, covering everything from the value of white space to the pure evil of tchotchkes, when I instinctively glanced at my wrist to check the time. My watch wasn't there.

I felt a tiny swell of panic. It had been my father's watch, an old stainless-steel Rolex I'd started wearing shortly after he died. My mind raced, trying to recall where I'd left it. It had it been on my wrist during the drive to Massachusetts because I recalled checking it. Since it was waterproof, I never took it off when I showered. The *massage*. Rather than leave it in the locker, I'd worn it into the treatment room and placed it on small stool in the corner. I would never fall asleep if I didn't retrieve it.

I dialed the spa number, which was listed on a panel on the phone. As I counted the rings, I leaned out of bed and glanced at the digital clock on the bedside table: 10:25. I wasn't surprised when no one picked up.

Plan B. I'd just head down there. There might still be someone on-site, cleaning up and not bothering to answer the phone.

I threw off the covers and dressed in the same clothes I'd worn earlier. My room was on the second floor of the inn, not far from a back staircase that ended near a side entrance to the spa. Hurrying along the corridor, I was surprised at how deadly quiet it was—no murmur of voices, no hum of TVs, and definitely no headboard banging. Guests here obviously preferred getting loofahed to getting laid.

The door to the spa was solid glass, and I could look directly into the small reception area that was reserved for the use of the inn's guests. It was dark, except for a backlight in a case of beauty products. I tapped on the door, then tried to open it. No luck. As I turned away, though, I thought I heard a sound, something thudlike that I couldn't identify, from deep within the spa.

It sounded as if someone *might* still be there, but I was going to have to try the main reception area, which could only be reached from the outside. Walking along the ground-floor corridor, I found an emergency exit and let myself out. I was on the edge of the parking lot, dark, except for a few perimeter security lights and a big puddle of moonlight. I headed around the edge of the building, toward the main entrance of the spa.

I was surprised at how cool the night was. The early-October temperature had hovered around seventy earlier in the day, almost balmy, but it had dropped at least twenty degrees. There was a stiff, choppy wind, making the tree branches shake. This was one of those nights that told you that if you'd been hoping the summery weather would last forever, you were a fool.

Before I even reached the door of the spa, I could see I'd wasted my time. There was a narrow window alongside each side of the front door, and it was dark inside. There were no cars at that end, not a soul in sight. It was totally silent, too, except for the wind and the faint yawning of cars speeding along a far-off highway. I felt nervous all of sudden, standing out there in the darkness all by myself.

I quickly broke into a jog and crossed the distance of the parking lot to the front of the inn. There were about twenty cars at that end, obviously belonging to guests. The front door was open, and I walked into the reception area, where a girl no more than twenty-five was sitting at the front desk, staring at a terminal screen. Like my massage therapist, she had bright red hair, held off her face with a tiny blue clip. Without giving her time to inquire if she could help me, I explained the situation to her and asked if she could open up the spa.

"I'm sorry, I'm not allowed to let anyone into the spa," she said. "But they open at seven. I can leave a note under the door asking them to look for your watch as soon as they get in. Who was your therapist?"

"Piper."

"Oh, I'm sure she saw it and put it up someplace. There's no need to worry."

"You're probably right, but I can't help it," I told her. "The watch has incredible sentimental value to me. Who *can* let me in?"

"Well, Danielle could, but—"

"I don't want to wake her. Is there someone else?"

She thought for a second, her blue eyes raised to the ceiling.

"Well, the manager had the day off. But I guess I could call Piper. She's an assistant manager, and she's got a key."

"But then she'd have to drive all the way back here."

"No, she wouldn't—she lives right here. There's a building out back where some of the staff stay. I don't think she'd mind coming over."

Natalie—that's what it said on her name tag—glanced at a phone sheet on her desk and placed the call. A machine obviously picked up after five or six rings because she left a message, detailing what had happened and asking Piper to call.

"She must have gone into town for dinner," she said, setting the phone back down. "I doubt she'll be gone long. There's another assistant manager, Anna . . ."

She let her voice trail off without asking if I wanted to track her down obviously hoping I wasn't going to push the issue even more.

"I can wait till Piper gets back," I said.

Once back in my room, I alternated between reading my book and fretting. I had just glanced at the digital clock for the about the four hundredth time—11:13—when the phone rang. It was Piper.

"Hi, Miss Weggins? Natalie said you left your watch in the treatment room."

"Yeah, I'm pretty sure it's on the little stool in the corner. You didn't see it?"

"No, but then I don't recall looking over there." She hesitated a second. "Why don't I run over and check—I'm just behind the inn."

There was something about her tone—resigned politeness—that told me she was doing it not out of any inborn generosity but because the inn encouraged staff to bend over backward for the guests.

"God, I hate to put you out, but I'd die if something happened to that watch. Should I meet you down there?"

"I'd be happy to drop it off in your room—but actually maybe it's best for you to show me exactly where you think you left it."

She said we should meet by the inn entrance to the spa. I'd kept my clothes on, so it took me less than two minutes to get down there. I had a five-minute wait, though, before Piper strode down the corridor from the front of the inn. It was funny how different she looked out of "uniform." Instead of a beige T-shirt and baggy beige pants, she was wearing jeans and a long-sleeve green jersey shirt, low cut with a ruffle. Her shoulder-length red hair, which had been tied back earlier, was spread around her shoulders like a brush fire.

She was courteous enough when she greeted me, but it seemed like that kind of phony politeness she'd displayed on the phone. She already had her keys out and unlocked the door, lifting the handle slightly as she pulled it forward, obviously familiar with the door's quirkiness.

She flipped on a light in the reception area, and I followed her down one of the corridors. The scent of green tea still hung in the air, and something else, maybe jasmine. The only sound was our footsteps on the stone floor. It felt kind of creepy to be there alone, after hours.

I wouldn't have been able to recall which room

we'd been in, but she seemed to know. As we reached the open doorway, she froze suddenly, like a gazelle picking up the scent of something possibly predatory.

"What is it?" I asked.

"There's a light on," Piper said in a hushed tone, using her chin to point down the hall ahead of us. I glanced in that direction and saw a chink of light coming from beneath a doorway.

"Is someone here?" I asked, my voice as quiet as hers.

"No. It's just funny. I swear I turned off the light and left the door open. Why don't you look for your watch, and I'll check."

She flicked on the light for me, and as she walked off down the hall, I made a beeline for the stool. I mouthed a big "Thank you" to the gods when I spotted the Rolex lying there, all by its lonesome. As I slid it onto my wrist, I heard a scream.

With my heart thumping, I stumbled out into the hall. Piper was standing paralyzed in the doorway of the room down the corridor, half in the room, half out.

"What's the matter?" I yelled.

She turned to me, with a look of absolute horror on her face, unable to form even a single word. I rushed down the hall, pushing past her into the room. It was also a massage room, though slightly larger than the other. The lights were dim, and at first nothing seemed amiss. Then I looked down.

Lying on the stone floor, absolutely still, was a body, or at least what I thought must be a body. Every inch of it was wrapped up in some kind of silver paper. I could see the outlines of the limbs and the torso and the head, and the outline, too, of the nose, protruding from the face. It looked like some kind of mummy. Like some horrible mummy from outer space.